NEANDERBALL
Sofia Diana Gabel

Neanderball

ISBN: 979-8-9893356-0-2

This book is dedicated to the three most favorite people in my life: Alexandra, Olivia, and Andrianna.

Chapter 1

Lucien stood outside his lab door, hoping his Neanderthal clones had survived to reach the five-day blastocyst mark. What made his cell phone alarm go off? He placed his chin on the plastic extension to the right and pressed the red button. With his retina scanned, a chime sounded. He straightened. Next came fingerprint verification. He placed his thumb on a small pad next to the retinal scanner and waited for the second chime. Last came the voice verification.

He stepped back and spoke, *"Bonjour, je m'appelle* Lucien Roux."

A split-second pause. *"Bonjour,* Doctor Roux."

Third and final chime. The door slid left into the pocket slot and closed after he entered the lab. For a moment, he stood and enjoyed the cool, unobtrusive, sterile comfort of the place where he'd spent most of his time over the past three years. His second home. Come to think of it, it was more accurate to call it his first home.

"Lights."

The fluorescent lights flickered on and illuminated the countertops crammed with glassware, notepads, microscopes, and computers. He dodged around the benches and stools to the incubator room at the far end of the lab.

He pressed a button beside the door. "Release incubator lock."

As he wrapped his hand around the incubator's door handle, his foot tapped. "Come on, come on."

To anyone else, it would look like a commercial refrigerator door, but looks were deceiving. He kept his incubator out of view in a separate room where only his voice would unlock it, tucked away from the potential prying eyes of the techs and cleaning crew.

The lock clicked open.

What had happened? Nutrients he'd deal with, but if he'd miscalculated the growth enhancers, it meant he'd lose the entire batch of Neanderthal specimens. If they lived, all sixteen would have developed further than any of the other clones that failed to thrive.

He swung the stainless door wide and hurried in. The interior lights flooded the cool, small space. There they were, his sixteen specimens, mounted vertically in silver-sided test tubes holding the growth medium, four high with four side-by-side, all males to reduce the variables that might come with both sexes. He peered closely through the small magnifying window in the first growth tube and then the next and the next.

"What the hell? That can't be right."

The clones were too big.

The telemetry readouts next to the tubes said they had developed into two-week-old embryos.

"*Mon Dieu*," he muttered.

Not possible. Such a huge increase in growth wasn't feasible. The cells couldn't divide that rapidly, even with the added enhancers. His research had a flaw. He slammed his fist against the table holding the telemetry system, which bounced up and crashed back down. Shit. He checked the machine, which thankfully hadn't broken.

"Control your temper, you idiot." He held his breath for a moment and exhaled slowly.

After a quick check of the fluid intake and growth hormone levels, he rushed to the lab computer, punched in the numbers, and sat back as a graph appeared. He fumbled with the top button on his shirt and mopped his forehead with a piece of lens tissue. Unbelievable. At such a growth rate, in four more weeks, they'd be almost full-term infants. Their organs and systems couldn't sustain such rapid development. He'd have to act quickly and extract as many stem cells and genetic material as possible before they grew any older because Bay Genetics policy forbade any experimentation on viable fetuses, even his. He ran another program to estimate the best time to harvest cells.

While he waited for the results, he pushed his chair back, bumped into the small desk behind him, and knocked a stack of journals to the floor. With a sigh, he picked up the top journal, *Paleogenetics*. Had it really been four years since they'd published the interview about his initial research design? He remembered all too well how the interviewer pressed him for details about using ancient DNA from Neanderthals.

The computer continued calculating. Time to get an upgraded system if he got more funding.

He flipped to the interview where a photograph of a younger him clad in a white lab coat standing beside a microscope adorned the first page. Right there under the photo sat his bastardized name, *Paleo* Roux, dubbed by the interviewer. When the media started to refer to him as such, he refused further interviews.

He checked again, but the computer program wasn't complete yet. "Come on!"

After another calming breath, he skimmed down through the article and found where he explained how Neanderthals were built like modern-day linebackers, their strength and endurance making them excellent test subjects, theoretically. He'd hedged around his real intentions:

Their body structure and musculature were specifically adapted for carrying heavy loads and running over rough, uneven terrain. It's those traits that made them perfectly adapted to their hostile environment, and because of their genetic make-up, I believe my preliminary research will indicate that they had superior immune systems, which may have allowed them to fight diseases like cancer. While researchers have found evidence that they had non-lethal ailments like arthritis, my hypothesis is to show how a Neanderthal embryo's stem cells could be manipulated to replace faulty neural cells in modern humans and be used to formulate cures to certain devastating diseases due to their potential inherent resistance to some fatal ailments.

He closed the journal and put the stack back on the desk. He'd never actually said that he'd intended to grow Neanderthals and he'd purposely left out that he'd manipulate the embryos' genetic code to carry the cancer gene he'd inherited from his maternal lineage, using his own DNA, which was risky. He'd then harvest stem cells for experimentation. Scientists and laypeople alike would come out of the woodwork if they knew all the details and declare him inhumane or make him out to be crazy. Or maybe both. He'd get no more funding if the truth got out.

Neanderthals were the perfect subjects to use. They were an extinct species; nothing more than skeletal remains. Sure they were in the *Homo* genus, but he wasn't using modern humans, *Homo sapiens*, or *Homo sapiens sapiens,* as he preferred, which might keep the moral naysayers off his back. If everyone could understand his motivation, they wouldn't object, and would probably laud him for being a hero. Nobody wanted to die or have their loved ones suffer from insidious diseases like cancer. It wasn't wrong to try to find a cure. If someone had found a cure eight years ago, his mother wouldn't have lingered for over a year, losing her once-brilliant self to the disease. As hard as it was, he was glad when she finally succumbed to the rare glioblastoma brain cancer that ate away at her mind.

The memory remained clear. He sat with her every night, holding her hand, dabbing her face with a damp towel, and injecting morphine into her IV when she moaned in agony from the constant migraines. He didn't want to go the same way, but when the genetic test said he'd inherited the same damn gene, the Stat3-beta2, he set about to find a cure before he became another statistic of the disease.

With the calculations done at last, several harvesting scenarios appeared. Above them, an insistent, red blinking sentence: DANGER: Error in growth hormone.

Chapter 2

For the remainder of the day, Lucien puzzled over what went wrong or how he'd miscalculated the growth hormone, but nothing stood out. An anomaly? A mutation in the clones? Faulty reagents? Nothing made sense. The best scenario for harvesting the stem cells was within twenty-four to forty-eight hours. Around six, he packed up and went home, with his stomach growling and a headache that throbbed mercilessly.

He didn't even stop at the front security desk to say goodnight to Marlowe, even though he knew damn well the risk of rebuke from her. They'd only been dating for four months, but it was the most solid relationship he'd been in for years. Being Friday, he had the weekend to make it up to her. She'd forgive him, she always did. Of course, he had to figure out how to fix his experiment first.

In the morning, rested, head clear, he dressed in a pair of jeans and a linen shirt. He liked going into the lab on a Saturday because none of the other Bay-Gen scientists would be there to admonish him, the lone paleogeneticist, for his work, or for dressing too casually. They questioned the validity of his experiments and stressed the "paleo" part as if to say he wasn't a real scientist like them. But his experiments were every bit as important as any of theirs, even if he sometimes strayed into the unethical, their words, not his. They'd soon see what a *paleo*geneticist can do. This morning he'd pick up where he'd left off and salvage what stem cells were available.

He walked right past the dresser mirror because he'd rather live in denial that he was still young, instead of an overworked forty-two-year-old man with traces of gray peppering his hair. Although Marlowe said she liked the salt and pepper look and didn't care that he was almost ten years her senior. And that's all that mattered. He fired off a good morning text to her and tucked his phone into his jeans pocket. Within seconds, it rang.

It wasn't Marlowe, but he recognized the number. Why couldn't Harmond leave him alone?

Lucien answered, "This is Dr. Roux."

"Don't hang up. Good morning, Dr. Roux." General Harmond's voice grated on Lucien's nerves.

"I said I'm not interested." Lucien held the phone away from his ear and drew in a breath.

"Dr. Roux? Are you there?"

"Yes. There's nothing you can say that'll change my mind." Lucien began his usual count to ten. This guy wouldn't take no for an answer. "Besides, there might be an issue with my experiment."

Harmond paused before responding. "It doesn't matter. What about an unlimited budget to complete or fix your work?" Another pause. "Under exclusive contract to the United States Government, of course."

"Not interested." Lucien's voice boomed louder than he'd anticipated.

"Unlimited money and no one looking over your shoulder. No oversight, Dr. Roux. Think about that. I need your answer. Be smart, Roux, this is my final offer. You'll regret not accepting my offer."

"I already said no. Do *not* call me again." Lucien hung up.

Nothing Harmond had on offer would make Lucien surrender his clones and turn them into some sort of militarized obscenity. That wasn't the goal and never would be. A cure for cancer was. He'd worked too hard to perfect the sequencing to simply turn it over to the likes of Harmond for his super soldier aspirations.

Lucien went to the garage, climbed into his matte-black Jaguar XJ, and tossed the phone on the passenger seat. Even with the sun barely above the horizon, he knew Marlowe would be at Bay-Gen. Today she worked the weekend shift at the security desk and would be there absurdly early. She took punctuality, and her job as supervisor, seriously. In fact, she handled every aspect of her job with precision. He appreciated that about her. His work required the same type of dedication and gravity. Most of the women he'd dated were nice enough, but Marlowe had something special. They clicked. And she never complained about the many times he canceled their lunch dates because of his experiments.

He drove off down his quiet, tree-lined street, a blend of old oaks, magnolias, and ornamentals. He liked this particular Oakland neighborhood with its eclectic feel, partway between the ostentatious excesses of the *nouveau riche* and the stately homes of the old-money wealthy. His house hovered between the two, a remodeled Victorian with laminate flooring instead of hardwood, and a distinctive lack of antique furniture. He bought his house and the Jag with the remaining money from his old life of crime. They were his only luxuries.

Crossing the Bay Bridge into San Francisco on an early Saturday morning with light traffic presented the opportunity to daydream without worrying about getting into a fender bender. Early morning was his favorite time, when the ocean shimmered on fogless days as the sun silently crawled out from the depths of night. With the window down, he inhaled the cleansing, salty fresh air and felt one with the ocean, that primordial home to the beginnings of life.

The city, with its towering buildings and packed streets, triggered his favorite musing, about a time thousands of years ago when humans were scarce and roamed in small bands, not in massive two-ton chunks of metal, jockeying for the best lane on the freeways.

He turned down Montgomery Street, pulled into the underground parking structure of the mirrored high-rise that was Bay-Gen, and swiped his key card to open the iron gate. He loved his job, days spent peering into microscopes or gently teasing ancient-DNA strands apart. Tedious sometimes, sure, but also exhilarating and well worth it when he made progress as he had a few months ago. He knew he'd find the problem and fix it, and he also knew that someone like Harmond would never get their hands on his work.

He parked and sprinted up the stairs to the lobby, with its sickly gray and white marble floor shining under the overhead lights. Marlowe and the night guard were engaged in conversation. Lucien smiled at how good she looked in her supervisor's crisp white button-down shirt and black pants instead of the dark blue shirts and pants the other guards wore. She'd pulled her blonde hair into a tight bun, not her usual low ponytail.

He waved. "Good morning, Marlowe."

She gave the night guard a sharp nod. "You can clock out."

Lucien waited until the night guard vanished. "Sorry I left last night without saying goodbye. I had some issues that gave me a blinding headache and I went straight home. So, lunch today? There's that new Italian place down the block. I'll take a break around noon if that works."

"Not a problem, I was busy myself. Lunch sounds good, although I do prefer French." She smirked.

"*Est-ce que tu?*"

"Yes, I do. I wouldn't lie about that, Frenchie."

His cell phone vibrated in his pocket. "Hold on a sec." It better not be Harmond, again. "Oh, damn."

"What is it?" Marlowe leaned over the desk, peering at his phone.

"Nosy. It's my lab alarm. It's set to go off if there's a problem with my experiment."

"What kind of problem?"

He sighed. "I don't know yet. Care to come up while I check things out? No techs up there on the weekend."

She shook her head. "Can't. Gotta watch the desk. So, you're solo today?"

"All by myself." He glanced at his phone again. "Okay, I have to go. Lunch. Noon?"

"Noon."

If the clones died, he might not get another grant. He wiped his brow with the back of his hand to clear the beads of sweat. No more chatting, he had to get upstairs.

He jogged toward the elevators.

The elevator opened right away as soon as he pressed the up button and stopped on the fifth floor. He stepped out into the silence of the weekend and hurried down the hallway. The overhead recessed lights flickered on as they detected movement. At the end of the hall, his paleo-lab was protected by a biometric security system he'd commissioned as a precaution after the first calls from General Harmond.

Lucien never told the techs or other geneticists the exact truth about his experiment, because using Neanderthal DNA combined with some of his would be considered unethical. Another reason for the biometrics, but if he found a cure, it'd be worth it. Maybe overkill, but why take chances.

Once in his lab, he brought up the results from yesterday and checked what triggered the new alarm. Sure enough, the embryos had continued to grow, but more importantly, they were alive and apparently healthy.

His phone vibrated in his pocket. A video call from Marlowe. Oh, damn, he'd have to break their lunch date to harvest the stem cells.

"Hey, Marlowe..."

It wasn't Marlowe.

"Don't talk, listen, Dr. Roux." A strange woman with a stern husky rasp held a knife to Marlowe's throat.

His breath stuck in his throat and his hands trembled. The woman stood beside Marlowe, and at least a foot shorter. A huge muscleman dressed in black with a balaclava hiding his face held a gun to Marlowe's head.

"What do you want? Let her go!" Lucien shouted at the phone. "What's going on?"

The camera zoomed in. Marlowe flinched as the woman pressed the knife against her neck. A rivulet of blood made its way down to her collar. A bright red stain against the stark white fabric of her shirt.

With a smirk, the woman stared into the camera. "Be smart or your honey will bleed a lot more. What I want, *Paleo*, is your Neander-babies."

Chapter 3

Lucien's breath stuck in his throat. He couldn't think straight. How did the woman know anything at all about his experiment or Marlowe? And why call him Paleo? She obviously wasn't a reporter. Somehow it had to be General Harmond's handiwork. With the phone against his chest, he glanced around the lab. The woman had to have a hidden camera set up to spy on him.

"Come on, Paleo, play nice," the woman said in her hardened voice. "Yes, I've had your lab under surveillance and yes, I tracked down the company you hired to install your biometric system. With a little persuasion, I had them install my cameras while they were on site."

He glared at the phone's screen. "Why did ...? Let Marlowe go, she's got nothing to do with my research. Let her go."

The woman laughed. "This little honey is my insurance that you'll be a good boy and hand me those embryos. I believe you have sixteen that have mysteriously grown, according to your computer records. Is that correct, Paleo, all sixteen are alive and well? I wanted to have a camera in the incubator, but the techs swore it wouldn't work in there. Doesn't matter though, I'll soon have everything I need. Your babies will be mine."

The air flew from his lungs. She'd hacked into his computer as well. How? Who was she?

"I'm coming up, and you'd better have those babies all wrapped up with a bow by the time I get there."

The camera panned back to show the entire lobby again. Marlowe stood very still, not struggling at all. If not for her eyes blinking, he'd swear she was a statue. She'd told him once that her training in the Marines gave her "skills," and then didn't elaborate further, so why wasn't she using those skills now? He'd have to save her.

He steadied his nerves. "If you let Marlowe go, we can talk. Tell me what you want with the clones. Are you working for Harmond?"

"This isn't a Q & A session, Paleo. My client, not the military, paid me for a service, and I will deliver. I always deliver." She motioned to the clock on the wall behind the security desk. "You have five minutes to secure the embryos. And if they aren't ready by the time I get up there, the honey dies."

The video closed. Lucien dropped the phone on the counter and wiped his sweaty hands on his jeans. She knew Harmond was military, which meant she had to be collaborating with him in some fashion. He ran to the incubator and touched the first growth tube. The embryo had some of his DNA. They all did. How could he hand any of them over? Without special care, they'd die like the others. If the woman exposed his work before he had any results, it would be an ethical nightmare. But if he didn't surrender them, Marlowe would die.

He slumped to the tiled floor, shivered, and rested his head in his hands. "What do I do?"

He stood and glanced around. Every detail, every calculation, had been carefully planned to test their immune systems. It was unconscionable to take them out of the lab. He hadn't even run any tests yet, so why would anyone want his research? Harmond's idea of turning Neanderthals into soldiers stunk of absurdity on every level, but the woman in the lobby claimed she wasn't with him, so why did she want the specimens?

A sound in the lab caused him to abandon the incubator. His phone vibrated on the countertop. No more time. Sacrificing Marlowe for his research was out of the question. No one else knew how to keep the fetuses alive, so the woman would deliver dead Neanderthals to her client. And Marlowe would be safe. He'd ramp up his security even more to prevent anyone from ever gaining access again. He grabbed the phone and opened the video.

"I'm working on it! Don't hurt her."

The camera zoomed in on Marlowe and the woman. "You've almost exceeded your five minutes, Paleo. I see that you haven't been doing anything."

"I know." He tried not to sound desperate. "Give me more time. The specimens are on telemetry and feeding tubes. It takes time to—"

"Time's up." The woman displayed the knife. "Say goodbye, honey."

He shouldn't have delayed. "Wait! Wait! I'll get them ready for transport!" He stared at the screen. Did Marlowe wink? His chest hurt and his dry throat prevented him from swallowing, but she didn't seem worried at all. How did she accept impending death like that? "Don't hurt her, I'll do what you want."

He stumbled toward the incubator, eyes glued on the video. Then, Marlowe swept a leg out and smacked it into the woman's leg, causing her to fall and lose her grip on the knife. Lucien lost his breath. Marlowe had been waiting for the right time to act. The camera shook and then showed the ceiling of the lobby. All Lucien heard were grunts and heavy footsteps running.

A single gunshot rang out.

He ran full speed to the stairwell, flew down the stairs to the lobby, and burst through the door. Marlowe lay face down near the security desk, blood snaking its way out from under her, staining the marble floor. One step forward and someone grabbed him from behind.

The woman from the video strolled out from behind the security desk, a pistol in her hand. She glanced at Marlowe in passing. "I give her a couple of points for trying something. Not that her ridiculous attempt did anything except get her killed. I might have let her live, but she forced the issue."

"You fucking bitch!" Lucien struggled, but a hefty goon held him tight. "You didn't have to shoot her."

With another glance at Marlowe, the woman shrugged. "Apparently I did. Okay, Paleo, let's go up and get those Neander-babies and all of your research, or you'll receive the same treatment."

Marlowe wasn't moving and the blood had pooled into a sizeable puddle. Lucien's throat burned. He should have acted faster and secured the fetuses as soon as the woman told him to. Marlowe died because of him.

"Go ahead and kill me, but then you'll never get your hands on my research."

With a raspy laugh, the woman strode to him and got a few inches from his face. She smelled like an ashtray. "Your family owns a vineyard in Saumur, in the Loire Valley of France. Your father, Laurent, your younger sister, Nicoline and her brats, your younger brother Édouard, two cousins, Pierre and Diodore, and the family's loyal housekeeper, Amaline, all live on the property. It would be such a shame for the entire place to go up in flames in the middle of the night. Such a terrible loss of life ... a tragedy." Her wide-set eyes didn't blink, and her creased face was expressionless, like a hideous mask. "You lost your mother to cancer, what, eight years ago? Are you willing to risk the rest of your family?"

She wasn't the type to bluff, and he knew no one else should die because of him. But to lose years of research to the likes of her stung. No choice though. His family deserved to live. His father, a brilliant man, Nicoline, a caring nurse and a wonderful mother to three children, and Édouard graduated recently with his master's degree in finance. They had so much to live for. They had to be protected at all costs.

"Fine, take my experiment, take everything." His head drooped.

She backed away a few steps. "Well, thank you, Paleo. Pity the honey had to die, she had spunk and I admire that. But those are the breaks. One less dame in the world."

Lucien glared.

"Oh, don't be like that, Paleo. Everyone dies. Why don't we take a little stroll to your lab? It'll all be over soon." The edge of her thin lip curled up a fraction.

The goon behind Lucien let him go and shoved him toward the elevators. "Move!"

A drop of sweat made its way down Lucien's nose. He stumbled and staggered forward, glancing back at Marlowe. Every step took him away from her and closer to the end of his career, and possibly his life. Who else would want his research? Another healthcare company? Why not wait until he had something solid? Sixteen cloned Neanderthals wouldn't be good for anything with faulty experimentation. So why steal them now?

At the elevators, the woman pressed the *up* button with her knuckle and stood back, arms straight at her sides. Who was she? She didn't look like a typical assassin, not at all like those he'd seen in the movies, but she appeared easily as cold-blooded. The elevator door slid open, and he got a firm push inside.

He tripped and slammed into the back wall where he turned and kept his back flat against the hard surface. At least that way nobody had the opportunity to shoot him in the back.

"Look, I'm working with Banner Health Systems. If your client is a competitor, they won't get anything useful. Not yet. I haven't done any experimentation at this point. My research is to benefit everyone. If your client thinks they can make money off my—"

The woman interrupted in her monotone, frosty voice, "I get paid to deliver a product, no questions asked."

"Product? My research isn't a product. It's a way to help humanity. You don't have to do this, I can pay you. My family has money. I ... have money."

Her lips, pressed tightly together, parted barely enough to mumble, "Your family has money, Paleo, you live off grants. Your only worthwhile possessions are your car and your house. I don't want either."

She didn't say another thing, even when the elevator stopped at his floor. The goon tugged him out and nudged him forward.

He stopped in front of his lab and glared at the woman. "If you remove the embryos, they'll die. Or is that the real reason you're here? To destroy my research? Are you some sort of anti-science—?"

"I'm retrieving a product, Paleo, remember? Not a dead product, but a viable one. I asked you to get me the embryos and you didn't. I know you have battery backup systems, so you'll be using those to ensure the Neander-babies won't die. You should have done that when I asked, and your sweetie wouldn't be where she is now. Got it?"

He nodded. What else could he do? She'd thought of everything. "You didn't have to kill Marlowe."

"Oh, Paleo, we've gone over that. Time for you to move on. Now, open the damn door." She jabbed him in the ribs with her gun.

He knew what he had to do. Stay alive, call the police, and have the woman arrested for murder. That motivated him. After going through the biometrics, he stepped into the lab, the one place he'd always felt comfortable and safe.

The woman motioned to her goon, who stomped up to Lucien. "Be good, Paleo."

He went straight to the incubator and turned around. "The battery backup will only last for an hour."

She nodded and checked her watch. "I know. An hour is plenty of time. See? I know what's what. Now move. You've got three minutes now to secure the specimens into the backup containment cells. Go."

He swallowed and called out, "Unlock incubator door." He hesitated.

The woman poked him with the gun again. "Open the door now. You have two minutes and thirty seconds. If we get to zero, I'll kill your family and take the specimens anyway. Cooperate, and everyone lives."

"Except for Marlowe." He took a step inside the incubator and had the urge to slam the door behind him, but the goon followed him in. He reached under a cabinet and dragged out three metal cases, each capable of holding up to six growth tubes. Next, he pulled three battery packs from the wall charger and attached them to the cases. "The fetuses will die unless you have the correct nutritional formula and a complete growing medium setup. This is madness." He opened the cases.

The woman sauntered up to him. "One person's madness is another person's genius. Load 'em up."

"What guarantee do I have that you won't hurt my family?"

"I don't give guarantees." She peered into a growth tube. "I can hardly see the little buggers. Two minutes remaining, Paleo."

"Don't call me that."

Two minutes? As fast as possible, he disconnected one tube at a time, nestled them all into the cases, and connected the temporary nutrition supplements. He shut the lids.

"As I told you, they can only survive on the backup system for an hour, maybe less." He stared at the cases and thought of all the research he'd done. He should never have left France.

"They'll survive. My client wants living specimens. I win, Paleo."

Lucien touched the empty growth tube slots. She *had* won. A sharp crack rang in his ears and his head exploded in unbelievable pain. He hit the floor, hard. As darkness spread and his lungs ached for oxygen, he stared toward the hallway. He saw a figure crawl into the lab through the open door. Through his fuzzy vision, it looked like Marlowe. Wasn't she dead? A final bang! and then silence.

Chapter 4

A strange rhythmic sound broke into Lucien's dream of lying on a warm beach beside Marlowe. He fought it for a few seconds, but the incessant noise wouldn't stop. He gave up and fluttered his eyes open. A bright light stung them and forced him to close them again. The sound continued.

"Dr. Roux? Can you hear me? Dr. Roux?" asked a man in a gentle, soothing voice. "Can you hear me?"

The man was persistent, so Lucien opened his mouth to respond, but nothing came out. After having no luck speaking, he gradually opened his eyes again, blinking to clear his cloudy vision. He recognized the sound, a heart monitor beeping steadily.

He coughed and drew in a deep, ragged breath. "Wh ... where ... am I? Where's ... Marlowe?" Talking hurt his dry, raw throat. "Was I shot?" Someone pushed a small ice chip between his lips.

The head of his bed rose so he sat almost upright.

The man, whose nametag said Dr. Aquino, came close and shone a bright light into Lucien's eyes. "Welcome back, Dr. Roux. We've been expecting you to wake up soon. You've been administered a new cocktail of medication and it appears to have worked. Yes, you were shot. What do you remember?"

"Ah." Lucien remembered it clearly. The woman must have decided she didn't need him anymore and shot him. He reached up and felt his head. No bandages, but there were multiple electrode-like things attached to his hands and arms, front and back. "Where ... was I shot? My head ... what are these ... things?"

Dr. Aquino gave him a pat on the arm. "Muscle stimulators. Dr. Roux, you took a bullet to the head. It's a miracle you survived, let alone woke from the coma."

"Coma? A coma?" Lucien peeked under the blanket and saw more electrodes attached to his torso and legs, causing his muscles to jitter a bit. That was the pins and needles he felt. If he'd been shot, why wasn't there a bandage around his head? "How long?"

"Almost five months."

What? He must have misheard. "You mean five *days*. Five *weeks*?"

"Months, Dr. Roux." Dr. Aquino shut off the monitor's sound, pulled up a stool, and sat beside the bed. "It's natural for you to be disoriented and confused. Memory loss is another symptom of the coma, so don't stress it. It may or may not come back."

"Come back? I don't have any memory loss." He coughed again and Dr. Aquino handed him a cup of water. He sipped until it eased his sore throat. "I remember everything. A woman stole my research and then shot me. Wait, what happened to Marlowe? Marlowe Dunham. She's the security supervisor at Bay-Gen. I swear I saw her in my lab. She'd been shot. I saw a lot of blood when I got to the lobby. Where is she? Did she survive?" He sat up and felt remarkably strong for being in a five-month coma.

The doctor stood and glanced at the monitors. "Try to stay calm. You've experienced significant trauma. Ah, yes, Miss Dunham." Dr. Aquino nodded. "I treated her for a gunshot wound to the chest, close to the heart, but she still managed to get to your lab and fire off a couple of shots. Hit her target, too, but the assailant got away after Miss Dunham took another bullet. If Miss Dunham hadn't triggered an alarm, you'd be ..."

"I'd be dead. Did she suffer?"

With his forehead knotted, Dr. Aquino asked, "Suffer? Who? Miss Dunham?"

"Of course." Lucien closed his eyes. She'd helped him and ended up dead for her trouble. He'd never even had the chance to really get to know her.

"Dr. Roux, Miss Dunham is very much alive. She visits you every day, reads to you, and insists that she shave you herself. The nurses know to avoid her. As do I. Oh, and she has round-the-clock security guarding your door."

"She's alive?" Lucien touched his face. Sure enough, clean-shaven. "She's alive?"

"She's, ah, quite a force to deal with. Get some rest and we'll talk later." Dr. Aquino switched the monitor's sound back on but at a much lower volume. "I'll have some labs drawn and send physical therapy in. Miss Dunham is waiting to see you. She's been waiting for six hours since I administered the latest medication. I'm glad you woke up or I'd have to answer to her." He smiled and left.

A few seconds later, Marlowe, with dark brown hair instead of her usual blonde, came in. "Lucien, it's so great to see you finally awake." Her lips parted in a huge smile. "You look good."

He blinked and shook his head to clear his mind. "How? I saw you face-down in a puddle of blood. And the doctor said you'd been shot in the chest."

Her smile faded. "I'd lost a lot of blood, but when I came to and didn't see anyone around, I figured they'd gone to your lab. I tripped the silent alarm and then managed to get upstairs. I left a blood trail through the lobby, in the elevator, and the corridor. The cleaning lady hates me."

"No jokes, Marlowe. I'm not in the mood. You mean to tell me that you, half-dead and bleeding out, made it all the way upstairs, and shot those assholes?"

"You're welcome. Look, I'm not saying I had a fun time or anything, but I managed to shoot three of her guys and shoot her in the shoulder. My aim was off though. I'd aimed for her heart. I paid for that mistake."

"She doesn't have a heart, Marlowe. The doc said you got shot again."

"Yep. She got me right here." She parted her bangs and showed him a thin scar at the edge of her forehead. "Superficial. And here." She pulled up her sweater to show a jagged scar on her left side. "I went down, and she must have thought I died. Guess her aim was off too. She knew I'd tripped the alarm, Lucien. Right before she shot me again, she said it wouldn't make a difference because she had what she needed. I guess that's why she didn't hang around to check my pulse, or yours. That's *her* mistake, and one she'll regret."

"Unbelievable. Are you a superhero or something?" He reached for her hand and squeezed it. "Thank you."

Her face lit up with that beautiful smile. "Again, you're welcome. And no superhero, just a ton of Marine training."

"You thought she'd come back to finish me off. That's why you have a security guard..."

"Two guards, during the day. I take the night shift. She hasn't shown up though. Hopefully, that means she doesn't know, or care, that you pulled through." Her smile dropped. "Lucien, there's something else."

The "something else" had to be about the Neanderthals. "My research is gone, isn't it? She has it, doesn't she?"

"Apparently so. But there's more. You never exactly told me what your research is, but I heard the woman say she wanted your *Neander-babies*. What the hell does that mean?"

Lucien groaned. "Ugh."

"You found a way to reintroduce Neanderthals into the twenty-first century?" Her eyes narrowed and her lips pressed together.

He didn't want to tell her anymore. "Not reintroduced ... there's no point talking about it. The embryos would have died by now. The process to grow them and keep the nutrients and growth hormones at the correct levels had to be precise. No one else had the capability to duplicate it."

"Are you sure about that?" She arched an eyebrow.

"What are you getting at? Do you know something about them? Tell me."

The heart monitor beeped faster.

She handed him a computer tablet. "This is something you need to see. Steel your nerves."

For what? Had the woman, or her supposed client, published his research? His hard work, credited to someone else? "Okay."

She reached over and scrolled through several video files, stopped on one labeled Game II, and pressed play. "This one will do. Prepare yourself for Neanderball."

Chapter 5

Lucien stared at the video. Confused, he looked to Marlowe for answers, but when none came, he went back to the screen. Not exactly a sports nut, he'd only ever sat through one American football game to impress a woman he'd dated. She was the sports nut. Now though, his interest piqued. The playing field looked quite different, with small hills and mounds scattered about and a final larger hill leading up to the goal, with the posts on either side of the hill. Not at all like an ordinary football game.

Marlowe took his hand. "This is Neanderball. They introduced it about two months ago."

"Neanderball?" The field had no players, but the stadium was jam-packed with cheering people. He tore his eyes away from the video. "And who are the players?" His gut wrenched because he already knew the answer.

"Teenage Neanderthals. Your Neanderthals, I imagine."

A surge of anger shot through him.

Marlowe pulled her hand from his. "Ow. You're crushing my hand."

"Sorry." He loosened his grip. His embryos survived somehow. "Who's responsible? That woman who tried to kill us? General Harmond?"

She muted the volume. "Maybe, I don't really know. Who's General Harmond?"

"He kept pressuring me to work with the government to create ..."

"Government? Never mind. I don't want to know." She turned the volume back up. "The teams are owned by a father and son, Thomas and Jeremy Baker, sponsors of several MMA fighters and they co-own a real football team. I investigated them. They're into some shady shit. Anyway, they must be that bitch's clients."

"That's ... unbelievable. She said her clients needed the Neanderthals alive. I had no idea anything like this would happen."

Blood pounded in his ears. He took a breath and resumed watching. The crowd settled down and a troupe of cheerleaders, not Neanderthals, pranced around in short pink skirts, pandering to the audience, pom-poms waving. They split up, with half going to one side of the field, and the rest going to the other side.

The announcer declared, "Welcome to game two of Neanderball! Today's winning team will be matched with last week's winning. Then this winning team will battle the previous winners, in the first exhibition of the Neander-Games!"

The crowd roared and held up banners and signs with silly names on them.

Lucien wiped the sweat from his upper lip and swallowed. "Neander-Games?"

Marlowe took his hand again. "Sort of a Neanderthal Superbowl, but played every three weeks with the winning teams of the Neanderball games. There are four teams, each composed of four Neanderthals. Sixteen in all. The first two teams play three games on the first Saturday of the month. The other two teams play three games the following Saturday. The winning team from each of Saturday's games battle it out in the Neander-Games on the third Saturday. The fourth Saturday has exhibition games, a series of strength and endurance games, not that they're games at all. This isn't seasonal like football. They intend to play year-round."

"So, if Neanderball has been played for two months, that means my Neanderthals grew into teenagers in only, what, three months? And are playing football in twenty-first-century America?" He shook his head. "That's ludicrous."

Whoever continued his experiment must have created a new enhanced growth acceleration concoction. That had to be why they grew too fast in the lab. No way was that harmless. No hominid could go from embryo to teenager in so short a time without skeletal and organ damage or abnormalities, brain damage, and who knows what else.

She nodded. "Yep, it's ludicrous. And instead of carrying a football, they fight over a hundred-pound burlap sack of sand and run with it up and over the hills to the goal. Anything goes. They can tackle, punch, kick, anything. The more violent the game, the more the audience cheers."

Lucien dropped the tablet into his lap and slumped against his pillow, staring out the window near his bed. His Neanderthals were being exploited for entertainment. They'd become a commodity. He would never have exploited them. His scientific research did not exploit anyone. His was a noble goal, not like having them run around a field with a sack of sand. The team owners evidently knew about the abilities of Neanderthals and were smart to incorporate their brute strength into the game. Carrying a heavy load up and down hills was as natural to them as walking on level ground was to modern *Homo sapiens sapiens*.

"Lucien, watch the damn game."

"I've seen enough. I've got to get my work back. I can't give up on my research." He shifted and dangled his feet over the edge of the bed. "Where the hell are my clothes?" He plucked off the muscle stimulators.

"Hey, take it easy. You've been in a damn coma for five months."

He stepped onto the cold linoleum floor and wiggled his toes. "Relax, the doctor said the muscle stimulators kept my body in shape." He stood for a moment. His muscles trembled and he felt weak, but he refused to sit down. "See?"

"You're shaking all over. Besides, what do you think you can do? The team owners have money, a lot of money, and money always wins. Since they own the team, they clean up and make money off sponsors, merchandise, betting, and every other thing they can think of. All the money linked to Neanderball funnels straight to them. There's also talk of a kid's cartoon based on the fucking game. You'll never get close to the players or the team owners." She stood in front of him. "If you're not going to listen to reason, at least lean on me so you don't crumple into a pile on the floor."

He placed his hands on her shoulders and took a step. With each step forward, Marlowe backed up a step. He felt like a toddler. The trembling eased after about ten steps, and he decided to try it on his own. She stayed close but let him advance solo.

"Nice, Dr. Roux. But don't overdo it." She smiled.

He eased into a turn and went back to the bed. "Thank you for your help. Seems like you're always helping me out." He sat and drew in a breath, completely exhausted.

"Glad to do it." She picked up the tablet from the bed before he lay on it. She sat beside him and cued up the video again. "Now that you've had your temper tantrum, watch. Here they come."

He leaned close. He wanted to see them, see how they moved, and if there were any defects from the rapid growth. The cheerleaders on each side of the field stood in front of a tunnel entrance, but parted when four burly, hairy young Neanderthals came out. There were four from each side, running at what could only be called a full-on charge, toward one another. They were incredible specimens, short in stature, with pronounced brow ridges and muscles stretching the fabric of their jerseys. But there was something else. Their noses were wrong. They should have had wide nostrils to allow for better airflow, but instead, they had a narrower, slightly aquiline nose.

"That's my nose. They're ... my children," he whis-pered.

"What? Shush."

They never slowed at all, and collided into a mass of shoving, punching, and kicking. The crowd loved it. Lucien flinched. The cheerleaders seemed wary and scrambled onto elevated platforms where they would perform.

After a minute of brawling, a loud buzzer sounded. The Neanderthals lined up immediately, like football players, except there were only four players on each side.

"What the hell? ..." Lucien's voice trailed off.

"This is Neanderball," Marlowe said softly.

He swallowed a trace of bile rising in his throat and watched as a golf cart emblazoned with sponsors' logos zipped out onto the field and stopped between the teams. Two men hopped out, hefted a large burlap sack from the back, and placed it on the ground in between the teams. The players shifted weight from one foot to the other, eyes narrowed. They looked like they'd pounce any second. One of the men waved a red flag, and then they both ran to the golf cart and took off.

The Neanderthals, knees bent and arms flexed, readied themselves. Lucien fixed his eyes on the spectacle. What a mockery of an amazing species. Watching them gave him chills. When another buzzer sounded, the Neanderthals dove at the sack until it vanished, hidden under thrashing bodies.

"I think I'm going to be sick." Lucien wiped his brow. If he'd had time to salvage the genetic material and destroy the embryos when he'd realized they'd grown too fast, he might have saved his experiment. And made it impossible for the woman to have stolen his research. Too late now.

Marlowe handed him a cup of water. "As I said, there's nothing you can do. It's only a game."

He glared at her. "A game? My work ... Neanderthals developed tools, buried their dead, and created art. And they might have vocalized as we can. They're a *Homo* genus like us, did you know that? *Homo neanderthalensis*. Or *Homo sapiens neanderthalensis* to be more precise. That's why combining some of my DNA with theirs worked. They're not adapted to live in this climate or in cities. Look at them. Pounding on one another for a sack of sand!"

"I know. Trust me, I hate this damn game, too." She leaned against him. "You know, I have to ask ... what the hell were you thinking? Bringing Neanderthals back from the past? What did you hope to accomplish?" She frowned. "Wait. Did you say you added your DNA into the mix? That's not ... right. What the fuck, Lucien?"

"Let me explain."

"No. I can't ... while you were lying here, day after day, I got to thinking. Is what you planned any better than where they are now? You were using them, right? And you're aware of them being a *Homo* species. At least now they're not being experimented on. That's what you were going to do, wasn't it? That's what Bay Genetics is all about, right?" She got off the bed and pointed at the video. "Those players are your creation. You're the root cause of this, willingly or not. Take some damn responsibility for where they've ended up."

It was the truth. They *were* his creation. "I am taking responsibility." Didn't she understand how much time he'd spent in the lab? "You're right, I am the only one responsible for this ground-breaking research. Research, not ball players. I've got to stop Neanderball and get my work back."

"Your work? Is that all you care about?"

He slipped off the bed and half-crawled to the bathroom, dropped to the floor, and vomited into the toilet. A moment later, Marlowe knelt beside him and placed a damp washcloth on his forehead.

"I'm sorry, Lucien. I shouldn't have come down on you so hard. It's the whole make-money-off-the-downtrodden that gets to me. Okay, maybe not exactly downtrodden, but you know what I mean."

He took the washcloth and wiped his whole face. He flushed the toilet. "The helpless. That's more accurate. They belong to me and now those morons have them. The Neanderthals are helpless without me to care for them."

"Wait, what?" She glared. "They seem to be doing fine. You don't own them. They're not property, you know. If they're like us, and you think of them as property, you're condoning Neanderball and exploitation."

In no mood to enter into an ethical debate, he closed his eyes and shut her out for a moment. His head spun, and his stomach roiled. "Okay, listen, you don't understand. I meant they're similar to us, but they're not modern *Homo sapiens sapiens*. They're an extinct species. And don't ever say I condone their mistreatment or exploitation." He paused and replayed what he said. Of course there was a fine line between his research and what was morally right. He'd intended to use them when they were barely more than a few differentiated cells, and then destroy them. But now they were teenagers. So, what could he do now, assuming he'd get them back? "Damn, my head hurts. How can I fight for my rights?"

"Your rights? Are you forgetting the Neanderthals' rights?" She turned away and strode from the bathroom, leaving him on the floor.

She took the moral high ground when she had no right to. She worked at Bay-Gen and knew what went on. He'd told her on their first lunch date that he'd started working on a special genetic project.

She shouted, "The worst part is that it's become the most popular game in the world. It's broadcast everywhere. Vegas bookies eat it up and sports bars make a killing. I had a buddy of mine look into the legality of what they're doing, and it's legal. The Neanderthals were officially adopted by the team owners. Since they're not technically adults, the "parents" have the right to make them play."

"What are you talking about?" He dabbed his face again with the washcloth and shuffled his way back to the bed. "Legal? How is any of this legal?"

"Trust me, it is."

What a twisted world he lived in. He lay down and closed his eyes. "How do they explain where the Neanderthals came from?"

The bed creaked as Marlowe sat next to him. "Well, before you woke up from the coma, they kept it top secret. They evaded the question. There were rumblings that they'd divulge everything in time. Every now and then, a humanitarian group would get all and protest, but they were quickly slapped with a cease-and-desist order or something and quietly went away. I told you it's all about money. Expensive lawyers and threats."

"Or bribes. Hold on." A thought flashed through his brain. He opened his eyes and sat up. "You said they evaded the question, but they'd explain everything at some point?"

"Yep."

He reached for her hand and held it tightly. Things started to make sense. "What if that woman didn't come to finish me off in the hospital because I'd make the perfect scapegoat? It wouldn't matter if I lay in a coma. I can be blamed for engineering the Neanderthals, whether I'm dead, alive, or in a coma."

"Duh. I figured that out already. And it's the truth. You did bring those kids into the world." She squeezed his hand, hard. "Stop talking. I need to process."

Lucien wrestled his hand free before she shattered his phalanges. She thought him a monster.

She shook her head and shot him a glance, a little softer than before, and left.

"Marlowe!"

He slumped onto the pillows. The only way to redeem himself in her eyes meant getting his research back to show his intent had been honorable. Finding a cure for cancer would make society, and Marlowe, exonerate him.

In his younger days, he'd dealt with several evil-minded people. He'd learned that the best way to make them disappear meant destroying their credibility and reputation. Once he ruined the woman's standing in the criminal world, she'd be out of business and hopefully would leave him alone. He'd prove his original experiment had been tampered with and stolen, and then he'd have his life back. Finally, hope lay on the horizon. Now all he had to do was put a plan into action.

Chapter 6

Alone in his hospital room after Marlowe left, Lucien stood at the window and watched the world. Nothing seemed different. Below, a few patients sat on benches in the courtyard and enjoyed the sunshine, while birds flitted from tree to tree. It was all a façade though. The world was *very* different.

Without any street clothes, he wrapped a sheet around his hospital gown and stepped into the hallway to find a change of scenery, anywhere other than the stuffy hospital room.

"Dr. Roux?"

Lucien turned around and saw the doctor.

"Dr. Roux, where are you going? Physical therapy is on the way. Your muscles are strong, but you still need physical therapy to gain your balance back."

"I have my balance."

"You're shaking, unsteady. Let's get you back to your room."

Lucien shook his head. "No, I don't want to be here any longer. I'm leaving." He half-shuffled to the elevators down the hall.

"I haven't discharged you yet." The doctor jogged to him. "We need to make sure your body is capable of—"

"It's capable." Lucien pressed his finger on the down button. "I'm fine."

The doctor frowned. "You're leaving against medical advice."

The elevator door opened.

Lucien walked in. "I don't care." He pushed the ground floor button. "Thank you for everything you did for me."

"Well, ah ..."

The door closed before the doctor finished his sentence. Lucien clenched his jaw as the elevator descended. He was disappointed in humanity, but mostly in himself for allowing that woman to win.

On the ground floor, the door opened and Marlowe stood in the lobby, waiting for the elevator.

"Lucien? Where do you think you're going? I was coming back up to apologize."

He got out and drew in a deep breath. "It's all right. I deserved it. My lofty ideals need an occasional slap-down. Hey, I've got to get out of here. I hate hospitals."

She pointed to the sheet. "In that? I can bring you some clothes."

"No. I need to be away from here. Now. I want to go home."

"Oh." She motioned to some plastic chairs. "Sit for a minute."

"No. I'm going home."

"About that. You don't have a home anymore." She glanced away. "They foreclosed it. I didn't want to tell you before. Look, I would have helped out, but I barely make enough money to pay my mortgage. The auction house sold off your belongings as well."

Foreclosed? So now, in addition to everything else, he'd lost his house. Now what would he do? He had nothing left. "*Merde.*" He staggered to one of the chairs and flopped down, the excess sheet bunching at his legs. "Do I still have a job at Bay-Gen?"

No answer.

"Marlowe?"

With a heavy sigh, she shook her head. "You were let go. But they pay for your hospitalization since it happened at work. Worker's Comp covers most of it, but they help with extra care. The muscle stimulators are a Bay-Gen invention, state-of-the-art. They had to get the hospital to sign a memorandum of agreement to use them on you. So that's something."

He pulled the sheet around his shoulders a bit tighter. "That wasn't a magnanimous gesture on their part, they used me as their guinea pig for the stimulators. They've done the same with other inventions. I have no job, no house, no research" He knew his life had ended.

"Hey, hold on with the doom and gloom. I'll take you to my place and you can clean up." She took his hand. "I managed to hold onto your Jag and a closet full of your clothes."

He stared at her. "You did that? But you had no idea if I'd come out of the coma. And why did you stay with me at night for five months? I can never repay you for—"

"Repay? I don't want repayment. I want that woman's head mounted on my wall. I knew you'd snap out of your Sleeping Beauty routine sooner or later, and besides, two heads are better than one at figuring out who she is and what rock she's hiding under." She handed him the car's key fob. "Are you willing to help me find her or do I have to go it alone?"

He rubbed the Jaguar emblem between his fingers. "Of course, I'll help you. But first, I need to change out of this less-than-charming outfit."

"Totally agree with you on that. Are you good to drive?"

He sighed and stood. "I don't know. Let's get out of here."

He ignored the stares from a couple in the lobby and hurried toward the entrance. As soon as the door slid open, a swarm of reporters flocked toward him from the parking lot, jockeying for the best position to snap a photo of him.

"Dr. Roux, is it true you tried to commit suicide because you wanted to avoid blame?"

"Paleo! Paleo! What gives you the right to tamper with genetics? You're playing God!"

"Why have you been hiding? Guilty conscience, Paleo?"

"Do you still want to kill the players?"

A beam of sunlight stung him right in his eyes and the word *guilty* rang in his ears. He opened his mouth to speak, but Marlowe shoved him back into the hospital lobby, his mind whirring. Who'd tipped off the press and who said he'd tried to commit suicide? Nobody but Marlowe and the hospital staff knew he'd come out of the coma. Unless...

He shuffled to the chair again and slumped into it. "She knew. She's watching me."

Marlowe spun around and waited until the doors closed. "Who? The woman?"

Even with the doors closed, the cameras kept filming.

"Of course. Why can't she leave me alone?" He got up and hurried away from the front entrance. "Those people out there know about my research. And they were waiting."

The woman must have leaked the information about him to the media and had to be watching a broadcast somewhere, laughing her ass off. One of the reporters said he was playing God. Was he? He leaned against the wall and shrugged off the sheet. He felt hot and couldn't catch his breath. Even the skimpy hospital gown felt confining.

"Easy, Lucien." Marlowe placed her hand on his shoulder. "You've been through so much, and now this. I swear I'll make her pay."

He sucked in as much air as possible and shook her hand away. "The only thing I did wrong was cloning the Neanderthals in the first place. My research wasn't to turn them into football players. This is...it's—"

"Take a breath, you're hyperventilating." She looked him in the eyes. "Breathe."

A moment later, five security guards and two uniformed police officers rushed past them toward the entrance. Lucien concentrated on regulating his breathing so he wouldn't pass out and got up to watch the guards and police shoo the paparazzi away. One tenacious cameraman got urged to move with the threat of a billy club. That made him smile a little, but when the guards noticed him and strode toward him, the smile dropped.

"You Dr. Lucien Row-ex?" one of them called out.

He nodded. "It's pronounced roo. Like in kangaroo."

The guard scowled, waved to a police officer, and ordered, "Detain Dr. *Roo* like in kangaroo for creating a public disturbance and threatening the Neaderball team."

"What?" Lucien backed away. "I haven't done a damned thing. Arrest those people out there. They're a public nuisance. Or better yet, do your job and find the woman who shot me!"

The cop sauntered over with a pair of handcuffs dangling from his hand. "You're being detained, sir."

"This is bullshit," Marlowe grumbled. "What's he done? You have no probable cause to arrest him."

The cop turned to Marlowe. "He's not being arrested, ma'am, only detained for questioning."

"Then why the handcuffs?" She scowled at the cop. "I'll get you out, Lucien."

"Don't bother." He extended his arms to the cop. "I'm probably safer in jail."

The handcuffs clamped around his wrists in front, rather than behind his back, so that was something. The cop motioned to the door. "You going to come along peacefully?"

With a heavy sigh, Lucien nodded and jiggled his hands. "What do you think, I'm going to make a run for it with handcuffs on?"

"You'd be surprised," the cop mumbled. "It's for your protection. Ah, do you have a robe or jacket or something?" He motioned to the hospital gown and sheet. "You know, so you can cover up?"

Lucien shrugged. "*Je m'en fous.*"

"Huh?" The cop stared.

"I don't care," Lucien explained.

"Okay, then move." He prodded Lucien forward and motioned to Marlowe. "You stay here."

She continued scowling and draped the sheet over Lucien's shoulders.

He hung his head as he shuffled through the lobby between the cops, prepared for another onslaught of accusations. He'd woken up from a coma only to get detained for something he didn't do. Outside, the security guards did their best to keep the reporters at bay as he made his way through the doorway.

The first thing he noticed was a young, bearded man pushing his way to the front of the crowd. He wore a garish orange T-shirt with the slogan "I live for Neanderball" emblazoned across it. Below the slogan was *Team Orange*.

"You've got to be kidding," Lucien muttered to himself.

The young man hurled something at Lucien and shouted, "You can't kill Team Orange! Asshole!"

A plump balloon filled with orange paint splattered all over Lucien's hospital gown as it struck him in the chest. Lucien lunged at the young man and even with his manacled hands, managed to punch him square on the nose. He was aiming for his chin, but was hampered by his weakened muscles and the handcuffs. "I'm an asshole? What about you and the other fools who encourage the exploit—"

A bolt of electricity surged through him and he toppled to the dirty sidewalk in a quivering lump. After a few seconds, he regained control of his muscles and saw a Taser in the cop's hand. Could his life get any worse?

A police car screeched to a stop outside the hospital. A cop pulled Lucien to his feet and shoved him into the back of the car onto a hard vinyl seat. The paparazzi pushed in close, snapping photos as the car sped off. He saw Marlowe shove her way in front of the crowd and mouth the word *fuck*.

The cop in the passenger seat turned around. "You're the one who invented the Neanderthals?"

"Invented?" Lucien slumped in the seat and covered his face with his hands. "Are you serious? No, I didn't invent the Neanderthal species. I'm a geneticist. That's all." He looked up and saw the cop's scowl.

"That's not what I meant, smartass. Did you create the Neanderthal players?"

"Inadvertently, yes." Lucien gazed out the window. Maybe he shouldn't say anything. "I want a lawyer."

The cop didn't respond. He faced front and said something softly to his partner. As they neared the police station, another group of paparazzi swarmed and rushed at the car. The cop turned on the siren, which made them move out of the way, but not too far.

Lucien shielded his face with his hand but peeked between his fingers. There were more orange T-shirts among the crowd, but this time, there were also shirts in bright purple, green, and blue. Team fans. His Neanderthals were reduced to being represented by fanatics in gaudy-colored shirts.

"Idiots," Lucien mumbled.

"What's that?" the cop said after turning off the siren.

"Nothing." He shifted his weight to get away from the sticky orange paint that had dripped and pooled on the seat all around him. No use, he sat in a puddle. He pinched his nose because the paint stench gave him a headache.

Once safely in the underground parking garage of the station, he sat up and pulled the sticky hospital gown away from his skin, shivering. The sheet stuck to the seat where it had slipped off his shoulders. The car stopped near a doorway with a sign above it: Prisoner and Detainee Entrance.

His new life as a detainee. Only a few months ago, he was on top of the world, about to make a scientific breakthrough that would ease the suffering of the ill. Now, everyone on the planet loathed him. The fans hated him because they knew he'd intended to kill the embryos, and the humanitarians hated him for ... well, pretty much the same thing. The only person he had left was Marlowe, and at the moment, she wasn't all that fond of him either.

The cop opened the door and ushered him out. "Come on."

Lucien hesitated. Unlike the hospital, in this place, he couldn't leave at any time. Whether they called him a detainee or prisoner, it meant the same thing. They had him trapped. "I ... I'm innocent. I'm doing my job, that's all. I'd never hurt a fully formed fetus."

"Sir, exit the vehicle or I'll have to use force." The cop took a step back and lowered his voice, "Look, if you're the guy who started Neanderball, then you're my hero, even if you wanted to kill them. Thank God you didn't. Love the game. My kid and I watch it every Saturday. We're team purple. We cheer for Brutus, but all the team members are good."

"Brutus?" Lucien edged out, tugging on the sheet, and stood.

"Yeah, Brutus. You know, the one with the crooked fingers 'cause he broke them a couple of weeks back. They all break something eventually."

Lucien's legs trembled. He should have stayed in the hospital and waited for physical therapy. "What?"

"Yeah, Brutus got banged up pretty good. Didn't you watch it? Anyway, he cracked a few ribs, broke his fingers, and busted his nose." The cop laughed. "But he messed up the other team before they took him down. He still plays with broken bones!"

Lucien grabbed onto the car door. "What the hell sort of game is this?" He felt dizzy.

"Well, it's more of a blood sport, but there are some rules, so that makes it a game. Right?"

"Yeah, sure, that makes everything perfectly fine." Lucien's knees threatened to give out. "I ... I need to sit."

"You can sit in the interview room. We got a wheelchair if you need that. Hey, bring the chair, and a towel." The cop motioned to the driver, who went to the doorway and unfolded a portable wheelchair leaning against the wall.

Lucien stood for a moment to make sure his legs were working right, while the driver grabbed a towel from the trunk and spread in on the chair.

"Thank you." Lucien sat.

"I can't believe you're the guy. Can I have your autograph, for my kid?" The driver pulled a small notepad from his shirt pocket. "His name's David." He poked the notepad in Lucien's face. "Come on, it's the least you can do."

Lucien stared. "You think it's appropriate to poke that in my face after you handcuffed me and brought me here?" He snatched the notepad and tossed it as far as possible with the handcuffs on. "*Va te faire foutre.*"

"Huh?"

"Sorry. Fuck off."

The cop's eyes narrowed, and he grabbed Lucien by the gown, lifting him off the wheelchair an inch. "You rich, self-important guys are all the same." He leaned close. "Fuck you, too."

Lucien flinched. Great, he kept making more enemies. He knew he should apologize, but he no longer cared. "Lock me up for whatever false charges you've dreamed up."

A nurse wearing pale blue scrubs came through the door and went straight to the cops. "I got a call."

The cop let go of Lucien. "Yeah, this guy's sick or something and said he had to sit down. We picked him up at the hospital. He's the Neanderball guy. The inventor or whatever."

The nurse glared at Lucien. "Oh, really? That's a barbaric game if you ask me. Did anyone ask those Neanderthals if they wanted to play or if they even wanted to be brought into existence at all?"

"I'm a scientist, a geneticist. I do work for a healthcare company. I didn't "invent" Neanderball. I'm appalled that my research is used for this absurdity."

"Then why did you do it?" She pushed the handcuff aside and took his pulse, squeezing hard.

He grimaced. "I told you, I had nothing to do with any of this. I got shot. I've been in a coma for five damn months. You think I'd have any part in this?" The words kept coming, he couldn't stop. "A woman stole my research. She shot me and my ... the security guard at my lab. Marlowe and I almost died. Don't you dare accuse me of playing any part in using my Neanderthals for entertainment!"

"Calm down, sir," the nurse dropped his wrist and stepped back. "You look pretty good for being in a five-month coma." Her voice dripped sarcasm.

"Yeah, don't I though?" Lucien stood. "I am a French citizen. I demand you contact the French Consulate." Maybe they'd help him. Unless they hated him, too. "And can you get me a change of clothes? Something without orange paint all over it!"

The cop raised an eyebrow. "You're not even American?"

"You can't tell by my accent that I'm not from here?"

"I meant an American citizen." The cop sighed and motioned to his partner, the driver, who stood by the detainee's doorway. "Got a problem."

"Yeah? What?" The driver came over.

"French citizen."

"Oh. Sir, you're being detained, not arrested."

Lucien's face flushed hot as he held up his hands. "I know! But I'm handcuffed and they forced me into the police car! I demand to speak to my Consulate." He pushed the wheelchair away. "I'll walk."

"The cuffs are for your safety." The cop looked at his partner, shrugged, and took the cuffs off, clipping them into a holder on his belt. "No cuffs. Follow me."

The driver swiped a key card at the doorway and waited. "Inside, sir."

Down the hallway and up a flight of stairs was the interview room, a cold, sparse room with a metal table and two chairs. The only window was small and had thick bars covering it. Lucien stepped inside and began shivering all over again.

He motioned to the hospital gown. "Fresh clothes? Blanket?"

The cop nodded and motioned to his partner. "Yeah, sure. Wait in here while we call the Consulate." He left and shut the door behind him.

Lucien crossed his arms and paced. He stopped at the small, barred window in the door. He saw into the hallway and partially into another room across from his. A few cops wandered past, but otherwise, the hall was empty. He continued to pace and rub his body until his shivering eased. At the door again, he tapped the glass. Nobody heard. He was little more than an animal looking out.

If Marlowe had been allowed to go with him, he'd have someone to talk to, or maybe complain to. Hopefully, she'd find a way to get him out. He stayed at the window, hoping for help from the first human he saw. A moment later, a chill snaked down his spine. The assassin-woman strolled down the hallway, the hint of a smirk on her face.

Chapter 7

Lucien pressed his body against the wall next to the door and held his breath. If the woman came into the room, there was zero chance of escape. Why couldn't she leave him alone? He had no doubt now that she'd had him under surveillance. The only reason she'd be in the police station would be to kill him before he had the chance to talk.

He let out his breath. Why hide? It was a guarantee that she knew he was there. Surely she wouldn't do anything since there would be too many witnesses. Might as well confront her, but if she did try to kill him, he wouldn't go easily. He dashed to the table and picked up a chair. Not much defense against a bullet, but better than nothing.

About four feet from the door, he readied himself, his heart thumping, sweat beading on his forehead. A moment later, the woman's face appeared in the window. He jumped. She smirked and drew a stubby finger across her throat. What was that, intimidation? He motioned for her to come in, but she vanished. He waited, counting the seconds, until he reached his breaking point and carried the chair with him to the door, ready to attack. He peeked out, but she'd vanished.

"What the hell?" He dropped the chair. "Where'd you go!" She taunted him, but why? Did she get some twisted pleasure out of making him suffer?

A cop's face popped into view and startled Lucien. He caught his breath and shoved the chair with his foot. As it skittered across the room, the metallic scraping echoed off the walls.

The cop unlocked the door and scrutinized Lucien. "That outburst isn't going to earn you any good-behavior credit. Here." He tossed a bundle of clothes and a thin blanket onto the table and held the door as another man with slicked-back hair and a tailored business suit sauntered in carrying an attaché case.

The cop stayed at the door and said, "This is Mr. Basten from the French Consulate. I'll be waiting outside."

Basten, perhaps in his forties, nodded to Lucien and waited until the cop left before extending his hand. "*Bonjour.* You prefer French or English?"

Lucien shook his hand. "English is fine. Can you help me?" After slipping into a pair of grey sweatpants, Lucien let the hospital gown drop into a sodden pile and pulled on a blue T-shirt with "Police" stamped across the chest. "They say I'm not under arrest, but they won't let me leave."

Basten picked up the chair and placed it at the table. "Shall we?" He motioned for Lucien to sit in the other chair across from him.

"Sure. What do you know about my situation?"

Basten nodded thoughtfully. "Enough. I've been following the news and have been in contact with your family. Your father, brother, and sister intended to fly here to see you, but I stopped them."

Lucien stayed standing. "You what? Why?"

"Sit." It was more of an order than a request. "Your family is where they need to be, as you are where you need to be. You've got quite a thick skull. Incredibly, you survived a bullet to the head."

"Yes, it is incredible." Lucien sat, leaned his elbows on the cold table, and studied the man. The way he spoke, he wasn't from the Consulate, which meant only one thing. He was one of the woman's goons. "What does she want from me?"

"She?" Basten sat opposite Lucien and raised a trimmed eyebrow.

"Stop screwing around. I'm not in the mood. Are you here to kill me?"

Basten laughed. "Ha! Why would I do that? I told you, you're exactly where you should be. It took some planning to get everything in place. Bay Genetics was more than willing to use their experimental medication cocktail on you."

"Wait, what ...?" Did that mean Bay-Gen was in-volved?

"You are integral to the plan. Well, you became integral when you didn't die. There are rumblings about investigating the legality and morality of Neanderball. If Neanderball fails, the boss fails. And she doesn't like to fail. She has a reputation to protect." He smiled with teeth that were too white. "You can't make a move without her knowing. But, no, I'm not here to hurt you."

"Then why are you here!" Lucien pounded on the table.

"Oh, calm down. I'm here to pass along a message from our mutual friend." Basten pulled a plastic baggie from his attaché case and slid it across the table. "This is for you."

Lucien peered at the baggie. There was a folded piece of tissue inside, with a slight bulge in the center. His gut clenched. A cyanide pill wrapped up in there? Did the woman want him to commit suicide now? Were cyanide pills still a thing?

"What ... wh ... I don't understand ..." the words stuttered from his lips.

"Open it, Dr. Roux."

Lucien struggled to open the baggie. After a few tries, he succeeded and slowly pulled out the tissue. He glanced at Basten and unfolded it. "What the hell is that?" It wasn't a pill, but an oblong-ish object stained red on one side, about the size of a ... fingernail. "What did—?"

"I only deliver the messages. That belongs to your brother." Basten leaned forward and slid a photograph in front of Lucien.

The photo was of Édouard, strapped to a chair, his index fingertip bleeding. "You bastard!"

Basten placed his finger on the photo and dragged it back. "Here's what you're going to do, or the next baggie will contain something from your father. Maybe something more important than a fingernail. Listen carefully." He leaned over the table. "You will admit to replicating the Neanderthal DNA and growing the embryos. You were about to use them for experimentation when Thomas and Jeremy Baker offered to buy them from you out of pity, to save their lives. You took the money, but their bodyguards shot you when you tried to double-cross them after you assaulted Thomas Baker. Got it?"

The words tumbled around in Lucien's head. So that was how the woman played it out. The team owners were heroes and saved the Neanderthals from death. "You want me to be the bad guy? To get the heat off those men?"

A slight smile formed. "Not me personally. But you will do as I say, or the next bullet will be a lethal one. Oh, and I hear your elderly father is weak these days. Your mother's death was hard on him, wasn't it?"

"Shut the hell up." Lucien covered the fingernail with the tissue and pushed it away. "You leave my family alone."

"Oh, they'll be fine, so long as you cooperate. Don't try to contact them or the authorities. You do, and they ... well, use your imagination. And after, that bullet I mentioned will find you. I'll be holding onto your passport for safekeeping." Basten pulled the passport half out of his pocket, slid it back, and tucked the tissue into the same pocket. "As a representative of the French Consulate, I have arranged for your immediate release on the condition that you will repeat to the police, and the media, what I have told you." He stood and smoothed his jacket. "Remember what I said about ..." his voice trailed off and he turned to the door.

Lucien closed his eyes, images of his family flashing through his mind. They had to be terrified. He hadn't visited them in over two years, being too busy with his research. What was it all for? All he'd accomplished simply provided team members for Neanderball. He opened his eyes. "I'll do whatever you want. But don't touch my family again. Ever."

Without turning, Basten nodded and knocked on the door. "A deal's a deal, *monsieur*."

"Get out."

The door opened and Basten gave the cop a genial slap on the arm, then strolled out without another word. The cops were in the woman's pocket as well. She must have told them to hold off any questioning until Basten came to deliver the message. That's why she was in the police station.

A moment later, a man dressed in a creased off-the-rack suit came in, sat down, and placed a manila folder on the table.

"I'm Detective McAllister. I understand you're ready to give a statement."

"Ready? More like coerced. This is unbelievable." Lucien rested his head in his hands.

McAllister shrugged. "Unbelievable or not, your Consulate guy said you'd like to make a statement to clear everything up. Are you wasting my time? Should I get him back?"

Lucien stared at the tabletop, right where his brother's fingernail had been, and realized he didn't have a choice. "I'll make a statement."

"Okay, then. I have to say, this is the weirdest case I've ever worked on. Neanderball has pulled this country together, Dr. Roux. And those Neanderthals deserve to live their lives, not die at your hands. They didn't ask to be born, now did they?" He opened the folder. "Take your time and if you need more paper, let me know." He took out two pieces of blank paper and dropped a pen on them. "I'll be outside."

Lucien put his hand on top of the papers. "Sure." McAllister likely only knew what they wanted him to know. "Hey, can you shut off the air conditioning? I'm freezing."

"You got a blanket right there." McAllister knocked on the door and left without saying anything more.

Lucien wrapped the blanket around his shoulders and stared at the blank pages. False confession time. His life was in shambles. If he wasn't hated before, he would be now. All those years he'd put into studying and tweaking DNA strands were for nothing. Time to move back to France and start a new life, although that meant leaving Marlowe. She'd stuck with him and protected him, but now he had to protect her by getting as far from her as possible.

He picked up the pen only to drop it when he heard shouts and whoops coming from outside the room. He dashed to the door and peered out the barred window. A crowd of police gathered around a flat-screen TV in the room across the hall. A news broadcast played, and although he couldn't hear what was said, he knew Neanderball was the topic. Behind the news anchor, a video feed showed his Neanderthals wearing purple, orange, green, and blue T-shirts. They were standing on the playing field, occasionally shoving one another or pawing at the grass with their feet.

He banged on the door. "Hey!" Nobody came. They were all too interested in the Neanderball report. "Somebody! Please!"

The Neanderthals grinned at the camera as it panned past them and made awkward hand gestures like they were trying to do a thumbs-up, but didn't quite get it right. How devastating to see them acting like spoiled children, mugging for the audience, and reveling in the applause. These were no longer his experimental subjects, they were living, breathing people who had part of his DNA. If he wrote the confession as Basten wanted, he'd lose them forever. But if he didn't write it, his family would suffer, and he'd be murdered.

"Shit."

He paced around the room and thumped on the door each time he passed by. He was in an impossible situation with only one solution. The woman's power reached too far for him to disobey. He'd have to sacrifice himself and scurry away to some obscure part of the world where nobody knew him; so he'd live out the rest of his life in private, and maybe start up his experiment again somehow. Seclusion wouldn't bring shame to his family or anyone else who knew him. And then there was Marlowe. She'd be guilty by association, and that cut him deeply.

The paper and pen taunted him, waiting for him to accuse himself of a tainted version of the truth. There was no choice. He sat and scribbled the statement, loathing himself with each word. A smarter man would find a way to save his family and the Neanderthals, but no answer came to *him*. When they released him, the first thing he'd do would be to apologize to Marlowe for all he'd put her through. Next, he'd get his passport from Basten and be with his family before disappearing forever.

The door opened and McAllister came in with a Styrofoam cup. "All done?"

"Yeah, sure." Lucien pushed the paper away and accepted the cup. "What's all the commotion out there?"

McAllister glanced outside. "Oh. Press conference. An announcement said that the Neander-Games will be hosted right here in the Bay Area. Oakland." He leaned on the table. "Some say it'll be bigger than the Olympics." He laughed. "Rumor has it that Neanderball will become an Olympic sport in time. Dr. Roux, you should embrace this. You made a mistake wanting to kill those players, only a mistake. They're amazing athletes. Kinda scary and weird looking, but amazing."

Lucien sipped the hot black coffee and leaned back in the chair. "They're not athletes. They're prehistoric people. *Homo neanderthalensis*. Not football players."

"Whatever you say." McAllister took the paper, scanned through it, and motioned to Lucien. "You're free to go. What you wanted to do was wrong, but it's still an honor to meet you."

He nodded to McAllister and stood. "May I keep the blanket?"

With a shrug, McAllister stood aside. "A woman is waiting for you to take you home."

"A woman?" He pulled the blanket tightly around himself. "What woman?"

"I don't know. Let's go."

With McAllister leading the way, Lucien followed, hoping it was Marlowe and not *the* woman. They went to the lobby where, thankfully, it *was* Marlowe standing by the front desk, drumming her fingers on the countertop. Instead of smiling, she frowned.

"Are you all right?" She glared at McAllister. "These bozos wouldn't tell me a thing."

Lucien sighed. "Yeah."

She kept glaring. "You had no right to hold him. He's done nothing wrong."

"Really?" McAllister waved the paper in the air. "He already admitted he'd assaulted Thomas Baker after selling the Neanderthals to him. Luckily for you, Mr. Baker isn't pressing charges. Lady, your boyfriend here thought he'd take the money and then take the Neanderthals back to kill them." He clicked his tongue. "Maybe we should question you, too."

Marlowe stared at Lucien. "Why'd you write that?"

"Later, Marlowe. Please take me home, or somewhere other than here." He headed for the front door.

"Wait." Marlowe ran to him. "There are about a dozen camera-clicking vultures out there waiting for you."

He looked into her eyes. "It doesn't matter. I've got to talk to them."

"No, you don't." She put her hand on his shoulder. "You don't."

"I do." He took her hand and squeezed it. "I really do."

He opened the door, keeping the blanket around his body, and waved his hand to quiet the crowd. "I have something to say."

The paparazzi settled down enough for him to blurt his speech out, exactly how Basten wanted. Cameras and phones alike took his photo as he hurried to his Jag where Marlowe was in the driver's seat. She waited until he fastened his seat belt before pressing the ignition starter. A few people hung around the car, calling out questions that he had no intention of answering, but mostly the paparazzi moved off.

Marlowe revved the engine and turned to him. "I should have asked if you wanted to drive. You look a lot better now."

He concealed his face with the blanket. "I don't feel better. Go ahead and drive. Get me away from here."

She accelerated too fast and skidded on the pavement. He flinched and stopped himself from telling her to take it easy with his car; it was more hers than his now. When the sound coming from the tires changed, he dropped the blanket and saw they were on the main road. She stared straight ahead, her jaw tight.

"Is something wrong?"

At a stop sign, she slammed on the brakes. "Yeah. You lied back there. Why?"

Someone behind them honked.

"You're blocking traffic." Lucien waved to the car behind.

"Screw them." She glared at him. "Why, Lucien?"

"We'll talk when we're home. This isn't the time."

"The hell it isn't. Tell me the truth. What happened at the jail?" She flipped off the other car when it honked again. "I'm not moving until you talk."

The car zipped around them, honking the whole time.

Lucien slumped in the seat. "A man from the French Consulate came. At least I think he was from the Consulate. I can't be sure of anything at this point."

"And?"

"And, they'll hurt my family unless I cooperate with them. Oh, and the guy made a point of saying the next bullet would finish me off. They're trying to legitimize using the Neanderthals. This was all planned out when I didn't die. The man told me what to say to the reporters. They pulled out my brother's fingernail. God only knows what would be next." His throat burned. "I can't jeopardize my family." He coughed.

She gripped the wheel so tight the leather wrapping squeaked. "Why didn't you tell the police?" With her eyes on him, she reached into the glove compartment and tossed a small bottle of water onto his lap.

He took a drink, which helped calm his sour stomach. "You're seriously asking me that? The police are involved, too. *She* was in the police station." He looked out the side window.

"In the station? Why didn't you tell someone?"

"I told you, she owns the police." He didn't turn from the window. "I'm going back to France."

"France?" She took his hand. "Your life is here. You once told me that you wanted to stay in the U.S. forever, that this is your new home, away from the memories of your past. Hey, look at me."

He turned and squeezed her hand. "I did want to stay. But things have changed, and I have nothing now."

"You have me." She touched his face. "And you can't leave your Neanderthals. They're here and need you to liberate them from Neanderball."

He gazed out through the windshield where buildings, roads, and giant billboards cluttered the landscape. Neanderthals didn't belong in this world. "I agree with you, but they're not mine anymore. How can I liberate them? They're no good for experimentation now."

"Experimentation? Forget all about that crap. Lucien." She kissed him on the lips. "They never were yours." She faced forward and blasted through the intersection.

As the Jag sped along, he considered what she said. He had to stop thinking of them as experiments. The worst part was that he'd never get to know them. He watched Marlowe. He'd focus on starting a new life with her. It still hurt that his research had been bastardized for the sake of entertainment, but it could be time for a change. He'd use his skills from his youth to get into a new line of business, with her as his partner.

She turned down an unfamiliar street and stopped in front of a small condo complex, shut off the engine, and turned to him. "This is me. Not much, but it's mine."

He looked around. "Street parking? You park my car on the street?"

"Yeah." She got out and opened the passenger door. "You going to stay in there all day?"

Part of him did want to stay with the Jag to make sure it didn't get damaged or stolen, but when a lanky teenager passed by and stared, he unfastened his seat belt and climbed out so he wouldn't be trapped in the car if the kid tried something. "I'll come in with you, but please set the car alarm. Did you see that character?"

"This is a safe neighborhood. Your car has been here for five months and hasn't suffered even a scratch." She motioned to the teenager. "That kid's barely twenty and on his way to a Ph.D. in astrophysics, a genius. It's a good neighborhood." She tapped her foot. "Any day now."

He shut the door and sighed. "The car alarm?"

"Nervous Nelly," she mumbled. "There, done." She jangled the fob from her fingertips.

He took the fob and headed to the front path. "Thanks." He'd do his best to convince her to move to France after a while. It would be a new beginning for them both.

"Lucien ..."

"What?" He followed the direction she looked in and saw a black car crawling down the street with the driver's window down. "Is that ...?"

"It sure is. The woman."

He glanced at Marlowe. She had a gun in her hand, her finger ready on the trigger.

Chapter 8

Lucien turned his attention back to the woman in the car. She also had a gun, bigger than Marlowe's, equipped with a silencer. She fired a single shot into the Jag's front tire. When Marlowe let out a long breath, he knew she was ready to pull the trigger.

"Wait!" He pushed in front of Marlowe. "That bitch isn't going to hurt you again. She shot the tire, not us" He waved his hands. "What the fuck do you want? I gave the speech."

She stopped the car in front of the Jag, the barrel of the gun pointed at him. "Yes, you did. Consider this a friendly reminder that I'll always know where you are and I can blow your head off any time. I'll be calling on you from time to time when the need arises. Have a lovely day, you two. And get that tire fixed." She sped off.

Lucien let out his breath and faced Marlowe.

She still had her gun out and had a deep frown. "What the hell? That was stupid to jump in front of me and put yourself at risk like that! You okay?" She remained focused on the woman's car as it skidded around a corner.

"Yeah. No, I'm not okay." He took a few breaths, but his heart still thumped out a symphony. "Does she want to kill me or not? Fuck. My car."

"Your car? Damn it, Lucien, who gives a shit about the car. She's on a power trip and wants us to know it. Let's get inside." Marlowe finally reached under her jacket and holstered her gun. "I need a drink."

He nodded. "Me too." He glanced at the lopsided Jag. "Hey, how long have you been carrying that gun? I mean, at the hospital. The police station?"

She didn't answer.

Once inside the condo, she locked the deadbolt, drew the curtains, and told him to follow her to the kitchen. He wanted to know about the gun, but it was obvious she wasn't about to tell him.

"Consider this your house, too, Lucien."

Her home was nice, not as big as his old, restored Victorian, but comfortable. Of course, he didn't actually have a house anymore. He sat at the kitchen table while she took two glasses from the cupboard, grabbed a bottle of Scotch whisky, and sat opposite him.

He preferred wine to whisky, but at this point, a stiff drink sounded perfect.

She filled both glasses almost to the brim and pushed one to him. "Here."

"Thanks." He took a tentative sip. It went down smoothly and left his throat warm. "My life's over."

"Wow, that's a defeatist view." She took a long drink until her glass was half empty. She put the glass on the table and stirred the whisky with her index finger. "I see this as half full, but you see it as—"

"Needing a top-up." He filled her glass with half of his drink.

With a smile, she clinked her glass to his. "Okay, I'll give you that one. But seriously, we can't let that bitch win."

It was easy to say that, but how could he defeat her? She had too many resources. What did he have? Marlowe would help as much as possible, but that only made it two against an army. There had to be some way to stop the madness though. Some way to get his research back.

"Hey. You said you have my clothes."

"Yep." She motioned to a hallway. "In my room."

"Did you happen to save a black leather jacket?" He took another sip of whisky and stood. He'd tucked a flash drive in the pocket.

"Um, I think so. I know I grabbed a grey wool coat and a trench coat for sure. Why? That your favorite coat or something?"

"It very well might be my new favorite." He hurried from the kitchen and found the bedroom closet.

She'd kept everything pristine. He went hanger by hanger until he found the leather jacket. He held his breath and reached into the inside pocket. His fingers touched a small object that brought a grin to his face. It was the flash drive that he'd used as a safeguard. He'd taken it home two weeks before the kidnapping when there was a severe storm that he thought might interfere with the auto-backup system. He knew damn well that the computer servers had emergency generators and battery backups, but something had told him to manually back up most of his data anyway. Now he was glad for his nervousness.

Marlowe came up behind him and tapped him on the shoulder. "What you got there?"

He opened his palm and showed her. "My life."

"Does that mean you have your research on there?"

He turned the drive over. "Indeed it does. Most of it anyway. Do you have a computer?"

"Really? Who doesn't have a computer?"

"I meant can I use your computer?" He cradled the flash drive in his hand. "I have proof that my research was never intended to allow the Neanderthals to grow past the early embryonic stage. Now I can show the world and exonerate myself."

She sighed and tilted her head. "Listen, your research isn't the issue. The woman made you admit you were behind the Neanderthals and would have killed them. Proof isn't going to help you because you already admitted your guilt."

He shook his head. "Proof will clear my name. I have a detailed journal on here that states my intentions and each step I took. It describes the projected outcome of my research to use stem cells I'd harvest from the embryos, not fetuses. Embryos, Marlowe. It'll show that I'd calculated the correct growth hormone and that the woman tampered with it to make the clones grow too fast. This should be enough to exonerate—"

Marlowe held up her hand. "Stop right there. When you found out they grew too fast, what was your plan?"

"Ah. I never had time to draw up a plan. I got shot in the head, remember? I'm not a monster, I'm a scientist."

"Whatever helps you sleep at night." Her eyebrow arched. "So, what were you going to do, Dr. Roux?"

He looked away. "I ...I'd have to, well, there wouldn't be much time to collect—"

"That's not an answer." She put her hand on his shoulder. "You were going to kill them, weren't you?"

"Not right away. I'm sorry."

"I'm not naïve. I know how science works and how discoveries are made, but ... you were prepared to kill your embryos only after you got what you wanted. That's right, isn't it? Older embryos and fetuses are anathema to your work, but you didn't want to lose your research. I don't know what the right answer would be if I faced the same situation." She furrowed her brow, and her jaw tight. "But science or not, it's wrong."

51

Lucien shook his head. "I'm not the villain here." No explaining his way out of it, even if he wanted to. "It's a moot point now, isn't it? Those clones are sports heroes being exploited."

"Yes, they are. Okay, so what's your plan going forward? Show the journal to the press and risk your family in France? Not to mention your own life."

He knew damn well he'd have to find a way to keep his family safe. "Of course not." He wiped his sweaty brow. "My family."

"We'll figure it out. Hey, why don't you change clothes and rest for a while. You look a little pale and that tracksuit makes you look like a hobo. You've only just come out of the coma." She left the room.

"I'll change, but there's no time to rest. I feel strong and ready to do whatever it takes. Whatever Bay-Gen had in that drug cocktail worked wonders. And those muscle stimulators ..." He went back to the closet and took out a pair of jeans and a burgundy button-down shirt. "I don't suppose you have any of my underwear?" he called out.

"Bottom dresser drawer!"

Wow. She'd even saved his freaking underwear. "Thanks." He placed the flash drive beside the computer and opened the drawer.

After dressing, he stepped into the bathroom to wash his face and smooth his hair. He looked a mess; bloodshot eyes with dark circles underneath, hair sticking up in the wrong places, and a pallid complexion. He'd been through hell and come out the other side. It was a sign that he was on the right track to redeem himself.

He glanced at the flash drive, the key to ending the nightmare. Although he didn't know how yet. It nagged at him that evolution had taken tens of thousands of years to make him what he was, yet he'd only spent a couple of years making an extinct species come back to life. No matter how he spun it in his mind, he'd tampered with evolution and now the Neanderthals were paying the price.

He sat on the bed and called out, "Hey, Marlowe, did you know that people of European ancestry have a small percentage of Neanderthal DNA?"

She eyed him from the doorway. "You look much better. And yes, I did know about the DNA. You told me that during our first or second lunch together. In fact, I had a DNA test done a couple of weeks after that and I have two percent Neanderthal in me."

He straightened his shirt and rubbed the flash drive between his fingers. "Same as me. That's why I had no trouble combining my DNA with theirs. I'd tried to find a cancer cure ..." his voice trailed off.

"What's done is done. We've got to move forward." She motioned to the desk. "Use the computer. Be honest with me though, what are you going to do with the information on that drive?"

His first instinct was to apply for another grant and start over. Was that even possible now? "I'm not sure, but ... those Neanderthals need to be under constant care. The atmospheric levels are different in the twenty-first than when they originally walked the Earth and there's pollution and so much stimulus that they're likely in danger. Plus, my growth hormone was tampered with, and that amount of accelerated growth can't be healthy. I need to try to determine what that means to the development of the subjects."

With a deep sigh, Marlowe leaned against the door jamb. "Subjects? I'll leave you to it then. I've got work in a few hours. Bay-Gen isn't too happy with me these days, spending so much time at the hospital with you. But it's hard for them to complain much since we were almost killed on the premises. Truth now, are you going to be okay with me going?"

"I don't need babysitting, you know. Sorry, that sounded snippy."

Marlowe raised an eyebrow. "Yes, it did."

"I appreciate your concern. I'll be fine. Thanks again for everything." He sat at the desk and turned the computer on. "This is a damn good laptop. Expensive." He looked over at her.

She smirked. "Yeah, well, I occasionally do some surveillance work here and there. Need access to some, ah, shady info."

Shady? Was her shady anything like his youthful shady? "And that requires you to have a high-powered computer?" He inserted his flash drive and waited.

"Yep. Sure does. I'll make some coffee." She left without any further elaboration.

Lucien smiled. Knowing about her alleged shady dealings only made her more intriguing. He had a few skeletons, too.

The data files opened.

Before checking his online journal, he decided to run the last diagnostics he had to make sure the clones had been healthy the last time he'd backed up the files. He queried the data file and created a projected graph interpolating the physiology of the embryos to see how their growth compared to that of a modern human. He stared at the graph; his breath stuck in his throat. It showed that his embryos would have developed every organ better than a human's. The Neanderthals' hearts would be mature, their lungs would be far more efficient than modern humans, and their brains would be fully functioning. If they'd been allowed to develop naturally.

They were prehistoric miracles, enhanced of course by a touch of modern science. But he had to look at what repercussions early maturity might have, and he couldn't do that through projections.

Examining them at their current growth stage is what he needed, but he'd have to get close to them to do that. Marlowe admitted she had experience with surveillance. He was sure she'd find a way to get near them and take hair samples, or even better, blood.

She strolled into the bedroom and placed a steaming cup of coffee on the desk. "If I remember right, you like sugar but no cream."

"That's right." He looked up at her and smiled. "Hey, how good are you at surveillance and using those special skills you told me about?"

Chapter 9

Lucien waited for Marlowe's response. She stared at him for several awkward seconds and finally pushed his coffee cup aside, sat on the edge of the desk, and glanced at the computer.

"What exactly do you want me to surveil?" She poked the monitor. "That's your research?"

He nodded. "Yes. I want to see if the Neanderthals are healthy, so if you can—"

"Do what? I don't see how I can be of any help here. All I've been able to do is find out who owns Neanderball. That isn't much."

"It is. You're resourceful. I need my research. I've spent years in that lab. If you can get close to the owners, maybe ..."

She shook her head and stood. "This is about you? *Your* research? *Your* work? What about the Neanderthals?"

Did she think him heartless? Of course he thought about the Neanderthals, but they *were* his research. She didn't understand it was all mixed together.

He glared at her. "You know what goes on at Bay-Gen, don't pretend you're against it. How can I let what's happened be for nothing? That woman has hurt you, me, and my family. She must have sold my research to the highest bidder. For what? To use Neanderthals for entertainment? That's so absurd it makes me sick. But I'm not convinced that's her only agenda or end goal. There's more to this than a stupid game." He stood and went into the living room.

Marlowe followed. "Look, I'm sorry. I know where you're coming from, I do. This is your life's work, but this issue is bigger than your research now. It's about exploitation, pure and simple. We've got to find a way to expose the truth without dragging you deeper into the mud or having you end up in the morgue. As it stands now, you created prehistoric test subjects, and those test subjects run around beating the crap out of each other while mindless idiots cheer." She got in his face. "We have to free them."

He took a step backward. "Free them? They're Neanderthals. They don't belong in the twenty-first century. When you said liberate them, I thought you meant ... never mind."

"Christ, Lucien." Marlowe shook her head. "I didn't mean kill them."

"That's not what I mean either." He sighed. "I would have destroyed the clones when I finished with ... you know. But they're no longer my experiments, and I know that."

"No, they're not."

Lucien closed his eyes for a moment. They'd have to be kept in a secure lab and studied for the rest of their lives, but that wasn't what Marlowe would agree to. "Listen, I doubt they can speak very well or even if their bodies have adapted to the environment here. Their brains were shaped a bit differently than ours and then there are small genetic differences in their neurology, so maybe they can't think like we do, analytically or otherwise."

"Okay, okay, but they're in this century and must have been taught how to think and act." Marlowe raised an eyebrow. "Right?"

"I don't know. But, I'd rather not see them driving a pick-up truck on the freeway, playing bumper cars with another motorist because their brains can't comprehend the rules of the road. They can't live in this time. The last telemetry readings I have indicated that their organs would have been fully formed and functioning if they'd been allowed to grow into full-term infants. When I found out they'd grown too fast, I was, well, I ..." He paused to catch his breath. "Our environment is so different than the time when they evolved, they haven't had the time needed to physiologically adapt. I hate all of this. They don't belong in society. They should be secured and—"

"Wait, so what are you saying? You want to lock them away so you can study them like lab rats? They're teenagers." She frowned and let out a few breaths in rapid succession like she tried to calm herself. "You need to tell me everything. I mean everything about what you've done and why."

"I've already told you some." He slumped onto the couch and rested his head in his hands. The truth was hard. "These weren't the first test subjects I created."

"Excuse me?" She crouched next to him and pulled his hands away from his face. "Would you mind repeating that? You've done this to other clones?"

He stared at the floor. "Of course. I received a research grant to find a cure for a specific type of cancer. My goal was to verify if Neanderthal DNA was stronger than modern humans' and I had every reason to believe it was. I'd worked with Neanderthal specialists in France and throughout the world and tracked down another paleogeneticist in Berlin who'd done some preliminary work with Neanderthal DNA. He'd located a specific interferon protein derived from a host cell on a particular cloned Neanderthal cell. That protein wasn't found in *Homo sapiens sapiens*."

"Okay, I follow. Interferon is used to fight cancer, right? I read an article once."

"Sometimes. I believed this one protein would target a particular cancer gene." He looked up.

She gave him a sharp nod. "Go on."

"When I got back from Berlin, I went right to my lab to locate and reproduce the protein, but the first few recombinations didn't work and the subjects failed to thrive. That's when I took another tack and merged my DNA with the originating specimens since the DNA sequences weren't complete. I succeeded, after a few more trials, and got to the blastocyst stage where I extracted the stem cells. Next, I created an enhanced growth hormone to produce more embryos for stem cell implantation without much wait time. The next four trials started with strong cell division, but they failed."

"Yeah, but you didn't stop there. We have brutish Neanderball players now."

He drew a deep breath. "True, but you know that's not by my hand. Anyway, I had to tweak a few processes and then managed to get the next test subject cells to produce interferon that targets the cancer gene, but the interferon was still too weak. I speculated that slightly before the eighth week, while they were still embryos, the interferon would be stronger, and it was. I never would have let them mature into the fetal stage because of the contract I'd signed with Bay-Gen. No fetal experimentation. They'd been sued a few times. I played around with the stem cells some more and ... well, these Neanderball players were my next attempt. I planned to extract the stem cells, but you know what happened."

"They became teenagers in under five months. How's that possible? What did you do?"

"Not me, that woman. She had someone tamper with everything. A body simply can't grow that fast. The subjects need to be tested."

Marlowe sighed. "Well, whatever happened, there's no going back now. Hey, you said the protein targeted the cancer gene. Did it work?"

He shrugged. "I don't know, I hadn't gotten to the experimentation phase yet. And the woman knew that because she took the subjects right before I'd done anything. She knew they'd matured because she tampered with the growth hormone."

"Shit. I hate that bitch."

"Same. I had an alarm set on my phone so if anything went wrong with the embryos, I got an alert. She must have known that, too, because she was ready and waiting, knowing I'd come to the lab. What am I going to do? This was supposed to be a good thing." He drew in a breath. "I carry the same cancer gene that killed my mother, and so does my sister and thousands of people. I purposely added that into the subjects' codons to see how they responded to it. But unfortunately, I never had the chance to study the results." He shook his head and realized how cold he sounded.

"Wow. You gave them cancer. But why Neanderthals? Why not fruit flies or something?" Her lips pressed together, and she folded her arms across her chest.

"The DNA. We're compatible. But I didn't give them cancer, I gave them the gene. A lot of Neanderthal skeletons have been healthy and robust, the perfect test subjects. It's a way to experiment on human-like subjects without actually using a human subject, a chimp, or a gorilla. I refuse to experiment on animals."

"Hypocrite. They are animals, like you and me. Don't give me double-talk."

He groaned. "Experimenting on an extinct species isn't immoral. It can't be because they no longer exist."

"Really? Unless they do exist. And they grow up in the twenty-first century where people care about things like cloning for experimentation."

He didn't respond, there was no need to. Instead, he wandered back to the bedroom and scanned through his files again. The coffee she'd brought in earlier was lukewarm, but he drank it anyway. He needed a caffeine jolt.

"You've got quite the dilemma, don't you? I need some air," she called out.

The front door slammed. It would be good for her to get some distance for a while, at least until she calmed down and saw that his experiments came from lofty ideals, not from an uncaring mad-scientist agenda. But there were so many variables to consider now, like with them growing so fast, perhaps their bodies hadn't developed a fully functioning immune system and they had no ability to fight the disease. If that was the case, they'd be doomed, and he was the one responsible.

He went to the living room window and peered out. Marlowe paced back and forth on the sidewalk out front. If she wasn't willing to try to get biological samples, he'd have to do it himself. Best not to involve her anyway; he'd put her through enough.

Back in the bedroom, he pulled the flash drive and tucked it into his jacket pocket. He searched on the internet for the team owners. They were quite newsworthy judging by the number of hits. Thomas and Jeremy Baker were called the "most original gamesters on the planet" according to one website and "saviors" on another for freeing the Neanderthals from a research lab and a life of torture.

"Saviors?" Lucien thumped his hand on the desk. "Thieves, exploiters maybe, but not saviors."

He spent close to an hour reading through websites and articles until he found a lead, an email address for the Neanderball publicist. Now came the tricky part, lying, something that didn't come easy. Not anymore anyway. He'd left his old deceitful life behind.

He set up a new email address under a fake name and fired off a note.

Dear Ms. Goodson,

Greetings. I understand you represent Mr. Thomas Baker and Mr. Jeremy Baker as their publicist. I'm a newspaper columnist from France, here in the US to write an article on Neanderball. Could you please accommodate me and arrange a meeting with the Bakers and a photoshoot with the team members? I would be most appreciative.

Thank you for your time.

Jean-Paul Benoit

The name gave a nod to his maternal grandfather, who really had been a writer for a small newspaper. Before hitting send, he thought of his family. They'd always been there for him and had been supportive of his decision to move away and go into paleo-genetics. Except for maybe Édouard, always a little jealous, and let sibling rivalry get the better of him at times. Édouard was probably happy about him moving away.

When it was time to get out of his old business, his father was relieved, and his mother told him she wouldn't have to worry anymore. At least she'd died thinking he was in a safe profession. He pressed send and got up.

"Lucien! I took a long walk to clear my head," Marlowe said. "Where are you?"

"In here." He went to the doorway of the bedroom. "I've been thinking. I don't want you involved with this mess any longer. I'll go it on my own from here. But can you lend me some money for a hotel room and a bit of traveling cash? I'll pay you back somehow."

She stared at him for a moment. "No. I'm in this whether you like it or not. Besides, I saved your bacon before, and without me, you'll end up dead in a ditch somewhere. You need me."

"So, you don't think I'm some sort of mad, inhumane scientist?"

She smiled. "Maybe a little. Look, I thought about it, and we all get mixed up in things sometimes. I've certainly done things I'm sorry for, but I try not to dwell on them. What's done is done." She cocked her head. "Tell me what you need me to do."

"You're incredible, you know that? It's good to have you on my side. I mean it. Okay, I've got to find out if my Neanderthals are at risk for cancer and if they have strong enough immune systems to fight it, so I'll need DNA samples. Blood, hair, skin cells. If they test positive and have weak immunity, they need treatment right away."

"You do care about them, don't you?"

"Of course. I also care about you." He got up and placed his hands on her shoulders. "This might be dangerous though and I can't stand the thought of you getting hurt."

She laughed. "Danger's my middle name, Paleo."

"I don't doubt it. And don't call me Paleo." He frowned.

"All right, Dr. Roux. Hey, I care about you, too." She pressed her lips and made a kiss.

For the next two hours, they skimmed through the Internet for anything about where the Neanderthals lived and if it would be possible for Marlowe to get close enough to them. Lucien checked for an incoming email from the PR woman. Nothing yet.

He went to the kitchen and downed a hasty meal of canned soup and toast while Marlowe sent a flurry of text messages to friends. He had the feeling they weren't so much friends as colleagues. If she had someone who'd help, who was he to argue? The lives of sixteen prehistoric teenagers hung in the balance.

He lay down on the couch, closed his eyes, and ran his finger over the scar on his head. In a blink, his life might have ended.

A gentle hand covered his. He opened his eyes, craned his neck, and kissed her on her lovely lips. She returned the kiss.

"Lay here with me for a second." He put his hand behind her head.

She pulled away. "I would, but I have a meeting. Rest," she whispered. "A recon meeting with a friend in ten minutes. I called in sick at work."

"Recon?"

"Yep. Don't worry about it. I'll let you know what I find. See you in a few." She straightened and flashed a smile.

"Marlowe, wait." He sat up.

"No time, sweets. Gotta run."

"Wait! I can't let you do—"

"Let me? *Let* me? I make the decisions about what I will and will not do. And this is something *I* decided to do. Lie down and rest. You'll be worthless to this operation if you're all worn out and not thinking straight." She wasn't smiling this time.

"Fine. Promise me you'll be careful." He watched as she slipped on a black, snug-fitting tactical vest — similar to one he used to have in the old days — and picked up a matching black backpack.

"I promise." The final piece of her outfit was a black beanie.

What the hell was she going to do? She looked like a sniper or a cat burglar. With a parting smile, she left.

He wandered around the house, half-heartedly looking at her photos, trinkets, and books. Her taste ran all over the place. Classic books mixed with cheap romance, girlish figurines next to a grenade nestled under a bell jar. Hopefully, it wasn't armed.

Too wound up to concentrate on anything, he looked out the kitchen window into the small backyard for a distraction. It was overgrown and uninhabitable. To the left, covered mostly in thick morning glory vines, stood a small shed.

The kitchen door leading outside was stuck, but after tugging at it a few times, it creaked open. Didn't she ever go outside? He propped it open with an empty terra cotta pot he found on the deck and made his way to the shed. Like the back door, this door was stuck as well. He gave a good pull and it promptly slipped off its hinges. He leaned it against the shed and looked inside where there was a workbench with an assortment of tools hanging from hooks. No lawnmower, but he found a gas-powered weed whacker. He shook it. A little gas remaining.

It took a few tries to get it going and more than a few tries to knock down a substantial number of weeds. He continued until sweat drenched him and he gasped for breath. He shut off the weed whacker and examined his work. Not bad. He'd cleared a path and discovered a concrete bench and a birdbath near the far end of the yard. He dabbed beaded sweat from his face and stretched.

A bird twittered at him from the branch of a tree hanging over the bench. He smiled. "You're welcome. I'll put some water in the bath for you."

He jogged to the kitchen, fetched a saucepan full of water, and filled the birdbath. Instead of hopping into the water, the bird flew off. Oh, well, he tried. A twig snapped and he jumped. A bird? A person? He turned. Nothing there. Marlowe was right, his nerves were frazzled.

"Marlowe? Is that you?" Sweat trickled down his face. "Marlowe?"

He gripped the saucepan handle tighter, held his breath, and listened. No sound at all. No birds, no insects. After steadying his nerves, he went to the back door. It was closed. He'd propped it open. The air was still, with no gusty wind to blow the door closed. He exhaled in a jagged rasp and pushed on the door. It creaked as it swung inward, revealing the terra cotta pot to the side, moved by someone.

"Enough with the fucking mind games!" he shouted.

If the woman wanted to scare him, she'd succeeded. He'd played along with her demands, so what now? After peeking into closets and checking under the bed, he found no sign anything was amiss. Did he move the pot himself when he'd fetched the pan of water, making the door close, and he'd simply forgotten? Maybe.

Next on his list, securing the house. He locked the windows and doors but didn't feel any better. His nerves were jangled from the adrenaline coursing through his body. He ended up in the kitchen, found the whisky, and downed a large gulp straight from the bottle as he went to the bedroom to log into his email and found a new message from Carolyn Goodson, the Bakers' publicist.

Dear Mr. Benoit,

Of course we can accommodate you, one of our foreign correspondents. There is a press conference in Oakland, California tomorrow afternoon at five at the Oakland Arena next to the Oakland Coliseum. The next Neanderball game will be this weekend at the Oakland Arena and since the players have practice every day, if time permits, we will have a tour and perhaps a meet-and-greet with the players. You'll certainly be interested in our announcement about Neanderball going international. I'll be sure to put your name on the press list. Tell the guard who you are.

I hope to see you there.

C. Goodson

Goodson Public Relations

www.goodson_PR.com

• • • •

-NEANDERBALL, NOT ONLY a game, a way of life.

The warmth of the whisky settled inside him. He leaned on his elbow and reread the email. Tomorrow he'd see his Neanderthals in person.

A little unsteady, he wandered back to the kitchen and poured the whisky into a glass, but sipped it this time to maintain the slight buzz he already felt. He raised the glass. "Here's to you, my Neander-children. I'll see you soon. Providing nobody tries to blow my head off."

Chapter 10

For what seemed like hours, Lucien sat in a rattan chair in the middle of the living room, staring at the door, waiting for Marlowe to return. He gripped the saucepan-weapon, ready to bonk any intruders over the head. The whisky made his eyes heavy, and when he almost drifted off, the sound of footsteps on the stoop made him jerk wide awake and almost drop the pan. Maybe drinking wasn't the best idea. He relaxed a second later as a key turned in the lock. The woman wouldn't use a key, she'd have a battering ram.

"Lucien, hi. What's going on?" Marlowe stepped in, shut the door, and locked it. "You're holding an empty saucepan and you look, I don't know, weird."

He got up. "I feel weird. Too much whisky and too many synapses firing. I'm foggy and hyped up at the same time." He collapsed onto the couch and clutched the saucepan to his chest. "I thought someone was in the house. I was wrong."

"Okay. Did you check—?"

"I checked everywhere and made sure the doors and windows were locked." He paused and drew in a deep breath. What if he wasn't wrong and one of the woman's goons put a bug in the house? Did people really do that?

"Lucien?"

He put his finger to his lips and whispered, "Someone might be listening."

She nodded.

He stood, unsteadily, and motioned for her to follow him to the kitchen. He turned on the faucet. "Did you find anything?" he whispered again.

With a one-shouldered shrug, she stood by the sink and wrestled the saucepan from his clutch. "Found *something*. Are you sure you're all right?"

He nodded. "Yeah." His vision grew slightly blurry. "Maybe not so much. Talk to me while I get some coffee. No more alcohol. I drank to calm my nerves and I think it worked a bit too well." He poured a cup and took a sip.

She nodded and whispered, "Pretend everything is okay." Now she spoke in a normal voice, "Looks like you overdid the drinking a bit."

"Ah, yeah. Oh, that reminds me, have you ever stepped out into your backyard?" He rubbed his eyes. "That door was stuck, practically glued shut."

She stared at him for a moment. "What?"

"Never mind. I nosed around and saw an old, tattered book about Christopher Marlowe. Any link there with your name?"

She shrugged again. "Yeah. My mom was a fan of Elizabethan writers."

"Huh. Interesting. Must have been a huge fan to name you after an old dead guy."

He turned on the faucet more and whispered, "So, tell me what you found."

"I see you know the old running water background noise trick, eh? Let's get you settled in first. You're useless tipsy." She spoke normally again, glancing around the kitchen, "Have a seat. You know, my mom wrote a senior paper on Marlowe and Francis Bacon. I never cared for any of that stuff, but I'm stuck with the name. Glad she didn't name me Bacon."

He laughed and sat, curling his fingers around the mug. He downed most of the lukewarm coffee in one long gulp. "Well, I like it, it's unique. I think I told you that before. I'm settled."

"Good." She whispered in his ear again, "Well." She filled his cup again. "I know something about that woman. Me and my friends located her goons, and after tracking them, we found her."

He choked on his coffee. "Holy shit. That's big. Why didn't you lead with that? Now we can tell the cops everything."

"Lucien." She shook her head. "I investigated her dealings with the local cops who arrested you. We checked CCTV and phones. My associates found out that she's connected up the wazoo. Untouchable."

"Nobody's untouchable. Tell me her name. I have connections, too."

"You? Who? The review committee of one of the journals you wrote for?"

"Wow." He frowned and drank the rest of the coffee. "You really do think I'm a meek lab rat, don't you? I had a life before I became a paleogeneticist. I was a little off-center in my youth."

Her eyebrow shot up. "Off-center? I find that hard to believe, mister button-down scientist."

"I wasn't always a scientist. I fell in with the wrong crowd in my late teens. Illegal stuff." That was something he'd hidden from his colleagues, and Marlowe, but now, his past dabbling with an international theft ring could be useful. Every few years, he and his old friends met on the outskirts of Paris and chatted over old times, but out of the four of them, only Alexei stayed active and always had a knack for squirming out of tight spots.

Marlowe shook her head. "I had no idea. Okay, so how can your past illegal activities help us now? I'm telling you, she can pretty much do as she pleases without any repercussions. Don't know why, but it's a fact."

"We'll see. Let me contact a friend of mine and see if he knows anything about her. Her name?"

"Beatrix Fenwick."

"Thank you." He turned to go but spun around. "Beatrix? Who's named Beatrix? It somehow suits her. I'm tired of being scared. I'm going to find a way to keep my family safe and take down the Bakers at the same time."

"And the Neanderthals? What about them?"

"I'm including them when I say my family. I need to send an email." He gave her a peck on the cheek and strode off to the bedroom.

Alexei Ozerov had managed to stay off the radar by "donating" sizeable funds to various benefactors, another one of his terms. In truth, the donations were bribes and the benefactors were the authorities. It was because of this that Alexei had kept Lucien out of prison. Several times. Never as skilled as Alexei, Lucien accidentally left his fingerprints at one location and a blood smear at another after cutting his finger on a lock pick. Alexei did what he did best and made everything disappear from Interpol's evidence records.

After logging onto the Internet, Lucien connected to Alexei's proxy server and wrote a brief email.

Alexei, I hope this finds you well. I'm in trouble and need your assistance.
-Lucien

Send.

He sat back and rubbed his eyes. What a messed-up life he had. If he had his passport, he'd catch the next flight to France and go home. No, he couldn't do that. Basten said there was to be no contact at all. Being so helpless made his life that much more frustrating.

"Lucien!" Marlowe shouted from the living room.

"Coming!" He hurried from the bedroom and found her standing with her cell phone in her hand.

"Someone named Joe is calling for you. On *my* cell. My number's not listed anywhere."

Now what? Another order to speak to the press? He took the phone, put it to his ear, and drew in a breath. "Hello?"

"I wondered when you'd contact me."

"Alexei. Well, I foolishly thought I could handle it on my own." He gave Marlowe a nod to let her know everything was fine. "How did you get this number?"

"Don't ask questions you don't really want the answer to. I've kept up with your shenanigans, my friend. I know Ms. Dunham is offering you shelter. And I know Beatrix Fenwick has you under her thumb. You can't do this on your own."

Lucien went back to the kitchen and ran the faucet again. "I know that now. Fenwick had cameras installed in my lab and she knows every move I make and—"

"No more talking. I'll send an exterminator to the house. It's quiet time now, my friend." The phone went dead.

Quiet time. That phrase meant Alexei believed someone was listening in, and an exterminator was someone schooled in locating high-tech bugs. Lucien nodded to himself. Memories of his old life flooded back. Things were good then. The criminal life was one of freedom. No one to answer to, no committees or papers to write. What would his life have been had he continued in his old line of work?

Marlowe stomped into the kitchen. "Lucien! What the hell is going on?"

"Sorry." He handed her the phone. "Thank you." He placed his finger to his lips and whispered in her ear. "My friend also thinks Fenwick might have the place bugged."

"Your friend?"

"A good friend."

Marlowe frowned and kept her voice low, "Tell me what else your *friend* said. Is he going to help?"

"Not here." He motioned to the backyard. "Outside."

She followed him. As soon as she stepped onto the deck, her mouth gaped. "Wow. I mean, wow. When did you do this?"

"I got bored and had a whisky buzz going. Still do. You know, I made my biggest breakthrough with the Neanderthal DNA replication after I had a couple of glasses of wine. I also wrote most of my dissertation under the influence."

With a smile, Marlowe shook her head. "Alcohol and genetics. A glass of booze might just have helped me in school. I failed genetics."

"I'll be your tutor." He leaned in for a kiss, but she backed away.

"Too late, Dr. Roux, I'm so over genetics. Now, who exactly is this friend of yours and how did he know my number?"

He pointed to the recently uncovered bench. "Let's sit."

"I completely forgot about that bench." She unfastened her vest and slipped the beanie off. "Spill."

"Alexei is going to help us. I trust him with my life."

Marlowe locked eyes with Lucien. "Cool. Now, how are you involved with him?"

Without revealing too much detail, Lucien explained about his foray into the darker side of society and how Alexei taught him to pick locks and crack safes, scale a building using hooks and pulleys, pick a mark, and forge ID badges. "But I don't do that anymore."

"How come? I mean, I'm glad you did, but why? Alexei sounds like one hell of a guy. You had quite the life."

"I did, but my family needed me. My mother did anyway. She hated that I was always off somewhere, saying a young man should be studying or working."

"You *were* studying and working." She smirked.

He laughed. "True. Although I told my family another story. They thought I traveled across Europe, bumming money and food off people in a misguided attempt to discover myself."

"Yeah, I guess telling the truth wouldn't have worked out so well for you. My dad would have killed me if I ever did anything like that. My dad and my brother were Marines. Did I ever tell you that?"

"You mentioned it once. It explains your, ah, regimented style. My mother was the disciplinarian in our house. If I'd ever told her what I was really doing, she would have strung me up on the clothesline and beaten me with a broom!" He stopped laughing when he remembered his mother on her deathbed. "But that was a long time ago. I worked with Alexei for four years and finally went home at twenty-three, enrolled in university, and studied like mad." He paused, needing to change the subject. "Hey, I'm invited to attend a Neanderball press briefing tomorrow at the Oakland Arena. I want to get close to the players. All I need is a single strand of hair."

"Odd segue, but okay. A hair from each of them? That's not going to be easy."

"No, no, only from one. They're cloned. And no, it won't be easy, especially if someone recognizes me." Lucien kicked at the dead grass around his feet.

"Wait, how come you were invited to the press conference?"

"Oh. I created a persona, a journalist. Told you I know a thing or two." He glanced toward the house. "Was that the doorbell?"

Marlowe shrugged. "I didn't hear anything. You got super hearing, too? I don't think Fenwick would ring the bell, but any visitors, even your pal, at this point are suspect."

"Totally agree with you."

They got up and hurried inside. Sure enough, the bell rang again, followed by several hard knocks. Lucien peeked through the peephole and saw a tall man wearing a backward ball cap. "Who's there?"

The man looked directly at the peephole. "I am the exterminator." He had a strong Russian accent.

Lucien unlocked the door and opened it a few inches. "ID."

He felt Marlowe right behind him.

With a stern face and unblinking eyes, the man opened his jacket, revealing a large gun in a shoulder holster. He handed a cell phone to Lucien.

Alexei was on the phone. "Let Vitaly in, my friend. He'll sweep and eliminate any threat."

"Okay. Thanks." Lucien handed the phone back to Vitaly, who slipped it into his pocket and strode inside.

Marlowe grabbed Lucien's hand and pulled him aside, her voice low, "You trust that guy?" She motioned to Vitaly as he walked through the house with a small, black device in his hand.

He nodded and watched Vitaly stop near the TV and reach around behind it. "He's found something."

"Yeah, no shit. Just how did that woman get in my damn house? My locks are the best you can get." Her brow furrowed.

"She's damn good. Then there's the fact that I forgot to lock the door after you left." Lucien gave her a gentle nudge. "But we'll take her down, you and me."

"You got that right. And don't ever forget to lock the damn door. Absolutely no more whisky for you."

Vitaly continued walking to the bedroom while Lucien and Marlowe waited in the kitchen. After about fifteen minutes, Vitaly finished his sweep and dangled a box, remarkably like an old-fashioned metal lunchbox. in front of Lucien.

He shook the box. "Five bugs. Exterminated."

"Oh, ah, thanks." Lucien glanced at Marlowe and back at Vitaly. "So, what now?"

With no expression, Vitaly replied, "I examine and then dispose. Take this." He handed Lucien a hockey puck-sized object. "Lights flash if more devices are planted. You check every day. I come back if lights flash."

Lucien took the object. "Sure. Ah, Vitaly, since you work with Alexei, any suggestions how I can infiltrate the Neanderball team tomorrow without getting recognized? Alexei used to handle that stuff. I've been out of the life for a long time."

"Neanderball?" Vitaly gave one sharp nod. "Mmm. Good game. Suggestion is to disguise with glasses, mustache, hair dye. I go now." He strode to the front door and left.

Marlowe shut the door and whistled. "Disguise with glasses," she imitated Vitaly's accent and glanced sideways at Lucien. "Who *are* you, Dr. Roux?"

"A pissed-off scientist."

"With questionable Russian friends."

"Yes, with questionable Russian friends." He smirked.

Marlowe's phone rang. "Ten to one says it's for you." She handed it to him.

"Hello?" Lucien winked. "Alexei."

"My friend, Vitaly said he collected five bugs. These people are serious. You'd better watch your back."

"Yeah." Lucien glanced at Marlowe, who watched him with an eyebrow raised. "Do you think I can pull it off? Obviously, I can no longer euthanize the subjects ... the Neanderthals. Which leaves me to be a humanitarian. If they're sick, they need treatment. And ..." his voice trailed off. "They have to be freed."

With a chuckle, Alexei agreed, "*Da*, they do. Freedom for Neanderthals!"

"Freedom for Neanderthals," Lucien repeated. "You and me, Alexei, we'll take down Fenwick and get my research back."

"Christ," Marlowe mumbled. "I'm involved, too. And now there's two of you to worry about."

Lucien hung up and smiled. "Wrong. It's Fenwick who should be worried."

Chapter 11

Lucien and Marlowe made a midnight trip to a twenty-four hour drug store for supplies: hair dye, burner phones, notepads, and a pair of novelty glasses. Back home, she helped him become a sandy blond, something he never imagined he'd be.

"I look ridiculous." He sighed and combed his wet hair.

"You look fine."

He lifted a few strands of hair. "And I thought I was humiliated before. Now I really want to murder Fenwick for forcing me to do this."

Marlowe laughed. "It's a temporary dye. A few washes and you'll be back to your handsome self."

"So, I *do* look ridiculous."

She didn't answer.

"Marlowe?"

She smiled. "Not ridiculous, just different."

"All right, that helps my ego a bit. Hey, ah, I'll take the couch and you can have the bed."

"Are you being chivalrous, Dr. Roux? Or is it because we haven't slept together yet and you feel awkward us being in the same bed?" Marlowe raised an eyebrow.

He brushed his hair out of his eyes. "A bit of both, I think. You've already done so much for me, it's time I did something for you. I want our first experience to be special, not spur of the moment in the middle of turmoil." A partial lie because he'd imaged making love to her after their third date.

"Well, I did mean *yet*. But this isn't the time for sex. And while I appreciate your offer, I'll be staying on the couch, near the door, in case Fenwick decides to pay a visit." She smiled again.

He sighed. "All right." He'd rather they snuggle together under the sheets all night, but with all that happened, he wouldn't be firing on all cylinders.

Marlowe flashed a brief smile and put her gun on the side table. Lucien found spare sheets and a blanket in the hall closet and made up the couch while she peered out the front window. He stood with her and gave her a kiss goodnight, then went to bed.

Every sound, real or imagined, made sleep near impossible until pre-dawn. When Marlowe thumped on the bedroom door at seven, he wanted nothing more than to hide under the blanket. That wasn't possible though because she strode in and stood at the foot of the bed.

"Come on, sleepyhead, time to work on your alter ego." She wore a navy-blue tailored suit, a stark white blouse, and heavier-than-usual makeup. "Stop staring. If I'm accompanying a foreign journalist, I have to look the part. I'm your editor-in-chief."

"You are?" He eased out of bed. "Are you supposed to be French?"

"No. I'm American, working in Paris. I fell in love with the city while on spring break in college and moved there after I graduated. And don't get me started on the French men." She fanned her face with her hand. "Ooh la la."

He resisted the urge to correct her that the real meaning of *oh là là* was an exclamation of surprise rather than a romantic gesture because he didn't want to spoil her playful mood. "You've got your cover all worked out, haven't you? Done this sort of thing before?" He stretched.

She shrugged without answering the question. "The burner phones won't be traceable, not even by your Russian friend. I've put my number in yours and vice versa." She reached into her pocket and tossed a small paper bag on the bed. "Here. I wasn't sure what you might need."

"I need a morning kiss."

Without hesitating, she puckered her lips and gave him a peck. "That's all you get until we have the DNA."

"Fine. It'll do." He touched his lips and smiled.

He opened the bag and took out several plastic test tubes with stoppers, and a sealed DNA swab. He stared at her. "When did you get these?"

"While Prince Charming slept."

"Oh, so now I'm—"

"We'll leave around four, Dr. Roux. I made you an ID card as well. Get showered and dressed. You need to get into character and practice what you're going to say. I got my hands on a schematic of the Oakland Arena, so while you're rehearsing, I'm going to study every inch of that place. Got it?"

He nodded. "I know who I'm supposed to be and what I'll say. Don't underestimate me, *mademoiselle*. Hey, are you taking another sick day from Bay-Gen?"

She frowned. "Fuck those people for using you as their medication guinea pig."

"So, yes, then?"

No answer.

When she left, he took a hot shower and recalled the video of the Neanderthals playing Neanderball. They truly were the perfect athletes and seemed in good health, but how? They grew too fast. Fenwick didn't know a damn thing about cloning and yet she had someone increase the growth hormone.

He dressed in a pair of jeans and a pale blue cotton shirt and went to the kitchen where Marlowe's strong, black coffee jolted him fully awake. The Oakland Arena schematic lay out on the kitchen table with red marks drawn all over it, indicating entrances, the locker room with adjoining physical therapy room, and the security offices.

He stared at the schematic. "They used to have basketball games at the Arena. Now they have concerts and I guess Neanderball."

"That's right. I figured you for the anti-sports type." She sighed. "I wouldn't have thought it'd be big enough for a football game to be played in there."

"It's not exactly football, is it? Neanderball is a compact game compared to a regular football game. And I watch sports. Soccer mostly, though." He forced the rest of the coffee down and stood. "Is this a fool's errand? Am I kidding myself?"

"About what?"

"Everything." He looked down. "I created this absurdity. Am I being too optimistic to think I can do anything about it? Who am I to judge whether Neanderball is bad for the Neanderthals? If they enjoy it, what's the harm? It's not like they can go and get jobs at the local fast-food restaurant. What kind of life can they have? I ... I didn't think ..."

She came up behind him and wrapped her arms around his waist. "I know what you're saying, but they *are* being exploited. I swear, one minute you want to destroy them and reclaim your research, the next, you want to leave them alone. Make up your mind, I'm getting whiplash."

"I'm fighting against my instincts as a scientist, Marlowe. The scientist wants to recover what I can of my research and continue looking for the cure."

"And what does the non-scientist want?"

"He wants to help the Neanderthals have agency of their own lives. But seriously, I don't know how they can."

She pressed in close. "They never had a choice whether they wanted to play or not. And they're not allowed to leave, even if they understood that they could. They're prisoners. I'm helping you because this isn't right. It's not right."

Her warm breath tickled his ear and he leaned into her. "Yeah."

"Get into your new persona until you believe it's who you are."

"You mean blond-headed Jean-Paul Benoit?" He ran his hand through his hair. "Maybe I'll keep it this color."

With a firm shake of her head, Marlowe pulled away. "Nope. I like you in your natural state. Now, rehearse."

"Fine, fine." He grabbed one of the English muffins she had on a plate and went to the living room.

He plopped onto the couch, took a bite out of the muffin, and licked off the butter that dripped onto his fingers. The press conference might be the only chance he'd have at reaching the Neanderthals, and if he blew it, he might never see them. What if he did manage to get a DNA sample and find a fatal error? So what? It wasn't like the Bakers or Fenwick would simply relinquish them for treatment. But at least he'd have proof that they were sick and shouldn't be playing Neanderball. He'd still be the most hated man on Earth, but the Neanderthals wouldn't be used as players any longer.

A single knock on the front door brought Marlowe rushing into the living room. "Don't answer it." She had a pistol in her hand.

He jumped up. "Damn, Marlowe, it might be a Girl Scout selling cookies."

She frowned. "This isn't Thin Mint season."

"Oh. Then, do you have a gun for me? I know how to shoot."

"You do? I'll handle the gun, so stand back." She strode to the door. "Who's there?"

No response.

Lucien got beside her and kept his voice to a whisper, "It's Fenwick, isn't it? Seriously, give me the gun."

Marlowe's phone rang.

She glanced at Lucien, kept her gun aimed at the door, and answered the phone. "Yes?" With a grunt, she handed it to him.

He didn't take his eyes off the door as he put the phone to his ear. "Alexei?"

"Of course, my friend. Open the door."

Lucien motioned to the door. "Marlowe, open the door."

She peeked through the peephole and waved Lucien over. "Who the hell is that?"

Lucien checked. Standing in front of the door with a lop-sided grin was Alexei. Lucien unlocked the deadbolt and swung the door wide. "I thought you were in Russia."

Alexei, with tousled chestnut brown hair, a thin mustache, and an impeccably tailored suit, threw his arms wide. "When my friend is in trouble, I come."

After a brief and bone-crushing, hug, Lucien stood aside as Alexei pushed his way in and smiled at Marlowe. She did not reciprocate.

With the deadbolt locked, Lucien nodded to her. "This is my friend, Alex—"

"I know." She hadn't lowered the gun.

Without losing his smile, Alexei extended his hand. "You are more beautiful than your driver's license photo." He looked at the gun. "A Sig Sauer M17. Nice. But I prefer the civilian P320-M18."

"Civilian? So you haven't served. I have." She lowered her arm slightly and glared at Lucien. "He knows guns. And got my driver's license photo? Really? Who the hell have you brought to my door?"

What could he say? Or rather, what should he say? Alexei risked exposure to help and Lucien was grateful for it, no matter how it annoyed Marlowe. "Alexei is my friend and he's very good at what he does. I'm lucky to have him here. Let's leave it at that."

Alexei let out a laugh and finally gave up on shaking her hand. "Yes, let's. Lucien, I like the new look. Vitaly's idea?"

Lucien nodded. "He suggested a dye job. I look like a haggard old surfer."

"No, it looks good on you." Alexei turned his attention back to Marlowe. "Any friend of Lucien's is my friend, too." He cocked his head. "You have the steely eyes of a mercenary."

Marlowe's frown deepened, and she still held the gun. "Lucien."

"Take a breath, he's here to help. You can put the gun away." Lucien nudged Alexei into the kitchen. "Did you ever think I'd end up like this?"

Alexei turned and faced Lucien. "As what, the founder of Neanderball? Got to say no to that. I'll help you clear your name, my friend, but I have to say, I've made a sizeable amount of money from that game, and I stand to make a lot more."

"What are you talking about?" Lucien groaned. "You're betting on the game?"

Alexei nodded. "Of course. You know me, I never pass up a chance to make legitimate money."

"Legitimate?" Marlowe stormed in. "The whole thing isn't legitimate! Cavemen playing football? For the love of—"

Alexei spun around, his face flushed. "Cavemen? My friend spent the better part of his life working day and night to perfect his techniques at DNA recombination and cloning to create those beautiful people. They are not cavemen. They are early humans and anyone who thinks otherwise is a fool." He winked at Lucien. "See? I follow your magnificent work."

Lucien slipped in between them, not the safest place to be. "Marlowe, I see your point of view, and Alexei, as always, I thank you for defending my honor. But really, we need to concentrate on the Neanderthals."

"I thought that's what we were doing?" Alexei raised his eyebrow.

"No, you were antagonizing Marlowe." Lucien ran his hand through his hair, still feeling self-conscious about the color. "For God's sake, Marlowe put the gun away."

She tucked the gun into a pocket. "I'll keep it right here." She patted the pocket.

Lucien shook his head. "Now, if you two can get along and help blond-me finalize my plans for this afternoon, I would be most appreciative."

"Anything for a friend." Alexei poured himself a cup of coffee. "Ms. Dunham, darling, if I have offended you in any way, I apologize. Oh, and I do have some information that might be helpful."

Lucien watched Marlowe to gauge her reaction.

With a deep sigh, she visibly relaxed. "Apology accepted. What information?"

Alexei continued, "I know Fenwick's weakness." He took a sip of coffee. "Oh, this coffee blend is delicious."

"Alexei, what do you know?" Lucien held his breath for a moment. Was this the catalyst to get everything going? Or only another one of Alexei's complicated schemes that might get them all arrested.

For three more sips of coffee, Alexei said nothing as Lucien tapped his foot and waited. Finally, he put the coffee cup on the counter.

"Well?" Lucien prodded, a spark of hope teasing him at the idea that Fenwick wasn't as untouchable as Marlowe thought.

Alexei sat, swung his legs onto the kitchen table, and leaned back. "As I'm sure the lovely Ms. Dunham here has already discovered, Fenwick has her fingers in a lot of pies."

She hovered near Lucien. "You're right, I do know that. And get your filthy feet off my table."

"Do as she says, Alexei." He sat in the chair opposite. "How many pies?"

Alexei removed his feet and motioned for Marlowe to sit next to Lucien. "Well, she's wanted by every major law enforcement agency on the planet, yet nobody has ever so much as brought her in for questioning. Why, you might ask?" He paused. "A woman like Fenwick makes certain to cover her behind by assuring she is kept alive and off the radar."

"What does that mean?" Lucien pulled out the chair for Marlowe. "What are you saying?"

Leaning on his elbows, Alexei looked directly at Marlowe. "I'm saying that's why I'm here." He turned to Lucien. "You can do nothing by yourself, or even with the help of Ms. Dunham. You need me and my expertise. Fenwick is a collector. Like our old friend Dobroslav, if you remember that piece of work."

A shiver snaked up his spine at the mention of Dobroslav, a Czech arms dealer who'd crossed their path a few times in the old days. The man was a sociopath; cold and calculating. But that wasn't the worst part of him. He was a collector extraordinaire. Among the more honorable thieves, collectors were despised for burrowing into the darkest hidden parts of a person's life and then holding onto the secrets to remain immune from prosecution. Even Alexei had no idea how many secrets Dobroslav had collected.

Marlowe thumped on the table. "Excuse me, who's Dobroslav, and what's he or she got to do with Fenwick?"

Lucien watched Alexei for a moment before answering. "Dobroslav's a he. A collector has, ah, the dirt on a lot of very, very important people. If the collector is captured or killed, the dirty secrets are revealed in one way or another. Nobody knows how, but nobody is willing to risk exposure. This is how collectors can move around without being harassed. You said Fenwick was untouchable, that's why."

"But she has a weakness?" Marlowe stared at Alexei.

With a nod, Alexei smirked. "She does. And I found it."

Lucien wiped a trace of sweat from his forehead. He'd been out of the business for so long that he wasn't used to the intrigue and risk anymore. "Wait. How did you find the one thing that'll bring her down when nobody else could? Are you a magician now?"

"I have a host of near-magical powers, my friend, as well you know." He got up and poured himself a fresh cup of coffee. "Have you heard of a town called Samobor?"

Lucien shook his head. "Nope."

He continued, "It's in Croatia. I had some business to attend to at a museum in Zagreb." He turned to Marlowe. "That's a large city in Croatia. Anyway, I had dealings with an old colleague who'd been a target of Dobroslav's, and he mentioned that another collector had been spotted in Samobor."

"You've been to Croatia several times as I remember, Alexei. Once you told me you went to visit an old flame." Lucien nudged Marlowe. "He's quite the flirt. Always has at least one lover on standby."

"Shall I continue, or do you want to mock me some more?"

"No, please, continue." Lucien leaned forward. "And it's not mocking, it's admiration."

With a slight grunt, Marlowe pushed her chair back a few inches. "Why is it good-looking men can't settle for only one woman?"

"Ah, so you think I'm good-looking, Ms. Dunham?"

"Shut up."

He continued, "I can't settle for one woman, Ms. Dunham, because I prefer beautiful young men."

Marlowe's mouth gaped. "Oh. Ah, sorry. I didn't figure you ... I mean ... it doesn't matter if ..."

Lucien laughed. "He made a pass at me when we first met. Remember that, Alexei?"

"Indeed I do. Shame you're straight. We'd have torn up Europe together."

"We did all right regardless. Please finish your story about Fenwick. I need to know what I'm up against." Lucien stood and stretched, feeling more relaxed than he had all day. It felt good to be with his old friend again, it made him feel young. Sort of. "If we can get Fenwick out of the way, I can get to the Neanderthals." He sat back down and took Marlowe's hand.

"I know. That's the plan, my friend." Alexei swirled the coffee around in the cup. "Back to my story. I took a side trip to Samobor and poked around a little but came up empty-handed until my last day. I'd been wiling away the afternoon at a sidewalk café enjoying a glass of delicious Dingač when I noticed the unmistakable secretive slither of a collector. An unsightly woman who would have passed as a matronly governess to anyone with an untrained eye."

Marlowe nodded. "Fenwick."

"Exactly. Of course, I didn't know who she was at the time, but I placed her under surveillance and extended my stay in Samobor for three more days. For two days, Fenwick played the part of a tourist. Visited a museum, strolled the streets, even took a fucking boat ride on the river. But on that third day, she must have been confident nobody followed her. She stayed in her hotel all morning, finally leaving at half-past two." His lips turned up into a slight smile. "Any guesses where she went?"

Lucien let go of Marlowe's hand, groaned, and drummed his fingers on the table. "Come on, Alexei."

The smile grew. "A sanitarium. Right on the river. Upscale, not one of the ghastly places for indigents. More like a country club really."

Lucien made a mock gesture with his hands that he would strangle Alexei. "Don't make me hurt you."

"You could try." Alexei glanced at Marlowe.

She rolled her eyes. "I'm still having trouble processing you two gallivanting all over Europe doing God-knows-what."

Alexei chuckled. "She has a brother." His arms spread wide. "She has a fucking brother."

"So what?" Marlowe pushed her chair back further and stood. "So fucking what?"

Lucien stood and smiled. "This is huge. Collectors have zero attachments for a reason. No family, no real friends. Connections like that are detrimental to someone in her line of business. And the fact that she visits her brother means she cares. Someone with evil on their mind might use that against her."

Alexei's smile had relaxed. "Evil on their mind? It's good to have you back, my friend."

"Hold on. I know exactly what you're thinking." Marlowe shook her head. "Jesus Christ, you're going to go after the brother? In a sanitarium? The poor guy's sick."

Alexei raised an eyebrow. "We're all sick in one way or another, my dear. Do you want Fenwick off your back or not?"

"We do," Lucien answered.

With all that Fenwick had done, he wasn't about to allow her to continue terrorizing him, or anyone for that matter. Because of her, he had nothing. Surely Marlowe understood that. Preying on an innocent mental patient would be one of the lowest things he'd ever done, but in this case, it was necessary.

Alexei glared at Marlowe for a moment before returning his attention to Lucien. "Of course, I had no idea of what importance Fenwick would have, until now. I stored that information away in case I should ever need it. And now I do. It's serendipity, my friend."

Pacing around the kitchen, Marlowe stopped near Alexei. "She's Croatian?"

"No, as American as you, my dear. But who would look in Croatia for a family connection? Damn smart if you ask me. But I'm smarter. When I learned it was Fenwick who had you in her web, Lucien, I knew I could help. I waited for you to ask."

Having a friend like Alexei was worth its weight in gold. Lucien checked the clock on the wall. "The press conference is at five. There's no time to get Fenwick's brother. Great idea, but we can't pull it off in time."

"Oh, my friend, your lack of faith in me disappoints." Alexei feigned a frown. "You remember a colleague of mine, Janko? I've mentioned him before."

"Janko?" Lucien searched his memory, but Janko didn't sound familiar. "I don't recall."

"No matter. Janko works with Vitaly. I met with Janko when in Croatia. He had something I needed for the museum job. Anyway, that's not important. What is important is that it'll only take a phone call to have him visit the sanitarium. There's always time to work a job."

A trickle of sweat rolled down Lucien's back. He'd now involved his friend, and by extension, a nefarious colleague who was evidently prepared to kidnap a mentally ill man.

"Lucien," Marlowe said softly. "Are you all right with this? I mean, I have no qualms about putting a bullet between Fenwick's beady eyes, but using an innocent man, and a mental patient at that, doesn't sit well with me."

Alexei had his phone out. "Should I make the call?"

"Make the call." Lucien motioned to Marlowe. "Come out back with me. We should talk."

"You got that right." She stormed out without waiting for him.

With a slight laugh, Alexei put his phone to his ear. "You're in trouble now, my friend."

"I know. Make sure Janko doesn't hurt the brother." Lucien went to the doorway and saw Marlowe pacing near the bench.

Alexei came up beside him. "I can do that."

"Thanks."

"Now go and take care of your lady before she buries you in the garden."

Lucien drew in a breath and headed toward the back of the yard. He knew he'd get a verbal lashing that would sting more than a physical one.

Chapter 12

Lucien walked toward Marlowe, the fresh outside air tickling his sweaty skin, but when she spun around with narrowed eyes, even the air couldn't make him comfortable.

She glared and confronted him. "Don't think for one minute that I'm not fully aware of how dangerous Fenwick is, but—"

"I know, I know." He sat on the bench and patted the seat beside him. "Sit. Alexei isn't a murderer. He promised me the brother won't be hurt. It's a bluff, that's all, but if it'll get Fenwick to back off, then I've got to do it. I'm responsible for the Neanderthals being here in the first place and if I can get them back, there's still a chance I can verify if their genetics hold the key to producing a cancer cure. I'm not taking any of this lightly. But Fenwick started it. She almost killed you. I can't forgive someone for that. As I said, she started it."

"Yes, she did, but I don't want us sinking to her level. And for fuck's sake, I can't believe you're still trying to salvage your precious research. You can't screw around with someone like Fenwick. Did you forget that she put you in a coma and has your family held hostage?"

"Of course I haven't, but that only makes me want to destroy her all the more. And trust me, I realize those clones ... Neanderthals ... are no longer lab experiments. But if some good can come from this, then that's a positive thing. Right?"

She sighed. "I understand. But you're a target and that bothers the hell out of me."

"Damn, Marlowe, I can handle myself."

"I'm sure you can, but if there's a way to get those Stone Age teens away from Neanderball and take out Fenwick at the same time, then I'll be happy to help. So long as you don't lock those kids away and stick them with probes and electrodes." She sat next to him and let out a deep breath. "If this plan of yours is the only way to keep you safe, then I'm in. I don't like it, but I'm in."

"That means a lot. I have no intention of hurting them." He took her hand. "When this is all over, and if we're both still alive, how about a romantic vacation somewhere exotic?"

Her frown lightened. "You're on. A fancy, exclusive, and awfully expensive island paradise. Your treat."

"I know the exact place to go. You might have to spot me some money though." He leaned into her and pressed his lips to hers. "And only after my hair is back to normal."

"Deal." She kissed him back. "I want the old Lucien back."

"Did you have to say old?"

She laughed and snuggled against him. "What if Fenwick doesn't back off? What then?"

"Let's enjoy a peaceful moment here under the trees. Okay?" He glanced toward the house when Alexei called his name from the deck. "Well, the peaceful moment has passed." He got up.

She stood and stretched. "You should be rehearsing anyway."

He gave a nod and jogged to the house. "What's up?"

With a serious expression, Alexei whispered, "Janko will acquire the brother within the hour." He looked at Lucien for a moment. "Everything will be fine."

"I trust you." Lucien watched Marlowe, who strode around near the bench with her hands clasped behind her back. "She's worried about me, but she's with us. I want my Neanderthals back and I want Fenwick out of my life."

"Fenwick will pay. And we'll get your brutish teens back." Alexei sighed. "I feel like I owe those boys something. My winnings from Neanderball bought me a new speedboat and a cabin in the Alps."

"Don't you have enough luxury in your life already?" Lucien pointed to a diamond Cartier watch on Alexei's wrist.

He shrugged and held his wrist up so the sunlight glinted off the diamonds. "One can never have too much. I have an extra if you'd like it."

"No, thank you." Lucien rubbed his eyes. "I have a headache and a fancy watch won't make it any better."

"But your Neanderthals will?"

"I hope they will. They might hold the key to everything I've worked for. I've got to know for sure. I need to test their genes."

"I understand the importance to you. This research of yours is some sort of repentance for your misspent youth, isn't it?"

"I don't know, well, perhaps it is. Some of us in my family carry the gene, as well as a lot of other people. I want to give back and I don't care for any notoriety or diamond watches."

"There's your Jaguar."

"Okay, except for that. I used up all my savings from our time together to get that car and a hefty down payment on my house. The house is gone, but Marlowe saved my Jag."

"Bless that woman." Alexei smiled and pulled his sleeve over the watch. "Then we shall talk no longer of luxuries. Go and practice being your alter ego and I will keep in touch with Janko." He motioned to Marlowe. "And what about the lovely Ms. Dunham?"

Lucien slowly shook his head. "Don't mess with her. She needs time to get her head straight about all of this." He lowered his voice, "Fenwick almost killed her. That's not a forgivable act. I want that woman to suffer."

"Don't worry, my friend. I'm here now. Everything will be as you desire." He turned and went back inside.

While Marlowe continued to wander around the yard, Lucien did what he was supposed to and sat in the kitchen dreaming up a few questions to ask at the press conference to add legitimacy to his ruse. It wouldn't be the first time he'd used a fake persona. He'd be ready, even if Marlowe doubted his ability to lie.

After an hour or so, Alexei came into the kitchen and sat down. "Janko has the brother. It was not an easy grab."

"What do you mean?" Lucien glanced out the window and saw that Marlowe sat on the bench plucking petals off a flower. "What happened?" If someone got hurt, he'd never forgive himself.

"Fenwick's brother was under very tight security in a locked ward for the criminally insane."

Lucien sat on the edge of the table. "Wait. What? Criminally insane? That sounds about right. Is it a prison?"

Alexei shook his head. "No. But the ward is run like one. Janko said the brother's real name is Bernard Fenwick, but he is registered as Luka Duvnjak, a convicted European serial killer."

"What does that mean? I'm completely confused."

"Duvnjak is a real person, but according to Janko, he's never been found. Understand? Fenwick placed her brother in the facility as the serial killer. Very clever. Even the personnel believe he's Duvnjak. That's why it was rather difficult to get him out of the place."

"But Janko did?" Lucien let out a deep breath. "And nobody got hurt?"

Alexei looked down and sighed. "I didn't say that, my friend."

"Oh." He checked on Marlowe's location. "We won't share that with her. Who got hurt?"

"Two security guards, a male nurse, and a patient who tried to jump on Janko's back." He shrugged. "Nobody's dead though."

"I guess that's something." He watched Marlowe but turned when Alexei cleared his throat. "Is there more?"

With another shrug, Alexei continued, "By now, Fenwick knows about her brother's abduction. That means you must be vigilant."

"She won't know he was kidnapped on my behalf though."

"Perhaps not, but she's smart. It would be quite a coincidence. Now, try to relax and get into character. I have some things to take care of, but I'll return before you leave for the Arena." He got up and wrapped Lucien in a bear hug. "Be safe, my friend."

"You too."

Marlowe strode in, glanced at them, and continued to the living room, calling out, "I thought you liked beautiful *young* men, Alexei."

When Alexei burst out laughing, Lucien pulled away and followed her. "I'm not that old."

Sitting on the couch with her feet on the coffee table, she flashed a teasing smile and a wink. "I know. I like to ruffle your forty-two-year-old feathers. Okay, *Monsieur* Benoit, what's your plan for the press conference?"

He sat close to her, kissed her on the cheek, and whispered, "I'm going to steal back my research, liberate the Neanderthals, and cure cancer in one fell swoop. That's my plan." He placed his hand under her chin, leaned in, and planted another kiss. "So long as you're with me, I have no doubt I'll succeed."

Chapter 13

The rest of the day went too quickly, and Lucien didn't feel as confident as he had before. He knew what to say and how to act but getting close enough to the players to grab a hair sample was the tricky part. And judging by what he'd seen on TV, they were strong and violent, not the sort who'd willingly part with anything, even a strand of hair.

"Marlowe! Do you have anything for an upset stomach?" he shouted from the kitchen.

A moment later, she walked in with a bottle of bright pink liquid. "Sure do. Drink a capful of this stuff. We've got to leave in about fifteen minutes. You ready?"

He shook out his hands and rolled his neck. "Of course. I'm about to meet my—"

"Neander-children?"

"Yes. Neander-children. You know, they have no idea who I am or why I created them in the first place. I don't even know if they've been taught to speak yet."

"What do you mean? They can talk?" She took an empty coffee cup off the table and placed it in the sink. "Lucien, can they talk?"

He shrugged. "Not sure, but I thought I told you before that they probably had a language. The latest research points to them having had the ability to make sounds, like us."

"Yeah, okay, I remember you saying something like that. That's ... cool. I guess. Hey, if they're smart, you can explain everything to them. Who knows, maybe they'll come with you willingly." She ran water into the coffee cup and dried her hands on a dishtowel.

"That certainly would make it easy."

She stared at him for a moment. "When this is all over and the Neanderthals are safe wherever they'll be safe, we'll go on that romantic trip. You can rest and I'll catch some rays on the beach."

"Sounds heavenly, but I'll be on that beach with you. I've been sequestered in my lab for too long. How about we go to France? I'd love my family to meet you."

"I'd like to meet them."

A shiver ran through his body. Fenwick had them. "Oh, hell. If Fenwick finds out that I'm involved with her brother's ..." He'd have to call it off. There was no other way. "I can't ..."

"Breathe. You're as pale as an Englishman."

The headache that never seemed to go away sprung to life with renewed vigor. He massaged his brow. "My family, Marlowe."

She reached into the sink and flung the coffee cup across the room. It shattered against the wall. "Damn it! I'm sorry, I wasn't thinking about them. You've got to contact Alexei."

"No need." Alexei strode in from the living room. "I am sorry, my friend. I like your father, even after he called me a good-for-nothing thief and threatened to have my genitalia removed, with a rusty saw if I'm remembering correctly."

"What have I done, Alexei?" Lucien grabbed the medicine bottle and took a long swig of the pink stuff.

"This might not be as bad as it seems." Alexei glanced at the broken coffee cup. "Fenwick won't dare harm your family until she knows if her brother is alive or not. Therefore, we must keep him breathing. I'll contact Janko and request a photograph showing proof of life."

With a broom and pan, Marlowe frowned at Lucien. "Jesus. Proof of life? Sounds like you've done this sort of thing before."

"Not me." Lucien took the broom and swept the cup shards into a pile. "Alexei's right though. So long as Fenwick's brother is alive, she won't dare touch my family. How are we going to end this, Alexei?"

With a casual shrug, he answered, "You get your Neanderthals and your family, and Fenwick gets her brother. Simple."

Marlowe frowned. "It's not simple! She won't hand over the Neanderthals, not after all the trouble she went to. They belong to the Bakers now anyway." She threw the dustpan at Alexei.

It smacked him in the chest. "Ouch. My dear, I've done this sort of thing a time or two before. It will require a delicate orchestration, but I'm an excellent conductor."

Lucien jumped in front of Marlowe. "Okay, everyone take a breath. I need to call my father." He scrambled through the house and found

Marlowe's phone, dialed his father's home number, and waited. It answered on the third ring.

"Papa, it's Lucien. Are you all right?"

"Hello, Dr. Roux." A man with an American accent responded. "The elder Roux cannot come to the phone right now."

"Put him on the phone!"

A pause. "It's evening here. Your father has retired for the night. But he's alive. For now."

Lucien clenched his fist and swallowed hard. "I need ... proof of life." The words stung. "Let me speak to him."

"I don't think you're in any position to make demands. I don't take orders from you." The man hung up.

"Damn. Shit!" Lucien caught himself before he threw the phone against the wall, reconsidered, and tossed it onto the table instead. He checked the time. They had to leave.

"What's wrong?" Marlowe took his hand. "Is it your father?"

He squeezed her hand gently. "They won't let me talk to him. He might be—"

"Don't say that." She looked into his eyes. "Let's call it off."

He clutched her hand to his chest. He needed her support now more than ever. If he left the whole Neanderball thing alone and Janko released Fenwick's brother, there'd be no reason for Fenwick to go after his family. That might be the only way to protect them now.

Alexei asked, "What is it you want to do, my friend?"

"I don't have a choice." Lucien dropped Marlowe's hand.

So what if he lost his research? At least he'd have his family. There'd be time to start over again if he found more funding. Neanderball proved his success at cloning, which would hopefully convince some of the healthcare companies to put up a grant or two. Maybe he'd move back to France for a fresh start.

"Lucien." Alexei had his cell phone in his hand. "Lucien," he said louder.

"What?" Lucien hurried to his friend. "You have news?"

There was no mistaking Alexei had bad news; eyes cast down, shoulders stooped. "My friend, I texted Janko about Fenwick's brother ..."

"And?" Lucien's stomach tightened.

Without speaking, Alexei handed the phone to him. A single text from Janko:

Verification from contact that Roux's family believed dead and vineyard on fire. Orders?

Lucien dropped the phone. His knees shook and he collapsed onto the floor. Was it true? He felt Marlowe beside him, but comfort wasn't what he needed. He wanted to scream. He wanted revenge. He pushed her hand away; there was no comfort.

"Lucien," Alexei said softly. "I wish there was something to say to ease your suffering."

"Me too." Lucien's voice came out raspy. He wiped his eyes and drew in a breath.

He wished he'd seen his family one last time to tell them how much he loved them and missed them. They were always in his heart regardless of the distance between them. And his sister, she'd never done anything but love her children. Now they were dead. He'd never walk through the vineyard with his father or play tennis with his brother again. Fenwick took everything from him. No doubt left, she had to pay.

He drew in a breath and looked up at Alexei. "Kill the brother."

"What?" Marlowe crouched beside him. "Don't do this, Lucien. You're emotionally raw right now and lashing out. Stop and think for a minute. Hurting innocent people is wrong. The brother hasn't done anything."

He got to his feet and glared at her. "And neither did my brother or my sister or my father. I have no family left now."

Standing beside Marlowe, Alexei placed his hands on Lucien's shoulders. "Ms. Dunham has a point. Reacting out of emotion will create more trouble, and that's something you don't need right now. You want your research back? Then continue with the plan. Once you have what you want, I'll go after Fenwick with everything I have."

Lucien locked eyes with Marlowe. For a tough woman, she had a sensitive, kind side to her. It balanced the hardness, and that's what he loved about her. She *was* right, Fenwick's brother hadn't done anything, and revenge-killing him wouldn't accomplish a single thing. He didn't want to be like Fenwick. But he did want to face her again. One minute alone with her would be enough.

He wiped his eyes again and drew in a deep, ragged breath. "All right. Nobody dies but Fenwick. Marlowe, will you drive us to the Arena? I can't drive right now. I need some time to compose myself. I'll do the best I can, I promise." He stared at his trembling hands.

Alexei patted him on the arm. "We will fly to France and hold an appropriate memorial once this is all over." He raised an eyebrow. "Yes?"

Lucien embraced Marlowe. "Yes. For now, I can't think about my family. I need to destroy the Bakers and Fenwick and rescue my Neanderthals. I have to do this; otherwise my family died for nothing."

"There's no I, it's *we*. You're not alone," Marlowe whispered in his ear. "Can you compartmentalize this?"

He sucked in a cleansing breath. "I can."

She kissed his forehead. "Okay then. To the business at hand. You'll need a journalist's notepad, the one we bought should work. And I've already made you the fake ID."

"I knew I liked her, my friend." Alexei went to the front door. "We leave in two minutes."

"I'll be ready." Lucien pulled back and looked into Marlowe's eyes. "*We'll* be ready."

Once Alexei left, Lucien staggered to the den and found the notepads they'd bought at the store. Hopefully, it looked like the type a journalist would use. He stood for a moment in front of a framed photograph of Marlowe as a young girl, on a beach somewhere, standing waist-deep in the surf with a man beside her. Her father, he assumed. Could he possibly push his own family from his mind and pull off the ruse at the Arena? What if he saw Fenwick? What if she saw him? He closed his eyes and inhaled.

When he opened his eyes, he felt a sense of purpose, a drive to finish what he'd started. His father had been proud of his work and would have been excited to say his son found a cure for cancer. *For you, Papa, I'll get my research back on track and take care of that swine of a woman.*

"Lucien! Time to go." Marlowe peeked into the den. "Can you do this? Can you really stow your emotions?"

He turned with a sigh. "I don't have a choice. The only family I have now are my Neanderthals. They're a part of me."

"Yes, that's true, but you have friends, too."

"Wonderful friends." He forced a smile, waved the notepad in the air, and went outside.

Alexei stood beside the driver's door of a silver Porsche 911. "I will follow behind in case there's any trouble."

"Appreciated." Lucien got into the passenger side of the Jaguar, strapped in, and cleared his head of everything except the Neanderthals. In less than half an hour, he'd be closer to them than he had been since they were stolen so many months ago. Soon, it would be over.

Chapter 14

The drive to the Coliseum complex gave Lucien some breathing room, but thoughts of his family crept into his head. It wasn't like he could simply forget what had happened, no matter how hard he tried.

Marlowe hadn't said a word, and he knew she realized he needed quiet. When she pulled up to the entry gate, he slumped in his seat as a small group of protestors swarmed them, shoving signs at the windows, and shouting that Neanderball violated the Neanderthals' rights, and genetic experiments should be outlawed.

He turned from the window and shielded his face with one hand. "At least not everyone is a Neanderball fan. I need this to succeed."

"It will." Marlowe motioned to a security guard behind the gate.

The hefty man, clad in a dayglow orange vest that strained against the snaps, and with a black baton gripped in his hand, unlocked the gate, and yelled at the protestors to stand back.

Marlowe edged the car forward and wound her window down. "We're here for the press conference."

"Name." The guard closed the gate once they were through. When he came back, he had a clipboard and repeated, "Name."

Lucien flashed his fake ID. "Jean-Paul Benoit and company." He pointed to Alexei's car. "Carolyn Goodson invited us."

"Fine, fine. Go to the left and straight toward the entrance. You'll see another security guy." He went back to the gate to let Alexei through.

"Okay, we're in," Marlowe said as she headed in the direction the guard indicated.

Sure enough, before long, another man in a bright orange vest, waving a smaller baton or maybe a flashlight, motioned them forward.

Marlowe glanced at Lucien. "Stay in character, *Monsieur* Benoit."

"*Oui.*" He gripped the ID. "I'm ready."

This was it, too late to turn back.

She slowed to a stop near the guard. "We're journalists from Paris here for the press conference. Jean-Paul Benoit and his editor-in-chief."

The guard scanned down a paper attached to a manila folder. "Ben ..."

Lucien leaned across and showed the ID. "B...e...n...o...i...t."

The guard nodded. "Here it is. Never would have guessed you spelled it like that. Go ahead and pull into a parking space closest to the main entrance. Is the guy behind you with you?"

"Ah, *oui*." Lucien looked through the rear window. "He is our security."

"Sure, sure," the guard mumbled, waving them forward.

Marlowe drove toward the main entrance. "That was surprisingly easy."

"Lies are believable when you're confident."

There were about twenty cars parked in the lot, one a shiny red McLaren Spider.

He leaned forward. "You see that car? It's a McLaren. It's beautiful." He tucked the ID into his pocket. McLaren was a favorite of his brother, not that he had the money to buy one. "Beautiful car."

"Yeah, okay. Like I said, getting here was easy, but now comes the hard part."

He nodded, his eyes still on the McLaren. "Is Alexei behind us?" He glanced out the back window.

"Did you think he wouldn't be?"

He focused again on the McLaren. "I don't know."

"Don't get distracted by every shiny object you see. I need you focused."

"I am." He turned and watched Alexei pull up beside them.

After Marlowe shut off the engine, she drummed her fingers on the steering wheel. "I have to know, can you maintain control if you see Fenwick? I know this is a difficult time, but ..."

Could he? He had nothing but pure hatred for the woman. "Can *you*? Look, if she's here and recognizes me, Alexei will handle things."

"That didn't answer my question." She raised an eyebrow.

He wiped a trace of sweat from his upper lip. "I will not cause any disturbances if that fucking cow is here."

"Thank you. Your disguise might throw her off for a minute anyway."

"Let's hope. I told you, I won't do anything to draw attention to myself if I see her." He opened the door and climbed out.

Alexei opened his door and grinned. "A McLaren Spider. Goddamn, it's a thing of beauty."

"That's what I said. Marlowe isn't impressed though." Lucien shrugged and motioned to the entrance to the Arena. "Shall we?"

"After you." Alexei patted him on the shoulder. "You're doing well, my friend."

Marlowe strode to them. "Bring your A-game, boys."

"Always," Alexei said softly.

Lucien stared up at the Arena. Even though the Coliseum was bigger, the Arena still towered. He'd never been inside but saw a photo once of a country music concert and was amazed at how many seats they managed to fit into the space.

At the entrance, a uniformed guard stood to one side and a man in a dark blue suit blocked the way. He held up his hand as they approached. "ID."

Lucien held out the ID and flashed a smile. "Jean-Paul Benoit, my editor-in-chief, and my personal security. Can't be too careful these days." He added a heavier accent for effect.

The man in the suit remained stone-faced, but after checking the ID, he opened the door and ushered them through without another word. Security was tight, but they'd made it so far.

Alexei sidled up to Lucien as they walked. "So, we're in."

"We are. Keep a sharp eye." Lucien noticed a sign on a large easel ahead of them and to the right.

Neanderball Press Conference

"I guess we go right," Marlowe whispered as she moved in front and took the lead.

Another sign about twenty feet further down led them in front of an open door. Lucien hung back a little and waited for the all-clear from Marlowe, which he got a few seconds after she peered into the room. Chattering voices came from the room and the few words he picked out were mostly *Neanderball* and *Neanderthals*. He wiped his sweaty palms on his pants and stepped inside.

The room wasn't much bigger than his lab. Crowded in the space were twenty or thirty people gathered in small groups. He immediately felt like an outsider. A young woman, late twenties or thereabout, with blonde hair, bright red lipstick, and a tight-fitting business suit, sauntered up to the podium and attached a microphone to her lapel.

"Ladies and gentlemen of the press, may I have your attention please?" She had a slight southern accent and maintained a smile while waiting for the chatter to stop. "Welcome to the second official Neanderball press conference. I'm Carolyn Goodson."

A round of applause went up and the crowd pushed forward as a group. Lucien followed Marlowe to the side of the room where there was a gap, but Alexei didn't come. Instead, he circled in the opposite direction. As Goodson waited, Lucien adjusted his novelty eyeglasses and smoothed his hair, glancing around the room now and then. Thankfully, no sign of Fenwick.

"All right, all right, let's all settle down." Goodson's smile never faded. "Before I take questions, I have an exciting announcement. Neanderball is going international!" She flourished with both hands.

The ensuing cheering and whistling forced Lucien to cover his ears. After a minute or so, the noise finally stopped, and Goodson continued.

"The first stop for the international team will be Japan, followed by Scotland, Ireland, and Germany. We're hoping to pick up the market in Australia as well. And," she paused, "we'll breathe new life into this international team with improved Neanderthals. They'll be bigger and stronger, far superior players. We'll have teams based in Europe and America. Our Neander 2.0s are slated to make an appearance in about six months! Now, let's hear it for your Neanderball team!"

More cheering.

Lucien leaned close to Marlowe. "Did I hear that right?"

She nodded. "Yep. How is that possible?"

"Because Fenwick took my research." He balled up his fists and wanted to punch the closest thing, but before he did, Alexei grabbed him in a bear hug from behind.

"My friend, do not react. We will stop this." He let go. "Trust in me."

Lucien spun around. "I do. But my intent wasn't to build a team of Neanderball players. Especially *enhanced* ones. This is out of control."

"Yes, it is." Alexei frowned and pulled him away from the crowd. "I despise people who don't play by the rules."

Lucien lowered his voice, "Same here. For them to be creating more Neanderthals, they would have had to duplicate my work. Exactly. I created hybrids using my Y-chromosome codons and my cancer gene. I tested the procedure over and over again to make sure of the genome's stability. These people are crazy. If they don't perfect the recombinant technique with modern human DNA, there'll be catastrophic results. Not to mention I have no idea if these Neanderthals are developmentally intact."

While the crowd continued to celebrate, Lucien caught movement in his peripheral vision, a flash of something in the light. His breath hitched when he saw a man he recognized, with a shirt full of shiny medals. "What the hell is *he* doing here?"

"Who?" Marlowe glanced around.

Lucien motioned with his head. "Guys, I think there's more going on here than simply a game. I hope I'm wrong, but I have a terrible feeling that they're manipulating the sequences to create paramilitary super-Neanderthals."

"Para ... super Neanderthals?" Alexei leaned in. "Tell me what you mean." He pulled Lucien away toward the doorway.

Marlowe soon followed them, her eyes constantly moving around the room. She glanced at Alexei and back at Lucien. "What's going on?"

Lucien wiped his brow. "Things have escalated. I saw this guy, General Harmond. Early in my research, he approached me and then barraged me with phone calls. He's been doing his best to get my research, even offering to give me an unlimited budget, but my work would be under the government's scrutiny. I refused numerous times. He initially asked me about my research and asked very odd questions about the physical stature of Neanderthals and whether it would be possible to manipulate the genes to make them even stronger and fiercer. And obedient. He wants an army of expendable non-human super soldiers to run murder squads. I told him to go to hell."

Marlowe nodded. "Yeah, that sounds like the military."

He continued, "I'd bet a year's salary that Harmond found a renewed opportunity with me out of the way to get my work. Fenwick's got to be working with him." He wiped his face again. "I was furious when he said it wouldn't be like sending humans into battle, but an expendable and legal alternative to having real soldiers dying. As if that made it okay. Living drones is what he said."

"Damn it." Marlowe frowned. "And I thought Neanderball was bad enough."

With a twitching lip, Alexei slammed his fist into his other hand. "Super Neanderthal soldiers. You can't make this stuff up. We need to put an end to this. Now."

"No shit." Marlowe nudged Lucien. "What do you want us to do?"

Before he answered, four members of the Neanderball teams were paraded out behind Goodson. Lucien stared, shocked at how big they looked in real life. They truly were magnificent; burly, barrel-chested, and fierce. The absurdity of Neanderthals in the twenty-first century, wearing football jerseys, was hands-down the most ludicrous thing he'd ever seen.

He turned to Marlowe. "I want you to help me kidnap those players."

Chapter 15

L ucien stared at the players. Each of them wore a different colored team jersey; purple, orange, green, and blue. The crowd was out of control, pushing, high-fiving, and shouting. He flinched as they cheered for their favorite team and pushed toward the podium. Goodson held her ground with a broad, smug smile.

"Focus." Marlowe tugged on his arm. "How are we going to kidnap those ... those—"

"Anachronistic young men," answered Alexei. "Big, strong young men. Brutish, but lovely in their own way."

With a nod, Lucien brought his attention to Marlowe. "I'll go along with young men. Obviously, we can't kidnap all of them, but if we can get at least one player, I can run some tests and try to convince him that he, and his brothers, are being abused and exploited. Then ..."

She rolled her eyes. "Then he'll ride in on a white stallion and set his brothers free? Really? A bit naïve, aren't you?"

"All right," Alexei started. "So if we can wrangle one of them into submission, you'll have access to the DNA you wanted. But I have to tell you, my friend, those boys are rather ... muscular."

"Afraid to get your hands dirty, Alexei?" Marlowe scoffed.

A chorus of screams rose from the front of the room. Lucien craned his neck and saw two men from the crowd grabbing onto the arms of the player in the green jersey. Before security got there, the player twisted free and slammed his fist into the nearest man's nose. A fountain of blood erupted and sprayed over the crowd. Silence fell as the player did the same to the other man and knocked him to the ground. Standing over the man, the player raised his leg and stomped on the man's throat.

"Stop!" shouted a middle-aged man in a red and white striped jersey and matching ball cap. "Team green! End game! End game! Locker room, now!"

The Neanderthal glared, kicked the downed victim one last time, made a few guttural grunts, and sauntered out of the room through a side door. The others followed. If the man in the jersey was the team coach, it seemed like he only had a tenuous amount of control over the Neanderthals.

"Jesus," Marlowe whispered. "Brutal."

"That's an understatement." Lucien got a good look at the bloody victim as the crowd parted to let EMTs pass. His nose wasn't only broken, it was smashed almost flat against his face, and his neck crushed to the point where he couldn't be alive. "What do they expect, they're Neanderthals."

The confusion and medical emergency, were the perfect distraction. Lucien didn't see Harmond anywhere. He gave Alexei a nod and pushed his way through the curious onlookers and out through the side door. It led to a short hallway where, at the far end, the Neanderthals were slowly walking, occasionally elbowing one another in the ribs. The presumed coach trotted after them and attempted to get them under control by repeating *end game* over and over. It didn't seem to work too well because one of the players spun around and charged at the man, breaking off before he made contact. The man dropped and cowered with his arms covering his head.

"Lucien, stop." Marlowe grabbed him from behind and turned him around. "Those *young men* are unpredictable, and you saw what that one did back there. They've been trained to be violent. You can't go up to one and ask him politely to come home with you."

"Why not? What do I have to lose at this point? They understand some language. What if I can make them understand—"

Alexei interrupted, "Understand what? That you're their papa? No chance, my friend. But I have an idea." He reached into his pocket and pulled out a small glass vial of yellowish liquid. "A special blend of mine."

"Special blend of what?" Marlowe peered at the vial.

The corner of Alexei's lip turned up. "Can you make sure the Jag is unlocked, my dear?"

She glared at Lucien. "What the hell ...?"

With a shrug, he mumbled, "If he wants it unlocked, unlock it."

"I hate this. No plan, just spur-of-the-moment idiocy." She scowled and strode back into the press room.

"Did she call me an idiot?" Alexei smirked.

"She did, but I think she aimed it at us both." He motioned to the vial. "So, what is that stuff?"

"Neanderthal-strength knockout drops."

Lucien smiled. He should have known his cohort would come prepared for anything. "How do you ... administer it?"

"Carefully. Very carefully." He slipped the vial back into his pocket and proceeded forward.

Lucien drew in a deep breath and followed. All they needed now was a phenomenal amount of good luck. When they reached the end of the hallway, Alexei put his finger to his lips and pointed to an open doorway. The coach's voice held a stern tone, not quite yelling.

"What do you think you were doing, Rascal? You might have killed that man."

"Kill," came a throaty reply. "Rascal kill."

"No, we don't kill. Ever. Got it?"

Lucien's skin prickled. They spoke. Actually spoke.

He heard a familiar voice speak next. It was Fenwick. "Coach MacIntyre, don't be too hard on them. Boys will be boys, after all."

"Ms. Fenwick, you didn't see what happened."

"I did. And so did my VIP client."

Lucien peeked into the room.

Fenwick chuckled. "He's very pleased. Very pleased indeed. He's been watching the games and this last display clinched the deal. They're ready to proceed with their program of Neander-soldiers. You've done well with them, MacIntire, and will get that bonus I promised. And you, Rascal, good boy."

"Rascal obey lady."

Holy shit. Lucien couldn't breathe. Fenwick *wanted* Rascal to kill someone. Did that mean the whole thing was staged? Did she get some poor idiots to lunge at Rascal, knowing full well what would happen? "Alexei," he said softly. "Neanderball is a way for Fenwick to showcase the Neanderthals to the military."

He whispered back, "Shhh. We may be too late to save them, my friend."

"Never." Lucien reached into Alexei's pocket and pulled out the vial. "We have to get those players alone."

He stared at the liquid in the vial. The only way to stop further abuse of the Neanderthals was to get them away from the team owners and Fenwick.

"What are you doing?" Coach MacIntire's voice rose. "You can't have a gun in here."

Lucien held his breath. What did Fenwick have in mind? She had to be stopped. But how? He watched Alexei pace. This might be the only chance they'd have of getting the jump on Fenwick. And getting the Neanderthals away from her.

Fenwick spoke in her gruff voice, "I can do whatever I want. You've become a liability." A pause. "Rascal, kill your coach."

"Rascal obey lady," came the throaty response.

"No," Lucien breathed. "We have to ... do ... some ..."

Alexei grabbed the vial and charged toward the room. He skidded to a stop in the doorway, tossed the vial, and threw his body on the floor as the vial shattered onto the tiles. Unfortunately, Fenwick and Rascal escaped through a back door, but Lucien watched as the other three players wobbled and collapsed.

Marlowe ran up next to Lucien. "What's ... why's he on the floor?"

"He ... we're going to ... I don't know what we're going to do. Why did you come back?"

Alexei didn't move.

"Alexei?"

Marlowe dangled the Jag's key fob from her fingers. "The doors are unlocked. Now tell me what the hell is happening."

After a few seconds, Alexei got to his knees and looked around. "It worked. Don't worry, it dissipates fast."

"Wow. You continue to amaze me." Lucien hurried into the room.

"You wanted me out of the way, didn't you? Dick." Marlowe scowled.

Everyone but Alexei was unconscious. The room looked like a gym with large burlap sacks, weights, and treadmills. At least they had three players.

With a gasp, Marlowe came up beside Lucien. "Oh, shit. How are we going to move these beasts down the hallway and into the parking lot? They've got to be at least two hundred and fifty pounds."

Alexei grabbed onto Lucien's arm, slightly wobbly. He blinked and looked over at Marlowe. "No time to waste, my dear."

"How are we going to pile those guys into the Jag?" She took him by the arm as he swayed. "Um, are you okay?"

"Breathed in a bit of my brew." Alexei knelt beside the Neanderthal in the blue jersey. "We'd better move fast. I have no idea how soon the mixture will wear off."

"Pardon me?" Lucien placed his fingers on the neck of each Neanderthal. Steady pulse, but faster than what he'd expected. "If you don't know ... let's move."

A finger twitched on the player in the orange jersey.

"Now!" Lucien dashed around the room looking for anything mobile that would hold a full-grown Neanderthal.

In one corner, behind a stack of padded mats sat a wheelchair. Only one. He kicked the mats aside and wheeled it out. Before he said anything, the Neanderthal with the twitchy finger rolled onto his side and groaned.

No words were necessary. Alexei and Lucien tugged on the unmoving Neanderthal in the purple jersey and dragged him near the wheelchair. With Marlowe's help, they managed to slump the player into the chair.

Marlowe checked the hallway. "All clear."

Lucien shoved the wheelchair forward and rolled it into the hallway but in the opposite direction to the press room. There had to be another way out, one that wasn't crowded with spectators, EMTs, security, and press. At the end of the hall, a short corridor led directly to an emergency exit. Exactly what they needed.

Chapter 16

As fortuitous as finding the emergency exit was, once Lucien opened the door, a shrill alarm sounded. Without hesitating, he pushed the wheelchair outside and ran as fast as he could. He'd come out near the side of the building, a fair distance from where the Jag sat.

"Run, Lucien!" screamed Marlowe above the alarm. "Go!"

He wanted to make sure she was okay, but he dared not slow down. Alexei would make sure nothing happened to her. Out of breath, Lucien spied the Jag, but several security guards were milling around the entrance, scanning the parking lot with binoculars. One stood only a couple of feet from the car.

Lucien stopped so suddenly that he almost lost his grip on the wheelchair. Marlowe ran past him, tossed the key fob at him, and shouted for him to keep going. She tackled the nearest guard to the ground. With Alexei right behind him, he made it to the car. Together they managed to shove the Neanderthal into the back seat and slam the door shut. Lucien jumped into the driver's seat and Alexei rode shotgun.

"Move it, boys!" Marlowe yelled as she slid into the seat beside the Neanderthal.

Lucien stared in the rearview mirror for a few seconds until she smacked him across the back of his head. He pressed the ignition starter, screeched out of the parking spot, and pressed on the accelerator. Unfortunately, the exit gate was closed. "What do I do?"

Alexei held onto the dashboard. "Go faster."

Two guards, one with a walkie-talkie in his hand, stood in front of the gate and didn't appear to have any desire to move until Lucien sped up and drove right toward them. Better judgment prevailed and they darted aside just as the car crashed into the gate, breaking through with no trouble. The protesters were still hanging around but jumped out of the way as Lucien sped past them. He skidded out of the parking lot, sliding on some loose gravel, and knocked Alexei into the passenger door.

Alexei let out a whoop, apparently unharmed. "We're clear, my friend. Best to slow down so you don't flip us." He turned around in his seat. "How are you doing, dear?"

Slowing, Lucien glanced in the rearview and saw Marlowe with a trickle of blood on her forehead. He braked and pulled off the road. "You're hurt."

She shook her head. "No, only a bump from slamming into the window when you tore out of the lot. I think our friend here smacked his head pretty good, too."

The Neanderthal slumped to the side, not moving.

Lucien hopped out, opened the rear door, and checked for a pulse. "Strong. He's okay. Are you sure you are?" He touched the bump on her forehead. "I didn't mean for you to get hurt."

Sirens wailed in the distance.

"We need to move!" Alexei shouted. "Now!"

She grabbed her seat belt and fastened it. "I'll be fine. I'll do my best to keep your ... this Neanderthal from bouncing around back here. Go."

By the time he got back into the driver's seat again, several police cars had caught up and were no more than a thousand feet behind them. "We can't make it."

"We can." Alexei started the engine. "Drive, my friend, and let me do what I do best." With a hint of a smile, he wound down the passenger window and pulled something from his jacket pocket.

With no time to think, Lucien sped off and got to seventy miles per hour within seconds, but he kept accelerating to ninety to gain some distance between himself and the cops. "This takes me back," he mumbled.

"What are you doing, Alexei?" Marlowe called out.

"Remember Deggendorf in Bavaria, Lucien?" Alexei hung half out the window.

He did remember, too well. They'd barely escaped arrest by Interpol, but they did, thanks to Alexei's less-than-conventional plan. "Are you crazy? You almost got us killed!"

"But we're still alive to tell the tale. Now, slow down and let them catch up." Alexei pulled the stopper off a vial with his teeth.

Lucien slowed until the cops were close enough.

"Get ready." Alexei tossed the vial up in the air. "Move!"

Sweating, Lucien floored it. His hands gripped the steering wheel so tightly that it felt like his fingers would break. "Are we clear?"

Alexei eased back through the window, chuckling. "We were clear about fifty meters ago. Wonderful driving, my ..."

Before he finished, a series of explosions let Lucien know the plan worked. "Is anyone hurt?"

In a shaky voice, Marlowe shouted, "What the hell was that?"

Decelerating a bit, Lucien checked in the rearview and saw one police car on fire, and several others sideways on the road and the shoulder. Nobody followed. They'd made it.

After securing his seatbelt, Alexei rubbed his hands together.

"Seriously, what the hell was that?" She slapped Lucien's shoulder.

Alexei answered. "Another special concoction of mine. When we stopped back there, I scooped up a handful of pebbles from the side of the road, mixed them with a little nitro, a touch of triacetone triperoxide, a few other ingredients, and a thickening agent, and let the little devils swim in the mix."

"Wait." Marlowe got close to Lucien's ear. "You didn't tell me he's a bomb maker."

"He isn't." Lucien slowed down to take a curve. "He's a thief. But even thieves must have an escape plan."

"He's right, my dear. I've never been to prison in my life, and that's because I believe in being prepared. I had a feeling we might need a getaway plan. You see, the mix coats the pebbles, and they scatter and explode on impact. Rather effective, and they don't generally do too much damage."

A groan came from the back seat. Lucien pulled over under a large oak tree and turned around. "Is he waking up? This isn't the best time."

Marlowe leaned in close and carefully lifted an eyelid. "He's still out, but I don't think for long. Where are we taking him? This guy isn't going to be too happy when he wakes up. And I'd rather not be the first person he sees when he does."

Alexei ran his fingers through his hair. "Especially with the headache he'll have."

"Headache?" Lucien put the car in park but kept the engine running. "I don't suppose anyone has any zip-ties or rope."

"No, but we can get some." Marlowe pointed straight ahead. "There's a tactical supply warehouse in Emeryville on 65th, not too far from here. We can pick up a few things."

"Oh, I knew I liked her, Lucien."

Lucien nodded. "Tell me where to go."

With directions, he found the warehouse, although he wasn't sure it was the place he wanted to be at the moment. There were three men, dressed in black with holsters on their hips, guarding the front entrance, and another two men at either corner of the building with rifles slung over their shoulders. In the parking area were three camo-painted Jeeps and a black Hummer. A Jaguar would stand out.

"Park on the street." She waited until he stopped and then hopped out.

He wound his window down. "Wait. Are you sure about this? I don't like the look of those men."

She rolled her eyes. "They're fine. Mostly ex-Marines, like me. I'll only be a minute." She jogged straight to the building.

"My friend, that lady of yours is good to have on a mission such as this."

"That's an understatement." He let out a sigh. "I don't like her mixed up in this. Fenwick nearly killed her. I can't lose her. It's bad enough my family is … but what if—?"

"No. We don't think of the *what-ifs*. You know that. Concentrate on the mission. Revenge for your family will come soon enough." Alexei leaned back. "We have to ditch the car."

"I know. And by now they know you were involved. Your car is back at the arena."

Alexei winked. "I wouldn't worry about that. I stole the car and I used gloves. No fingerprints or ties to me whatsoever." He took out his cell phone and spoke in Russian, hanging up a moment later. "There now. Problem fixed. Vitaly will locate us a new ride and keep an eye on Ms. Dunham's house."

"Good idea. That's the first place Fenwick will go." Lucien shuddered.

The mission was supposed to be a quick DNA sample snatch-and-grab, but it had turned into a public kidnapping. He stared out the window and saw Marlowe jogging back with a large black duffle in her hand.

He swiveled in his seat and watched as she put the bag on the ground, unzipped it, took out several zip-ties, and fastened them around the Neanderthal's beefy wrists and ankles. They didn't look like ordinary zip-ties. "Marlowe, what are those?"

"I figured we needed something stronger. These are stainless." She grinned. "If he breaks out of these, I'm running."

"I'll be ahead of you, my dear." Alexei chuckled and answered his cell. "*Da*." He slipped the phone into his pocket. "We have a new vehicle waiting at the Claremont Country Club."

Marlowe grunted. "We're stealing a car?"

"Are we, Alexei?" Lucien hadn't boosted a car in years, but if it was the only way to escape Fenwick, then he'd go along with it.

With a slight shrug, Alexei answered, "It's a metallic blue Audi SQ5, keys on top of the rear passenger side tire. It's fast. And I doubt it's stolen, Vitaly has a way of convincing people to relinquish things."

Marlowe closed the duffle and slid it on the floor in front of her seat. "Let's go."

Lucien found the country club's address on the GPS and took off. Now and then, he looked back to check on Marlowe and the Neanderthal, wondering what else she had in the duffle.

After about fifteen minutes, he pulled into the Claremont Country Club and drove up and down the parking rows until he found the Audi. Unfortunately, there were patrons everywhere, coming and going, standing around in crisp white tennis outfits, chatting. Transferring a two hundred and fifty-ish pound Neanderthal from one vehicle to the other wasn't going to be easy. He parked behind the Audi.

"I'll be your distraction, my friend." Alexei got out and wandered down the lot, instantly engaging a couple of women.

"That's our cue." Lucien jumped out and opened the back door while Marlowe unlocked the Audi.

Teamwork paid off and they got the hefty Neanderthal into the Audi, only losing their grip once. Lucien drove the Jag into an empty parking spot and got in the Audi's passenger seat as Marlowe backed out.

Honking for Alexei might draw attention, so Lucien leaned out and shouted, "Hey, we're ready."

With a dismissive wave, Alexei kept up his conversation and entered something into his phone. He gave a parting kiss on the women's cheeks and sauntered to the Audi. "Lovely ladies."

Marlowe sped off once Alexei got in. "I thought you were a man's man, Alexei."

"I'm a thief first, my dear. Those ladies are trophies to wealthy men, which makes them a new source of revenue for me."

"Seriously, you're going to rob them? We're in the middle of a kidnapping and you're setting up targets for a job? Lucien, did you hear that?" Marlowe screeched onto the main road.

Lucien knew he had no chance of controlling Alexei, but she didn't. He shrugged. "Scouting marks is simply a way of life with Alexei. Don't worry about it. He never loses focus of the mission." He turned and smiled at his friend. "What were you this time, photographer, talent scout?"

Alexei laughed. "Hollywood exec looking for actresses. They were more than happy to give me their phone numbers." He stopped laughing. "Uh-oh."

"What?" Lucien turned partially around in his seat.

Alexei kept as far from the Neanderthal as possible, pressed against the door. "He's waking."

"Shit." Marlowe slowed and pulled into a strip mall.

Lucien jumped out first. He opened the rear door and felt for a pulse. Strong and fast. With any luck, Alexei's drug would keep the player drowsy for a while. As he peered closely, the eyes sprung open and the teen head-butted Lucien, catching him on the jaw.

Chapter 17

The hit stunned Lucien for a moment and he fell backward, landing hard on the pavement. In a flash, Marlowe and Alexei were beside him, dragging him out of the way as the Neanderthal rolled from the back seat and slammed to the ground right where Lucien had been.

"Who you?" the Neanderthal growled.

"Shit. You can speak." Lucien scrambled to his feet. "Do you understand what I'm saying?"

With narrowed eyes, the Neanderthal nodded. "Rock understand." His voice, raspy and slightly slurred, was clear enough.

Marlowe crouched. "Your name is Rock?"

Another nod. "Rock. Who you?"

Half in shock, Lucien, rubbing his jaw, crouched beside Marlowe, and tried to calm his thumping heart. "I'm Lucien Roux. This is Marlowe and Alexei." He motioned to each of them. "And you're Rock. It's ... an honor to meet you. I don't mean you any harm and I apologize for your treatment."

Rock struggled against his bindings, but soon gave up and wriggled into a sitting position. "Lady be mad if Rock gone."

He had to mean Fenwick. Lucien pointed to Rock's head. "You have a bump. Are you in any pain?"

Alexei whispered, "Probably has a rager of a headache from my concoction."

Rock shrugged. "Some pain. Why you bring Rock here? What you want?"

"Lucien, this is crazy." Marlowe straightened and glanced around. "We can't stay here."

It *was* crazy. But a good crazy. It was the most exciting moment Lucien had felt in a long time and he didn't want it to end. Having a conversation with a living, breathing Neanderthal was beyond anything he'd have imagined. But Marlowe had it right, they needed to move.

He motioned to the car. "Rock, we need to get you back in the car. I promise we aren't going to hurt you. I want to talk. Can we do that?"

"Talk? I talk, you talk." He looked at Marlowe. "I talk to new lady."

With a one-shoulder shrug, Marlowe said, "Okay, sure. But not here."

Rock eyed Lucien for a moment. "You give Rock hands and feet back and we talk."

"Oh." Lucien knew Rock wasn't trustworthy yet. Unfastening the zip-ties wasn't an option. "Perhaps we can give you your hands and feet back when we get to a new place. Would that be all right, Rock?"

"Rock will wait."

Lucien smiled, adrenaline spiking hard through his veins. He motioned for Alexei to help him lift Rock into the back seat, which wasn't an easy feat, but once safely inside, Lucien shut the door, raced around, and climbed in next to Rock, letting Marlowe drive.

"Rock," Lucien started, catching his breath, "Has anyone explained exactly who you are?"

He nodded. "I am player. Star player." He emphasized the word player, but in a way that sounded like it took effort for Rock to pronounce. "I am here to play game."

"You like to play?" Lucien looked into Rock's eyes and didn't see a Neanderball player, or an experiment. He saw a person, an intelligent person. A person who'd grown and learned to speak in a matter of months.

Rock sighed deeply and turned to the window. "Brothers like. People like. Rock not so much like."

That was surprising to hear. Lucien didn't look at Rock and stared down. "If you don't want to play, you don't have to. Ever. I'll see to that." He looked up.

Rock's shoulders slumped. "Rock always play."

Lucien noticed Marlowe watching through the rearview mirror, her face etched with concern. He felt the same.

With his voice low, he edged close to Rock. "I'm sorry you've had to live like this. Not my intent. I'll find a way to make it up to you."

"What mean you? Why you sorry?" Rock stared at Lucien with a look between suspicion and confusion.

Explaining genetics and cloning to an extinct species that had been created in a lab didn't seem possible. Lucien decided to give it a try anyway. "I am the person who brought you into existence. You and your people died out thousands and thousands of years ago." He stopped and waited. "Do you understand any of what I'm saying?

With a slow nod, Rock looked past Lucien, out the window. "Rock understands. Neanderball players not like others. Bad man, you, made us. Lady say to hate you." He paused. "I no hate. I no hate any peoples. I learn. Brothers no learn. No want learn. Rock want learn. Rock talk on paper."

Lucien allowed himself a moment to comprehend what Rock said. They taught the kid to hate his creator. Maybe that was right. "I'm not a bad man. I'm ... wait, Rock. You write? Is that what you mean? You can write, talk on paper? Put words on paper?"

Another nod. "Rock use stick to talk on paper."

"Holy shit," Marlowe mumbled.

"Yeah, holy shit." Lucien reached into his pocket for the notepad and pen and handed it to Rock. "Can you talk on the paper for me?"

Rock twisted his hands to move the twist-ties and awkwardly held the pen. He precisely formed the letters R O C K. "I talk on paper. Lady and Coach no see Rock talk on paper."

Alexei turned in his seat. "You are a special boy, Rock. Smart to hide your secret talent from those moronic twits. Perhaps I can teach you a thing or two—"

Marlowe interrupted, "Don't you even think of it."

"She's right, Alexei." Lucien shook his head. "Rock isn't your student."

"Rock no hate you." Rock motioned to Lucien. "Lady say you bad. Lady say I kill peoples. I no kill."

"Kill?" Lucien wiped his brow. "She wants you to kill? Like what happened on the stage? Damn it."

"Ah, a gentle soul. Not unlike you, my friend." Alexei turned back around. "That woman's a menace."

Rock slumped slightly in the seat. "Why Rock go with you? Where brothers?"

"Guys!" Marlowe shouted. "Exactly where are we going? We can't go to my place. So, ah, where?"

By now, they were far away from the arena, but Lucien knew Fenwick would be looking for them. He patted Rock on the arm.

"I'll make sure nobody hurts you, Rock. And your brothers." He leaned forward. "Marlowe, find an inconspicuous motel."

Without turning, Alexei said, "It feels right being back together with you, my friend, committing capers. My fondest memories are of you and me."

Rock grunted softly. "You brothers?"

"What?" Lucien leaned back again. "Oh, ah, no. Alexei is my friend. Do you understand what friend means?"

With a puzzled expression, Rock thought and then nodded slowly. "Not brothers, but like brothers. No hate, no kill. Like brothers."

Alexei chuckled. "That's right. Lucien and I are like brothers. I, the slightly older and far better-looking one of the two." He turned and flashed a sly grin.

With another nod, Rock stared at Lucien. "Lu-c-ien. You Lucien?"

"Lucien. Yes, that's my name. And that's Alex-ay and Mar-lowe. My friends."

Rock repeated, "Lucien, Alexei, Marlowe." He paused for a moment. "Why Rock not same?"

Before he answered, Marlowe pulled into a nondescript motel, drove around the back, and parked.

She unfastened her seatbelt. "Well, boys, here we are, the Bay Breeze Motel. Looks like a one-star, if that. Alexei, you go and secure us a room while I keep an eye out for trouble. And Rock, we're all different in one way or another."

Alexei took off his seatbelt and opened the door to get out, but hesitated. "I need to contact Janko and make sure Fenwick's brother is safe. But first, a room in this less-than-desirable establishment." He sighed, climbed out, and headed to the motel office.

When Rock slumped further down into his seat, Lucien's gut tightened. "Marlowe, do you have something to cut through these ties? Rock doesn't need the restraints any longer."

"Seriously? You've known him all of ten minutes." She unlatched the glove compartment and withdrew a pistol, waving it in the air so Lucien saw. "You won't mind if I keep this handy, will you?"

"Put that away. You won't need it." He watched Rock. "A knife or wire cutters?"

A heavy sigh. "In the duffle."

It was awkward with Rock taking up most of the back, but Lucien managed to stretch his arm and unzip the duffle bag. He felt around until his fingers touched on a handle. He pulled out a large knife in a leather sheath, like the sort of hunting knives he'd seen on TV documentaries about poachers or redneck alligator hunters.

"You expect me to cut through the zip-ties with this?"

"Well, there's a compact bolt cutter in there, too. Use that."

He glanced at Rock and shrugged, then reached back into the bag. Sure enough, he found a pair of short-handled bolt cutters. They cut through the ties with no trouble. Once free, Rock rubbed his wrists.

"Rock has hands back."

Lucien cut the ties around his ankles and gave him a pat on the back. "And your feet. I see no reason to keep you restrained. I promise you, you've been treated badly for the last time."

After a few minutes of silence, Alexei returned, glancing around as he approached. He opened the passenger door and leaned in. "We have what passes for a suite; two rooms connected by a common door." He straightened and looked past the car toward a small grove of pine trees. "I have an uncomfortable feeling. Let's get inside."

"Yeah, right with you." Marlowe hopped out, pistol in hand, and waited for Lucien. "Hurry up."

He got out, dashed around the car, and opened Rock's door, motioning for him to exit.

"Come on, Rock, we'll go inside and talk some more." He waited, standing back a bit in case the Neanderthal decided to charge at him.

Luckily, Rock complied and walked beside him to the motel room, but stopped short of going inside. He turned and glared toward the same trees Alexei had noticed.

Marlowe, gun by her side, moved in front of the group. "Is there something there that I need to worry about?"

Without warning, Rock pushed past her and ran full speed across the parking lot to the pine trees, never turning or faltering as Lucien shouted for him to stop. With a crash of snapping branches, Rock disappeared.

"Shit!" Lucien took a step but Marlowe stopped him.

"You're not going anywhere." She raised her arm and aimed the pistol. "If that bitch is there, she has Rock now. You'll make yourself a target if you go running after him."

Alexei opened the motel room door. "She's right. I already like that boy though."

More than anything, Lucien wanted to go after Rock, to make sure he wasn't ever going to be hurt again. If he'd been captured, there would never be another chance to save him.

"I ... damn it. He's gone." Lucien leaned against the wall. "I've lost any chance of recovering my research and now that intelligent boy will be a prisoner of Fenwick and the Bakers forever."

Taking a step back, Marlowe whispered, "Fuck your research. You two get inside and lock the door. I'll circle around and get a look at ..." She stopped talking, her mouth gaped slightly. "Lucien."

"What?" He saw where she looked and gasped.

Rock, carrying a full-grown squirming raccoon by the scruff of its neck, walked to them, a huge smile on his face. "Rock bring food for friends."

Alexei burst out laughing.

When he got close, Lucien noticed scratches on Rock's arms. "Rock, you didn't ... you shouldn't ... thank you. That's very nice of you, but we don't want to hurt any animals. Why don't you let that raccoon go and we'll order a pizza or something?"

"Pizza?" Rock looked at Lucien, then at the raccoon, which let out a long growl. "Rock like pizza." He dropped the raccoon and watched as it scampered away, turned, and growled again before continuing back to the trees.

Alexei laughed so hard words wouldn't come.

After lowering her arm, Marlowe sighed. "So, I guess it wasn't Fenwick in the trees."

Calming down, Alexei shook his head. "No. Apparently, the boy's hearing is far more acute than mine." He winked at Rock. "Come inside, Rock, and we'll order that pizza. Pepperoni?"

With a smirk, Rock pointed to the trees. "Raccoon pizza?"

Lucien smiled. "You made a joke. Rock, you amaze me."

Rock let out a guttural laugh and barged into the room. Lucien followed, relieved that Fenwick hadn't found them. Of course, it would be hard to hide a famous Neanderball player for long, especially one who caught live raccoons.

The room, small and rundown, had two twin beds, an old television, and a stained coffee pot on the desk near the TV. The other room wasn't any better. Marlowe insisted on keeping the adjoining doorway open so any sound would be within earshot, which made perfect sense and gave Lucien a slightly heightened sense of security.

He pointed at Rock's arms. "We'd better get those scratches cleaned."

With a shrug, Rock let Lucien clean the wounds with soap and water. "You good man, Lucien." He smiled and took the bed near the window, plopping down on the mattress, causing the springs to creak. He stretched and closed his eyes.

Weirdly, Lucien felt a connection to the boy, a paternal feeling, and knew he'd do anything to keep Rock safe.

"Lucien," whispered Alexei. "A text from Janko."

They stepped outside, regardless of Marlowe's frantic hand signals that they should stay. Alexei held out his phone. The message was in Russian.

"Alexei, you know I can't read Russian." Lucien pushed the phone away. "What does it say?"

"Janko's at your family's home. He's done a little poking around. It is indeed burned to the ground, but ...," he paused. "A boy from the nearby village reported having seen a truck speed away with several occupants that were bound and gagged in the rear seat. He said one looked like your father, whom he knows from working at your vineyard. Good news, no?"

Lucien's knees shook and he had to grab onto Alexei for support. "I don't understand. Janko said my whole family was killed."

"A dastardly ruse, I'm afraid. That's why Janko went there in person. He's very good at sniffing out deception, and the truth."

The phone rang.

"One moment, my boy. It's Janko." Alexei answered and spoke in Russian at length.

Lucien paced, a renewed sense of purpose surging through him. But now the question was, why lie about having his parents killed? What did Fenwick hope to gain by pretending she'd had them all killed?

After slipping the phone into his pocket, Alexei sighed. "Are you ready for more complications in your life?"

"What on Earth do you mean? It's fucking complicated enough."

"Not quite. The people who've absconded with your family appear to be American military, and it seems they are circumventing Fenwick. That bit of news might be a good thing since we know what a psychotic piece of work she is. Janko followed as far as he dared and knows the location where your family is being held. At least your father, but I'm hoping it's your entire family."

"Goddamn it. Why haven't they contacted me then? Fenwick has the Neanderthals, I don't. Well, except for Rock. What do they want from me?" Lucien wiped his hands on his pants and kicked a plastic trash bin halfway across the parking lot.

"Better?" Alexei wrapped his arm around Lucien's shoulder.

"Not at all."

Marlowe opened the door and peeked out. "What the hell is going on out here? You almost woke Sleeping Beauty." She stepped outside. "Seriously, what's going on? Both of you look a tad anxious. Fenwick?"

Lucien shook his head. "Hardly. Well, sort of, in a convoluted way." He explained what Janko said and waited while she processed it.

It took all of thirty seconds for her to work it out. She nodded thoughtfully. "They're cutting Fenwick out and will now contact you to do their dirty work, getting the Neanderthals. And they'll probably want you to kill Fenwick while you're at it. They took your family so she couldn't get them and now they're a bargaining chip. Smart. Really smart. But Fenwick's a collector, so she mustn't have anything on Harmond and that's why he's screwing with her. If that's the case and he has your family, we'll be dealing with him from now on. There's a chance he'll protect you from Fenwick. Until he gets what he wants. Wow. Shit just got real."

"Complicated is how Alexei put it." Lucien groaned. "At least I know my family is alive."

With a wink, Alexei smiled. "The one bright spot in all this mess. Janko will continue his surveillance to make sure everyone is safe."

Lucien went back inside and lay on the empty bed next to Rock's. The boy snored and twitched in a dream state, like any normal teenager, unafraid of anything. And why shouldn't he be? He was strong, capable of incredible feats of strength, and one of the most beloved people on the planet.

A few minutes passed with nothing but the snoring and Alexei's pacing outside the room. Marlowe had come inside and fussed with the duffle bag. She pulled out several scary-looking firearms and laid them on the dresser. While Lucien was trained in most common weapons, including knives and pistols, thanks to Alexei, he'd never dealt with military-type firepower. Marlowe, however, seemed comfortable around any weaponry.

Quietly, she crept over to him and motioned to Rock. "How are you going to explain to him where he came from and that this is thousands of years in the future from when his people lived? He's a bright kid, but come on, explaining genetics to a Neanderthal has to be impossible. He knows he's different but ..."

He shrugged. "I've been trying to come up with a way, but everything I think of is too ... complex. Maybe one day he'll learn to read and I can show him my journal articles and research. For now, though, we've got to keep him safe and as far from Fenwick and those military idiots as possible. I don't know if Fenwick has given them my research or promised it to them. Either way, they have my family, so they want something from me."

"Agreed." She sat on the bed and grasped his hand. "We'll get your family back. I'll tap my buddies for extra help, and Janko is exactly where he should be." She grew quiet. "I never imagined the military would go to these lengths. There've always been rumors about creating super soldiers, all the way back to MKUltra, but genetically engineering Neanderthals as soldiers is seriously messed up. You said they're a *Homo* genus, like us, so maybe we have a legal leg to stand on."

"It's accepted now that they're *Homo neanderthalensis*, but not by everyone. What the hell is MKUltra?" Lucien sat up and kissed her hand.

"You know, that program where they drugged up a bunch of guys. It doesn't matter. What does matter is that we can't let your Neanderthals get turned into mindless grunts for the military."

"Come on, you know I'd never let that happen. I'll do whatever it takes to stop it, and Alexei will, too." He watched Rock for a moment, stunned at how similar he was to modern humans. "I hate myself."

Alexei stepped into the room. "No, you don't. You hate that your scientific self became blinded to the fact that sometimes experiments are taken too far without forethought as to the welfare of the subjects." He gave a lopsided grin. "I belong to PETA."

"Really?" Marlowe raised an eyebrow. "Never would have guessed that in a million. Okay, boys, we'll bivouac here overnight and bug out at 0500. I'll take watch."

There was no room to argue with her matter-of-fact tone. Instead, Lucien nodded, relieved that he didn't have to make any decisions for a while.

Alexei checked his phone and announced, "Two large non-raccoon pizzas will be here in twenty minutes." He noticed Lucien staring. "Pizza phone app. I can order and check delivery time. Don't you have one? Considering your propensity for pizza, I figured that would be a necessity for you."

"You like pizza, Alexei, I tolerate it once in a while." Lucien smiled. "But I'm starving, so pizza sounds amazing."

While waiting, Lucien turned on the TV, which did not wake Rock, and found a local news special report about the incident at the arena. Lucien's old driver's license photo was displayed, with the words "Dr. Paleo Roux-Suspected Kidnapper" underneath. One video showed him rushing down the corridor — the blond hair making him look like an aging rockstar — with Rock slumped in the wheelchair. A grainy enlargement of his face, frozen on the screen for all to see remained as the reporter stated harshly that Paleo Roux wore a disguise to get close to the players, used two accomplices to drug them, and kidnapped star player Rock.

"That's a very unflattering photo, my boy." Alexei sighed.

"That's all you can say?" Lucien shut off the TV, went to the bathroom, and splashed cold water on his face. "And they're still calling me Paleo!"

Marlowe groaned. "Unflattering or not, your photo's now on everyone's TV set and I'd bet plastered all over the Internet by now as well. At least they didn't broadcast my photo and Alexei's from the security footage."

"Give them time." Lucien dried his face and stared in the mirror. The blond man looking back was infamous, a devil among men for his once well-intentioned work.

The bed creaked and Rock jumped up. "Rock have secret. Lady secret."

Lucien watched through the mirror. "What secret, Rock?"

"Secret mean secret." Rock stomped to Lucien and touched his shoulder. "Lady say secret."

Lucien turned. "She's a bad lady who wants to use you and your brothers for bad things. You can tell us the secret."

Lucien saw that Rock wanted to tell, but something held him back. He wandered away and stood by the window, his broad shoulders slumped.

Finally, he spoke, slowly, "Brothers have secret like Rock. Secret kill when Lady make secret kill."

"What the hell is he talking about?" Marlowe kicked a small wire trashcan. "I hate riddles."

"Me too." Lucien retrieved the trashcan and set it upright. "Rock, tell me what you mean. What does secret kill mean?"

Rock turned with a dark expression. "Lady bad?"

"Yes, very bad." Lucien glanced at Marlowe. "She almost killed me and Marlowe. She's bad, Rock. Tell me, what does she make you do?"

"Rock go away to bad place if Rock say secret."

Alexei jumped in, "Listen to me, young man, I've done plenty and nobody's ever put me away. You're with friends, tell us the secret." He squeezed Rock's shoulder. "You are solid muscle, aren't you?"

Rock looked at the ground. "Rock hurt people for lady. Brothers hurt people for lady. Lady say ... brothers and Rock get locked away if people know."

Lucien let out a heavy sigh. "So she has you doing her dirty work? I hate her more with every passing second. I'll stop her from making you do anything bad ever again. I promise."

"Rock like that."

With a grunt, Marlowe sat on the bed. "Why does he have to speak in third person? Rock, say *I* instead of always saying Rock. It's driving me fucking nuts."

Hesitantly, Rock nodded. "I hurt people. I no want to hurt people. I want to learn speak ... talk like other people. Lady say no, I speak like Neanderthal. Good for business." He sighed and turned away.

"Oh, for God's sake." Marlowe went to Rock. "You don't ever have to listen to that bitch again. You want to talk like us, then do it. Complete freaking grammatical sentences. Rock, I want that woman put away, or better still, six feet under. Lucien, explain to him who you are. It's about time he knew."

Rock's expression changed to curiosity. "Tell Rock. Tell *me*."

"All right." Lucien hadn't wanted to rush into an explanation, but if there was ever a right time, this was it. "I'm a scientist. That's a person who—"

"I know scientist." Rock locked eyes with Lucien. "Scientist make Rock and brothers. What Lucien do?"

"Oh, boy." Lucien took a deep breath. "I am the one who made you, not anyone else. The lady stole my research and used it to force you and your brothers into playing Neanderball so some bad men would see how you perform and take direction, and hurt people at her will. But listen, I never wanted this for you."

Alexei approached and gave Rock another shoulder squeeze. "Lucien is a good man. You can trust him. We're here to help him free you and your brothers. The lady, Fenwick, is not a good woman. She's been using you and we're going to stop her."

"How? How you stop Fenwick lady and how you help brothers?"

Marlowe smiled. "We'll find a way to take out Fenwick and save your brothers. But we need your help, Rock. Will you help us?"

Lucien watched as his small group of friends grew by one, a Neanderthal teenager. Rock nodded and said he'd do whatever they needed him to do, so long as he didn't have to hurt anyone. Who would have thought a Neanderthal would be so gentle? The familiar feeling of guilt swept over Lucien again. If things had gone to plan, Rock would never have survived. That brought up another issue. Once he realized the awful truth, would he ever forgive Lucien?

Chapter 18

While Alexei stood outside and placed a call to yet another of his nefarious friends, Lucien sat with Rock, trying to explain the life history of the ancient Neanderthals. Rock listened and nodded, seemed confused at times, and angry at other times, but sat on the bed attentively, taking it all in.

"Do you have any questions so far, Rock?" Lucien glanced at Marlowe, who typed on her phone.

With a thoughtful sigh, Rock gave a slow nod. "I do. The Neanderthals went away long time back. You made Rock and brothers come back here. You no say why? Why, Lucien?"

"I had good intentions."

With his brow pinched, Rock shook his head. "That not say why."

Alexei barged into the room. "Attention, please! Gentlemen, and lady, my associate has conveyed a message to Fenwick that her brother is safe for the time being and if she wants him to remain that way, she will retract the slanderous meanderings about Lucien and release all the players."

"She won't do that," Marlowe scoffed and held up her phone. "I reached out to some associates of *my* associates, and they've agreed to back us in retrieving the rest of the Neanderthals."

"By brute force, no doubt," Alexei grumbled.

"Oh, come on." Marlowe got in Alexei's face. "Your guy used brute force to grab Fenwick's brother. Hypocrite."

"That's enough with the squabbling." Lucien motioned to Rock. "We have this young man to consider. I think we all know it's only a matter of time before Fenwick finds us. And this time she won't hesitate to kill us all, even if it means the end of her brother. We've humiliated her."

He drew in a deep breath and held it for a moment hoping it would help him regain his composure, but it didn't. They were holed up like trapped animals with nowhere to go. Whether they used brute force or not, any plan would be difficult and dangerous. If he proved Rock had a potentially lethal gene, Fenwick and Harmond would no longer be interested. What he needed was a lab to run tests, but he no longer had access to Bay-Gen. If he tried to buy some equipment, Fenwick would surely track him through the sale.

A single knock on the door startled everyone, especially Marlowe, who in an instant had her gun aimed and her feet planted firmly, the right foot slightly in front of the other. A shooter's stance, or at least he assumed that's what it was.

"Pizza," called a man's voice.

Lucien let out a sigh. "You can relax, Marlowe."

Alexei held up his phone and shook his head. He mouthed the words *not pizza*. He stood to the side of the door, jiggled the knob slightly, and quickly withdrew his hand.

Rapid-fire peppered the door around the doorknob and to the center. Lucien ran to Rock and urged him into the bathroom while Marlowe pressed her body to the wall on the other side of the door. Peering out from the bathroom, Lucien held his breath. If the door was breached, they wouldn't stand a chance. He let out the breath in one huge exhale.

"Rock, stay in here. I'm going to go and help my friends," he whispered.

"Rock help. Not afraid of guns."

"Well, I am, and I can't have you getting injured." Lucien stepped out but was pushed aside by Rock.

Before anyone stopped him, Rock charged at the door and flung it open, grabbed a stocky man dressed all in black, and dragged him into the room. The assailant, obviously stunned, stared up from the floor. Marlowe wrestled the gun from his hand and passed it to Alexei. Rock still had the man by the hand, twisting the wrist. A loud snap, and the man screamed out.

"Rock!" Lucien ran to the door and slammed it shut. "I told you to stay in the bathroom."

"Rock no want you or friends hurt." He released the man's wrist.

"Thanks, but we're supposed to be protecting you." Lucien sighed and crouched beside the man on the floor. "I know Fenwick sent you, but how did you find us?"

Clutching his wrist, the assailant sat and glared at Rock. "I've been tracking you. I intercepted the pizza guy. That creature is the property of the Bakers."

"Rock not prop ... er ... ty." He glanced at Marlowe. "*I* no property."

She smiled. "That's right, you're not. And you can say *I'm not anyone's property*. Complete sentences, sweetie." She turned to the assailant. "Tell me how you tracked us or I'll let Rock have another go at you."

After scooting backward, the man grimaced and cradled his bruised, bent wrist. "I work for Thomas and Jeremy Baker. Fenwick is a means to an end. I have no loyalty to her."

"And what's the end?" Alexei peered out the window.

"For us, the Neanderthals. For her, it's making a shit ton of money selling the proprietary data to the U.S. Military. They're the perfect foot soldiers and assassins. They don't ask questions and kill without hesitation. Look what it did to my wrist. It would have killed me if you hadn't intervened."

"It?" Lucien hovered over the man. "Rock is a he, not an it, or a creature. They're not commodities for you to use."

With a strained smile, the man let out a small laugh. "Really? Everyone knows you were using them for experimentation. There's no difference between what you were doing and what we're doing. You think because you're a scientist, you're innocent? Bullshit." He sneered.

Lucien balled up his fists. "At least I didn't shoot into a room without knowing where Rock stood. You don't give a shit if you kill him or not, do you?"

The man shrugged. "If my boss can't have it, then no one can. Alive is better, but whatever. We still have the others."

"Dickhead." Marlowe glared.

"You can't win, Roux." The man shrugged again. "We can track them anywhere, thanks to Fenwick. They have implanted nano-transponders. You've lost. Give that thing to me and walk away."

Rock stomped over and grabbed a handful of the man's hair. "You get nanos out of Rock."

"Call off your caveman!" the man yelled.

"Rock," Lucien paused. "Do whatever you want to do with this piece of garbage."

"No! You can't ..." The man struggled with his one good hand to pull Rock off, but it wasn't possible.

Lucien watched for a moment and considered what the man said. Nano-transponders? Technology was out of control. Humanity focused on progression, pushing the envelope toward a brighter future, when in reality, only the greedy wanted to use technology to make themselves richer. Was there no good left in the world? Rock came from a place of simplicity where survival depended on acquired skills, not artificially created technology.

"Hold on, Rock. We can use this piece of trash." Lucien patted Rock on the arm and glared at the man. "Can the nano-transponder be removed?"

A long pause. "Yeah. But it's not me you have to worry about. If one Neander goes offline, Fenwick's end protocol goes into effect."

Marlowe hovered over the man. "What the hell is that?"

The man shook his head. "Nope. You get nothing more out of me unless you let me go."

With a loud grunt, Alexei leaned against the door. "We don't give a damn about you. You can go, but let me tell you, if you try to warn Fenwick, you'll regret it. You've left your fingerprints all over the place, so we can frame you for the kidnapping. And if you double-cross us, my colleague will make you long for death."

The man laughed. "Roux? I can take him, broken wrist or not."

Alexei continued, "Not Dr. Roux, although I have first-hand knowledge that he can handle himself in a multitude of situations. The colleague I referred to is this fine, strapping young Neanderthal. Now, answer the damn question."

"Fine. It's your funeral, or should I say *his* funeral." The man pointed to Rock. "The end protocol is designed to destroy the Neanders if the tracker signal ever got lost, in case one of the players escaped or got stolen. I don't know how it works, but once a signal is lost, they die. Drop dead. Allegedly."

Lucien looked over at Alexei and then to Rock. Every time he thought he had the upper hand, it slipped away. Every single time. Rock's life had been in jeopardy since the moment he'd been created in the lab.

"Wait." Lucien knelt beside the man. "How do we disable this end protocol?"

The man struggled to his feet. "Told you I don't know. Fenwick's techy goons created it, I guess. My goal is to save the Neanders because if they die, my bosses are out a lot of money, which means I'm out a lot of money. Your best bet is to give Rock back to the Bakers and try to find a way to get the end protocol info from Fenwick or her guys. Not that it'll do any good, because we'll strengthen security now. I heard her tell my boss that she'll initiate it if things go sideways. We're not going to let that happen. Like I said, the Neanders are money. That's all I know. Rock isn't going to the military, neither are the other players, so you don't have to worry about them. The military is getting enhanced Neanders. Look, we only care about Neanderball. Fenwick's working with someone who has their own agenda and she's using our players as examples. I'd prefer to have her out of the picture. We've got what we want. If you take out Fenwick, the military deal will fall through, and everyone wins."

Marlowe sighed. "Except Fenwick."

"Except Fenwick." The man edged closer to the door. "We got a deal?"

They were backed into a corner, and Lucien had no idea how to get out of it. He still had to find a way to keep his family safe from the military faction who'd kidnapped them. "What guarantee do we have that you won't go right to Fenwick?"

"Told you. I hate that sick loon. I have no loyalty to her." The man supported his wrist. "Take her out. Then the players will be safe. We'll keep them, but they'll be safe."

Lucien went to Rock. "It's up to you what we do. This is your life we're talking about."

After pacing back and forth for a minute, Rock stomped to the man. "You told my friends about this to help. You no like lady Fenwick. I no like lady Fenwick. I listen. You go." He pointed to the broken wrist. "I do that to all of you if you lie."

The man took a step back and bumped into the wall. "Shit. I'm not lying. At first, I thought the Neanders were some freaky ballplayers, and it was only publicity calling them Neanderthals. I know differently now, but you still gotta give Rock back. I'm supposed to call Fenwick when I have Rock. She can track him, too, so even if I don't call, she'll come. And trust me, she won't hesitate to put a bullet in your skull if you get in her way. That goes for all of you, including Rock. You can't escape her. Let her come and get him. I don't want anything more to do with this."

Lucien looked at his friends and back at the man. "Go." He motioned to the door and sat on the bed.

"I'll let her know she can come and get Rock." Without hesitating further, the man dashed from the room, leaving the bullet-hole-ridden door open.

Marlowe began to close the door but hesitated. "Well, our pizza's here."

She waited for the pizza guy, who stared at the door with a gaping mouth.

The guy held out the two pizza boxes. "What ...? The door's all ... that guy gave me a hundred bucks to wait ten minutes. Why is the door ...?"

"Oh." She motioned to the door. "It's really stuffy in here, we needed some air circulation." She grabbed the boxes and handed him a tip. "Thanks."

The guy continued to gape and hurried away.

She slammed the door shut, placed the boxes on the bed, and sat next to Lucien. No words were necessary because they all knew what had to happen. Rock sat on the bed beside Marlowe. The springs creaked. He opened a pizza box and took out a slice, then wrapped a huge arm around her shoulders.

"You no worry about Rock. I play game and be with brothers again." He stared off into space and took a large bite of pizza. "I play game, you be safe."

"This is bullshit." Lucien looked over at Alexei. "There has to be—"

Marlowe jumped in, "We can't hurt Fenwick until we know more about that end protocol."

"She's right, my friend." Alexei leaned on the dresser. "Once we have what we need though, then it's open season on that piece of rubbish."

Lucien sighed. "But I still don't understand why my family is involved. My damn head hurts from all of this."

He had no idea how to orchestrate a plan to get his family free without getting everyone killed. He was always a step behind the bad guys, and that frustrated the hell out of him. And on top of everything, he had to let Rock go back to playing Neanderball. The Bakers would continue making money and Fenwick would win. Again.

"I'm so sick of all of this." Lucien stood and faced Rock. "I'll find a way to undo it. I'll find a way to stop that end protocol and get you and your brothers away from the Bakers and make sure people like Fenwick can never bother you again."

Rock got up. "I not mad at you. I be with brothers again. That not so bad."

"Fuck it all." Marlowe jumped up and kicked the nightstand, making a cheap lamp that wasn't bolted down topple and fall. "Shit! I'm not letting her win, Lucien. Alexei, you have resources, right? Then let's—"

Alexei interrupted, "We will figure something out, my dear, but it'll take time. For now, Fenwick wins." He lowered his head, looking completely defeated.

Lucien had never seen Alexei admit to a loss. He always had a way out. Another plan. One redundancy after another. As hard as it was to acknowledge, he knew his friend had no options. "I appreciate everything you two have done for me, but we need to step back now and re-evaluate. My family should be safe until the military approaches me and makes whatever ridiculous demand they have. And so long as we don't stir the pot, Rock will be safe with the Bakers. I'm sorry I failed you, Rock."

With a huge shrug, Rock smiled. "You got Rock free. I no have that before. I be free again, I know. I play game now until you get me free again."

Lucien returned the smile, although he sure didn't feel happy or confident. "You're a good kid, Rock. You deserve so much more than this."

Even though his biological family lived in France, the incredible people in the motel room were his family, too. Now he had to come up with a solution to the convoluted problem he'd been given. One that would save all members of his family.

Chapter 19

After leaving Rock in the motel room to wait for Fenwick's goons to pick him up, Lucien, Marlowe, and Alexei drove off down the street to the nearest diner to regroup, and get some coffee and real food. The stress of the day took its toll and all three were mentally exhausted, unable to speak as they ate an all-day breakfast and sipped hot, black coffee.

"Lucien." Marlowe slid her near-full plate to the center of the table. "This is bullshit. That kid, he's special. We have to save him."

"And his brothers," Alexei added. "Don't fret, my dear lady. I'll contact Janko and we'll come up with a plan to force Fenwick to cancel the end protocol."

Lucien shook his head. "Nothing that'll risk my family, Rock, or you two. I can't be responsible for anyone else getting hurt. This is all so surreal."

Marlowe pressed in close. "What is? That Neanderthals are playing a competitive ball game? Or that we're dealing with a murderous psychopath? Or that the military took your family hostage? Or that we had Rock and let him go? What exactly is surreal, Lucien?"

Alexei clicked his tongue. "Ease off him, my dear."

Taking a bite of dry toast, Lucien shook his head. "I deserve it, Alexei. A verbal lashing is the least I should get. I'll never forgive myself if I don't help those Neanderthals."

Alexei's phone chimed. "Excuse me." He got up and stepped away.

"I'm sorry." Marlowe nudged Lucien. "I'm tired and cranky. I like that kid. And I hate Fenwick. I shouldn't be taking out my frustrations on you. I know we're on the same page."

"Well, thanks for the apology, but I'm ... I ... ugh, I can't think anymore." He lay his head on her shoulder. She was the one thing good in his life, the only thing he had to cling to.

She motioned to Alexei, who huddled in a corner near the bathrooms, curling his fingers into a fist one minute and pulling the phone away from his ear the next. "Hey, look. Alexei doesn't seem too happy with that phone call."

"Fabulous." Lucien sighed and watched his friend's mannerisms. "My family better be all right. I still can't believe they're alive."

While the waitress cleared away their dishes, Alexei wandered back to the table with the phone clutched tightly in his hand. He slumped into his seat, avoiding eye contact with everyone.

Lucien's stomach tightened. He reached across the table and tapped Alexei on the arm. "Well?"

After a pause, Alexei looked up, his face expressionless. "Janko's dead."

Marlowe wrapped her fingers around Lucien's wrist.

"What? How? When?" Lucien felt like he'd been punched in the gut. "Fenwick."

Alexei nodded. "Her people tracked him. They retrieved Fenwick's brother and then shot Janko in the back of the head."

"Wait." Marlowe let go of Lucien. "How do you know this? Wasn't Janko working alone?"

With a shake of his head, Alexei wiped his eyes. "No. Another colleague, a man I did not know well, sold him out. That call was from him. Janko told me many times that he thought of Pieter as a brother."

"Damn it." Marlowe slammed her hand on the table. "Damn it! Everything we do, Fenwick finds a way to beat us." She drew in a deep breath. "Alexei, I'm very sorry about Janko."

Lucien rested his head in his hands and mumbled, "I'm sorry, too. He put his life on the line for us. How many more people will suffer?"

The waitress came over. "Is one of you called Paleo?"

"Oh, what now?" Lucien raised his hand. "That would be me."

She continued, "I got a phone call from a woman named Ms. Fenwick. She said to tell you that Rock is back where he belongs and nobody else needs to die if you behave." She lowered her voice and glanced around the room. "Um, what did she mean by *die*? Are we in danger?"

He shook his head. "No. You're fine. You have nothing to worry about. Thank you." After the waitress walked away, he whispered, "We should leave her a very big tip."

"Agreed. How did Fenwick know we were here?"

Alexei placed his phone on the table. "I can't sit here and let Janko's death go unpunished. Revenge is what I need. Pieter used Janko's phone. I have a GPS tracker on Janko's phone."

Marlowe nodded. "So, we know where Pieter is."

"We do. And I plan to *question* the hell out of him." Alexei looked at Lucien. "We've lost our leverage that Fenwick's brother gave us. I know you don't like this part of the business, my friend, but ..."

"No, no, I'm in." Lucien glanced at the phone. "I'm sick of Fenwick being one step ahead. It's about time we got in front of this, no matter what it takes." He slid the phone to Alexei. "Where is that bastard?"

"Manhattan." Alexei gulped some ice water. "Luckily I have a few friends of questionable character in New York."

"So do I." Marlowe nodded. "Ex-Marines that freelance now."

Alexei smiled. "Ex-Marines, eh? Mine are ex-Marines also. It's a small circle, do you suppose we have the same nefarious friends, my dear?"

She shrugged. "Have you ever heard the code name Sky Warrior?"

With a laugh, Alexei clapped his hands together. "John Largette. AKA Sky Warrior. I have him on retainer."

"Retainer? You have a mercenary on retainer?" Lucien shook his head. "What a world."

Alexei finished his water. "A lot has changed since you and I ran together, Lucien. Mr. Largette has an uncanny ability to locate and seize a target quickly and quietly. I'll give him a ring." He got up and stepped outside.

As awful as everything was, Lucien's entire body tingled with adrenaline. For years, he'd been locked up in his lab, isolated and alone. Sure, he'd written the odd paper or given an interview here and there, and he'd made a point to attend several conferences for a little socialization, but basically, he'd led a solitary, uneventful life. Then came Marlowe. She'd been the bright spot that kept him going each day. And working with Alexei again was the proverbial cherry on top.

"What are you grinning at?" Marlowe poked him in the forehead.

"What? Oh, I remembered when we first met. You made me show you my ID before you'd let me go to my lab. I knew I'd like to get to know you better after that first interaction. I wasn't sure you even liked me. I'm still not sure."

"What? Are you serious? We've had lunch together and a couple of dinners for almost five months. I like you, otherwise, I wouldn't have gone out with you and wouldn't have flirted with you. Our relationship is what it is. Is that what you want to hear? Good, that's settled, so let's get back to the topic at hand."

Lucien sighed. He knew she wasn't the romantic type, but he'd hoped she'd have a bit more involvement in their status as a couple. Maybe he tried to force the issue as an escape from reality; after all, what did he have left? A failed career and reputation, stolen research used to build a ball team scouted to become expendable foot soldiers. And no wife or children.

"Lucien, stop daydreaming, Alexei's signaling he wants to leave." She pointed out the window.

Alexei knocked on the diner's window and motioned to the car.

"Yeah, he looks a bit anxious." Lucien reached into his pocket to pay for the food but remembered he didn't have any money. "Damn."

With a roll of her eyes, Marlowe plucked a couple of twenties from her pants pocket. "Don't worry, I got it. When this is all over, you'll need to find a job so you can pay me back."

"There's no way I can ever pay you back for what you've done."

She smiled and walked off toward the exit. He followed, catching up to her outside where Alexei nodded and shoved the phone in his pocket.

"Good news, I hope." Lucien closed his eyes. "Please let there be good news." He opened his eyes and saw Alexei's smile.

"Very good news, my friend. Sky Warrior is standing by." Alexei's smile faded. "Janko was a good man. He didn't deserve this."

Lucien shook his head. "No, he didn't. But we've got to be careful now. Fenwick's still watching us. She knew we were in the restaurant. She knows everything. I should stick around in California, so she doesn't suspect we're cooking up something."

Alexei strode to the car. "I agree. It's only right that I track Pieter down. Now that we've lost any leverage we had with Fenwick, I'm not sure which direction to go anymore."

"I hate this. Every single bit of it." Lucien rubbed his temple as his perpetual headache began to grow.

"Okay, mister doom and gloom, let's not get off track and start sulking again." Marlowe gave Lucien a gentle push toward the car. "Here's how it's going to play out. Alexei is going to New York to revenge-kill Pieter, you and I will stay here and wait for Sky Warrior, and one way or the other, rescue the

Neanderthals, and take care of Fenwick when the timing's right. I'll do that last part if you don't mind."

Lucien opened the passenger side door. "Oh, well, that sounds incredibly manageable."

"Stop being snide, it's not helping." She gave Alexei a nod. "What about you? Sound good?"

He glanced at Lucien and back to Marlowe. "I already said I'm going to take care of Pieter. Once I've completed my task, I'll head back this way. Sky Warrior is at your service. My treat."

Lucien raised his hand. "A question. What do you predict the odds of success?"

"This isn't Vegas." Marlowe bit her lip. "In all seriousness, I'd say we have a fifty-fifty shot at pulling this off. And that's with Sky Warrior's help. As Alexei said, we don't have Janko or Fenwick's brother. And now we're dealing with a military faction who kidnapped your family from Fenwick for whatever reason, so we're starting from scratch."

"Then how in the hell did you come up with a fifty-fifty chance?" Lucien paced.

She shrugged. "I was being optimistic."

"Be realistic."

"Eighty-twenty. In their favor."

Lucien groaned and got into the passenger seat. "I guess twenty percent is better than nothing. Let's go home and plot the perfect caper."

Chapter 20

After driving back to the country club to retrieve the Jag, Alexei took the Audi and headed out. Lucien wasn't worried about Fenwick surprising them with a blitz attack anymore since she'd be content that she had Rock and her brother and was under the impression she'd won.

By the time they got back home, the dark street was deserted, giving off a creepy vibe that made Lucien shiver. Marlowe parked on the street and shut off the engine, staring straight ahead for a moment.

She turned. "Five months ago, I would never in a million gazillion years have imagined I'd be embroiled in a kidnapping, knee-deep in paleogenetics on steroids, and working with a Russian thief. What's my life become?"

"I can only apologize so much."

"Apologize? This is a fucking dream come true. I haven't worked with Sky Warrior in years." She smirked and winked. "We might have increased our odds."

"To fifty-fifty?"

"Now who's being optimistic?" She handed him the key fob. "We need to nail down exactly who took your family and what they're after. That's where Sky Warrior comes in."

"You, ah, have a thing for this Sky Warrior?"

She tilted her head. "You have nothing to worry about. He's not my type. Nerdy science types with shady backgrounds are what gets me hot."

He took the fob and smiled. "I will never question you again, *my dear*," he mimicked Alexei's accent.

She let out a small laugh. "French is sexier. Let's get inside. I have a bottle of wine in the fridge. We need to celebrate our impending victory."

Seeing her in a playful mood made sweat trickle down his back, and the hint of an impending erection caused him to shift awkwardly in the seat. He climbed out of the car and walked quickly to the house, unlocked the door, and held it open.

She paused at the threshold and leaned into him. "Wine is boring. I have another way of celebrating in mind." She pressed against him and kissed him passionately, teasing his mouth with her tongue.

Breathless, he whispered, "I do hope you mean what I ..."

Another kiss interrupted him. She took his hand and led him inside, slamming the door closed with her foot. Without a word, they went to the bedroom. She raised an eyebrow and pulled her shirt off over her head, revealing a practical, but still sexy black bra. Lucien lost his breath.

He kicked off his shoes and began to unbutton his shirt, but she grabbed his lapels and pulled until the buttons popped off and his shirt hung loosely, half untucked. He couldn't hide his arousal anymore and unzipped his jeans. He watched while she slipped out of her trousers and seductively crawled onto the bed, her backside swaying as she accentuated each movement.

As much as he wanted her, his mind drifted back to his family, Rock, Janko.

"Yo, Dr. Roux," Marlowe called from the bed.

"I'm sorry. It's—"

"Lucien, I'm trying my best here to distract you. Turn off your brain for a minute." She slinked across the bed, took hold of his hips, and pulled him on top of her. "Turn off your brain." She worked his jeans down a bit and placed her hand over his erection.

Without hesitating, he wriggled out of his jeans and underwear, pressing into her as she moved her body against his. He'd been hoping for this moment for a long time. Propping himself up, he slowly slipped her bra straps down her soft arms and kissed her bare shoulders.

"You are the most beautiful woman on the planet," he whispered, noticing that her bra fastened at the front.

With a twist of his fingers, he undid the clasp.

She took his penis in her hand and firmly, but tenderly, massaged the shaft, slipping a condom on at the same time. "You're bigger than I thought. Glad I had a magnum handy."

Dizzy with desire, he couldn't even manage a response. He definitely wasn't magnum but appreciated the compliment, nonetheless. With a swift movement, he had her breasts exposed and began teasing her with his tongue while she pulled her arms out of the bra straps and wriggled out of her panties. He gently traced his fingertips over the scar on her chest and noticed several others on her abdomen and shoulder. Battle scars.

With a breast in his mouth, he positioned himself and entered her, thrusting slowly at first, then increasing speed with her hip thrusts. They settled into a rhythm and when her breaths came in quick gasps, he released at the same time she orgasmed. She wrapped her arms around his neck, bringing him to her to kiss him.

He lay next to her, eyes closed, his breathing ragged.

"Oh, you are not going to sleep," she rolled on top of him. "I'm not done with you yet."

With a smile, he opened his eyes. "I'm all yours. But give me a minute." He propped himself up on an elbow. "So, you know about my family, tell me about yours."

She glanced away and sighed. "Well, my dad raised me. My mom died when I was little. I don't remember her at all." She turned back and brushed a strand of hair off his forehead.

"Oh, I'm so sorry."

"Don't be. It's hard to miss someone you don't remember. My dad died a few years ago and my brother lives in England with his wife. I got out of military because I wanted a family of my own and the life of a soldier isn't exactly conducive to raising a houseful of kiddos. But, as you can see, my plans haven't exactly panned out."

"No, I suppose not." He gazed at her for a moment, taking in every inch of her. "You are a remarkable woman. Why are you with someone like me?"

She scoffed. "Your self-esteem has been shattered, Lucien. I know a good guy when I see one. Now, shut the hell up."

They made love through the evening until they both agreed to take a break to rest and eat a late dinner. He set about making grilled cheese sandwiches and a pot of coffee while she took a quick shower and came into the kitchen wearing a skimpy silk robe.

"Damn, you're getting me hard again." He winked and flipped a sandwich so it flew up into the air a few inches.

"You're good at that."

"Getting hard?"

"Flipping the damn sandwich." She laughed. "And the other."

"All Frenchmen are good in the kitchen, and the bedroom." He winked again and slid the grilled cheese on a plate. "This is the happiest I've felt in a long time."

"Same here, but unfortunately, it's back to reality."

"Yeah. But thank you for giving my brain a break, even if it was short-lived." He finished cooking another sandwich and sat at the table beside her. "So, tell me about this Sky Warrior. What can we expect from him?"

She nibbled on the sandwich and sipped the coffee he'd brewed. "Delicious. John Largette flew helicopters and served as a paratrooper in the Marines until they dishonorably discharged him for conducting an unauthorized mission."

"Really? He didn't go to jail, or prison, or whatever?" He kissed her on the cheek.

"No. Turned out the mission was a success, so they didn't want to publicly punish him, but they had to make an example of him in some way. Booting him out of the Marines was worse than prison for him."

Lucien nodded and took a bite of his grilled cheese. "So, he found an outlet for his skills in another way?"

She shrugged. "Yep. I can't believe Alexei knows him. I guess these disreputable characters run in the same circles."

"Does that include you?"

She shrugged again. "Well, I ran ops with Sky Warrior in the Marines and he helped me out of a few jams. After he was discharged he worked as a contractor. After I left the Marines, I worked with him as a ... I mean ..."

"You worked with him? As a mercenary? Who are you, Marlowe Dunham?" He was fascinated to delve into the unknown parts of her life. He'd always felt there was more to her than a mere ex-Marine security guard. "Come on, spill. You know my history with Alexei, now it's your turn."

With a laugh, she finished the food and pushed the plate away. "Who'd have thought we'd both have secretive pasts? I assumed you'd always been a dedicated, albeit somewhat plain, geneticist."

"Plain? Wow. Well, I am a geneticist. But plain?" He leaned over and kissed her, hard. "Let me show you how *not* plain I am."

"You already have." She smiled. "Several times. But we have the rest of our lives for you to prove yourself to me. For now, though, we've got to get back on track."

He groaned. "I know you're right, but living in a fantasy, even for a little while, is wonderful. What do you think Rock's doing? You don't suppose Fenwick would punish him, do you?"

"No idea. But he's a tough kid."

"Yes, he is." He arched an eyebrow. "You know, I'm still waiting to hear about your past."

She got up, cleared the dishes, and poured more coffee. "I come from a military family, as you know. I enlisted at nineteen, then deployed in Afghanistan for one tour in combat infantry, served back home for a few more years, and then ... recruited by ..." she paused.

"Largette? Sky Warrior?" Lucien shook his head.

"The money, incredible. And I got to do things I couldn't do in the Marines."

"Like commit felonies?" He took a long gulp of hot coffee. "Sorry. I didn't mean it like that. I'm one to talk. Like you, I too strayed from the righteous path." He smirked. "For a while there, I truly enjoyed my life with Alexei as my mentor. He showed me a life I never knew existed."

Marlowe sat back down, scooting beside him. "Money, expensive restaurants, flying first class."

"And the finest wines." He laughed. "I think we've shared the same life!"

"I knew I liked you, Dr. Roux." She snuggled against him. "When we find your family and make sure they're safe, we'll get Fenwick. Together."

He agreed with a nod. But would their lives ever be normal again? While he sat, enjoying the warmth of her body pressed into his, he thought back to what the man at the motel had said about the end protocol for the Neanderthals. It had something to do with the nano-transponders. Were they triggers? Some sort of subcutaneous weapon?

The man said Fenwick had tech guys, so it wasn't so far-fetched to think they might have invented a device that would kill the Neanderthals if the nano-transponders were disabled. After all, they'd successfully grown fetuses into teenagers in a matter of months. But without Rock, there was no chance of studying the technology. Of course, getting the tech before getting rid of Fenwick was imperative. Once they disabled the end protocol, the Neanderthals would be easier to rescue. And this time, Rock would help.

Marlowe nudged Lucien. "Dearest, what are you thinking? You have a wistful look on your face."

He straightened and sighed. "I would love to wake up in my lab and have all of this be a dream. Nightmare really. Except for the last few hours. I don't want to lose those."

"Well, it's not a dream. The way I see it, we have a couple of days to either stress out or enjoy the time and block out everything except you and me." Her lips formed a hint of a smile. "I'm all for the latter."

Without a word, he got up and extended his hand. "Let me show you which way I'm leaning."

Chapter 21

For a day and a half, Lucien pretended his life wasn't a catastrophe. He made a few French-inspired meals, sat out in the backyard with Marlowe, and made love at every opportunity. While he relaxed in the living room and enjoyed the morning sun streaming in through the window, he sipped a cup of café au lait. His cell phone rang, disturbing his moment of peace. It was Alexei.

"News?" Lucien clutched the phone and held his breath.

Alexei paused before speaking, "Definitely, my friend. Pieter sang like a songbird, after being properly motivated."

Lucien swallowed. "I won't ask how you motivated him. So, what did you find out?"

"Not what I expected. Turns out Pieter worked for the military, not Fenwick or the Bakers. He's the one who got your family away from Fenwick's thugs."

"Well, that's good news, right?" Lucien got up and paced.

"Not so good, my friend. The military is holding your family as leverage, like we thought."

"What sort of leverage? Fenwick doesn't give a shit about my family. She has what she wants." He couldn't breathe. His heart pumped furiously. "My family, Alexei."

"I know, I know. Pieter was a small fish, we need to find the whale."

"What the hell does that mean?" Lucien stomped his foot.

Marlowe hurried to him and wrapped him in an embrace. "What's going on?"

He put the call on speaker.

"Alexei, Marlowe's here with me. What can we do to get my family?" He turned to her. "Pieter was working for the military."

"That's good, right?" She raised an eyebrow.

"That's what I thought, but Alexei says no." He drew a breath. "Alexei, who's the whale?"

Marlowe pulled back and tilted her head. He waved a hand to let her know he'd explain later.

Alexei spoke, "I don't know. The military went to some lengths to get your family away from Fenwick's people, but there have been no ransom demands, threats, or anything. Whoever is in charge is the whale. We need that whale to figure out what's going on. Understand?"

Lucien nodded. "Yes ... no. I don't know. Did Pieter at least say where they're being held?"

"They were in France, then Belgium, then Germany. That's all he knew. He became worthless after that."

"Wait." Marlowe grabbed the phone. "Did you kill him, Alexei?"

"Of course I did. He met with an unfortunate accident. Fell from a seventh-story balcony. I got everything from him before though."

"Are you sure? What if—?"

"He didn't know anything else, dear." Alexei cleared his throat. "Sky Warrior is delving into the situation with the military. I'll be there soon with him in tow. If anyone can track down these bastards, he can."

Lucien closed his eyes for a moment in a pathetic attempt to calm his nerves. "I'm done being the nice guy. I want in. All in. Whatever it takes, you can count on me."

"Good to hear, my friend. Welcome back to the fold. I'll see you tomorrow." He hung up.

Tomorrow would be an interesting day.

Lucien put the phone on the coffee table and looked out the front window. What sort of leverage did the military need? If they'd only asked him, he'd have given them whatever they wanted so long as he got his family back. It had to be more than that. They knew he didn't have his research anymore, except for what he had on the flash drive, but that didn't hold the most up-to-date information. And they didn't know he even had the flash drive. So, what the hell were they after?

He let out a deep breath. At least he had Sky Warrior on his side, who both Alexei and Marlowe vouched for, which held a lot of weight. But what if Largette was reckless and got everyone killed? That was a very real possibility.

"Marlowe, would you trust Sky Warrior with your life? With my family's lives?"

She came up behind him and draped her arms over his shoulders. "Look at it this way, we need all the muscle we can get. Military-trained muscle. It takes one to defeat one. I've seen Sky Warrior rappel down from a helicopter right in the middle of a firefight, laying down cover fire on the way down to give five marines the chance to make it to safety. He saved five soldiers, me included, and didn't get a scratch. So, yeah, I'd trust him with my life, and your family's."

"Shit. Okay then, glad to have him on board." He turned and wrapped her in his arms. "Can we win this fight?"

"I don't like to lose, sweetness."

"You didn't answer my question. I don't like to lose either, but lately, it seems that's all I've been doing. I need a win. A big win." He kissed her and wandered to the couch, flopping down, exhausted. "Or maybe a do-over."

She stood at the front window with her head tilted. "A do-over? What exactly would you do differently? You're a scientist, and while I don't agree with your methods, your heart was in the right place. We are who we are." She sat beside him. "And I fell for you, no matter who you are."

"Thanks for the ego boost. You're too good for me, you know that? But what I meant was that if I knew about Rock and his brothers and how they're no different than us, I would never have used them as I did. I would have found another way to do my research." He shrugged. "I didn't want anyone to suffer like my mother. She was always so vibrant and full of life. Did I ever tell you how she developed a varietal wine that became one of my family's best sellers?"

Marlowe smiled. "No, you never told me that."

"She held our family together. Even when I ran with Alexei, breaking the law, she never had a harsh word for me. She pretended she didn't know what I was up to, but she did. She had a sixth sense about things like that. She worried but made a point to tell me that she loved me and she'd be waiting with open arms when I came back home. I'm going to make my mother proud and get us out of this mess." Lucien stretched his legs out. "I'm out of shape. Care for a jog?"

"Love to."

After borrowing a pair of men's sweatpants from Marlowe, he looked in the bedroom mirror. "I won't even ask who these belonged to. Are you ready?"

She came out of the bathroom, dressed in snug black yoga pants and a grey tee shirt. "Nobody. They belonged to nobody. I ordered sweats online last year and got men's instead of women's. It wasn't worth the trouble to return them."

He wasn't sure if she told the truth or not but decided to believe her. It was easier.

They left the house and jogged down the street in the warm afternoon sun, their footfalls the only sound breaking through the quiet. It didn't take long before he became exhausted, and his knees felt like they were pricked with glass shards.

"Hold on. I need to rest." He stopped and bent over, hands on his sore knees.

She continued for a few strides but turned and jogged back to him. "Maybe we should have gone for a walk instead."

He sucked in a few deep breaths and straightened. "Maybe."

The roar of an engine belonging to a large, black SUV with heavily tinted windows, interrupted the stillness of the afternoon. It headed down the road toward them. It didn't fit the neighborhood.

He shuddered.

Marlowe alert, her watchful eyes on the vehicle, stayed focused.

"We should get moving," he whispered.

Before she responded, the SUV accelerated and screeched to a stop beside them. Two burly guys with hooded masks jumped out. One grabbed Marlowe and the other dragged Lucien to the car and tossed him into the back. The guy got in beside him, clamped a handcuff around his wrist, and secured it to a metal loop on the ceiling. Helpless, he saw Marlowe shocked with a stun gun to her neck. She crumpled to the sidewalk as her assailant got into the back on the other side of Lucien. The car took off.

"What the hell!" For his outburst, Lucien received a slap on the back of his head. "Marlowe! Bastards! Let me go!"

"Shut up," growled a shadowy figure in the passenger seat. "You don't speak unless I tell you to, Dr. Roux."

With his jaw clenched, Lucien tested the strength of the handcuffs but got another smack for his trouble. He twisted around but couldn't see Marlowe any longer. Exactly who were these new assholes? His heart thumped and sweat dripped into his eyes. All he thought of was Marlowe lying on the sidewalk.

Nobody spoke as the SUV wove its way through the residential streets to the closest freeway entrance, heading east on Interstate 580. Where were they going? They hadn't told him anything. What did they want with him? They didn't seem like military guys, and they didn't seem to be with Fenwick; she mostly did her own dirty work. Was there another faction of thugs?

He couldn't stay calm, but he did his best by silently reciting a special mantra: *I'll make them all pay, I'll make them all pay.*

After a short while, the car ended up on the I-80, toward Sacramento. Still no explanation, no questions, no demands.

"Hey," Lucien said, hoping he'd be allowed to speak.

The guy on his right poked a gun into his ribs. "What?"

"My hand's numb. Can you take off the handcuff? It's not like I'm going anywhere."

From beneath his mask, the guy's eyes narrowed slightly. "Nope."

"For fuck's sake, what do you ...?"

"Shut up." The gun jabbed his ribs again.

The guy in the passenger seat turned, without a face mask, and glared. Young, maybe early thirties, with a pierced left eyebrow and a crooked nose. But his eyes were an oddly brilliant blue, like a male model's instead of a punk's. Lucien glared back.

Blue Eyes raised the pierced eyebrow. "Dr. Roux, our orders are to not harm you, but if you continue with these outbursts, I can assure you, the remainder of the trip will be most unpleasant." He had a slight accent, hard to figure out.

"Tell me what you want from me." Lucien tugged on the handcuff again. "Who gave you your orders? Fenwick? Harmond?"

Blue Eyes turned back around with a sneer. "No. You'll see soon enough."

The goons were teasing him, but why try to build suspense? They said they weren't allowed to hurt him. If it wasn't Fenwick or Harmond, then who? What the hell did someone else want? He had nothing left to give.

He sat in uncomfortable silence, searching his brain for any clues about what was to come, but there was nothing. The SUV zoomed through the city of Vacaville but switched to the slow lane after a few minutes as they neared the college town of Davis. He knew Davis very well, having been a guest lecturer at the university three times over the years. The SUV took the exit near the university, but they drove in the opposite direction, took a right, a left, and another right into a residential area.

"Are we dropping in for an early supper?" Lucien mumbled, trying the handcuffs again.

"Shut up," came the response from Blue Eyes.

After passing a few pristine homes, the SUV turned into the driveway of a lavish, yellow and white house with overflowing flower boxes hanging from every window. A sign out front said *Come in and check out our beautiful model homes*. There weren't any children playing or other cars anywhere on the street. An entire model neighborhood?

Blue Eyes turned around with a finger to his lips. "Keep your trap shut when we exit the vehicle or I'll rip your tongue from your mouth."

"I thought you weren't allowed to hurt me."

"Boss said nothing about your tongue." Blue Eyes sneered and climbed out.

The thug beside Lucien unlocked the cuffs, got out, and yanked Lucien by the wrist, forcing him to slide across the seat. Once on solid ground, he scanned the neighborhood for an escape route, but black SUVs blocked each end of the street. He was boxed in.

Herding Lucien toward the house, Blue Eyes stayed close. Lucien judged the man to be at least six foot five, or even a bit more, with broad shoulders to match his height. A pointless endeavor to make a run for it.

The front door opened and another goon, shorter, but not by much, ushered them inside. The interior was in total opposition to the outside. Computers were streaming what looked like live feeds of freeways, city streets, and most disturbing of all, Marlowe's condo.

"What is this?" Lucien wandered around, as far as they allowed him to, and groaned at one computer playing a Neanderball game. "That game is a farce, a shameful exploitation."

"I completely agree with you, Lucien," a soft voice said from the hallway.

Lucien spun around, recognizing the voice immediately. "Édouard?"

Édouard, his younger brother, stepped into the living room. "You've been having quite a difficult time of late, haven't you?"

"What the hell is this?" Lucien glanced around, but the goons weren't rushing Édouard and seemed to be waiting for instructions. "Is this your doing? You brought me here? Why? Are you here to help?"

"Have a seat, Lucien. We need to chat." Édouard motioned to a leather recliner. "Seriously, we need to chat."

Chapter 22

Lucien sat, bristling under the watchful eyes of his brother, a billion thoughts shooting through his brain. Was Édouard being a hero, or with Fenwick, or the military? Did he have a plan to help their family? What part did he play?

Édouard sat opposite. "Confused?"

"That's an understatement." Lucien glanced at the goons, jumped up, and grabbed Édouard by the front of his shirt. "What the hell is going on? You used a stun gun on Marlowe!"

Blue Eyes instantly leapt to action. He grabbed Lucien and tossed him back into the leather recliner. "Sit."

Édouard half-smiled. "You'd do well to behave, big brother. My men can be somewhat volatile when provoked."

Lucien collected himself and sat up, glaring. "So can I."

With a chuckle, Édouard straightened his shirt. "This is Armani."

"I don't give a shit. Tell me what's going on. Do you know where Papa is? Nicoline?" He leaned forward. "If you had anything to do with this whole mess, I'll—"

"What? You'll do what?" Édouard got up and wandered around the living room. "You won't do a damn thing. You're only in a position to listen."

"Fine. I'm listening."

Édouard sat again and stretched his legs. "Mother and Father were always so proud of you, no matter what disgrace you brought upon our family. I know about your crimes. Oh, Mother tried to cover for you by saying you were traveling around to learn about the world, but I knew the truth. You were running with a criminal gang."

"That's all water under the bridge. So, what is this, you want to find a way to rescue our family? How did you escape?" He sneaked a look toward the front door, but another goon blocked it. More than anything, he wanted to get back to Marlowe to make sure she was okay.

"Brother," Édouard started, "You misunderstand. I didn't escape. I arranged for Fenwick to set our home ablaze while I swooped in as the hero and freed our family. All while you did nothing but place them in mortal danger."

What exactly did he say? Lucien squeezed his eyes shut and replayed the words. Édouard worked with Fenwick all along? And the military? How? Fenwick wouldn't work with a nobody like Édouard. She was self-serving.

Édouard continued, "Father and Nicoline have hailed me as their savior since I pulled them all from the conflagration. The youngest boy rises while the eldest falls."

Lucien opened his eyes and looked at his brother's fingers. All his fingernails were intact. "That guy from the consulate said Fenwick pulled out your fingernail. You staged it. So, this is about jealousy? You're jealous of me? I have nothing, Édouard, nothing. I'm ruined, professionally and financially. What's there to be jealous of?" He placed his elbows on his knees and rested his head in his hands. "I'm quite sure Papa won't be so proud of me next time I see him."

With a laugh, Édouard jumped up. "There won't be a next time! You'll never go home again. I've been working on this for some time, ever since I heard about your research. You see, brother, my financial degree has proven most beneficial. Not only am I the bookkeeper for our once-glorious vineyard, but I've made quite a sum on the side as a money launderer for miscreants such as Fenwick. I put an idea in her head about the Neanderthals, *your* Neanderthals. It's the perfect way of undoing you. The most wonderful ridicule of your work."

"You dreamed up Neanderball?" He stared. "You did this to me? You had Fenwick shoot me? And Marlowe?"

His head spun. His own brother, hatching such deceit, all for the selfish reason of shining in the family's eyes. Édouard had always been the meek one, never straying from the path, never taking a risk. But he certainly proved himself to be a back-stabbing piece of rubbish now.

"Oh, yes, Fenwick. I didn't specifically tell her *not* to kill you or your bitch girlfriend, but I was overjoyed when you survived. So much better to watch you suffer. Yes, it's because of me that the world knows what a spectacular failure Paleo Roux is."

Standing, Lucien glared at his brother. "So how is the military involved? Do you launder money for them, too?"

"On occasion. But more like pure dumb luck, my brother." Édouard got up and looked out at the backyard through the glass doors. "General Harmond, who I believe you know quite well, approached Fenwick and she asked me to broker the deal. Neanderball proved to be the perfect venue to see the true nature and power of those Neanderthals. Fenwick has been training them to kill her enemies on the side. I'm content to see your life's work turned into a ridiculous team sport, but having your creatures turned into army grunts put the icing on the cake. You see, I have many talents, none of which impressed Mother or Father."

Lucien rushed forward, lashed out, and caught his brother on the jaw with a right hook. "You ruined me because of sibling rivalry?"

Blue Eyes jumped to action and threw Lucien to the floor, a foot to his throat. "Give me a reason," he snarled.

Édouard rubbed his jaw and motioned to Blue Eyes. A second later, the foot lifted, and Lucien received a fist to his left cheek. The impact twisted his neck and almost made him pass out. It took several seconds to recover, but when he did, he jumped to his feet, furious, and rushed at Édouard again, knocking him down. Like when they were children, older brother pinned younger brother's arms to his sides.

"You're my brother, Édouard. How can you do this to me? And to the Neanderthals?"

The moment the words left his mouth, Lucien got dragged off Édouard by his feet and pressed to the ground with a firm foot. Looking up, he saw no smile on Édouard's face this time.

"I've always been second to you. Even while you were off running around, it was always *can't you be more like your brother* or *Lucien wouldn't do that*. All my life ... well, no more. I've had your lab at Bay Genetics under surveillance for over a year now. And since I know your habits better than anyone else, I easily set you up for failure. Fenwick had connections who knew how to hack your computer systems to alter your growth hormone and enhance development. Really high-tech stuff. Your lab became mine."

Lucien struggled. No getting up this time. "You can end this right now."

Working his jaw, Édouard arched an eyebrow. "Oh, I plan to end, well, you."

"You're sick. You hate me so much that you want me dead?"

"Yep. But once you thwarted death, I figured I'd make you responsible for endangering our family." He stood over Lucien. "I keep winning, *brother*." He spat the last word like poison in his mouth.

"Then why hasn't Fenwick killed me? She's had lots of chances." His chest hurt from being pressed onto the floor. "Let me up."

With a gloating chuckle, Édouard motioned to Blue Eyes. "You can let him up, Brock."

Brock? Of course a goon would have a name like Brock.

Édouard continued, "She wanted to, and in fact, I insisted she end you once I had all the pieces in place. But, when you abducted her brother, she wasn't going to kill you. Things have changed now that she has him back, none the worse for wear. So now it seems the appropriate time to wrap things up."

When Blue Eyes moved his foot, Lucien got up and faced his brother. "*You're* going to kill me? You're a fucking coward."

"Not me. You're going to take your own life. Such shame you keep bringing to our family. Suicide is the final stain to darken your shattered reputation. Oh, and know that your pet Neanderthal, Rock, has been punished quite severely for his little foray into the outside world. And that's completely on you."

Lucien boiled down deep, the veins in his neck pulsing, his hands clenched. This world didn't deserve someone like Rock. Or Marlowe. But one thing for certain, the world was too good for the likes of Édouard.

"I had a firm rule against ever hurting family." Lucien checked the location of the goons in his periphery. "Had."

As quick as possible, he lunged forward, out of Blue Eyes' reach, grabbed Édouard by the throat, and shoved him hard into the glass doors. They shattered as Édouard flew backward. Suddenly, an opportunity. Lucien wasn't about to miss it. He charged through the broken doors into the backyard as several bullets whizzed by. At the far end, a wooden fence about five feet tall. Even out of shape, he managed to scale the fence and drop down on the other side, into another yard.

Amazingly, he didn't even twist an ankle. He sprinted through the yard and around the side of the house, emerging into the residential area behind his captor's house, completely disoriented. He stopped for a second to catch his breath and figure out which way to go. That was a mistake because a matte black truck with tinted windows screeched around a corner and stopped right in front of him.

CRITICAL

Chapter 23

Without hesitating any longer, Lucien took off in the opposite direction, but the truck sped up and followed, sliding on the pavement to block his way. The passenger door opened, and Alexei motioned for him to get in.

"Hurry, my friend!" Alexei jumped out and got in the back seat.

Lucien dove into the passenger seat and slammed the door shut a second before the truck spun around and took off.

From the back, Alexei reached over and placed his hand on Lucien's shoulder. "Too close for comfort."

"What ...?" Lucien swallowed. "What the hell? How did you find me? Marlowe ..." He looked at the driver, a well-built man in his forties or early fifties, with dark hair graying at the temples, and a dour expression. "Who are you?"

Alexei responded, "Take a breath. This is Sky Warrior. He discovered Édouard wasn't in France with the kidnappers and is here in America. We were searching for him to interrogate him about the rest of your family, but Marlowe phoned and said you were abducted."

"Okay," Lucien started, "But how did you know I'm here? I mean, right *here*."

Sky Warrior skidded around a corner and accelerated. "Marlowe has a tracker on you, Dr. Roux."

A tracker? "What?" Lucien slammed against the door as the truck took another corner. With shaky hands, he put on his seat belt.

"Keep breathing." Alexei leaned forward. "You're bleeding."

"I am?" Lucien saw blood all over his shirt. "I'm shot?" He felt his left shoulder where most of the blood appeared. "I've been shot, Alexei."

Alexei pushed him forward slightly. "Looks like the bullet went through the back and out the front. Lucky for you."

"I don't feel lucky." He accepted a cloth from Alexei and pressed it to his shoulder. "*Mon Dieu*, it hurts." He squeezed his eyes shut, suddenly feeling dizzy. "Why do I keep getting shot?"

Sky Warrior turned another corner, slower this time. "You didn't feel it before because of your adrenaline. Take a few deep breaths, Dr. Roux, and keep pressure applied. Alexei, check on the wound."

Alexei pulled down the collar of Lucien's tee shirt. "It's not bad. Hit the muscle." He shoved a cloth under the tee shirt behind Lucien's shoulder. "All right, what the hell happened back there?"

"My brother." Lucien opened his eyes and turned to Alexei. "He's behind all of this. He isn't satisfied that he's ruined me, he wants me dead. I barely got away from him."

"Édouard? That little simpleton? Perhaps we should go back and I can teach him a lesson."

He shook his head and checked on his shoulder. "He's got bodybuilder types surrounding him and is working with the military. And Fenwick."

Sky Warrior slowed and pulled into a parking lot. "How did you escape, Dr. Roux?"

"I remembered my old life with Alexei." He wiped his face on his good shoulder. "Remember that night in Monaco when you were caught with the sheik's son?"

"You mean you jumped through a window?" Alexei handed him a handkerchief.

Lucien mopped the sweat from his brow. "I did, after I tossed my brother through first." He closed his eyes as a wave of nausea hit him, but at the sound of his door opening, his eyes sprung open.

Marlowe immediately leaned in and kissed him. "What happened?"

He kissed her back. "My fucking brother, that's what. Are you okay? You're not injured?"

She pulled back and checked his shoulder. "I'm fine, but that wound needs care."

"After I put my brother in the ground." He got out and took in a deep breath.

Alexei climbed out and stood by Marlowe. "The lovely lady is right, my boy, we need to patch you up first. Fratricide can wait."

"Fine." He moved his shoulder and felt an instant jolt of pain. "Damn. It really hurts."

"Then stop moving it!" Marlowe slapped him on his good arm.

"Ow. Hey, they said you put a tracker on me. Where?" He looked over his clothes.

"On the tongue of your shoe. Good thing I did." She bent down, peeled a small button off his shoe, and handed it to him. "Now let's get that shoulder fixed."

Sky Warrior walked over to them with a first aid kit. "Mar, you want to do the deed?"

She looked at Lucien with an eyebrow raised. "You trust me?"

He turned the tracker over several times and glanced at Alexei, who shrugged.

When Marlowe opened the first aid kit, Lucien shook his head and backed away. "Here? You're going to ... do it here? We're in a restaurant parking lot."

"Oh, I'm sorry, princess, would you like a luxury suite at the Hilton?" She put on a pair of gloves and unraveled a length of suture thread without waiting for his response. "Don't be a baby."

"Marlowe." Lucien glared.

She didn't respond, but Sky Warrior did. "Dr. Roux, when evading an adversary, it's best to be somewhere they wouldn't expect. Like a restaurant parking lot."

"But ... Alexei?" He kept his eyes on Marlowe, who waited with a suture needle in her hand.

"My friend, we can't go to the hospital. And the restaurant is closed. This locale is a good one. You know it is."

"Yes, but ... Marlowe, you don't have to be so passive-aggressive. One minute you're kissing me and the next, calling me ..."

She leaned toward him and kissed him again. "There's no time for pleasantries, darling. You're bleeding and I don't feel like losing you today. Okay?"

"Okay. Was that so hard?" He drew in a breath and prepared himself for parking lot surgery.

Working efficiently, she cut his shirt to reveal the bullet hole, poured half a bottle of disinfectant over the wound, and began stitching. It hurt like hell, and when Alexei offered his hand, Lucien took it gladly and squeezed so tightly that his friend groaned. After she'd finished with the exit wound, she repeated the excruciating process with the entry wound on his back. Finally, she injected him with a dose of antibiotics.

Satisfied, she removed the gloves and tossed them onto the floor of the truck. "Not too bad, eh?"

"No, it was a delight." He gave Alexei an *I'm sorry* look. "Is your hand all right?"

Shaking his hand, Alexei smiled. "I'll live. How about you?"

"Well, other than an atrocious bedside manner, Marlowe makes a capable field doctor." He wiped the sweat off his face and checked his shoulder. "Those stitches will leave quite a scar, won't they?" He exhaled and smiled.

"Adds character, darling." Marlowe gave him a quick kiss and looked around. "We should get moving. Here's some ibuprofen for the pain."

Lucien swallowed the pills, gently worked his shoulder, and rolled his stiff neck. "I can't believe my brother is behind all of this. He orchestrated everything." His mood darkened. "He told me they severely punished Rock."

"What!" Marlowe paced. "Son of a bitch."

"We have to get that boy." Alexei motioned to Sky Warrior. "We'll get them all now that we have help."

"I hope so." Lucien went to Sky Warrior and extended his hand. "Nice to meet you. Are you on board with mounting a Neanderthal rescue?"

Sky Warrior shook his hand, roughly. "Ten-four."

Lucien looked at his friends and his newest accomplice. "We'll get those boys, but Fenwick and my brother belong to me. Understand?"

With a big smile, Marlowe winked. "Tough-talking paleogeneticist."

Alexei chuckled. "Tough-talking, and tough-acting, my dear."

"Only when properly motivated, Alexei." Lucien sighed. "And I'm plenty motivated."

Chapter 24

Lucien considered his next move, forcing Édouard to make Fenwick hand over Rock and his brothers. The details were missing though, but one step at a time. After finding an open restaurant, Sky Warrior parked the truck around back, away from the street, and ushered them all inside while constantly scanning the perimeter.

"Hey," Marlowe tapped him on the shoulder. "You've been staring at the menu for five minutes."

He leaned into her. "My mind isn't on food. And my shoulder still hurts like hell. Don't you have any stronger painkillers?"

"No. I can't have you in a haze." She kissed his cheek. "But you can have whatever you want off the menu."

Alexei, across the table, took the menu and put it down. "Once we rescue that fabulously muscular boy and his equally impressive brothers, we'll celebrate with an absurdly expensive bottle of wine in the finest restaurant, but for now, a cheeseburger will have to suffice. You need to eat to keep up your strength so your wound heals." He reached into his pocket and slid a small plastic container across the table. "Enjoy."

"Whoa. What did I just say?" Marlowe scolded.

Lucien opened the container and recognized oxycodone pills. He swallowed one right away. "Thank you. Sorry, Marlowe, but I'm about to pass out from the pain. How could my brother do this?"

"That's the kind of betrayal that hurts most," Sky Warrior said softly.

Lucien nodded. "Exactly. I'm still trying to wrap my head around all of this. Édouard had our vineyard burned and then faked a rescue so he'd be the hero." He opened the menu. "I didn't know he had it in him."

The waitress, an older woman with gray hair piled up on top of her head and thick, black-rimmed glasses, came over with a computer tablet in her hand. "Are you ready to order?"

Alexei flashed his charming smile. "We are, my dear." He motioned to the tablet. "Looks like even restaurants are modernized these days."

She shrugged. "Not my idea. Took me three weeks to learn which buttons to press. Even those Neanderball ape-men are better than me at computers."

Lucien abandoned the menu. "Excuse me?"

The waitress sighed. "Oh, you know, how they've started using smartphones now and doing that social media stuff."

As bright as Rock was, it didn't seem like he'd be the type to blog about his experiences in the twenty-first century. Lucien cleared his throat. "Do you mean the Neanderthals are actually doing the posting, or do you mean the team owners?"

"It's supposed to be the players themselves, but I think they have some assistant doing the actual typing. They read the fan posts though. They were on the news doing it. Reading those twittering things. It's amazing, but I still think we were better off writing old-fashioned letters instead of this impersonal technology junk. People don't know how to talk to each other anymore."

"Alexei," Lucien started, "I have an idea."

"Can't wait to hear it. But first, food." He motioned to the waitress.

"Of course." Lucien ordered a burger with fries and a glass of orange juice and waited anxiously while everyone else placed their order. When the waitress left, he leaned forward. "If they're on social media, we can use it to our advantage. Contact them ..."

Marlowe interrupted, "Yeah, I don't think so. Does anyone else think that sounds too simple? I can guarantee the social media pages are monitored by assistants like the waitress said."

"You didn't let me finish." He winked at Alexei. "Remember that time in Switzerland when we set up that thief and made him think he'd meet up with a fence?"

Marlowe shook her head. "What? I thought you guys were the thieves?"

With a shrug, Alexei said softly, "We are, my dear. Lucien, perhaps you should give her a little background."

Shifting in his seat so he faced her, he lowered his voice, "Alexei and I had taken possession of a lovely diamond necklace, but our car got broken into while we were in a café and the necklace was stolen from a strongbox we had in the trunk."

Marlowe sighed. "I really don't know you, do I?"

He continued, "We saw who did it. This novice punk, Manuel, who followed us around, trying to break into the business. He thought he knew better than us, arrogant fool."

Alexei grunted. "He wasn't exactly stealthy when he broke into our car, and he set off the car alarm."

Lucien smirked, remembering how Manuel, only a year younger than him, thought he'd gotten away with the greatest score ever. But he soon suffered for his arrogance. "He reached out to a local fence we knew and used."

With her head cocked slightly, Marlowe stared and raised an eyebrow. "And?"

"Manuel didn't know we were associates of the fence." He glanced at Sky Warrior as he texted on his phone, but when Marlowe nudged, he continued. "You see, we had an inside man."

Alexei smiled. "Correct me if I'm wrong, but you're thinking that Rock is our inside man in this case, *n'est pas*?"

"*Oui.*" Lucien returned the smile. "If we can contact Rock, we can get him to tell his brothers what's going on. They can find a way to escape, and we can meet them at a predetermined location, like with Manuel and our fence."

Marlowe held up her hand. "Hold on. You still think you'll be able to send a message that won't be intercepted? Are you for real?" She shook her head.

"Hear me out. Rock is highly intelligent. I'll work up a coded message I'm sure he'll figure out. Don't underestimate my Neanderthals." He turned away, suddenly irritated and feeling protective. Rock had surprised him with his speech and understanding, and his reluctance to hurt people. He wanted a normal life, not one playing a stupid ball game where he had no choice but to fight his brothers. Rock had a kind soul. Of course, there was still the end protocol to worry about, but one thing at a time.

Sky Warrior slammed his phone on the table. "Mission failure."

Lucien stared. "What?" Hearing the word failure made him grip the edge of the table, his fingernails gouging into the cheap laminate.

Sky Warrior slid his phone across the table. "I had ordered my men to secure your brother, but he eluded them in a firefight on the highway. A five-car pile-up. He has a special forces team, equal to, if not better than my men. Three of my guys were injured, critically."

"Shit." Lucien let go of the table. "He'll go after Rock, to punish me for ruining his plans. I've got to warn ..." He reached for the phone.

Marlowe pushed his hand away. "Stop. You said your brother set this whole thing up, right? But that's all he did, set it up. If he makes a grab for Rock now, Fenwick or the team owners will stop him. They're not about to lose a valuable member of the team and jeopardize the millions Neanderball generates. Remember what that idiot back at the motel said about loathing Fenwick? We need to slow down and think this through."

He knew she was right, but sitting around eating burgers went against his instinct. "All right. Sky Warrior, I don't know you, but Alexei and Marlowe have vouched for you. Can you come up with a plan?"

"Already working on it, Dr. Roux. My men are plenty pissed and itching to get back into the fight. I'll have something for you by the time the busboy clears our dishes."

Marlowe leaned into Lucien but didn't say anything.

A moment later, the waitress returned with their food. "You were asking about those cavemen. Look." She pointed to a small TV mounted on the wall in the corner behind Lucien. "You can see them using those phones to look at the social media stuff."

Lucien spun around. The first thing he saw, Rock with two black eyes, his left arm in a sling, and his upper lip swollen nearly twice its size, holding a computer tablet in his right hand. The other players seemed unharmed, although they were all sitting a few seats away from Rock, an obvious pariah. As if it wasn't bad enough seeing Rock battered, a shadowy figure almost out of view, hovered in the background.

"My friend, isn't that ...?" Alexei pointed to the TV.

Lucien turned back around, elbows on the table, his hands curled into fists. "My brother."

Chapter 25

Lucien squeezed his eyes shut and counted to ten. It didn't work. Too much adrenaline in his system. Seeing his brother's smug face on TV elicited a guttural reaction that he hadn't expected, and at the moment, he really didn't want to suppress his feelings. Being fired up gave him an advantage, and once he caught up with Édouard, the extra energy would help him do what he had to.

"Hey," Marlowe whispered as she wrapped her arm around his shoulders.

"Ow." He wriggled his injured shoulder away.

"Sorry. I forgot." She took his hand instead. "We need a plan. Fast."

He stared at her. "Of course we do." He motioned to the waitress. "Excuse me, but do you know how we can see what the Neanderthals are posting on social media?"

The waitress shook her head. "Sorry, I don't keep up with that. But Liam might." She pointed to a young busboy clearing dishes from a table. "Liam!"

He put down a dishrag and came over.

Lucien forced a smile. "Hi. Ah, I wonder if you know anything about the Neanderball players posting on social media and if I can contact them."

The look Liam gave, eyes squinted and mouth in a frown, made Lucien regret opening his mouth.

After staring for a few seconds, Liam finally spoke, "Yeah, I thought I recognized you. You're that crazy guy who invented Neanderball and then tried to kill the players. Asshole."

"Liam!" shouted the waitress.

"It's all right. I'm used to the abuse." Lucien drew in a deep breath. "I didn't invent Neanderball and I didn't try to kill ... can you answer the question, please?"

Liam rubbed his stubbly chin. "Yeah. I follow Brutus and Rock and leave comments sometimes. Rock got hurt though, so he's not doing much posting. I don't think the players can type, but they must tell someone what to post."

Sky Warrior slid out of the booth with his phone in his hand. He towered above Liam. "Show me."

Liam backed away but took the phone. A few seconds later, he handed it back. "Here you go. You got to follow the players to leave comments."

"Lucien," Marlowe whispered. "I don't see how you can convey a secret message to Rock. Every fan who follows him will see it. Not to mention, we don't know how Rock thinks or processes information."

Lucien shook his head. "Trust me."

Everyone underestimated Rock. He'd shown signs of advanced thinking, compassion, and humor. Whether from the modern DNA thrown into the mix, or that Neanderthals were smarter than people gave them credit for, was up for debate. But he felt certain Rock would figure out clues.

Now, to come up with a message that couldn't be cracked by anyone monitoring the feed. When Marlowe nudged him and motioned to Sky Warrior, he realized he'd been staring into space and hadn't heard a single word.

"Sorry, what did you say?"

Sky Warrior waved the phone. "You're all set, Dr. Roux. I have the social media accounts linked to Mar's and my phones." He paused, then explained, "I can monitor from wherever I am and track you as well. I also have a team of my guys heading to the arena to reconnoiter. Do you know what you want to say to the players?"

"Not yet." Lucien sighed and took Marlowe's phone when she offered it. "Wait." He smiled. "I have it." He typed a message and showed them. "Rock will know."

Alexei laughed and read the message, "I bet you like raccoon pizza. You should come get it where you had it last."

Sky Warrior shrugged. "I don't get it."

"An inside joke." Marlowe nodded. "Clever. But what about a date or time?"

Lucien thought for a moment. "What about tomorrow night at ... midnight? Security should be less stringent late at night. If he's as smart as I think, he'll find a way past his security." It was entirely possible that Rock wouldn't remember where the motel was, but they had to try.

Sky Warrior frowned. "Unless he's on complete lockdown."

Lucien sank into the seat. Fenwick had beaten Rock as punishment for escaping, so keeping him under lock and key wasn't an unlikely prospect.

"My friend, do you think that strapping young man can find the motel? Most of the trip he was unconscious." Alexei let out a sigh. "I must say, this is the strangest, and most frustrating, week I've had in a long, long time."

Lucien nodded. "I can't disagree with that. I didn't think this through. There's something else, too. We don't even know where the players live. What if they're housed even further away? Rock will never make it to the motel." He thumped his fist on the table. "Damn it."

Liam came back over. "Hey, guys, they said there's a special press conference tonight at ten to announce something about the players. Thought you might be interested." He shrugged and sauntered away to the kitchen.

"Now what?" Lucien let out a long sigh and gulped some water. Whatever the press conference was about, it had to be Édouard's doing. But maybe it was also an opportunity. "Sky Warrior, your men are going to the arena anyway, can you arrange for them to be at the press conference?"

"Not a problem, Dr. Roux." Sky Warrior picked up his phone and texted something. A moment later, he looked up. "I've got a squad of three heading to the location for recon. But without clearance, if you want entry, it would be a covert ingress."

Lucien looked over at Marlowe.

She smiled. "A break-in."

"Oh." He smiled back. "If there's a way for your men to get a message to Rock, then the social media angle isn't necessary. Maybe we can give him an easier locale to find."

"My friend, you're plotting like in the old days!" Alexei laughed.

Lucien continued, "Sky Warrior, can you find out what the protocol would be if one of the players suddenly became ill?"

"What are you thinking?" Marlowe shifted in her seat like she couldn't settle.

"Thinking out loud." He leaned into her, hoping to settle her down. He knew she wasn't used to seeing him in such a different role. "We can't risk the end protocol, but an illness wouldn't arouse suspicion."

With a sharp nod, Sky Warrior slipped from his seat and wandered away.

Lucien lowered his voice and motioned to Sky Warrior outside on his phone, "I think that if one of his guys can slip something to Rock to make him sick, he'd be taken somewhere immediately. We'd intercept. Alexei?"

"Damn." Marlowe leaned back. "I thought the social media thing was dumb, but this ..."

"It might work, my dear." Alexei smiled at Lucien. "You're thinking about Ibiza."

"Oh, my God. You're getting all your ideas from your prior dalliances. This is crazy." She shook her head.

"Yes, I am. I knew my past would come in handy one day." He'd used a similar ruse back in Ibiza when he'd escaped custody for trespassing. "So I was pinched by the local authorities when I set off an alarm in a very beautiful seaside mansion. I had a back-up plan, in case things went awry, which of course they did. Alexei had a special concoction of two capsules, one containing concentrated mustard and the other salt. I have to tell you, I never had anything so awful. An extreme bout of vomiting. I'd kept the capsules concealed in a secret compartment at the back of my watch. Luckily, the authorities didn't take my watch."

Marlowe raised an eyebrow. "I'm stunned."

Alexei chuckled. "Haven't you noticed, my dear, how Lucien never eats mustard? He must have vomited for two days straight!"

Lucien groaned. Thinking about it made his stomach queasy. "But it worked. They whisked me away to the infirmary where Alexei was waiting, as a replacement doctor. For some reason, the on-call doctor never showed up."

"For some reason, eh? You two." Marlowe shook her head.

With a smirk, Lucien said softly, "Alexei corrupted me in my youth."

"My friend, you were easily corruptible."

Sky Warrior came back in and slipped into the booth beside Alexei. "Good and bad news."

"Of course." Lucien sighed. Nothing was ever easy. "Good news, please."

Sky Warrior continued, "The players have a team physician who's always on hand, but nurses that come and go, but they're vetted."

"Okay. Now, bad news." Lucien sighed again.

"Security has been heightened since Rock's kidnapping." Sky Warrior paused. "But that's not all. Fenwick has a platoon of paramilitary personnel surrounding the arena and in position all around her and the team. I'd wager they're your brother's guys. At this point, inserting a replacement nurse would not be easy, and breaching the secured areas would require force."

"Force?" Lucien looked at Alexei. "Force won't work. We need stealth so she doesn't trigger the end protocol."

Sky Warrior patted the table for attention. "Dr. Roux, one of my team extracted intel from one of the scientists hired by Fenwick to develop the end protocol."

"Wait, what?" Lucien glared at him. "And you're only telling me this now?"

"You did bury the lead." Alexei frowned.

"I only found this out myself just now." He glanced at Marlowe. "Shall I continue?"

She took Lucien's hand. "Of course. Right, dear?"

He didn't answer, so Sky Warrior continued, "As I said, after questioning, the scientist revealed there is a component in the nano-transponders that, when triggered, will release a neurotoxin."

Lucien wriggled free of Marlowe's grip and slammed his hand on the table. "How does that help?"

This time, Alexei spoke up, "Give the man a chance. Please go on."

After a pause, Sky Warrior leaned forward, staring directly at Lucien. "The nano-transponders must be recharged every night. They're about the size of a quarter, inserted subcutaneously in the shoulder. Each player has four transponders, two front, two back. A charger is attached to the skin above the transponder and after six hours, they're fully charged." He raised an eyebrow.

Lucien glanced at Alexei. "So if we interrupt the charging, there won't be an end protocol. This is exactly the information we need!" He looked over at Sky Warrior. "Sorry. Sometimes I get a little—"

Marlowe finished the sentence, "Over emotional?"

"No. Anxious." Lucien leaned back in the seat, his mind churning. "So, how long does the charge last, and when are the players hooked up?"

"A full charge will last through the day and be too weak to trigger the protocol around midnight. The charging happens while the players sleep." Sky Warrior texted on his phone and a moment later, he nodded slowly. "It says players are kept under guard in the headquarters in Pacifica." He shrugged. "Anyone know where Pacifica is?"

"Yeah." Marlowe used her finger to draw an imaginary line on the table. "San Francisco, go south to the coast, Pacifica. It's a small town, great restaurants."

Sky Warrior smiled. "Maybe we can celebrate once the op's completed."

Lucien watched the interaction and had the urge to kiss Marlowe and punch Sky Warrior, but he stopped before making a complete ass of himself. "Our plan will still work. We can get Rock before he's taken to Pacifica and hooked up to the charger tonight. He'll be free. But we have to still get him a message so he'll be ready."

"It might work," Sky Warrior started. "Although we're still faced with the issue of how to get a replacement nurse approved. If we can't work it out, we'll be left with a forceful entry."

Lucien thought about alternatives. Somehow, they had to get Alexei's concoction to Rock, let him in on the plan, and find a way to rescue him from the infirmary before anyone realized.

He sat up and smiled. "I have an idea. I think we can use Sky Warrior's brute force after all."

"Lucien, darling, what the hell are you talking about? If Sky Warrior goes in hot, Fenwick can trigger the end protocol. Those nano-transponders might still have enough juice to trigger." She stared at him.

"The unexpected as a distraction—" Lucien was cut off.

Alexei finished the sentence, "Is a way to salvation."

"You're like an old married couple." Marlowe groaned.

Alexei burst out laughing. "More like a well-oiled machine of deception."

Lucien sipped some water and massaged his forehead. The headache was now a part of him. "But we'll have to make sure Fenwick can't trigger the end protocol. We still have no idea how she does that."

He took Marlowe's phone and logged into the team's social media account and found Rock's posts. "We can get a message to Rock about what we're doing."

"What?" Marlowe shook her head. "The raccoon pizza thing? Exactly what are we doing? I thought we gave up on using social media."

"I never said that." Lucien motioned to Sky Warrior. "There has to be a place with less security where we can leave Alexei's vomit-capsules for Rock to pick up. He'll get sick, go to the infirmary, and our nurse will get him out while everyone is distracted with Sky Warrior's invasion. Ideas?"

Sky Warrior smirked. "I'll go over the intel again. I've worked on some crazy shit with Alexei before, but nothing compares to this."

Marlowe rolled her eyes. "You're enjoying this, aren't you?"

He smiled. "Aren't you?"

She placed her hand over Lucien's. "I would if it wasn't for the obvious danger to Lucien, the Neanderthals, and pretty damn much everyone else. Fenwick's bat-shit psycho. You'd better not underestimate her."

"Come on, Mar, you know I take every precaution necessary." Sky Warrior winked and slipped from the booth, phone in hand.

Mar? Lucien rolled his eyes.

"The testosterone in the air is stifling," Marlowe mumbled.

Alexei grinned. "Dear lady, I see light at the end of this prehistoric tunnel. All will be well, you'll see."

Lucien nodded, even though he wasn't as confident. The new plan, loose as it was, had a chance of working, but everything would have to go like clockwork, without any bumps or errors. He leaned back and scanned through the player's posts. Nothing earth-shattering, just the regular, mundane chatter about upcoming games, injuries, and how excited the various players were for the next game. Rock's account stayed silent.

The thought of Rock being alone and beaten made Lucien queasy. "I need some air." He put the phone down and got out of the booth.

Sky Warrior paced outside the door, so Lucien moved about twenty feet away, needing solitude. He looked up at the bright blue sky, punctuated with puffy cumulous clouds, and wondered what Rock would have been doing if he'd been born a hundred thousand years ago in Europe. Would he still have the same intelligence and dry sense of humor? Or would he have grown up completely different, surrounded only by his own kind, living off the land, making stone tools, and living in complete freedom?

There were times when the simple hunter-gatherer life sounded wonderful, although being unsure whether you'd eat or not, not to mention a lack of fine wine, would take the shine off it. Still, it would be a pleasure living in a world where Fenwick hadn't been born.

In his peripheral vision, he saw Sky Warrior waving and heading in his direction. "Dr. Roux, we've intercepted chatter about the Neanderball players."

"Chatter? What sort of chatter?" He knew it wasn't good news.

With his voice low, Sky Warrior explained, "The players are being transported overseas to Budapest to play an exhibition game for the new international start-up."

"When?"

"Tomorrow." Sky Warrior shook his head. "It's now or never if you want to mount a rescue. Once they're out of the country ..."

"I know, I know." Lucien groaned. Even with Alexei's contacts in Europe, it would be near-impossible to arrange a kidnapping and escape plan.

"Dr. Roux." Sky Warrior grasped Lucien's forearm firmly but in a friendly manner. "My team's ready to go at a moment's notice. We can be at the Arena in time for the press conference." He let go and pointed to his watch, a large, military-type device with several small dials within the larger one. "Your call."

They still had so much to do. They had to get the message and emetic capsules to Rock and get him out of the building, all without raising suspicion. And, they had to have a safe house ready.

He stared at the watch. "What time do they leave?"

"The chartered airliner departs at 1300 tomorrow."

This was their only chance. He looked through the window at Marlowe and Alexei. "Okay. Do it. Get your guys ready. I'll make sure everything is in place."

"Roger that." Sky Warrior strode away, phone to his ear.

With a parched throat threatening to choke off his air supply, Lucien leaned against the restaurant window, lightheaded, and drew in deep breaths. He watched a little girl go by, three or four years old, wearing mismatched clothes and hugging a ratty teddy bear, with a huge smile plastered on her face, holding hands with her mother, not a care in the world. That's how children should be, free and happy to be themselves. Rock had to be free, like the little girl, so he'd control his own destiny.

Lucien pushed away from the window and waved to the little girl. Now, to set the plan in motion.

Chapter 26

Lucien readied himself to go back into the restaurant. Marlowe came out and stood beside him. She stared straight ahead, her eyes slightly narrowed, and her brow pinched. Her focused look.

"Sky Warrior filled us in." She bit her lower lip. "Things are about to get real interesting, Dr. Roux."

"No argument there." He closed his eyes and took a deep breath. "But, whatever it takes."

"Christ, Lucien, you sound like a broken sound byte."

He opened his eyes and stared at her. "You mean broken record?"

The hint of a smirk played on her lips. "That's so twentiethcentury, old man."

He grabbed her and pulled her close, planting a kiss on those smirking lips. "I couldn't do any of this without you. You know that, right?"

"Of course. I'm the brains behind this whole operation. Well, your unusual past skill set is coming in handy." She kissed him back. "This has to run like a precision timepiece or it won't work and we'll likely all end up dead."

"Doomsayer. I would have said *clockwork*, but precision timepiece works, too." He winked and headed back inside.

Alexei and Sky Warrior were deep in conversation, occasionally nodding or shaking their heads, sliding a sheet of paper back and forth between them.

Lucien slid into the seat beside his friend. "Let's rescue some Neanderthals."

"That's the plan," Alexei said softly. "We've been strategizing while you were canoodling with the lady."

"Canoodling?" Lucien raised an eyebrow.

Alexei gave a one-shouldered shrug. "It seemed appropriate. Anyway, we can't use Marlowe as a replacement nurse because Fenwick knows her, so I've come up with another operative I've used a few times."

Sky Warrior placed his hand on the piece of paper and tapped it with one finger. "I've worked with Sami, but ..." He paused for a long time. "Sami and Mar don't exactly get along."

"Did you say Sami?" Marlowe came over and placed both palms on the tabletop. "Sami? You serious? Absolutely not. That bitch can't be trusted. Not at all. Lucien, this isn't happening."

Placing his hand over hers, Sky Warrior drew a breath. "We need her, Mar. You'll have to look past your issues with her."

"Issues?" Marlowe straightened, her breathing coming in quick gasps. "I'd rather cut off my hands, or better yet hers, than have her involved. You know what she did."

Lucien groaned. "Well, I don't. What's so bad about this Sami?"

Marlowe glared at Sky Warrior, then continued, "She left me for dead after I got wounded by an IED. She's a fucking coward and should have been court-martialed."

He shook his head. "Okay, I agree with Marlowe. I'm not going to rely on someone *un*reliable. We can't have any mistakes, and this Sami sounds like a mistake waiting to happen."

"Well put, darling." She slid into the booth beside Sky Warrior, causing him to look extremely uncomfortable. "Anyone but Sami, John, anyone."

"Mar, don't you think I considered that? I know your history. There is no one else and we don't have the time to find an alternative."

She bristled. "Listen, misogynists, we don't need a woman nurse. Men are nurses, too." She looked at every man at the table, daring them to contradict her.

The plan was not off to a good start and Lucien considered calling it off, but that would be leaving Rock's future in Fenwick's and Édouard's hands. He'd never let that happen, even if it meant angering Marlowe by using her nemesis. He glanced at Alexei, who shrugged.

"Marlowe." Lucien reached across the table and took her hand in his. "My brother has betrayed me and my entire family, and Sami betrayed you. We're both dealing with a horrible situation. Can you do this? Can you work with Sami to save Rock and his brothers?"

She pulled her hand back. "You don't have to work with your brother. That's a big difference, Lucien. And stop with the guilt-tripping."

Alexei offered a slight smile. "My dear, I'm probably the least misogynistic man here, so when I say Sami is the best one for the job, I mean it. And it's not because she's a woman. She's unassuming and has played the

176

part of a nurse before. She knows the lingo. And she's lethal. Not to mention she's available. She's the best choice."

Marlowe sighed heavily. "This is killing me, but I can do it for Rock's sake. Once we're done though, I'll take care of Sami."

"You are definitely my sort of woman," Alexei smirked and let out a light chuckle. "You two can hash it out after the caper."

"Don't encourage her," Lucien whispered.

Sky Warrior tapped on the table. "All right, all right, we're a go. I'll finalize everything with Sami and get her in as a replacement nurse, somehow. But Dr. Roux, you've still got to let Rock know what's what and make sure we get Alexei's concoction where he can get at it."

"No problem," Lucien lied. "Alexei and I will handle it. Marlowe, can you arrange for transport and a safe house?" He hoped that by giving her a task, she'd ease up.

"You know I can."

He took her phone and logged into the player's social media account. If they managed to pull it off, they'd have to keep Rock safe until the transponder powered down, unless they found out how Fenwick triggered the end protocol. Yet another issue to consider. But one thing at a time. Getting a message to Rock, one that he'd understand, was vital to the plan. So how does one communicate to a Neanderthal that an escape plan is in the works? Lucien scrolled through the multitudes of messages until his eyes ached.

He blinked a few times. "I'm useless right now. I need a quick shower. Let's all meet at nine thirty tonight at the raccoon pizza motel."

"The what?" Sky Warrior leaned back.

"I'll explain it," Alexei said with a grin.

Lucien handed the phone to Marlowe. "Let's go home."

Chapter 27

After the group separated to prepare their respective parts of the plan, Lucien and Marlowe went back to her condo where he took a quick refreshing shower and opened a bottle of wine. Rather than dull his synapses, wine always helped him focus, with the calming effect blocking out distractions. There were many times when he and Alexei would drink the best French wine they'd get their hands on the night before a caper. By morning, they were primed to go.

Lucien sat on the couch and scrolled through the numerous posts on Rock's account, while Marlowe sat beside him cleaning a pistol.

"I've put you in so much danger. You can walk away at any time. I won't hold it against you." He took a sip of wine and stared at the deep red liquid. "I want you to know that."

She placed her hand under his chin and made him look at her. "Stop. I told you before, I have a personal involvement in this and I need to take care of Fenwick or I'll never be able to move past what she did. And Sami. She's on my shit list, too. Understand? I'm here because I want to be."

He put the wine down and showed her the phone. "I thought I'd give you one last chance. Look at this. Rock's account is on fire with fans wanting to hear from him and complaining about the team going overseas. How do they know? They haven't even announced it at the press conference yet."

"Hey, these days nothing's a secret. Why are they ticked off? The team's coming back."

"Not for months. And that means no more Neanderball until they come back." He scrolled to the last message. "This guy, Neander-Fan#1, says he'll protest at the arena tonight with a bunch of his friends. That might give us an advantage. We can use the crowd as a diversion. I have an idea. Want to hear it?"

"Duh." She picked up his glass and handed it to him. "A toast to devious minds and treacherous actions."

He clinked his glass with hers. "Are we the devious minds or the treacherous?"

She smiled and downed the remaining wine until her glass was empty. "Both, silly man."

"All right, so here's what I've come up with. A couple of Sky Warrior's men can pose as protesters; Sami will be the nurse, replacing the usual nurse who will mysteriously become ill, I presume; Alexei will create his disgusting concoction and hand it off to one of our protesters who will get it to Rock as the team is exiting the arena."

Marlowe's mouth gaped. "What?"

"Let me finish. I'll get a message to Rock so he'll be expecting a protester to charge out from the crowd and hand him the capsule of vomit-inducing gunk. Sky Warrior can create a disturbance that'll allow the guy to get to Rock. Once Rock swallows the capsule, he'll become ill, trust me on that, and be rushed back inside to the team doctor. While everyone is distracted dealing with the crowd and Sky Warrior's assault, we'll get Rock out to a waiting escape vehicle."

She filled her glass to the brim and drank half. "That's ridiculous. It's too complicated. Too many variables. Simple plans work better."

"This is all we have. We have to make it work. I'm going to reach out to Rock and hope like hell he understands what I mean. And you can explain everything to your old flame."

"Jealousy doesn't become you." She got up, finished the remaining wine, and strode to the kitchen.

After a few minutes of thinking, Lucien typed a message into Rock's social media account.

Hey, Rock, I know you like raccoon pizza so I'll bring you one tomorrow at the Arena! A friend of mine will deliver it to you.

He reread it several times, hoping it wasn't too obscure for a teenage Neanderthal to comprehend, or too obvious for the people monitoring the account to figure out. Marlowe hadn't returned, leaving him alone to worry. Once they had Rock, they'd try to remove the transponders, in case Fenwick decided to trigger the end protocol.

He had another thing on his mind, something he didn't want to share with Marlowe. He planned to grab a sample of hair or skin cells to conduct a DNA test to confirm whether Rock had the Stat3-beta2 gene or not.

If he did, Harmond wouldn't want to continue his program of cloning Neanderthals to use as cannon fodder.

Even though he chose science, he'd give it up in a second if Rock and his brothers would be set free. He wouldn't mind living a simple life. Replant the vineyard, tend to the vines, and with Marlowe by his side, he'd create the world's best wine. It would be a good life.

Lost in his dream of better times, he didn't notice that she'd crept into the living room until she cleared her throat.

Wearing nothing but a skimpy thong, she tossed her loose hair and let it tumble seductively over her shoulders and breasts. He dropped the phone. Her body was perfect and he'd never get tired of seeing each sensual curve, the toned abs, firm breasts that fit his hands as if they were created for that singular purpose, and the scars and old bullet wounds that gave her the imperfections that made her who she was. The last of the sunlight through the window caught her eyes and made them glow.

Without another thought, he picked up the phone, hit send, and stood. "You are the most beautiful sight, Marlowe." He closed the living room curtains, his eyes never leaving her. "Come here."

She approached slowly and dropped her eyes to his crotch. "I see my feminine charms have had the desired effect."

"Always," he whispered breathlessly, unzipping his jeans to relieve the building pressure against the fabric.

He embraced her, running a hand down the length of her back to her incredible backside, and pulled her in closer until her body meshed with his. She nuzzled his neck, small kisses teasing his flesh. He gently pushed her back and took a breast in his mouth, working the nipple with his tongue, his excitement growing as she tilted her head back and moaned.

Without pausing, he slipped her thong down and deftly explored her, massaging her clitoris until her moans grew louder. He couldn't take any more foreplay and swept her up in his arms, laying her on the couch.

"You reduce me to an animal," he breathed, straddling her.

She smiled and helped him out of his jeans, taking his erection in her mouth.

He pushed her down and thrust inside of her, rougher than he ever had before. His desire was on overload and for a moment, he felt guilty about thinking only of himself, until the rhythm of her hips and her gasps conveyed she enjoyed it every bit as much as he did.

After they both released, he collapsed half on top of her, exhausted. They lay still for several minutes, eyes closed, their breathing in harmony. When the phone rang, he groaned and edged off the couch. The peace had ended.

"Hello?" he rasped into the phone.

"Did I wake you, my friend? You sound like ..." Alexei's voice trailed off.

Lucien cleared his throat. "No, I'm fine. Do you have any news?"

"Of course. While you were otherwise engaged with the lovely Ms. Dunham," Alexei chuckled lightly, "I set everything in place. Well, with Sky Warrior's help."

"What makes you think I was ... never mind. So, we're ready to go?"

Alexei paused. "Only if our strapping young Neanderthal understands your message. I read it on the social media site. If Sky Warrior's man charges up to him without Rock's knowledge, it won't end well for any of us."

"Don't underestimate Rock." He accepted a glass of water from Marlowe and took a long gulp. "He'll understand."

"I hope you're right. I'll text you the details and meet you at the arena at half-past nine. Do not be late. Get some more rest, or something else, until then." He snickered and hung up.

Marlowe wrapped her arms around his waist. "It's a go?"

He nodded. "It is."

The phone chimed. Alexei's text.

He checked the details, which were simple enough and seemed flawless, although it was hubris on his part because he wanted it to work out. Nothing had gone smoothly so far, so why would this?

He got ready to explain the scheme when someone jiggled the doorknob. Instantly, Marlowe stepped to the side, searching presumably for her gun. He motioned for her to go to the bedroom, out of sight, but she hesitated.

"I'm not going anywhere," she whispered.

"We're both naked, Marlowe. Go and put some clothes on and get back out here." He grabbed his jeans off the floor.

She nodded and sprinted down the hall.

No sooner had he zipped up his jeans, than the front door smashed open. It swung wide on only one intact hinge. He stood, dumbstruck, as Édouard sauntered in behind Blue Eyes who held a black metal battering ram.

"Brother, nice to see you again." Édouard stood in the living room, a pistol in his hand.

Taking a few steps backward, Lucien purposely avoided looking at the hallway so as not to give away Marlowe's position. "What the hell do you want?"

Édouard laughed and aimed the gun at his brother. "I'm completely secured as the family hero and I intend to keep it that way. I can't have you attempting to undermine me at this point. Which means you must make an ignoble exit from this world." He feigned a frown that quickly turned into a smile. "No suicide this time, but an execution. Bullet to your cranium." He let out a self-congratulatory snicker.

"You haven't the balls to kill me." Lucien backed into a chair, overcome with the fight or flight response of a cornered animal. He rushed forward toward his brother but was tackled long before he reached him. Sprawled on his back, Blue Eyes knelt on his chest and pressed the barrel of a gun against his forehead.

"Any last words?" Édouard crouched beside him. "No? Well, goodbye then. You won't be missed."

Chapter 28

Lucien struggled to breathe from the weight of Blue Eyes on top of him. "You want me dead, do it yourself. Or are you still the little coward? I've always bettered you."

With Édouard focused on Lucien, Marlowe crept out dressed in her black stealth outfit and sneaked up behind him. Lucien saw her but did his best to keep Édouard's attention. It worked, because she struck Blue Eyes on the head with the butt of her pistol, then wrapped a garrote wire around Édouard's throat, pulling him off balance. Lucien rolled Blue Eyes off and jumped to his feet, drawing in a deep breath.

For a moment, he did nothing, his eyes burning into Édouard's and his adrenaline surging. When his brother's face turned scarlet red and he stopped struggling, Lucien waved his hand. "Let him go."

Through clenched teeth, she growled, "Why?"

"Because he needs to pay for what he's done. Death is the easy way out."

Reluctantly, she loosened the garrote wire. "This is against my better judgment."

"Understood." He hovered over his gasping brother, blood snaking down his neck from where the wire had cut into his flesh. "I've beaten you again, little brother."

When Blue Eyes groaned, Marlowe whacked him again. She pulled a zip tie from her pocket and secured his arms behind his back. "This, I was not expecting."

"Yeah, me either. So, Édouard, what am I to do with you?"

Holding his throat, Édouard sneered, "You should have let her kill me."

"Tempting." He glanced at Marlowe, whose deep frown and narrowed eyes chilled him to the bone. "Don't worry, you can do to him what you did to that thug."

Lucien watched as Édouard attempted to move away, but Marlowe pounced on him too fast. She smacked him a couple of times with the pistol and threw a few punches to his face for good measure. Once she had him secured and lined up next to Blue Eyes, she brushed off her hands and glared at Lucien.

"He's still my brother. I can't kill him."

"Why the hell not? He set you up, stole your research, kidnapped you, tried to murder you once already, and you still call him your brother? I don't understand you, not one little bit." She gave Édouard a half-hearted kick in the ribs. "He's a worthless piece of shit."

Lucien approached her but didn't get too close. "I agree. But I'd rather see him rotting away in a dank jail cell somewhere, a stain on the family name."

"Get real. He's not ever going to jail. You can't prove his involvement in all of this. Everyone on the planet thinks you're a crazed loon. In this scenario, you're the bad guy." She let out a frustrated sigh.

"I'm aware of how I'm perceived. But I plan on making sure my family knows how we've all been betrayed by him. Maybe he never will go to jail, but if I can undermine his scheme, then—"

"What? You'll be vindicated? Seriously, there's no good way this ends. We'll likely die at the hands of Fenwick or somehow manage to get Rock, and then he'll live the rest of his days hiding from everyone and never be free. And that'll be us, too. Your brother and Fenwick will be strutting around like heroes, and we'll be watching from our self-exile."

He drew in a breath and held it for a few seconds, but his heart still raced. Édouard didn't deserve to live, but as evil as he was, the fact remained, he was still family. Lucien looked at his brother, bound and beaten. If he let Marlowe have her way, he'd never have the opportunity to speak to his brother again. What should he do?

Lucien sighed. "If Édouard was out of the picture, what, in your expert opinion, do you think would happen?"

"I honestly think everything would unravel. He's the brains behind it all. Without him as her client, Fenwick might abandon the whole Neanderball thing. If she withdrew the security detail, we'd have the opportunity to march right in and take possession of the players. In a best-case scenario."

He nodded, still watching Édouard. "In a worst-case scenario?"

Without hesitating, she continued, "Fenwick would keep going and fulfill the deal with the military because it's already in place and paid for. We'd lose."

"Well, you're always the voice of reason. The likelihood of winning seems to be getting further and further away. But you've also made my mind up for me. There's no reason to murder my brother."

"The hell there isn't. He's the reason you and I were shot and your Neanderthals are playing a ridiculous ball game, destined to live their lives as prisoners for the entertainment of the masses. That alone should put your brother in the ground." She leaned over Édouard, who stared up at her. "I don't like you."

He laughed and coughed, bloody spittle spraying into the air. "Feeling's mutual. I only wish Beatrix had splattered your brains all over the lobby. And you, Lucien." He coughed again. "I should have killed you when I had the chance."

"You should have. You did what all cinematic villains do, you wasted time explaining your treachery instead of ending me. You should have watched a few more movies to see how it always ends for the villain. You're sick, Édouard."

"Perhaps. But I masterminded your downfall, quite successfully I might add. Our family is ashamed of you. Whatever happens now, you'll never recover. *I* win."

"Sibling rivalry," Marlowe spat the words. "What kind of monster wants to kill his brother because he's jealous? Lucien's right, you're one sick asshole." She stomped off down the hallway.

Édouard snickered. "*C'est une salope.*"

"Shut the fuck up, brother." Lucien went to the broken door and managed to get it to close. He peeked out through the curtains at the quiet neighborhood. "I think it's you who's the bitch."

All of the commotion and not a single person had left their house. People saw what they wanted to see and heard what they wanted to hear, which gave him the confidence he sorely needed to continue with the plan. The crowd at the arena would never suspect an escape right in front of them because they'd be too concerned about protesting the temporary loss of the players overseas.

"You're smiling. Don't get it in your head that you can survive this. Even if Beatrix doesn't end your miserable life, I'll find a way to do it."

Lucien turned away from the window when Blue Eyes groaned. "For years, I've been living a decent life, doing the right thing. I've been working at finding a cure for—"

Édouard interrupted, "Mother's dead, so I don't give a shit what you've been doing." He laughed. "You *would* like to kill me, wouldn't you?"

"With my bare hands." Lucien knelt beside his brother. "You were always a mean-spirited little boy." He imagined what it would feel like to commit fratricide, to take his brother's life. Would he feel guilty or relieved?

"Lucien." Marlowe came into the living room and glanced at Blue Eyes first and then Édouard. "I contacted Sky Warrior. He's sending a few of his team to watch these dickheads while we execute our plan. Hear that, dickheads, we're going forward."

For a moment, Édouard looked surprised but then smiled. "Doesn't matter. You might destroy Neanderball, but the deal with the military is done."

"What do you mean *done*?" Lucien stood and looked down at his brother. "Have you arranged for the military to kidnap the players overseas?"

"Oh, that would draw a lot of attention, wouldn't it?" Édouard sneered. "Try again."

Marlowe shook her head. "Don't play his games. No matter what he has planned, or thinks he does, we will win this thing. I don't like to lose and I'm sure as hell not losing to this little turd."

"You've already lost." Édouard smirked. "Do you think I would have come here without telling my team?"

"Shit." Lucien ran to the window and parted the curtain enough to peek out.

There didn't appear to be anyone around. Maybe Édouard lied. But then, the sound of a slow-moving vehicle heading down the street, tires gripping at the pavement, made him back away.

He whispered, "Someone's coming."

In a flash, Marlowe grabbed a roll of duct tape and gagged Édouard, her gun to his head. "Lucien, get out of sight, I can handle this."

"No. This is my fight, too. We'll stand together." His mind focused with sudden clarity.

He took Édouard's gun, made sure to take the safety off and positioned himself across from Marlowe. Whoever came through the door wouldn't stand a chance. He gave her a nod and sucked in a deep breath.

Instead of the door crashing in, someone knocked. Then again.

"Are you lovely people home?"

Alexei.

Lucien let out a huge breath and opened the door, which swung pathetically on its only operable hinge.

Alexei motioned to the door and then Édouard and Blue Eyes. "Unwelcome guests?"

"Definitely."

Marlowe lowered her arm and frowned. "I almost shot you."

"But you didn't. I'm here at the behest of Sky Warrior."

"You?" Marlowe groaned. "What for?"

With a flourish, he motioned outside. "I bring presents."

Lucien peered outside and smiled. Three fatigue-clad guys who had to all be well over six and a half feet tall strode up the front walk. They came inside and instantly gathered around Édouard and Blue Eyes, towering over them, looking as menacing as possible with deep-set frowns and hands resting on hip holsters.

"So, brother," Lucien started, his heart slowing to a regular pace, "I think we'll be ready for anything."

Édouard stared. "Whatever the outcome, your reputation is forever sullied."

Alexei stared at him. "You're a hateful piece of rubbish, aren't you? Lucien will always be a better man than you. I knew one day you'd show your true colors."

Together, Alexei and Lucien closed the broken door.

In a low voice, Alexei said, "I should like to take care of your brother if you will allow me."

"No, like I told Marlowe, he's family and I can't have him killed. I know you think me a fool for letting him live."

"You won't be conducting that task, my friend. Leave that to me. He's dangerous and has committed innumerable atrocities. To allow him to get away with his life is criminal."

"I know you're right, but, what if, I mean, he can change. If I can get through to him, maybe ... although he did want to kill me." He turned away.

How long had Édouard been harboring that much anger? Most of their lives? It would be easy to let Alexei put a permanent fix on the issue.

"I need some air." He went through the kitchen to the back door and stepped into the yard.

The birdbath, still full of water, had a sparrow happily splashing about, spilling water onto the soil below. The earthy smell of damp soil made the moment idyllic. He sat on the bench and considered what Édouard said. The military deal was done. That meant several things, one of which was that they were currently actively cloning more Neanderthals using the Neanderball players' DNA. In that case, freeing Rock and his brothers, and exposing the truth of what the military was doing, became imperative. With any luck, and it would require an incredible amount of luck, somebody would listen.

Shouts came from the house, followed by the sound of gunshots. He froze for a second before running toward the fray. All he thought of was Marlowe. When he reached the back door, several shots struck the doorjamb, splintering the wood. Small shards pierced his neck and shoulder, but it didn't slow him down. He charged into the kitchen where Alexei and a guy dressed in black were exchanging gunfire. Lucien hadn't been seen, which gave him the element of surprise. He plucked a butcher knife from the wooden block, ran around the island, and thrust the knife deep into the back of the assailant's neck.

Blood spurted, drenching Lucien's shirt and hands. The guy died before he hit the floor. The only other time he'd killed a person was by accident during an escape in Paris when he drove a getaway car too fast around a corner and it skidded into a pedestrian, an older man carrying a bag of groceries. He'd suffered debilitating nightmares for years after that, even with Alexei's assurance that the man's family had received an obscenely large anonymous donation. This incident, however, was no accident.

"Well done, my friend," Alexei blurted, reloading his weapon. "Thank you. Are you all right?"

Lucien dropped the knife and quickly rinsed his hands under the faucet. "I'll be all right. Marlowe?"

"She's battling four other thugs alongside Sky Warrior's men. That brother of yours told this deceased gentleman here that you went through the kitchen. I followed."

"Glad you did, but I have to help Marlowe."

"*We* have to help." Alexei tossed the dead guy's gun to Lucien. "Will you let me finish Édouard now?"

Lucien shook his head.

As the gunfire continued, they stood on either side of the doorway leading to the living room. Lucien took a quick peek but couldn't see Marlowe. However, one of Sky Warrior's men lay face down, bleeding on the carpet. Waiting wasn't an option. He took a chance that nobody would be expecting him and charged out ready to fire. He sensed Alexei beside him, which gave him an eerie sense of calm. After surveying the area, he fired off a shot at a man in camo who cut the bindings off Édouard. Direct hit to the head.

Édouard struggled to get free and shouted to another man, "Shoot him!"

The man turned and aimed his gun at Lucien but fell backward as a growing bloodstain appeared on his chest. Marlowe stood from behind the chair and winked. Her sleeve, covered in blood. One of Sky Warrior's men and Alexei took care of the final two assailants, while Lucien went to her.

He tore her sleeve. Only a graze. "Will you be all right?"

"Of course. But you ... is that ..."

He shook his head. "Not my blood."

"That's a relief." She gave him a peck on the cheek and rushed to Sky Warrior's remaining team. "Thanks, guys."

Sky Warrior's men went to their fallen comrade.

Alexei wrested the gun from Lucien. "You won't need this, my friend. This went relatively well."

Édouard laughed. "There are more coming, you fools."

"We're not the fools." Lucien wiped his sweaty forehead with his hand. "I'm the only one keeping you alive, so show a little appreciation."

Sky Warrior's men carried their injured friend outside, their stature solemn as they conducted their duty. Marlowe followed them to the door and watched while Lucien knelt beside his brother. Blue Eyes gasped for air from a chest wound. Nothing to be done for him.

"I won't let you get anywhere near the Neanderthals. Whatever you're planning, I'll see to it that it'll fail. I'll double the guards and keep those creatures under lock and key." Édouard laughed again.

Lucien glared. "You won't win. Whatever it takes, I'll save them and make sure you're the one under lock and key for the rest of your miserable life. How do you think Papa will feel about you then?" He got up and went to Marlowe. "You need medical attention for your arm."

She leaned against the door jamb, still watching as the men reverently placed their friend inside an SUV. "Don't think I didn't see you've been all cut up on your neck. What the hell happened?"

In all the excitement, he'd forgotten about the wood splinters. "It's nothing." He touched his neck and realized there were several thin pieces of wood sticking out of his skin. "You patch me up, I'll patch you up."

"Deal." She stepped inside and lowered her voice, "Your brother ... how much more are you going to take? Because of him, one of Sky Warrior's men is down."

"I'm aware. Let me worry about him. We can't stay here now and we can't leave him. If he's telling the truth, more of his people are coming."

"Agreed. We need to move before the cops show up, too."

When Sky Warrior's men returned, Lucien explained how they had to take Édouard with them. The news wasn't received well, but they agreed and dragged him by the feet out to the SUV where they loaded him in the back, roughly. Seeing the look on Édouard's face as they shoved him in was priceless.

Still, no neighbors appeared, although in the distance were sirens. Within seconds, the small convey headed out with Lucien and Marlowe in the Jag.

They drove a few miles and pulled over under a tree, with Sky Warrior's men standing guard while Lucien and Marlowe performed first aid on one another. With each splinter that she removed from his neck, his anger grew. Each of them had been a whisker away from ending up dead. If she'd been killed, he would have retaliated and killed his brother, no question about it. Alexei and Marlowe were right that keeping him alive was reckless. Édouard had done nothing to redeem himself and instead continued to hunt them down at every opportunity. It would only take a second and it would be over.

Lucien set the alarm on the Jag once he was patched up and got into Alexei's car, this time, a stolen, or borrowed as Alexei put it, Range Rover. With his head spinning, Lucien leaned into Marlowe in the back seat while Alexei drove and one of Sky Warrior's men sat shotgun. The reality of rescuing Rock slipped further and further away. It really would take a miracle for all the pieces to fall in place.

He rested his hand on her leg and whispered, "This must work. If it does, we'll get married."

She put her hand over his, kissed his cheek, and whispered back, "Lucien, darling, what the hell makes you think I want to get married?"

He didn't get the response he expected. As Alexei snickered from the driver's seat, Lucien straightened and gazed out the window. It was painfully obvious to him that while he navigated the complicated world of paleogenetics with ease, he knew nothing at all about women.

Chapter 29

Lucien rolled his neck and shifted in his seat as Alexei drove to the *raccoon motel* as they now called it, and parked around back where Sky Warrior waited. They had almost an hour before they had to be at the press conference, not much time to finalize all of the details. But he had a good team and felt confident for a change.

While Sky Warrior and Marlowe chatted, Lucien spoke with Alexei, "I'm nervous as hell. If one part of this fails, it all fails."

"I'm aware." Alexei motioned to a faded red sedan approaching slowly. "Prepare for some fireworks. That's Sami."

"Oh, shit." Lucien rushed over to Marlowe, who hadn't noticed the sedan. "Hey, can I see you for a minute, in private?"

She stared at him with slightly narrowed eyes, her suspicious look. "Why? We're in the middle of tactical planning here. I need to know exactly where everyone will be because I'm running point on logistics." She looked past him. "Oh. You didn't want me to see Sami. Do you think I'd risk the mission by smashing her face into the sidewalk?"

"Ah, no, that's not at all what I was thinking. But it seems like you were." He stepped back and pointed to the car as it stopped near Alexei's car. "Why don't you introduce me?"

Sami, a much smaller woman than he'd expected, stepped gracefully from the sedan, shook her short-cropped auburn hair and glanced around. She seemed out of place in a pair of light blue scrubs. Alexei waved her over, said something to her, and then walked with her to the group.

"Lucien, this is Sami. Sami, Lucien. You already know Marlowe and Sky Warrior."

"I do." She extended her hand to Lucien. "Nice to meet you." Next, she went to Sky Warrior. "Glad to work with you again, John."

"Likewise." Sky Warrior watched Marlowe. "Mar, you okay?"

She paused for a few seconds. "Sure."

Sami extended her hand to Marlowe. "No hard feelings?"

Rebuffing the handshake, Marlowe turned to Lucien. "Have you checked social media lately?"

The awkward meet-and-greet ended with everyone now present. Lucien took a deep breath and checked Rock's page. Only one response.

Bring Rock raccoon pizza

Lucien's breath caught in his throat. "*Merde*. Shit. I mean, shit. Marlowe, look." He showed her the phone.

"Okay, so he either really wants pizza *ala* raccoon or he understands that you're cooking up a scheme." Marlowe signaled to Sky Warrior and side-stepped around Sami.

Standing alone, Lucien did his best to seem amiable. "So, Sami, you understand what we're doing?"

"Of course, you think I'm a dipshit?" Her voice carried a harsher tone than expected in response to a simple question. "You're used to dealing with Ms. Congeniality over there, but I'm not her. I have a job, I do it. Anything else?" She raised an eyebrow.

"Ah, no." He edged away and made a hasty exit to Marlowe. "Damn, I don't like *her*."

"Thank you for that, darling." Marlowe smacked a kiss onto his cheek. "I would have no objection to her getting caught in the crossfire or being the victim of friendly fire. Either would work."

With a grunt, Sky Warrior looked past Lucien to Sami. "Mar, stow your fury. At least until the op is complete."

"I'm a professional, so don't school me." She looped her arm around Lucien's and pulled him away from the group. "If Sami screws this up, Rock will be gone forever. We'll never get another chance."

"I'm well aware of the precarious situation, but we don't exactly have any other choices, now do we? And I'm betting everything on her being a professional, too. I forgot to ask, have you arranged for transportation and a safe house?"

"It's all set. I'll be waiting in a blacked-out van near the Arena. That means windows heavily tinted."

"I figured that." He watched Sami sulking away from everyone else. "What the hell is her problem?"

A pause.

"Marlowe?"

"Fine. She had a thing for Sky Warrior. Still does."

"And? I feel like there's more to the story." He waited. "And? Look, I need to know that I can trust her."

She exhaled. "I thought you said you believed she's a professional. Anyway, when I recovered in the hospital after Sami left me for dead, John stayed with me day and night. That didn't sit well with her. Up until then, she'd been a great soldier, bright and tactically adept. Her skills were almost instinctual. But something happened."

"Like what?" He glanced at Sami again. "Like what?"

"Are you sure you want to hear this?"

Did he? How bad was it? "Of course."

"Okay. John and I had a fling. She must have found out and that's why she left me on the side of the road after the explosion. You asked."

He did ask, and now he regretted it. He shook his head. "Jealousy? Oh, come on. She's jealous of you and Édouard's jealous of me. The few times I've been jealous of someone, I've never wanted to kill them. Hurt them maybe, but not kill."

"Yeah, because you're a normal, good person. Some people can't act reasonably." She tilted her head. "I'm going to make sure that bastard of a brother of yours is secured." She wandered off to Sky Warrior's SUV.

A sinking feeling settled over Lucien because the whole plan hung by a frayed thread. It seemed cowardly that his part of the plan was simply to type a message to Rock while everyone else risked their lives. Marlowe would be in the escape vehicle and Sky Warrior's men would mingle with the crowd, with one of them handing off the vomit pill to Rock. That brought up an issue.

"Hey! Sky Warrior." Lucien jogged to him. "How are you getting Sami into the infirmary?" He squinted at Sky Warrior's military watch. "Shouldn't she be there now?"

Sami sidled over. "Five minutes."

"What?" Lucien stared at her.

"I'll be called in five minutes."

He glanced around, but no one offered any further explanation. "Okay. Wait, no, how is this working? I thought the nurse had to call in sick. Wouldn't she have already done that?"

With little in the way of expression, Sami sighed. "The nurse shows up half an hour before the press conference. By now, she knows she's not going to recover and will call in. The on-call nurse, me, will receive a call to go immediately to the Arena. That should be in about three minutes now. Anything else?"

Marlowe came back and placed herself between Lucien and Sami.

Even though he didn't like or trust Sami, she did appear to have everything under control. "No, no that's fine. Thanks."

She stared at him for a moment. "You're French?"

"I am."

"I don't like the French." She spun on her heels and strode away as her cell phone chimed.

With an I-told-you-so look, Marlowe shrugged. "Charming, isn't she?"

Sami hopped in her car and screeched from the parking lot as the team watched.

"So, how is Édouard?" Lucien watched Sami until he lost sight of her car.

"Pissed. He almost chewed through the duct tape, so I applied several additional layers. Listen, he'll only bring us trouble. I totally get the whole family thing, but seriously, if one thing goes wrong ..."

"It won't. I have to believe it won't or I'll never get through this. Hey, I'm involved in this. I'm coming with you."

She shook her head. "Nope. You're not. I need to know you're safe."

"With you in the van, I'll be safer than anywhere else." He raised an eyebrow. "You know I'm right."

"I wanted you to wait in the safe house, but maybe you've got something. Once Rock sees you in the van, he'll be less afraid. Okay. You're coming."

He winked. "Thank you."

"How's the shoulder?"

"Not so bad at the moment."

"Good. You're not getting any more drugs."

"That's mean. Look, I need to speak with my brother before we leave." He didn't bother mentioning that he still had some of Alexei's pills.

She shook her head but didn't stop him, so he wandered to the SUV and opened the back. Édouard glared at him and strained against the bindings. It was satisfying seeing him like that, and sad. Lucien always thought their family was tight-knit and perfect. How wrong he'd been.

"Édouard, once this is over, you and I will have a lengthy conversation. And then I'll turn you over to Harmond. I doubt he'll be forgiving of your failures."

The duct tape over Édouard's mouth crinkled slightly. He smiled.

Lucien slammed the hatch shut, his chest feeling tight. He turned around and wiped fresh beads of sweat from his forehead. He knew his brother well enough to know he wasn't bluffing. Something was afoot and it wasn't good.

"Marlowe!" He hurried to her. "You know how you had that tracker on me, and how Rock has a transponder? What if there's something on Édouard?"

"Oh, shit!" She motioned to Sky Warrior. "Search that piece of crap for any trackers."

He nodded and with two of his men, pulled Édouard from the back, rough enough that Lucien smiled. It didn't take more than a minute or so for them to locate two tiny trackers; one in the heel of his shoe and the other attached to the underneath of his shirt collar.

Lucien felt the intensity of Marlowe's stare even without looking at her. He wiped his face again. "We have to go right now, don't we?"

"Yeah, we do. If you would have let me take care of him back at the house..."

"Let's not go there. Not now. Where's the safe house?" He cocked his head. "Wait. Do you hear something?"

"I don't hear a thing. You're paranoid. So, the safe house isn't exactly a house, but it's definitely safe." She held up a hand. "Maybe you're not paranoid."

"You hear something, too?" He listened to the faint sound of a car engine but couldn't tell its location. "We should move."

"Yep." Marlowe signaled to Sky Warrior with her hand making a circle in the air. "Get in the car with Alexei. I'm riding with Sky Warrior."

"Are we going to the Arena?"

"Not yet. I want to make sure we're not being followed." She had a deep-set frown.

Lucien knew she blamed him for not dispatching Édouard, and while she had a good point, she wasn't understanding the finer point of family loyalty. If there was a chance Édouard wasn't too far gone, he might be brought back from the brink, after a suitable prison sentence. Killing him would be easy, but it eliminated any chance of rehabilitation. Marlowe only saw the logical solution.

Before he said another word, she'd climbed into the passenger seat of Sky Warrior's SUV. She never turned or waved. Had he forced her to create distance from him, to cling to her old life with John Largette? As if things weren't complicated enough, he had that to worry about.

"Lucien! Hurry, my friend. Bad guys on the horizon." Alexei had the passenger door of the Range Rover open and motioned in a restrained, but still somewhat frantic fashion.

The engine noise came closer, so Lucien jumped into the car and fastened his seatbelt in preparation for Alexei's driving. Sure enough, the moment he closed the door, Alexei sped off after the SUV, squealing the tires around a corner. Lucien glanced at the speedometer; seventy. Behind them, two pick-up trucks and a desert-camo-painted Jeep raced after them. As Sky Warrior sped through the streets, Alexei managed to keep up, but so did their pursuers. After zooming through a stop sign, a motorcycle cop flipped on his lights and siren and took a position directly behind Alexei.

Lucien held onto the dash. "That's all we need."

"It may work to our advantage. Those dastardly fellows might back off." Alexei continued to stay on Sky Warrior's tail without slowing.

The cop closed in behind them, motioning for them to pull over. He either wasn't aware or didn't care, that they were being chased. Lucien turned and noticed that Alexei had been right, the other guys slowed, working out their next move. When they were a sufficient distance behind, Alexei slowed.

"My friend, would you mind calling Ms. Dunham and let her know we're pulling over to receive a speeding ticket?"

"On it." He had Alexei's phone out and dialed her number.

"What the fuck!" she shouted.

"Not our fault. We're pulling over." He hung up. "We are pulling over, right? What if the cop is with Fenwick?"

"We'll deal with that if the need arises." Alexei edged the car to the shoulder and stopped. "Be calm."

"Impossible."

Sky Warrior flipped a U-turn and pulled over about a hundred yards ahead in the opposite direction.

Lucien let out a breath. "Looks like we have help if we need it."

"I figured. Sky Warrior is always the pre-eminent professional and worth every penny I pay him."

The cop shut off the siren, stepped off his motorcycle, hand on the butt of his pistol, and cautiously approached the driver's side. Alexei wound the window down and placed his hands on the top of the steering wheel, a stance he'd always do to show he didn't have a gun.

"I clocked you at seventy-five in a thirty-five. Any explanation?" The cop leaned a bit closer. "More than twice the speed limit means I can run you in."

Lucien squirmed, his eyes on the SUV. He saw Marlowe in the passenger seat, staring right at him. He faked a yawn, doing his best to seem innocent.

"Am I keeping you awake, sir?" The cop took Alexei's license, insurance card, and registration.

"Oh, no, not at all. I'm ..." Lucien faltered. "I'm ... a journalist. We're heading to the press conference at the Arena to see the Neanderball players."

The cop nodded, turned, and looked at the SUV. "They with you?"

Alexei answered, "Our escort. We're international journalists and have our own security team. Can't ever be too careful these days with the populace distrusting the media. I apologize for speeding, but we're late and I wasn't paying attention. Are you a Neanderball fan?"

"Not really. Hold tight, I'll go run your license." The cop sauntered back to his bike.

Lucien pressed his palms against his thighs. "I've always been impressed with how nothing fazes you. I'm about to pass out."

"It's practice. I've been at this a lot longer than you have. But, you're doing fine." He patted Lucien's arm. "Keep your eyes on the prize, as they say."

"Wait, you didn't give him your actual ID, did you? And where did you get a fake registration?"

"Oh, sweet, innocent boy. I don't carry any real ID. I always have appropriate documents on hand."

The cop came back and gave the license and papers back. "Okay, Mr. Sarris, I'm giving you a citation for excessive speed and reckless driving. It'll be a hefty fine."

Alexei slipped the license into his wallet and feigned a frown. "Well, it's my fault, officer. You're only doing your duty."

It took several minutes to write the citation, but once the transaction was completed, Alexei pulled out, slowly, into traffic. The cop followed, but after a minute did a U-turn and headed back in the other direction. Sky Warrior spun around and soon caught up, passing to get in front. As they passed, Marlowe shook her head.

"She hates me, Alexei. She blames me for everything, doesn't want to marry me, and ... and ..."

"Give her time. You haven't known each other that long and right smack in the middle of your budding romance, all hell broke loose. It's no wonder she's a tad mixed up. Be patient." He smiled. "Not to mention you proposed at the worst possible time. She's a smart lady who knows what she wants. And she wants you, trust me in that."

"I'm not so sure. I think I like her more than she likes me. I can imagine being her husband." He turned around and looked behind them. "I don't see the other vehicles. Did they turn back?"

"Doubtful. I'm sure they're keeping their distance this time. Sky Warrior will handle them."

"Handle them? What does that mean?" He kept peering behind.

"Let's not worry about that. So, tell me more about the lovely Ms. Dunham."

He knew Alexei changed the subject to ease the tension. "I feel so emasculated around her. She's always saving me or telling me off for some stupid thing I've done. I don't know how to make things right."

With a gentle chuckle, Alexei slowed and turned a corner, then accelerated again to keep up with the SUV. "My dear friend, be yourself. That's who she fell for. You mark my words, when this is all over, you two will jump into a loving relationship with both feet. For now, though, keep out of her way and let her work."

"Words of wisdom. You've always known what to say to get my mind right." He looked around. "So where are we going?"

"No idea."

He leaned back and gazed out the window. After a while, he recognized the area. "We're heading to the Bay Bridge. Wait, are we going to Bay-Gen? Is that our safe house?"

Alexei smacked his hand on the dash. "Ha! I told you she has brains. I doubt Fenwick would think we'd hide in there. It's also somewhat fortified, no?"

"Well, Fenwick got in, shot Marlowe and me, and stole my research, so I don't think it's too fortified. This is a mistake." His phone rang. "Marlowe?"

"Keep your pants on, darling. By now you know we're holing up at Bay-Gen. Don't fret, dear, some of Sky Warrior's men took care of those unwanted guests behind us, and a team is on-site right now."

"Wait." He sat up and stared at the back of the SUV. "Fenwick had surveillance cameras all over my lab. They're probably still there."

A pause.

"I hadn't thought of that. But your lab was decommissioned so I'm sure everything was cleaned out. Besides, we're not going to your lab."

He glanced at Alexei and back at the SUV. "No? So where then?"

"A couple of my coworkers have secured us an office on the executive floor. Oh, and Bay-Gen had to shut down early today due to a gas leak."

Gas leak? She'd thought of everything. He decided to take Alexei's advice and stop worrying about everything. "It is the perfect place. You're amazing."

"I am, aren't I? Okay, Dr. Roux, we have enough time to drop you off and get you settled."

"Wait, what? You agreed I'm coming to the Arena." His fingers tightened around the phone.

Silence.

"Marlowe?"

"It's too dangerous. Sky Warrior and I agree that you're ... extra baggage. You'll be safer ..."

He put the phone against his chest and turned to Alexei. "She doesn't want me to come. She thinks I'll be in the way." He shook his head. "Not happening. Turn around."

Chapter 30

Lucien sat quietly, keeping an eye on the SUV as Alexei slowed to let them get ahead. When Sky Warrior turned a corner, Alexei screeched the car into a U-turn and sped away toward the Arena.

"Are you sure about this?" He checked the rearview mirror.

"Look, Rock needs to see me or he might panic. I'm useless babysitting my brother at Bay-Gen. Do you disagree?"

"Not at all, my friend. But this will not curry favor with your lady-love."

He turned around. "I'm aware. I don't see the SUV. They're not following us. I appreciate Marlowe's dedication to keeping me safe, but this is about more than only me. I started this and I must end it." He turned back around and looked straight ahead. "It should be me that gives Rock the capsule."

Alexei stayed quiet for a moment. He reached into his coat pocket and took out what looked a lot like a matchbox. "Here it is. I made three, all containing the mustard and salt, in case one isn't enough to induce a strong enough reaction in a Neanderthal." He handed the box to Lucien.

"Thank you. Can I borrow your sunglasses and that weird ascot?"

Without answering, Alexei slipped off the sunglasses that were perched atop his head and untied the blue and white ascot.

They drove on as Lucien worked on an impromptu disguise. He pulled some hair down over his forehead and examined himself in the vanity mirror under the visor. Shampoo had faded his hair to dirty blonde and without shaving, he had a trace of stubble. With the sunglasses on, at first glance, no one should recognize him.

They neared the arena where a crowd of fans wearing team colors had gathered at the gate. He drew in a deep breath, held it, and let it out. The roar of an engine made him spin around in his seat. The SUV zoomed up inches from their rear bumper.

"How the hell did they get here so fast? I thought they were dropping off my brother."

Alexei sped up. Sky Warrior mirrored the speed.

"Oh, dear, I believe we're in trouble, my friend."

"Understatement." Lucien waved, but Marlowe's gesture included a finger that wasn't a return wave. "Slow down and let them pass."

"You read my mind." Alexei decelerated and pulled to the shoulder enough to allow the SUV to zip past. It almost grazed the fender as it swerved in front. "Reckless bastard."

"They're making a point." Lucien prepared for the oncoming dressing down he'd get from Marlowe, but this time, he'd defend his actions rather than simply bow down to her demands. Nobody understood his feelings or how he *had* to be involved. He'd been manipulated like a marionette, with his strings tugged this way and that. He'd had enough.

The SUV slowed as they neared the crowd and pulled in behind a row of parked cars lining the Arena's driveway. Alexei parked behind the SUV and once both vehicles were stopped, Marlowe jumped out, one hand on her hip, the other tapping her thigh. She didn't move toward Lucien but continued her nervous stance. Or was it fury? Hard to tell. Either way, she wasn't happy.

With the matchbox clutched in his hand, he ventured out of the car but didn't approach. "Don't say a thing, Marlowe. I know what I'm doing."

"Do you? Sky Warrior's guys had to fight off your brother's goons and shoot out their tires, flipping the Jeep, which might have killed the occupants. Not that I mind, but we're all risking our lives to keep you safe and then you decide to play hero on your own. Selfish—"

"That's enough!" He glanced around as several fans in the crowd turned and stared. He took one step closer. "I didn't ask to be protected or coddled. You did that on your own. This is my problem and I intend to do what I can to make it right. If you don't like that, then you can turn around and leave."

For once, she was at a loss for words.

Alexei got out of the car and stood between them. "We're here now and we need to proceed with the plan or all of this will be for naught. Lucien will pass the capsules to Rock and the rest of the plan will go like clockwork. It's one small change, my dear, that's all."

Lucien stood his ground. "I'm going to blend with the crowd."

With a twitching lip, she pointed down the street. "The blacked-out van is parked about a quarter mile that way."

"Perfect." He walked off, mingling with the throng.

Through the gates, he saw Carolyn Goodson, the Neanderball PR person. She climbed up the steps to a platform erected in the Arena parking lot and spoke into a microphone at a podium.

"Settle down, settle down! Your Neanderball team players will be here shortly. Please form a single line and do not rush at the stage when the gates are opened." Her eyes darted from side to side. "Open the gates!"

The crowd, totally disregarding what she said, pushed and shoved their way to the platform, shouting and chanting "Bring on the players!" Lucien got trapped between an orange team fan and a blue team fan and was forced forward with the throng. Several people around him were taller, hiding him from view. When the crowd finally settled down and spread out a bit, he had enough room to maneuver closer to one end of the platform. He didn't know where Sky Warrior or Marlowe were but knew they'd be in place to create the distraction when needed.

While Goodson repeated "settle down" about a dozen more times, he took a few shallow breaths, any deeper and he'd inhale too much of the stale sweat from the rabid fans. After a few minutes, a bus drove from behind the Arena and parked about thirty feet from the platform. A couple of minutes after that, the Arena doors opened and a new coach strode out, followed by the players. Rock was last in line, the swelling and bruising of his face mostly faded. He scanned the crowd but apparently didn't see Lucien. Lucien wanted to wave or call out, but he maintained his anonymity and edged a little closer.

The coach took a position with Goodson and motioned to the players, who began a half-hearted exhibition of shoving one another and growling like animals. Rock was ignored. Even his brothers had turned against him, or they were told to shun him. When Goodson stepped down and stood to the side, the coach told the players to go up onto the platform. They complied without any hesitation. They even stopped their previous behavior and stood in a line, staring straight out at the crowd.

Next, Thomas and Jeremy Baker strolled out, with the elder Baker taking the microphone. He grinned and presented the team. "Your Neanderball players!"

Cheers and whoops rose to a near-deafening level and for a moment it sounded like Sky Warrior had begun his assault. Lucien strained to see the platform but was blocked by waving arms and sweaty bodies.

Thomas Baker continued when the noise subsided, "I'm sure you've heard the rumors that Neanderball is going international, and while it's true, these players will return in one month and brand-new players will take their place on the world stage. We have new teams in the works, waiting to be trained by our experienced team!"

The crowd roared and Lucien squeezed through the mob to the side closest to the bus. If another team was ready, it meant Fenwick or Édouard had managed to clone new Neanderthals. And that meant Harmond likely had his Neanderthal soldiers as well.

"Lucien," shouted Alexei from beside him. "Concentrate, my friend, you look miles away."

"Sorry. Did you hear what Baker said?"

"About new Neander boys? Yes, I did. But we can't worry about that now. We've got to get to Rock. Sky Warrior is in place. Be ready. Five minutes. Get your backside to the van as soon as you've completed the mission." Alexei gave him a pat on the arm and slipped away into the crowd.

Lucien closed his eyes for a moment to clear his head, but the continuous din of the mob grew too distracting. He focused on Rock instead and tried to get his attention by sticking a hand in the air. Nobody noticed, not even Rock.

Time seemed to stop. The players made ridiculous poses; some fierce, some goofy. Such a demeaning display. The more he watched, the more he saw how content they appeared enjoying the limelight. Perhaps he got it wrong, and they weren't prisoners after all. But they did deserve the freedom to decide how they wanted to live their lives without Fenwick's control. Then there was Rock. He *had* to escape.

Time slipped by, but when a barrage of gunshots sounded, he sprung to action with the matchbox clutched in his hand. He pushed his way to the platform, but the security detail surrounded the players and began herding them to the bus, while several armed guards rushed toward the shots. An explosion right outside the Arena shook the ground.

Rock stayed the last in line, practically ignored by security as they urged the other players onto the bus. It was now or never. Lucien dashed out and touched Rock on the arm.

He extended his hand. "Rock, chew and swallow these. You'll get sick. We'll get you from the infirmary. Go to the infirmary!"

"Rock understand. You bring Rock raccoon pizza in pills." He smiled.

"Yes. We'll come back for your brothers. But we'll get you first."

Rock grabbed the pills and immediately put them in his mouth. An incredibly angry guard grabbed Lucien from behind and tossed him to the ground. He struggled to get up, but the crowd moved in and tried to get to Rock, trapping Lucien under a stampede of bodies. Someone stepped on his hand, another person tripped over him, and a foot kicked him in the face. Chaos reigned.

Injured and sore, he crawled free of the madness, stood, and looked around. Rock had vomited on three fans, drenching their faces. The pills worked. Baker ordered Rock to the infirmary and directed the bus to drive off. No sign of Sky Warrior or Marlowe, but Alexei paced outside the gate.

The commotion made the perfect cover for a getaway. Lucien took advantage. He rushed through the gate and headed toward his friend who stood beside a beat-up old car. Before he got far, Lucien felt a searing pain rip through his left side. He took a step and collapsed. Alexei rushed beside him within seconds but received a shot by another blast. Several more shots zipped by, striking the old car and two of the tires. They weren't bullets but something strong enough to burn through the metal and human skin.

Alexei shouted, "Get to the van!" Seared fabric clung to his chest where he'd been hit. "Now!"

"Not without you." Lucien managed to get to his feet and help his friend up. "My skin's on fire."

Supporting one another, they shuffled toward the escape van as several more shots screamed overhead.

"Great. One of those bullet things hit the engine." Lucien glanced around. "Who the hell shot at us?"

A truck screeched down the road toward the Arena and skidded to a stop near the van at the same time a black Jeep came through the Arena gates. The driver looked military, but who leaned out the passenger side window holding an odd-looking gun took Lucien by surprise. It was one of the players, wearing a camo ball cap and a frown. The Jeep stopped opposite the truck, trapping Lucien and Alexei between the vehicles. Fenwick hopped out the passenger side of the truck, a pistol with a silencer in her hand. She aimed and pulled the trigger. Alexei screamed out as her bullet burrowed into his right thigh. Lucien felt the full weight of his friend leaning on him. They were helpless and about to die. What the hell happened to Sky Warrior?

Chapter 31

Lucien, barely able to stand, pushed Alexei against the nearest car and glared at Fenwick. She had the chance to kill them both in a second, but she didn't. Instead, she approached.

"You never give up, do you Paleo?" She ordered the driver of the Jeep, "Get that Neanderthal back to the bus. Brutus, don't you dare fire that weapon again. These two are mine. Good shooting by the way."

Alexei whispered, "I have a surprise in my right jacket pocket." His knees gave out and he collapsed.

Lucien dropped down beside him to help, but also to reach into the pocket. His fingers wrapped around a small pistol. He checked to see if Brutus still had the weapon in play, then focused on Fenwick. It was one of those life-or-death moments romanticized in the movies, although this played out in real-time, and it definitely was not romantic. He'd been wounded by one of his Neanderthals.

He'd never been the best shot, especially when shooting blind, but he had to try.

Fenwick took a step closer, her cold eyes showing no emotion. "You can see how those experimental subjects of yours can be trained. They don't belong to you anymore, Paleo. Sad it has to end like this. I've enjoyed our little tap-dance. Édouard will be pleased though. He doesn't like you very much, Paleo."

"I know." Lucien felt for the safety and released it, his finger on the trigger, and moved his hand so the pocket faced Fenwick. "And stop calling me Paleo."

Her lips turned up at the corners and Lucien knew he had to take the shot. He sucked in a breath and pulled the trigger as he exhaled. The gun made more of a pop than a bang, and Fenwick stumbled backward and fell, losing her grip on her gun. He withdrew the gun and aimed at the driver of the Jeep.

"Good man," Alexei rasped.

"Drop the gun or I'll put a bullet in your brain! And tell Harmond he hasn't won yet!" Lucien shouted, his eyes moving from the driver to Fenwick. "Alexei, is she ..."

The driver hesitated for a moment. Brutus sneered and slipped back inside the Jeep. The driver spun around and drove back to the Arena.

Lucien watched Fenwick as she clutched her shoulder and got to her feet. "I think only a silver bullet would kill that one."

"Agreed." Alexei struggled to stand. "I'd like to get my hands on that weapon."

"I'd rather see it destroyed. Did you see Brutus? His loyalty is with the military."

Lucien's pounding heart reminded him he was alive and how much he wanted to stay that way. He had to see Marlowe again. He focused on Fenwick as she rushed to the truck and got in. His vision blurred and his sweaty hands made holding the gun difficult. A shot echoed in his ears and he swayed, no longer sure if his legs still held him upright. Another shot and he closed his eyes. The sound of a car engine echoed in his head, muffled, but distinct. Fenwick got away.

Tires screeched on the pavement.

"Lucien!" Marlowe shouted from somewhere nearby. "Lucien!"

He opened his eyes and felt her arms around him. "Marlowe?"

"Yeah, it's me. What the hell happened here?" She eased him down near unconscious Alexei. "Sky Warrior's man in the crowd said you delivered the package to Rock and then you were shot." She set about evaluating the wound. "That's not a bullet wound. What the hell? Alexei has a bullet wound and has a burn like yours, in his chest though. What's going on? How are you guys alive? We managed to fire a few shots at a truck and chase it away and saw a Jeep heading back to the Arena. Harmond's men I presume."

He accepted a bottle of icy water from Sky Warrior and took a small sip, enough to revive him somewhat. "Thanks. Fenwick's in the truck. The Jeep is with Harmond. One of the players has some kind of weapon that shoots burning rounds or something. He shot me and Alexei. I shot Fenwick, but she's still alive."

Sky Warrior groaned. "Damn. The military is using the Neanderball players? Unbelievable. At least you tried."

Lucien held onto Marlowe and looked around. The truck drove off in the distance. "She escaped."

The crowds near the Arena had dispersed and most people were running to their cars. Several fans who passed screamed and pointed, and one woman shouted for someone to call 911. Marlowe told them to shut up and mind their own business.

"You sure you wounded Fenwick?"

"Of course I am." He half-stumbled to where she'd been standing. "Look. Blood. I told you I shot her."

"Yeah, okay, I believe you." She took the gun from his hand and pressed a towel against his wound. "Alexei got it worse than you. I think his lung collapsed. I don't know any weapon that can burn like that. It's kind of like a cauterized bullet hole."

He stood by helplessly as Sky Warrior's men tended to his friend, skin pale, not moving. "I don't know what it is. It was a gun or something that looked like a gun. But it doesn't fire bullets. Wait. What happened to Rock? He took the capsules."

She pressed her lips together for a moment. "I hate seeing you like this. But we have him. Sami actually came through for once. The distraction worked, except for the part where you and Alexei almost got killed. I told you not to get involved, didn't I?"

"Yes, you did, but you know why I did this." He lowered himself to a crouching position and felt Alexei's forehead. "He's in bad shape." He glanced around. "The van's still here. How did Sami get Rock away?"

Sky Warrior helped him up. "Used her car when she heard the shots. And Alexei won't die. Neither will you if you let us tend to your wound. Rock is on his way to Bay-Gen and I'll get notification once they're secured."

"Tell me, have you ever seen a weapon that can do this?" He lifted his shirt where a seared hole smoldered.

Sky Warrior peered closely. "Maybe. I don't know. Next-gen weapons are being developed, but I've never seen one that can burn a neat hole like that."

Lucien groaned. "As if regular guns aren't bad enough."

Even though the plan had some unexpected consequences, he considered it a success. Mostly. He sat in the passenger seat of Sky Warrior's SUV while Marlowe patched him up. She scolded him again, but rather than feel emasculated, he felt cared for this time. Of course, Fenwick remained on the loose and might go into hiding now. But they had Rock.

After Marlowe jabbed him with a dose of antibiotics, he got up and watched as Sky Warrior himself worked on Alexei. A minute later, the news came that Alexei had to be rushed to the hospital and they loaded him into the rear seat.

Lucien slid in beside his friend. "I'm going with him." He peered into the back expecting to see Édouard hog-tied, but it was empty. "Where's my brother?"

Marlowe fastened his seatbelt. "At the safe house. Bay-Gen."

"Thank you for not ... you know."

"Don't you dare thank me. If not for that ass, none of this would have happened. Keeping him alive is an insult." She straightened, her lower lip quivering like she fought to maintain control. Her tone softened, "I'm really glad you're alive though."

"So am I. We did it. We saved Rock. I hope Fenwick is too busy taking care of her wound to think about the end protocol. I have to see him, to make sure he's okay." He forced a smile and took a deep breath. "But not before getting Alexei medical attention."

"No shit." She got into the passenger seat. "Let's move."

Sky Warrior stuck his hand out the window and made a circular motion. Two other SUVs U-turned and headed down the road ahead. Lucien leaned over and felt Alexei's neck for a pulse. Weak, but he was alive.

"I'm so sorry, Alexei. I should have anticipated we'd be seen. I keep underestimating Fenwick." Sweat dripped from his face. "I'm not feeling so well."

"You were shot with a flame thrower or whatever the hell that was, Lucien. You're not expected to feel well." Marlowe stretched her arm and felt his forehead. "You're feverish." She faced forward. "John, hurry."

Sky Warrior nodded. "Less than ten minutes to the nearest hospital."

The concern in Marlowe's voice made Lucien take a deep breath, wincing as pain shot through his side. She always stayed calm in a crisis, but her sense of urgency was disconcerting. He checked Alexei's condition again. Marlowe had to be worried about him, after all, he had two wounds. A few minutes ticked by and Lucien felt worse. Dizzy, disconnected as everything around him grew muffled and fuzzy. When Fenwick shot him at the lab, it happened so fast he hadn't time to process anything, but now, he felt his body shutting down.

"Lucien. Lucien, talk to me. You're shocky. Don't close your eyes. Hey, listen to my voice."

The fog lifted a bit, although his eyelids were too heavy to comply. He wanted to sleep, close his eyes for a minute. His body shook and he partially roused himself for a moment. Had someone lifted him? He had the vague sensation of movement around him. Silence descended and he felt at peace. Floating in the darkness soothed him, like the gentle caress of a warm blanket. His heartbeat thumped out a rhythm, a soft melody playing just for him. He wanted to stay in the moment and not let go, but a voice pierced his reverie.

"Please wake up, Lucien. Please."

No, he didn't want to.

"Lucien," came a forceful demand.

He surrendered his peace and urged his eyes to open. He lay in a hospital bed, hooked up to machines that clicked and clanked. Marlowe hovered over him and pushed something cold between his lips. He felt like he'd gone back in time.

"Stop trying to spit it out! It's an ice chip." She shoved another one in. "Surgery went great, but ..."

It took a moment to focus clearly on what she said. "Surgery? Alexei's all right then?"

"I'm talking about your surgery. Alexei is still in surgery. That shot to your abdomen shredded part of your spleen, and you had internal bleeding where the flesh didn't cauterize. But you'll recover, sans spleen." She leaned in close and kissed his cheek. "You had me worried."

He took a few breaths. "*I* had surgery?"

"Yes." She spoke slower, "You had your spleen removed. The surgeon said you would have died if we hadn't gotten here in time. Sky Warrior is standing guard and his men are watching the entrances. You're safe. There's a man outside the OR, too."

"Good. And Rock. How is he?" He swallowed and motioned for another ice chip.

"He's fine. I'm told he's watching cartoons on an iPad." She sat in a chair by the bed and dropped an ice chip into his mouth. "I thought I lost you. I don't want to lose you."

"I don't want you to lose me either." He smiled. "I feel pretty good."

"Drugs."

"Well, keep them coming." He smiled again. "I need to go and see Rock and explain everything." He sat up, his head spinning.

"Whoa. Remember, surgery. Splenectomy. You're down for a while." She kissed him again, gently pushed him down, and pulled the sheet up higher. "Rest. I'll be right here."

"I don't want to rest. I told you, I feel good. We have Rock, but we don't have his brothers, and we haven't stopped Harmond. And the end protocol. We're not done."

"You're done. For now. You know, Rock has an iPad. We can video chat directly with him. Sound good?"

He nodded. "Rock really is a twenty-first century Neanderthal. I'm proud of him. He's been through so much, but he never gives up."

She smiled. "Kind of like you." She kissed him again and stood. "I'm going to check on Alexei's progress and arrange for a video chat between you and Rock. You'll be all right?"

"I'm not going anywhere. Where's Alexei? Am I in a hospital?"

"Um, okay then, seems like the meds are really raging. We'll talk when you're a little more lucid."

"*Bien. Je t'aime.*" His tongue felt thick, and his extremities were numb.

Marlowe smiled at him. "All right, Frenchman. I'll see you in a bit. Rest."

She moved through the room in a fluid motion, trails of blue light coming off her as if she were in the rain and her shirt was made of watercolors. Such a beautiful sight, but he didn't want her to leave. As she stepped through the doorway, the light followed her until it dissipated into the air.

He closed his eyes. Everything seemed right in his world and pleasant thoughts of him making a gourmet dinner for Marlowe and Rock filled his head. They were at the table, anxiously waiting for him to deliver the feast. Of course, Rock couldn't drink the wine, too young, so he had a cold glass of milk instead. They were a family.

"Dr. Roux?"

Who intruded on his fantasy?

"Dr. Roux? Can you hear me, it's Sky Warrior."

The family dinner would have to wait. Lucien opened his sleepy eyes. "What?"

"It's Sky Warrior. Mar wants me to give you a message. Hey, can you understand me?" He peered closely. "Your eyes are glassy."

Lucien reached out and pushed him back. "That's because I'm flying on some outstanding medication. Now, what is it you want?"

"Mar wants me to let you know Alexei is out of surgery and in recovery. He should be fine."

"Oh. Good news. So where is *Mar*?"

"She's gone to check on Rock and make sure he's recovered from those pills you slipped him." Sky Warrior patted his shoulder. "You did good."

"Why, *merci*. So did you." He stared at Sky Warrior until his face came fully into focus. "Damn. I think the meds are wearing off. What about Fenwick? Any trace of her?"

A pause.

"My team's out looking for clues. Dr. Roux, there's another reason Mar went to check on Rock."

"Why's that?"

Another pause.

"Perhaps we should talk about this later."

"That's what *Mar* said to me before she left. Tell me." Lucien scooted up in bed and rolled his neck. "I'm awake."

"It's ... it's your brother. He slipped his bindings and attacked my guys."

"You let him get away?" Lucien's heartbeat ticked up a notch. "You have to find him."

"No, listen. He surprised one of my men and smashed him over the head with a glass pitcher. I had two men guarding him and Rock. My other guy reacted as his training taught him, and he opened fire. One bullet struck your brother in the throat and another in the head. I'm sorry, but your brother expired. Mar wants to make sure Rock wasn't traumatized by what he saw."

The words tumbled around, forming sentences Lucien didn't want to hear. He squeezed his eyes shut and tried to create a different scenario, but ultimately, the facts remained. His brother died. If he'd known there was even the slightest chance, he would have said kinder things the last time they were face-to-face, or at least tried to get Édouard back from the brink of self-destruction.

Tears clouded his vision. "You didn't have to be so specific. Where ... is my brother now?"

"He's still at Bay Genetics. We'll treat the body ... we'll treat him with respect, don't worry about that."

Lucien felt a surge of anger directed at Sky Warrior, but it subsided quickly. The fault belonged with Édouard. "I appreciate you telling me. Thank you for taking care of ..." He wiped his tears. "Taking care of his body. And you don't have to worry about Rock. He's a Neanderball player remember."

With a nod, Sky Warrior turned to the door. "I'll continue standing guard and will let you know when Mar ... Marlowe returns. The team uses satellite phones. They're more reliable. Thought you should know." He stepped outside and let the door close behind him.

Lucien wasn't sure why he needed to know about the satellite phones, but it sounded good anyway. He sat up as much as possible and grabbed the TV remote on the bedside table. He pressed the *on* button and scrolled through the channels, hoping for any news about the other players. Were they concerned about Rock? They'd shunned him, so maybe they didn't care, or more likely they'd been conditioned not to care. The most worrying part once Fenwick found out Rock had been kidnapped, again, is if she'd trigger the end protocol. Or maybe she wouldn't now that Édouard had been removed.

He pushed his brother from his mind and found a station with a *special report* banner plastered across the top of the screen and turned up the volume. A raven-haired anchor sat behind a glass-topped desk with a serious expression on her face as a video of the Arena incident played in the left-hand corner. The sound of gunfire, followed by the crowd running in panic, made him flinch. He didn't want to relive it.

The anchor took on a solemn tone, although it appeared a bit overacted, "The melee, credited to Dr. Paleo Roux, a shamed geneticist who has been known to target the players for experimentation, injured star player Rock.

Rock is being treated for his injuries and we're assured that he'll be in fighting shape for the next game. The whereabouts of Paleo Roux are unknown."

Lucien threw the remote across the room, shattering the mirror above a sink. They knew damn well how much he hated the nickname Paleo. Sky Warrior rushed in and looked around.

"Everything okay, Dr. Roux?" He motioned to the mirror. "Should I ask?"

"No." Lucien, now without the remote, pointed to the TV. "Can you shut that thing off please?"

After turning the TV off, Sky Warrior stood by the door. "Marlowe said she'll come right back here once she's sure Rock's okay. Can I ask you something?"

Lucien nodded.

"You and Marlowe. Are you ...?"

"Honestly, I'm not sure. I think I drive her crazy." He slumped against the pillow. "She deserves better than me."

Sky Warrior gazed out the window from across the room. "She deserves better than either of us. But she cares for you. I see it in her eyes. She never looked at me the way she looks at you." He placed a hand on the doorknob. "Treat her well, will you?"

"I'm not sure I'm the one for her, John. I have a dark cloud hovering over my head and it throws a shadow over her when she's around me. What would you do in my position?" He felt a strange friendship with Sky Warrior, maybe because they both loved the same woman or because they were both in the proverbial trenches together.

"I'd hold her tight and let her know how much she means to me. Then I'd make it clear that if she wants to leave, I wouldn't try to stop her."

Lucien sighed. That wasn't the advice he wanted to hear. He'd expected more of an ego boost like *of course you two are meant to be together* or *you're a good man and deserve a woman like her.* "What if she leaves?"

Sky Warrior shrugged and left the room, leaving Lucien alone with his thoughts. He closed his eyes and tried to doze, but Sky Warrior's voice questioning someone in the hallway put an end to his attempt. The fight-or-flight response kicked in, but he wasn't able to sit up, let alone run. He listened and realized a nurse wanted to get in. The door opened and a middle-aged woman in blue scrubs walked in. She glanced back at Sky Warrior, who stood in the doorway staring at her.

"It's okay," Lucien said.

"I'll be right here if you need me." Sky Warrior closed the door.

The nurse approached the bedside and motioned to the door. "Your security guy is intense."

"Yes, he is. Oh, do you have any news on my friend, Alexei Ozerov?"

She shook her head. "That's not the … you were brought in with a man named Ivan Volcov. Is that the man you mean?"

Damn. He'd forgotten about Alexei's fake IDs. "Yes, I'm sorry, I had my other friend on my mind. How is Ivan doing?"

"We got a briefing that he's in recovery and semi-conscious. He hit on one of the lab techs, so there's that." She checked the IV drip. "You understand you had a splenectomy?"

"I do." He smiled at the thought of Alexei feeling well enough to seek out a new companion. "Can you tell Ivan that I'll visit him as soon as I can?"

"That won't be for at least twenty-four hours." Satisfied with the IV, she examined a monitor. "We'll be drawing some labs on you to make sure there's no infection."

"Okay. Thank you."

"Is there anything you need? I can bring you juice or Jell-O. Bedpan?"

He shook his head. "No, I'm good."

"All right. I'll be back to check on you in an hour. And the lab tech should be here in a few minutes." She smiled. "I know you. You're the Neaderball guy. My kids love that game. It's too violent for me, but they eat it up."

He held his tongue and simply smiled.

She turned and left.

Sky Warrior poked his head in. "No word yet from Mar. It's not like her to miss a check-in."

"So, what does that mean? Is everything okay? Should we …?"

"You won't do anything, Dr. Roux. I'll make contact and let you know the status." He ducked back into the hallway.

Naturally, something would go wrong. He felt the bandages over his incision and pressed gently. It didn't hurt much at all. In fact, most of his left side was numb. He eased himself up but instantly felt dizzy and lay back down. He'd become useless.

A few minutes went by before Sky Warrior strode into the room, his face set in a frown. "Dr. Roux, I can't reach my men or Marlowe. I even tried Sami. We were never on radio silence, so this is a problem."

"Totally agree it's a problem. What are you going to do about it? I can't move so I can't help. You have to do something."

"I've sent a backup team to Bay Genetics to reconnoiter. They'll arrive in under five minutes. Hold tight." He spun around, phone in hand, and strode back out.

Lucien glared at the closed door. "Yeah, I'll hold tight. What else would I do?"

He massaged his forehead as a tension headache grew. What if Rock escaped and they were all in pursuit? But that scenario didn't explain why Sami couldn't be reached.

"Sky War ... John!"

Sky Warrior barged in, scanning the room with his hand on a holster beneath his jacket. "What?"

"This is Sami's doing, isn't it? She's working with Fenwick."

With a furrowed brow, Sky Warrior approached the bed. "I vetted her myself. She has no ties to Fenwick or the Bakers. I've known her for years."

"Then why can't you reach her? You don't think it's a bit strange that everyone, including her, is unreachable? If she's hurt Marlowe, so help me—."

"Stop right there, Dr. Roux," his voice changed, loud and stern. He checked his watch. "My backup team should be reporting in soon. Let's wait before drawing any unfounded conclusions."

"I hope they're unfounded." Lucien lay down again because his head throbbed. "This can't be happening. We had Rock."

Sky Warrior pulled up a chair and sat beside the bed. "I'll personally take care of Sami if she's double-crossed me." His face looked like an angry statue. He gripped his satellite phone and stared at the wall across the room.

Rather than look at Sky Warrior, Lucien turned enough to see through the window and wanted more than anything to be out of the hospital where he'd do some good. His daydream shattered when the phone chirped.

"Report." Sky Warrior listened for a moment, stood, and paced. He hung up and shook his head. "Not good. There's no body, no blood. The room has been cleaned."

"What the fuck, John." Lucien tried to get up but fell back against the pillows. "You're supposed to be a professional. How did you let this happen?"

Silence.

Someone knocked on the door and Sky Warrior aimed his gun. Lucien automatically shrunk down as far as he could into the bed. Another knock. The door opened, but no one entered. Sky Warrior stayed near the door, waiting. A second later, an arm appeared with a pistol aimed straight ahead. Sky Warrior leaped to action, grabbed the arm, and wrestled the gun away. He tugged and Sami flew into the room and slid across the floor.

Chapter 32

I f Lucien had a gun, he would have shot Sami before she had the chance to stand. Sky Warrior was prepared though and had his gun pointed directly at her head as she looked up at him. She held her hands out in surrender. Lucien glared. She didn't deserve mercy after what she'd done.

"Shoot her," he said, then reconsidered. "No wait. Where's Marlowe?"

Sami turned and looked at Lucien. "What? I didn't do anything to her."

Sky Warrior took a step toward her. "You didn't answer your phone."

She continued, "They seized my phone."

"What? How?" Lucien managed to sit up without feeling dizzy.

"I stood guard at the front desk at Bay Genetics like I was supposed to. Marlowe came and said she was informed by you, John, that Roux's brother was killed and one of the team was injured. After she went upstairs, two businessmen entered the lobby. My cover as a security guard meant I had to check them in, but ..." She paused. "Can I get up now?"

Sky Warrior backed away but didn't take his eyes off her.

She got up and stood against the far wall near the window. "One of the guys pulled a gun, took my sat phone and sidearm, and bound me with zip ties."

Lucien shook his head. It sounded like a replay of what happened when Fenwick originally stole his research and left him for dead. "You're lying."

"I'm not." She held out her red wrists. "I know I'm not trusted by either of you, but I'm telling you the truth. After I was trussed like a holiday turkey, two other guys came and went up to the safe room. No more than fifteen minutes later, down came Marlowe, Rock, and your brother, very much alive. It seems your guys are traitors, John."

Sky Warrior lowered the gun. "What are you talking about?"

She shook her head and looked at the floor. "Your guys that were supposed to guard Roux's brother and Rock came down with guns on Marlowe and Rock. They had Rock in a straitjacket thing. They gave Roux's brother a gun. They're working for Roux's brother."

"Wait a minute." Lucien mentally sorted through everything. "My brother's alive? Why did they say he died?"

She focused on Lucien. "To get Marlowe. Your brother wanted to get his hands on her to punish you. While I was tied behind the desk, I heard him say that he's glad Fenwick insisted on implanting a tracking chip in his arm and that now you'd suffer since he had Marlowe. I think they left me alive so I'd tell you about it. Rock's pissed and kept saying he'd pound them into the ground. I'm sorry, John. I would have put a bullet between their eyes if I could."

Lucien lay back, overwhelmed, and closed his eyes. Not only was Rock captured again, but Édouard had Marlowe. "I'm ashamed to say I mourned my brother when I thought he died." He opened his eyes and drew in a breath. "What now? What do we ... what can we ... there has to be something we can do."

"Give me a minute." Sky Warrior slipped his gun into the holster and paced, keeping a watchful eye on Sami. "All right. At the moment, the only people I trust are in this room. Dr. Roux, I'll need you to be our central command since you can't be in the field. Sami, I need you to remember everything you saw and heard. If Mar knew you were listening, she would have given a clue."

The door swung open and a young man in white scrubs came in. Both Sami and Sky Warrior were on him before Lucien had the chance to stop them. With a gun pressed against his cheek, the lab tech dropped his plastic tray filled with vials and syringes and screamed. The vials skittered across the floor.

Lucien waved his hand. "He's the lab guy, here to draw blood."

"Oh." Sky Warrior holstered the gun again. "Carry on."

The lab tech, visibly shaken judging by the ashen skin tone and trembling hands, attempted to pick up the vials, but kept dropping them with his shaky hands. "I ... have to get sterile ... vials. Can I ... what's going on?"

"We're security, that's all you need to know." Sami motioned for him to leave.

More than willing, the tech left his supplies and scurried from the room.

"I appreciate your alertness, but this *is* a hospital." Lucien sighed. "Let's continue the planning."

Sami rounded up the empty vials and deposited them into the plastic basket. She stopped and examined a small, glass bottle. "He came here to draw blood?"

Lucien nodded. "Yes, why?"

She held the bottle between her fingers. "Unless you were getting Botox injections, he came here to poison you."

"I don't understand." Lucien peered at the bottle when she came close. "*Clostridium botulinum*. Wait, botulism?"

Sky Warrior took the bottle. "Unbelievable."

"Sorry, dude. Looks like somebody wants to make sure you don't recover." Sami seemed sincere in her sympathy. "Your brother, I presume."

"I'm getting used to it." Lucien withdrew the IV from his arm. "I'm not taking any chances."

"Dr. Roux, you're just out of surgery." Sky Warrior took the dripping tube. "Then again, better safe than sorry." He wound it around the IV pole. "All right, it's obvious one of us has to stay with you. Sami?"

She nodded. "I think that's best. Marlowe might react like you did if she saw me. Providing she's still alive. Sorry."

Lucien pressed the sheet against his arm to stop the drops of blood that seeped from the site. "Someone has to watch Alexei as well."

"I'll arrange for him to be brought in here." Sky Warrior glanced at Sami and marched from the room.

She sat in the chair by the bed. "Dr. Roux, we got off on a bad note." She extended her hand. "I will do everything possible to keep you safe."

He shook her hand. "Thank you. And please accept my apologies. I'm more than a little distrustful of people these days."

"Understood."

"So, do you recall anything Marlowe said on her way out of Bay-Gen?" He mentally had his fingers crossed.

"Not really. Rock was the vocal one. He said something about the bad lady taking him to get raccoon pizza. I did hear Marlowe mumble that she hoped they got the door fixed. Any idea what that means?"

Lucien smiled. "Yes, I do. They're going to the motel. Get Sky Warrior!"

She got up and peeked out the door. "He's coming." She waved.

"What's going on?" Sky Warrior burst into the room as Sami shut the door. "Problem?"

"Not at all." Lucien motioned to Sami. "She saved the day. They're taking Rock and Marlowe to the motel we went to when we kidnapped Rock."

"You sure?" Sky Warrior checked his watch. "I know where it is. I can get a team in assault position within the hour."

"An hour?" Lucien shook his head. "That's too long."

"Dr. Roux, I can't trust some of my team. I'll handpick only those I know won't betray me. That takes time to rally them together and bring them here."

"Oh. And that'll take an hour?" He glanced at Sami, who nodded.

Sky Warrior paced. "At least an hour. I have a small unit on maneuvers in Bakersfield. By copter, they can be here in half an hour or so. But we need more firepower. Hold tight." He glanced at Sami and went into the hallway.

"John knows what he's doing, Dr. Roux. An op like this takes precision. It's best to take the time necessary to make it a successful mission." She raised an eyebrow. "Right?"

"I know you're right, but an hour is a long time not knowing what's happening to Marlowe and Rock."

"Trust me, Marlowe's tough. She can take whatever they throw at her and then some. We may not see eye-to-eye, but I respect the hell out of her." She checked her watch, an identical one to Sky Warrior's.

A moment later, Sky Warrior opened the door and held it while an orderly wheeled in Alexei's bed, raised so he sat upright. He had pale skin, but otherwise looked ready for a dinner party. His hair had been combed and he wore a red silk dressing gown with a matching ascot. Lucien smiled, wondering how he'd managed that.

"Ah, Lucien, my friend. It's good to be bunkmates with you. How are you feeling?"

"Evidently not as good as you." Lucien kept smiling. "Who did you sweet talk to get that?"

"Not important." His face softened. "I understand Marlowe and Rock have been taken. We'll get them back. I've called Vitaly and he's rounding up some rather unsavory types to help out. Fenwick and her ilk will be in serious trouble."

"What about Édouard? He's the one responsible for this." Lucien slumped.

"Don't worry, my friend, we'll do what we can, but the outcome is up to him."

Lucien nodded. Édouard had compromised their familial ties for the last time and as hard as it was, those ties were about to be cut.

Once the orderlies left, Sky Warrior finished a phone call and gave a thumbs-up. "All set. My tac team is on the way. Our checkpoint's Terminal 1 at Oakland International Airport." He reached under his jacket, pulled out a gun, and handed it to Sami. "Here's your gun back, and a new sat phone. Hold the line if the enemy infiltrates, and SOS if you need to."

Alexei whispered to Lucien, "I love this military jargon. Perhaps I should have enlisted."

"I don't think the uniforms would suit you." Lucien motioned to Sami. "She's turned out to be a benefit."

"Agreed. This might help to mend broken fences between her and Ms. Dunham."

"One can hope." He watched as Sami and Sky Warrior synchronized their watches and high-fived.

Sky Warrior stopped in the doorway. "Stay safe, Dr. Roux. Sami will get intel as we collect it."

"Okay. Thank you." His gut tightened. They were ready with a rescue operation that had every chance of going wrong. In other words, a normal day.

Sky Warrior left and Sami, with sat phone and gun in hand, stood beside the door. No one said a thing for what seemed like forever. Lucien took several deep breaths and rolled his neck a few times.

He let out a sigh. "Alexei, Rock sent us a message where he'd be. His intellect is incredible. If we fail, he'll be treated like an oddity and condemned to a life of misery. How do I live with this?"

"My friend, you're doing the self-pity thing again. It's most undignified and somewhat off-putting. We all make mistakes, but we learn not to make those same mistakes. You've learned, so stop this constant self-deprecation." Alexei turned to Sami. "Tell him."

She took a step away from the door and shrugged. "He's not wrong. Look what I did to Marlowe, and yet here I am, doing my part to help her. I know what you did, Dr. Roux, and I know why. You had good intentions, but you were blindsided by your brother of all people. You hadn't considered all of the possible variables, especially betrayal, and that's on you. But you didn't act out of malice and that's what counts. We'll get Rock back, and Marlowe."

He wanted to believe her, to trust that everything would work out, but with the constant problems that popped up, staying optimistic got harder and harder. "Well, I will agree that I have learned not to tamper with cloning Neanderthals ever again."

"There ya go." Sami smiled and peeked out the door. "All's clear."

He closed his eyes and tried to relax.

More time passed when finally, her phone chirped. "Sami here." She listened and nodded a few times. "Roger that." She put the phone away. "Sky Warrior is at the checkpoint. He'll call again after the rendezvous with the rest of the team. The mission's a go."

It sounded like they were at war. Well, in a way they were. Édouard's cruelty in faking his death was unforgivable. It didn't matter to him who he hurt, so long as he got what he wanted. He'd always been a conniving boy growing up, pushing his way into conversations that didn't concern him, cheating on his exams in school, and openly criticizing anything Lucien did.

"I think I hate my brother," he mumbled.

Alexei leaned over and patted him on the arm. "About time, my friend. Family is a genetic construct, that's all. You, better than anyone, should know that. It doesn't mean family must be devoted to one another. In the animal kingdom, some parents eat their young."

Lucien stared. "Damn, Alexei."

With a snicker, Sami agreed, "I wish my parents had eaten my sister. My whole family is dysfunctional. My older sister is an addict and my parents have enabled her since her teenage years. She's stolen from them more than once. But they still give her money and pay for motel rooms. I kept telling them to cut her off, but instead, they sent *me* to a shrink when I was a teenager. He told me that I have an attachment disorder. I call bullshit because I *can* form relationships, but not with shitheads. But what do I know?"

Lucien glanced at Alexei and back at Sami. She'd revealed a lot about herself, personal things, which meant she'd become comfortable enough to open up. He knew he could trust her.

After Sami's revelation, a hush fell over the group. Alexei turned on the TV and found an old western movie that he seemed to enjoy, and Lucien had a visit from the nurse, under Sami's constant scrutiny. She interrogated the nurse about the lab tech, but the nurse claimed he hadn't come to the room yet. No real surprise since they all knew he wasn't a real hospital employee.

Time crept on until Sami finally received a call from Sky Warrior. She kept the phone to her ear and announced, "They're in position. There are three blacked-out vehicles around the rear of the motel and two more at the front. The desk clerk gave up the info, eventually. Two adjoining rooms are occupied."

Lucien wiped his palms on the bed sheet and waited. The air in the room felt charged as if a bolt of lightning would strike at any second. "Sami."

She put her finger to her lips.

Turning to Alexei, he whispered, "This is killing me."

"Patience."

Time stopped. Sami eventually hung up the phone and shook her head.

"What?" Lucien would have jumped up if he had the strength. "What happened?"

She stood between the beds. "Neither Rock nor Marlowe is there, just the thugs who came to Bay Genetics. Sky Warrior is questioning them."

"Oh, for fuck's sake." He slammed his fist onto the mattress. "Where are they?"

The next second, the door opened and two large, ski mask-wearing goons stomped in. One grabbed Sami, unarmed her, and had her wrists zip-tied within seconds. The other stood by the door with an automatic weapon in his hand, pointing down, but still intimidating. The next person through the door made him cower into his pillows. Fenwick, wearing her trademark suit that seemed a size too small, closed the door behind her.

"We need to talk, Paleo," she said, her cold eyes focused directly on him.

Chapter 33

Lucien glanced at Alexei and noticed him visibly bristle. Neither of them could do a single thing, and with Sami out of commission, they were at Fenwick's mercy, not that she had an ounce of mercy in her.

"What have you done with Marlowe and Rock, you twisted bitch?" He forced himself upright regardless of a shock of pain that stabbed at him in his side. "If only my bullet had managed to crack your head open."

"Oh, now, Paleo, is that any way to greet a visitor? Your aim is lousy, the bullet only grazed my shoulder." She sidled up to Sami. "This one I don't know."

Sami glared. "Unbind me and I'll be happy to introduce myself."

Fenwick laughed. "You continually surprise me with your circle of rough friends, Paleo. But I'm not here to discuss your friends, I'm here to discuss your brother."

"My brother is a back-stabbing piece of shit."

"Yes, I know. And that brings me to my proposition." She stood at the foot of his bed and glanced at Alexei. "Alexei Ozerov, you little pickle dick. You won't die, will you? I'll get back to you." She looked at Lucien again. "Now, to business. Édouard isn't playing by the rules. He's holding Rock hostage and dealing directly with Harmond. And I'm sure you know that the end protocol can't be triggered anymore, so there's little I can do."

Alexei groaned. "What *are* you talking about, you insidious thing?"

"Well, I wasn't addressing you for starters, but since you need to be spoken to like a three-year-old, I'll slow down." She pulled up a chair and sat. "Paleo, your kid brother is a fumbling moron, but he does have my client's property, and that creates a delicate issue for me. If my clients aren't happy, I risk losing my stellar reputation. Little Eddie tried to off you and failed, and now wants me to deliver you in exchange for Rock."

Lucien glanced at the door, hoping security, a doctor, or a nurse would barge in. When they didn't, he shook his head, realizing he had nothing to bargain with. "Why not kill me and send my corpse to my brother? You've been trying to kill me since this started. Alexei and I are here because of you."

"Yes, yes, I shot dear Alexei, but he deserved it. A little payback. Besides, Paleo, I told you if you play ball, excuse the pun, we can all get along swimmingly. That incident at the Arena you cooked up was fairly well executed, but you ended up here, so it wasn't your best work. Harmond's toy soldiers came after you with an experimental weapon and cooked your innards, am I right?" She paused for a moment and continued, "You shot me, Paleo, so I think that makes us even for shootings. Anyway, your baby brother wants you alive. If you ask me, it's because he wants to make you watch him torture the cutie before he finishes you. He's a sicko."

"You're a fine one to talk. You set me up, ruined my career and my life, tried to kill me, tried to kill my friends, and now you're going to deliver me to my brother. Who's the true sicko?" He hoped that if he goaded Fenwick into killing him, Édouard might no longer need to hold onto Marlowe. It would be the only acceptable scenario at this point.

"Water under the bridge. Here's a shocker, Paleo. Listen carefully as I don't like to repeat myself. I have no intention of delivering you to Édouard. He crossed a line and tried to change my rules mid-stream. The Neanderthals are proprietary and for him to muck around like this, well, as I said, he crossed a line." She leaned back in the chair and crossed her stubby legs. "I'm here to offer you a deal. I know you're working with Sky Warrior and his team."

"Jesus. Is there anything you don't know?"

"No interrupting, Paleo. Édouard's tracking chips are all gone and he must have removed Rock's because I can't locate him. I intend to capture him and ... have a long talk with him about his misguided attempt to manipulate me. And that brings us to the crux of my proposition." She leaned forward. "You're his brother. You have insight into his deviously rotten mind better than I do. I want you to figure out where he's hiding, in exchange for your life and the lives of your family and off-color friends. My team will work with Sky Warrior to extract the little shit and make sure Rock isn't harmed. Oh, and the cutie will be saved, too."

Even considering making a deal with Fenwick made Lucien's skin crawl, but what choice did he have? If there was even a small chance that Marlowe and Rock would survive, he had to take it. "Rock deserves his freedom. That's all I want for him. He doesn't want to play Neanderball. And what can you do about Harmond and the military using Neanderthals? If you won't let Rock go and can't stop Harmond, no deal."

"Paleo."

"No deal."

She sighed. "The military deal is done. My lab rats have recreated the cloning technology and the Bakers have the rights to the same enhanced tech. There is nothing I can do about that. What I'm offering is to save Rock and the cutie. If your brother sells Rock to Harmond, which he's threatening to do, then the proprietary data I referred to will be in the hands of the military. They can reverse engineer the enhancements. My clients don't want anyone else cloning Neanderthals. Take it or leave it." She stood and turned toward the door.

What should he do? He was about to make a deal with the devil, and not for everything he wanted.

Alexei spoke up, "Ms. Fenwick, you have been a dastardly adversary and have caused my dear friend Lucien more trouble than he deserves. We can live with saving Ms. Dunham and Rock. As a collector, you understand the nuance of keeping secrets and avoiding having secrets of your own."

She straightened and turned around.

He continued, "You have a secret. Lucien and I know that secret. I want your assurance that you will honor your promise not to come for us, Rock, Ms. Dunham, Lucien's family, or Sky Warrior ever again. Not just now, but in perpetuity. If you try, I have arranged it so news of your brother will be spread upon the wind where it will be dispersed throughout the circles where you operate. You'll be done."

Lucien added, "Honor among criminals. Bring me Marlowe and Rock." He had an idea brewing, but he needed Rock.

Fenwick's mouth twitched. "You drive a hard bargain, but I'm not unreasonable. You can have Rock, but he's never to speak publicly about anything. Hide him away and the deal will be set." She reached into her jacket pocket and brought out a phone. "Contact me with positive news about your brother's whereabouts." She tossed it onto Lucien's bed.

Fenwick's goon released Sami, but didn't unbind her, and opened the door.

Fenwick smiled a greasy smile, stared at Lucien, and left.

The room fell silent for a moment and a shiver went through him. "I truly hope I never see that woman after this. Sami, are you okay?"

She nodded and wriggled her hands for a bit until she had the zip-ties loose. "Idiots used cheap plastic ties."

"Lucien, dear friend, once we have Ms. Dunham and that sweet Neander-boy, you can resume your boring, suburban life with no worry about Fenwick." Alexei smiled. "All will be well."

Lucien smiled as well. "I need Rock so I can run some tests."

"What the hell?" Sami stomped over to the bed. "I thought you wanted him free?"

"I do." He frowned. "You didn't let me finish. If I can prove he has the fatal cancer gene, that means his brothers do, too. They can't play Neanderball if they're sick. They'll all be released. And that means the military will have to abandon their cloning project as well."

"Can't they simply remove the gene?" Alexei eased himself onto his elbow.

"I doubt it. I never planned on figuring out how to remove the gene. It would take years and the bad press would bring too much heat on Harmond. I set my research to test if their stem cells had the ability to battle the cancer gene, but I never had the chance to test the subjects. I mean, the boys. My DNA, the portion with the gene, is combined into their DNA. And there's something else."

"Go on, my friend. I do so enjoy watching your mind work."

"It's a popular acceptance now that Neanderthals are *Homo neanderthalensis*, a step away from *Homo sapiens sapiens*. I ran into this issue when I set up my experiment. They're a *Homo* genus, which makes experimentation on them a gray area since they're extinct. Were extinct. But we can now use that to counteract the military's stance that they're not human. Using non-humans as expendable personnel is their entire agenda."

"Wow." Sami went to the window and looked out. "You're actually responsible for bringing these guys into this world to experiment on them. That's a dick move."

"You sound like Marlowe. I'd only use embryonic stem cells, Sami, not fetal tissue." He glanced at Alexei. "Does every woman hate me?"

He laughed. "Not at all. Women are simply smarter than us."

"You got that right." Sami spun around. "So, where do you think your brother is hiding?"

"Um." He thought for a moment. "He'd need to be somewhere isolated, but defensible. When he had me kidnapped, he'd commandeered an entire block of vacant model homes. He's a creature of habit and not the brightest."

"Don't underestimate him, he did create Neanderball and sell your research to the military." Alexei motioned to Sami. "What's the time, dear?"

She pointed to the wall clock.

Lucien squinted. "Four. Is that a.m. or p.m.? I've lost all track of time."

"It's a.m." Sami took the phone Fenwick gave him. "One number in the contacts. Fenwick, I presume."

"All right, so we know the logistics of what Édouard needs, but now I have to figure out his mindset." Lucien took a sip of water from the cup on the nightstand. "He wouldn't go too far, but the Bay Area is packed with plenty of hiding places. He wouldn't go back to Davis because I burned that location when I escaped. Édouard always liked the comforts of home. The house he chose in Davis was a lot like the one we grew up in. After he finished his schooling, he returned to our vineyard because, he claimed, of homesickness and that he missed the French countryside. He's on the run now and must know that Fenwick is coming for him. He needs to feel safe, in familiar territory. I think I know where he'll be. If I'm right, he'll be holed up in a French-owned vineyard near the Bay Area."

"You're sure?" Alexei raised an eyebrow. "Not that I'm doubting your fraternal knowledge, but we must be certain."

"Not a hundred percent, but mostly sure. He's not comfortable here, but he is comfortable around vines and probably has a connection to a French family that owns a vineyard. I know my brother, he's insecure on his own. My father would know all vineyards around here, especially French-owned."

"But we don't have your father." Alexei sighed. "To the internet!"

Sami handed Lucien the phone. "Here. Find us that vineyard."

After connecting to the hospital's Wi-Fi, Lucien began a search that brought up pages of wineries, but he narrowed the search to French-owned and got three hits. One in Cupertino, one in Napa Valley, and one in Walnut Creek. Process of elimination; Walnut Creek and Napa Valley were further away than Cupertino. He dialed the number and waited.

"Welcome to *Maison de Vin,* fine dining with sommelier-chosen accompanying wines. Our business hours are ten a.m. to five p.m. for wine tasting and eleven a.m. to ten p.m. for dining in our three Michelin-star restaurant. Please contact us during business hours for reservations. *Bienvenue à la maison.*"

He hung up. "That's it. *Maison de Vin.* Welcome home, Édouard." He dialed Fenwick's number in the contacts.

She answered right away, "That was fast, Paleo."

"You were right, I know my brother. And stop calling me Paleo."

"Fine, fine. Address?"

He gave her the address. "If he is there ... what are you going to do to him?"

"Do you care?"

He did, but not as much as before. "It's more curiosity."

"Let's see how this progresses and I'll be in touch. Tell Sky Warrior the meeting point is Ortega Park in Cupertino in twenty minutes." She hung up.

He motioned to Sami. "I don't know Sky Warrior's number. Can you call him? The meet is at Ortega Park. Cupertino. Twenty minutes."

She took the phone and made the call.

"Lucien, you remain the lovely young man I knew all those years ago." Alexei laughed. "It's in your blood."

"What is?"

"The penchant for using that wonderful mind of yours for less-than-scientific endeavors."

He did get a certain satisfaction from working outside of his normal boundaries. "I never said I didn't enjoy it." He smiled. "I'll enjoy it less though if something happens to Marlowe or Rock."

"Agreed. So shall I."

Sami finished the call and shrugged. "All set. Sky Warrior is on board, no questions asked."

"Well, my dear," Alexei started. "That's because he's on my payroll and has a sizable retainer to burn through."

Lucien gazed out the window as the dawn gently turned the sky from black to a soft orange. He shifted in the bed but couldn't get comfortable. Anything might go wrong. Absolutely anything. Two of Sky Warrior's men had been compromised, Fenwick wasn't trustworthy, and Marlowe's and Rock's lives hung in the balance. Still, it felt good to be actively involved rather than being constantly threatened, chased, and shot. Alexei had it right, intrigue was in his blood.

He wanted to hold Marlowe in his arms again. It seemed so long ago since he'd seen her, and he planned to apologize profusely for everything. Maybe even convince her to move to France and replant the vineyard, with the two of them sharing a dinner table with his family, *sans* Édouard.

When Sami announced the twenty minutes were almost up, Lucien gulped the rest of the water and took a deep breath. The next half hour or so was critical. Nobody spoke. All heads turned when someone knocked on the door. The nurse entered.

She frowned and stood aside with the door open.. "You have visitors. It's not visiting hours, but I was told to let them in. I don't care if someone is a celebrity or not, hospital rules are hospital rules. Everyone should obey them."

In walked Thomas Baker, the owner of the Neanderball team, and his son Jeremy. Lucien stared. What now?

Chapter 34

Thomas Baker took a few steps, paused, and walked in a bit further. Something about his demeanor was unthreatening, a change from the usual people Lucien encountered. Instead of barking orders or gloating, Baker looked at him with eyes dark from lack of sleep, or worry. Hard to tell which.

Baker motioned for his son to wait by the door. "Dr. Roux, you know who I am?"

"I do." He glanced at Alexei and back at Baker. "What is it you want?"

With a slow gait, Baker got closer and lowered his voice. "I know what Beatrix has done to you, in my name, and for that, I apologize. Another man pulled the strings, and he suggested I get involved with using Neanderthals for sport. At first, I wasn't aware of your involvement, but I soon learned."

"But that didn't stop you, did it?" Alexei interrupted.

A long pause.

"No, it didn't. Neanderball took off and, well, you know." Baker looked at his son. "Neanderball is supposed to be my legacy to pass to my son."

Lucien had heard enough of the false sorrow. "My life is ruined. My friend and I have been shot, my girlfriend has been kidnapped, oh, and the "other man" involved is my damn brother. Your apology should be made to the Neanderthals you keep as prisoners. They are innocent and don't belong in the twenty-first, let alone playing a stupid game."

"You're right, but here we are." Baker sat and stared at his lap. "They're sick, Dr. Roux. At first, broken bones wouldn't heal, and then they said their joints hurt. Their bones snap like twigs. Two have heart murmurs and one of them is on a special diet or he gets violently ill. Every one of them is having problems. They're so much worse now. What's happening? I know you had something to do with Rock being abducted, again. He puked all over everyone."

Sami ambled over. "I'm the one who got Rock out of the Arena. He was only sick for an hour."

"An hour?" Lucien looked at Alexei. "I was sick for days."

"Anyway," Baker continued, "The others are still sick. The team doctor is running tests, but he thinks they might have ..."

"Cancer," Lucien finished the sentence.

Baker's eyes widened. "How did you know?"

He shook his head. "They have a faulty gene. They weren't meant to survive past the embryonic stage, and especially not as adults. The rapid development has had detrimental effects as well."

"That's why I'm here, Dr. Roux. I need you to fix them." Baker reached under his jacket and pulled out a checkbook. "Name your price."

"You are truly amazing." Lucien rubbed his forehead.

"Thank you."

"Not a compliment. You want a miracle cure so your game can continue to make you obscene amounts of money. Do I have that correct?"

"Ah, well, I want the players healthy, of course." Baker wriggled in the chair.

"Even after what I told you, you still want Neanderball to be a thing. They will die, Mr. Baker. A horrible, slow death. Being eaten away from the inside. You can't stop it. I can't stop it." He closed his eyes and thought of Rock suffering. "You can't grow a person in a few months and expect their bodies to be normal. You've had them putting extreme stress on their skeletal system and now they're failing. I can't do anything."

"You're not even going to try?"

Lucien opened his eyes. "Mr. Baker, why do you think I cloned Neanderthals in the first place? Do you have any idea? Didn't Fenwick mention my research?"

"I asked her when I found out she'd stolen your research. She said you wanted to see if it was possible. You know, for a theme park or movie or something."

"No, this wasn't some grand idea for a movie. And my brother involved you as a way of discrediting me."

Jeremy Baker stepped away from the door. "Wait, your brother did this to you? That's messed up, man."

"Understatement of the century." Alexei struggled a bit to sit up. "I've made a significant amount of money off your game, but only because I'm a greedy man and enjoy life's luxuries. I will gladly donate it all to cancer research. Will you do the same?"

Thomas Baker stood. "Ah, we've made billions."

"As I thought." Alexei slumped back on the pillows. "I may be greedy, but I have morals."

"Thank you, Alexei." Lucien focused on Baker again. "Is there anything else?"

"Well, I believe Beatrix is involved with the enhanced cloning. Are they going to get sick, too?"

"Most likely." Lucien pointed to the door. "I think you should go now."

Jeremy Baker opened the door. "I know the players. They're my friends. I taught them to play catch and play video games when they weren't practicing. They're pretty good, especially Rock. He likes to watch baseball and play video games. I don't want them to die, Dr. Roux."

"Neither do I." Lucien's whole body felt heavy, like it was burrowing into the mattress. So much death and sorrow, for what? He hadn't accomplished a single thing and had only hurt everyone around him. If they did get Rock away safely, he'd at least live what life he had left in peace and freedom. "Please leave."

With a hand on the door, Thomas Baker looked at him. "I am sorry, Dr. Roux." He turned and left, followed by his son.

"Assholes." Sami glanced at the sat phone. "We should hear something soon. John said he'll call as soon as they're ready to breach."

"Okay." He turned to Alexei. "I want to go back in time and stop all of this."

"I understand, my friend. But if you did that, you'd never have known what a wonderful person Rock is. I, for one, am glad to have known him."

"Of course, I am, too, but it hurts so much knowing what's in store for him. This cancer doesn't usually show up until much later, which means the acceleration I did, or rather Fenwick did, must have kicked it into high gear. I've killed them before they ever really lived."

"In some roundabout way, it's a blessing in disguise. You said it yourself. They don't belong here. This is nature's way of fixing that."

"It's not nature, Alexei, it's me. I did it. How can I explain this to Rock? How?"

Alexei shook his head. "I do not know. But you'll think of something. Sit the boy down, he's got a solid brain, he'll understand. And I know he won't blame you."

Sami rushed over, phone in hand. "Stop the pity party! They're breaching a cellar on the property." She put the phone to her ear. "I'm tapped into Sky Warrior's com."

"I can't stand this," Lucien whispered. "They'll be all right, won't they?"

"They will. Keep the faith. You'll see your lovely lady and Rock soon," Alexei's voice quavered.

"Flashbang grenade," Sami announced. "Shouting, gunfire."

"*Mon Dieu.*" Lucien held his breath and let it out slowly.

Silence.

"Man down." Sami stared at Lucien. "One of Fenwick's."

For the next few seconds, they watched Sami for news. She held up a hand and pressed the phone harder against her ear. Lucien imagined the worst but hoped for the best. Her expression gave nothing away.

"Sami," Lucien said softly.

She shook her head. "I can't tell what's going on. There are shouts and gunfire and explosions. Hold on."

"Easier said than done." He rolled his stiff neck and threw the blankets off, suddenly feeling hot. "Alexei, what do you think's happening?"

"No telling. We must wait." Alexei's brow furrowed. "It will work out, you'll see."

"Hey, guys." She pulled the phone away and looked at it. "I don't hear anything anymore."

"What does that mean? Is it over? Marlowe? Rock?" Lucien thought he'd pass out. "Did we win?"

"I don't know," her voice hardened. "I think Sky Warrior's down."

Lucien stared. "Wait, what?"

"I'm patched into his com. A firefight. Now there's nothing. Shit."

"Oh, no." His breathing sped up. "This can't be happening. Did he lose his radio?"

"Lucien, take a deep breath, you're hyperventilating." Alexei leaned over and reached for his arm. "Breathe, my friend."

Sami paced. "I don't know what happened. We'll have to wait and see if someone reaches out," her voice had a hollow tone as if the life had drained from her.

Lucien held out his hand. "Give me Fenwick's phone. She'll know. We can't wait."

It rang, but nobody picked up and it didn't go to voicemail. "Oh, come on." He dropped the phone on the bed. "This is a nightmare."

Sami continued to pace. The nurse came in at one point, checked the IV bags and monitors, and wandered out again. Only her visit broke the incredible tension, for a few minutes.

After about half an hour, Lucien struggled to get out of bed, ignoring the pain that stabbed his side. He wasn't going to stay in bed any longer, and managed to make a very slow circuit around the room, leaning on every surface as he passed by.

Every few minutes, he dialed Fenwick's number to no avail. Whatever had happened couldn't be good if she didn't pick up.

"Lucien, come and sit. You need rest." Alexei patted the mattress. "Sit."

"I can't sit. We've got to go to the vineyard." A drop of sweat dripped into his eye. "Maybe I should sit." He lowered himself onto the edge of Alexei's bed.

"Good. Now, we can't go to the vineyard, but I can reach out to Vitaly."

"Yes, do that." Lucien handed him the phone.

After speaking in Russian for a minute, Alexei handed the phone back. "Vitaly is on the way to the vineyard."

"Did you tell him to be careful?"

"Of course. He knows better than to charge into any situation unprepared."

Sami cleared her throat. "Who's this Vitaly?"

"A colleague, my dear."

"I can meet up with him. Yes?" Sami stared at Lucien. "Yes?"

"Yes, but ..." He turned to Alexei. "Does Vitaly have weapons?"

With a smile, Alexei nodded. "He is well equipped. He will have extra weaponry for you, too, my dear."

"Perfect. I'm off." She grabbed the phone and typed something. "I put a number in the phone where anyone on Sky Warrior's team can text to convey status or changes in plans. I'll let you know what I find out. In the meantime, keep checking to see if anyone on the team communicates." She handed Lucien the phone and dashed from the room without another word.

He sighed and used the end of the sheet to wipe his face. "At least we have two people now to find out what went wrong."

"Better than nothing. Vitaly and Sami will be an effective team. My friend, are you prepared for the worst?"

"No. Not at all."

He went to his bed and lay down, exhausted. He looked out through the window at the sun-drenched dawn. A new day. But what would it bring? His experiment had been a complete failure, the Neanderthals carried the lethal cancer gene and were sick much sooner than they should be. They had no immunity to fend off the disease at all. He'd convinced himself they were stronger, and experimenting on them wouldn't violate any ethical mandates. He wanted to prove his hypothesis was right, no matter what.

When two ravens flew by the window, it felt like an omen. Sure enough, not more than two minutes later, the door opened and Édouard shuffled in. Lucien hoped it was a fever-dream and blinked to clear his vision. It was not a dream.

Chapter 35

Lucien had become the proverbial sitting duck. Alexei attempted to struggle free of his bed, without much luck, while Édouard stood motionless, staring straight ahead. In a flash, Lucien had the phone and pressed *call*, knowing Fenwick wouldn't answer, but it was the only link to a lifeline he had.

"Fenwick's looking for you. So, are you going to kill me in a hospital? Cowardly, even for you." Lucien gripped the phone and heaved it at his brother.

He missed.

Édouard didn't say a word but glanced at the door.

"Well? Get on with it, brother." Lucien searched for anything within reach to toss. He had nothing.

Édouard flinched as the door opened.

Fenwick strolled in, followed by one of her broad-shouldered goons. "Hello, again, Paleo."

"What ... how ... where's Marlowe? And Rock?" He glared at Édouard. "Why did you bring *him* here?"

Fenwick stood beside Édouard. "I have no idea where the cutie and beast are. I got what I wanted."

"You left them there?" Alexei looked at Lucien. "I'm sorry, my friend. This is not what I expected."

"Shush, Ozerov." Fenwick slapped her hand down on Édouard's shoulder. "This is a present for you, Paleo."

Édouard took a step backward, but the goon grabbed him in a flash and pushed him forward. Lucien recognized a look of fear in his brother's eyes; pupils dilated, non-blinking, frozen stare. He had the same look from when they were children and Lucien had dared him to jump off a creek bank into the icy water below.

"I don't understand." Lucien swallowed. He'd hoped not to see his brother again. He glared at Fenwick. "Did you at least see Marlowe?"

"I did. But listen, Paleo, you've been a somewhat worthy opponent and you did help me retrieve this slimy slug of a man, so I thought I'd repay the favor." She reached into her jacket pocket.

Édouard stared directly at Lucien. "You haven't succeeded. The damage is done."

Of course, he was right, but success wasn't only about coming out on top. Édouard never understood that. Lucien watched as Fenwick withdrew her hand from her pocket, flipped open a switchblade, and plunged it into the opposite side of Édouard's neck. Blood spurted onto the wall and covered the goon who held him. Fenwick's hand dripped red. Neither Fenwick nor the goon seemed bothered. The goon released Édouard and allowed him to grab his neck.

Lucien shouted and struggled to get out of bed. "Help! Someone!"

"Isn't this what you wanted, Paleo? A fitting end to your familial nemesis? Your hands are clean." She held up her blood-soaked hand and laughed. "But mine aren't!"

The goon stared at Lucien and shook his head as if to say *don't try anything.*

"You're insane." Alexei reached for Lucien and grabbed his arm. "There's nothing you can do, my friend."

As Édouard collapsed to his knees, Fenwick rinsed her hands, and the knife, in the sink. Lucien sat in shock, horrified to watch his brother's blood drip down the wall and pool onto the shiny tile floor.

Fenwick dried her hands and turned around. "So, Paleo, we won't see one another ever again. I will honor the deal, providing you do. I thought you should see your brother one last time." She glanced down at Édouard. "Looks like he's about done now. *Adieu,* Paleo." She sauntered from the room, followed closely by the goon.

Trembling head-to-foot, Lucien managed to stand and edge closer to his brother, who lay on his side, staring up with cloudy, lifeless eyes. A second later, the door opened and the nurse rushed in.

"Is something ...? Oh, my God!" She leaned out and screamed for a crash cart, emergency team, and security.

"It's too late." Lucien sat on the bed. "He's gone." He turned to Alexei. "He could have told us about Marlowe and Rock. And Sky Warrior. But now he can't."

Alexei looked at the body. "He got what he deserved. But, if Fenwick got to him, that means Sky Warrior must have been successful in breaking through the defenses."

"True. But why did we lose contact? And where are they? Fenwick said she saw Marlowe. What if that meant she killed her?"

"Fenwick wouldn't do that. You heard her, she's sticking to the deal. She wouldn't jeopardize us revealing she has a brother." Alexei turned to the nurse, who held the door as several white-coated staff pushed in. "Madam, this is not our doing. I do, however, believe any valiant effort on your part would be wasted at this point."

She glared. "I know you didn't do this. You can't even stand up. That woman or bodybuilder guy did it, didn't they?"

A young man in white scrubs abandoned his pitiful attempt at CPR and announced, "Someone call time of death."

Lucien blocked out the voices around him and watched as they lifted his brother's body onto a gurney and covered it with a sheet that soon turned red. He had a mix of emotions that ranged from sorrow to anger to relief. Fenwick was gone, a good thing, but she left too many unanswered questions about what had happened at the vineyard. Not knowing was eating away at him and although he tried to stay hopeful, the realization that neither Marlowe nor Rock might have survived plunged him into despair.

Before long, two uniformed police officers entered the room as a crime scene photographer took a series of photos from every imaginable angle, complaining that the body shouldn't have been removed. A cleaning crew mopped up the floor and walls once the photographer finished. Once the cleaners had the room spotless, the cops, a slender young man with close-cropped black hair, and a middle-aged woman with sandy blonde hair tied back in a loose bun approached.

The woman cop pointed to Alexei. "I'm Sergeant Tanner. The nurse said you and this man were shot at the Arena during the Neanderball press conference. Can you confirm this?"

"I confirm." Alexei motioned to Lucien. "We were set upon by hooligans. There really should be more police patrols at events such as that."

Her eyes narrowed. "Yes, well, be that as it may, I'll need a statement and your contact information. And an explanation of who the dead man is and what he wanted. One of the hooligans perhaps?" She spoke to her partner, "Have them fill out the statement." She turned and left.

"I have to go." Lucien walked to a narrow closet near the sink and opened it. "Where the hell are my clothes?"

The young cop shook his head. "Um, you can't leave."

"Watch me." He wandered around the room. "I have to find out what happened to Marlowe and Rock."

"I understand, my friend, but perhaps it's best to wait." Alexei pointed to his midsection.

Blood had seeped onto his hospital gown. "Perfect. I've burst my stitches." He sat on his bed, defeated. "Édouard's dead."

"I'm well aware. You can grieve later if you feel the need. For now, Sami is on her way to the vineyard, so we should know something soon. Why don't you check the phone for messages?"

Lucien refocused his attention on the vineyard. There were no messages. He lay back and pressed his hand gently on his wound. When the cop gave him a pen and paper, he put his name at the top, but forgot Marlowe's address, so left out the contact information. Alexei jotted down something, but since they had to keep their stories straight, Lucien figured it would be best to wait until the cop went away before writing anything more.

It wasn't long before the phone chirped. Finally, a text.

SOS. Evac. SW unit. Casualties.

He showed the phone to Alexei, who nodded. "We don't know anything for sure. SW? Sky Warrior, I presume."

Lucien wiped his forehead. "Casualties. That's not good, no matter who's involved."

The cop came closer. "Casualties? What are you two on about? Give me that phone."

"None of your business, officer." Alexei grabbed the phone and shoved it under his pillow. "If you want it, you'll have to come and get it. Perhaps you'd prefer to bludgeon me with your nightstick."

"What?" The cop took a step back. "Smartass. Finish your statement."

Lucien smiled. "Officer, could you give us a moment alone, please? We'll complete the statements for you. We're certainly not going anywhere."

The cop shot a look at Alexei, nodded to Lucien, and strode from the room.

"Well done, my friend. That young officer seemed more than happy to depart."

"Better done with finesse than taunting." Lucien held his hand out for the phone.

"True, but you know how I love to play."

Lucien nodded and for the next several minutes, clutched the phone, hoping for another update, but when it didn't come, he decided to check on his wound, which throbbed. The bandage had a stain of blood, but it wasn't as bad as he'd thought.

The nurse returned, her face pale, and glanced at the floor where Édouard had been. "So, ah, who was that man? And the people who did that to him?"

Lucien gazed out the window. "My brother. The woman is someone he worked with. She's gone now though, and I doubt anyone will find her."

"That's ... horrible." The nurse paused for a moment. "I can't imagine what you're going through. Um, you have a phone call. It'll ring here in a moment."

He perked up and stared at the phone beside the bed. As soon as it rang, he grabbed the receiver. "Hello?"

"Dr. Roux, this is Thomas Baker again. Can you please help my players? Two are in the ICU and the others aren't doing much better. Please. If I get you your research back, can you do something?"

He gripped the phone. Why wasn't it Marlowe on the line? "At this point, it's too late. It would take months to study and all you can do is make them comfortable. There's nothing you can do. What hospital?"

"The one you're in. I'm not making excuses, but I'm a businessman and saw an opportunity. I regret—"

"Regret won't save those boys." He shifted in the bed. "They'll die because my brother made them develop too fast and had them kidnapped from my lab. And now I'm lying here with a burn wound that destroyed my spleen. What the fuck do you expect me to do?"

The nurse interjected, "You need to stay calm."

Alexei spoke up, "My dear, perhaps you wouldn't mind bringing us some water or juice. Yes?"

She hesitated, shrugged, and left.

Baker continued, "Please, Dr. Roux, you know the genetics better than anyone. You created them, you can fix them."

"I can't. This wasn't supposed to happen. None of it. We're all paying the consequences now, especially the Neanderthals."

"Dr. Roux, don't hang up yet."

"Oh, come on. What more do you want from me?"

Baker paused. "The military, the branch that has your research and the enhancement technology, well, rumor has it that the embryos they've grown are failing to thrive. That's good, right?"

Definitely the best news he'd hoped for. If Harmond failed with his super-Neanderthal soldiers, the program would be scrapped. "Yes. Good. I've got to go." He hung up, slamming the receiver more than he had to.

Alexei raised an eyebrow. "Good news?"

"More or less. Harmond's tinkering with my research failed. I need to get to the ICU."

"Excuse me? You're not that ill."

"Two of my Neanderthals are dying there. I need to see them."

"Oh." Alexei pressed the call button looped around his bed rail.

The nurse came back. "You pressed ..."

"Wheelchairs, please." Alexei threw off the covers.

Lucien did the same. "We're taking a road trip."

Chapter 36

Once the nurse saw the bloody bandage, she insisted on applying a clean dressing before she'd even consider bringing in wheelchairs. Lucien agreed, not that he had a choice. She informed him that he'd loosened several staples, left for a moment, and came back with a doctor who swept in, stuck the wound together with surgical glue, and vanished, all within the span of maybe three minutes.

Lucien sighed. "I'll probably get charged a thousand dollars for that visit."

The nurse glanced at him with narrowed eyes. "We have the best care here."

She went out in the hall and held the door as two orderlies brought in the wheelchairs.

With a slightly snotty tone, she said, "You shouldn't move around too much for the rest of the day, but starting tomorrow, you need to be up and walking. Pain or not, you have to start moving to prevent blood clots."

"Yes, ma'am." Alexei smiled. "We shall comply with your orders. Now, to the chariots."

The nurse rolled her eyes and left. The orderlies stayed by the wheelchairs.

Lucien had an easier time getting seated, but Alexei, being in worse shape, had to rely on an orderly to help him. After they were settled, they were wheeled upstairs to the ICU, followed at a distance by the young cop who he surmised was still curious about the casualties they'd mentioned. Lucien kept the phone on his lap, periodically checking for messages, but when he arrived at the nurses' station, his focus shifted to the two beds, side-by-side, where the Neanderthals lay hooked up to respirators.

Lucien's heart broke when he saw them, and he had to turn away for a moment to compose himself. "I *am* a mad scientist."

"Nonsense, my friend." Alexei placed his hand on his shoulder. "You're a dedicated scientist and science isn't always predictable."

"I've come to terms with it, but it doesn't make it any easier."

"I understand."

One of the nurses came from behind the desk. "I know who you are, but you still can't see the patients."

"No, I don't need to see them." He stood and shuffled to the glass wall of the room and watched the Neanderthals' chests rising and falling. He placed his hand on the glass. It felt cold.

How strange. They looked peaceful, a fitting end to a tragic life. At least they wouldn't be forced to play Neanderball any longer. He watched for several minutes until Alexei cleared his throat.

"A bit longer, please."

"Not that, my friend, there's a message."

"What?" He plodded to Alexei and took the phone.

S on scene with medical.

"Good news, no?"

"Yes, good news." Lucien let out a breath. "Sami made it. Come on, come on, tell us what happened." He stared at the phone.

Another message.

SW down. Medic tending. Chaos.

"What? What chaos? What does that mean?" He shook the phone, as if that'd make the message clearer. "How do I type a message? There's no place for me to type."

"Stay calm, Sami is right in the thick of it. Give her a moment."

No further messages popped up. Lucien kept the phone in his hand and watched the Neanderthals for a few more minutes before asking to be taken back to the room. After getting in bed with the phone on his lap, he turned on the TV to check for any news of gunfire at the vineyard, but there were only the usual reports of traffic jams and wildfire threats.

He flipped from channel to channel, interrupted occasionally by the cop or the nurse until he gave up and tossed the remote onto the nightstand. He and Alexei got their stories straight and completed their statements, to the relief of the cop who looked more than happy to leave, thanks to Alexei's continued teasing about police brutality.

"Lucien, do you remember Paris, on your twenty-fourth birthday?"

"Of course. Why?"

"Do you remember what you told me? After my magnificent toast?"

He thought back to that night. They had dinner with a few friends, drank too much champagne and ate too much rich food, then ended the evening with Alexei's overly emotional toast. But what he'd said after that had gone from his memory.

"I don't. Too much champagne."

Alexei smiled. "You told me you dreamed of changing the world. Making it a better place. At that moment I knew I'd lost you to your future. The thrill-seeker in you had disappeared. You wanted to settle down and make something of yourself."

"I said that?" He blew out a puff of air. "If I'd known then...well, it's all water under the bridge now, isn't it?"

Thumping footsteps out in the hallway made him jump. A second later, the door flung open and a burly man in desert camo fatigues burst in. He scanned the room and stood in front of the door.

"Dr. Roux?"

"That's me." Lucien raised his hand, too tired to be scared. "Whatever you want, I'm not in the mood."

"Huh?" The man looked around the room once more. "I received orders to come directly here to assure your safety."

"My safety?" He glanced at Alexei, who shrugged. Who's after him now? Fenwick was out of the picture, his brother too, the Bakers were harmless, and Harmond didn't need to use the research, so he wasn't a threat any longer either. "I don't need protection from whoever wants me dead now. Who are you?"

"Name's Parker. I'm in Sky Warrior's unit."

"What?" He sat up. "What's going on at the site? Who sent you?"

"Marlowe. She said to get my ass here ASAP or she'd shoot me in the foot. I chose to come here."

"Smart. Okay, Parker, so what's happening back there?" Lucien grabbed a handful of bedding, his heart rate increasing by the second.

Parker continued, "Sky Warrior is wounded, Marlowe's pinned down. I couldn't get to her. Three of my squad are dead. We didn't find your brother or the Neanderthal. I'll stay with you, but I need to dispatch our backup squad." He caught his breath and took out a sat phone.

While Parker spoke in a hushed but hurried tone, Lucien turned to Alexei. "At least Marlowe is alive. But Rock? What did my brother do with him?"

"What I can't understand is why they're still fighting. They must know Fenwick took Édouard. It's unlikely her people would continue the fight."

Lucien motioned to Parker. "Fenwick grabbed my brother. How did her goon squad swoop in and back out without being seen?" He checked the phone again for messages. "Nothing."

Parker took the phone away from his ear. "Dr. Roux, I don't know what the hell is going on, but there's a weapon on-scene that shoots lasers or something. It burns holes into everything."

"I know that weapon." He turned to Alexei. "It's Harmond's men. Has to be."

"That bastard. Parker will get reinforcements and we'll soon have Marlowe and Sky Warrior back. As for Rock, I'm at a loss, unless Fenwick's people or Harmond's have him."

Parker slipped his phone into a holster on his belt. "Done. Ten minutes. Why am I supposed to babysit you two?"

Lucien thought for a moment. "There's no need. All threats have been removed. Go back and help. And find Rock."

"The Neanderthal?"

"Yes!" The word came out as a shout. "Sorry. I'm a bit frazzled at this point."

"No problem, sir. You will tell Marlowe I came here?"

"Of course. I'll make sure she knows." He motioned to the door. "Now go."

As soon as Parker left, Thomas Baker rushed in, red-faced and breathing hard.

He took a breath, put a hand on the door to keep it closed, and faced Lucien. "I ... I don't know where to start."

"Mr. Baker, I've told you I can't help the Neanderthals. I am truly sorry, but there's not a thing I can do." Lucien genuinely commiserated with the man, so desperately trying to save their lives. In that, they were of one mind.

Baker continued, "That's not it."

"Excuse me." Alexei sat up. "What then? We're in no mood for games."

"Yes, say what you want and get out of here before I say something very rude."

"Dr. Roux." Baker drooped his head and stared at the ground. "It's my boy. He collaborated with your brother to take Rock."

"What?" He eased out of bed and faced the man. "What are you saying? Your son has Rock? How? When? My brother's dead."

Baker looked up. "Your brother never had Rock at the vineyard. My boy picked him up at some other location. He called me and told me. I had no idea. I swear."

"What on Earth does he want with Rock?" He grabbed Baker by the arm. "Call your son. You know Rock's as sick as his brothers or will be soon. He needs treatment."

"You said you had no treatment. Were you lying?" Baker wrenched his arm away.

Lucien went to the window and gazed out. "There's no cure. I didn't mean treatment, I meant to say he needs to be on medication to make him comfortable." He turned. "What does your son want with him?"

"That General Harmond guy said he wants him for genetic testing. Rock didn't show any signs of illness like the others. Well, other than the vomiting spree he had. Look, I didn't have to come here, but I did. I don't want any of my players experimented on. It's bad optics. Can you help?"

Lucien spoke to Alexei, "The men at the vineyard are definitely Harmond's men. They're keeping Sky Warrior's team occupied so they can't rescue Rock."

"I would agree with that assessment." Alexei waved his arm at Baker for attention. "You. Where is your son now?"

From Baker's demeanor, he didn't trust them. His eyes were narrowed and flitting back and forth from Lucien to the door. "What do you intend to do to my boy?"

"We're only interested in Rock." Lucien sat on the bed and sighed. "Once he hands him over to Harmond, Rock's gone forever. Please, Mr. Baker, help us."

"Promise me you won't hurt Jeremy."

"Promise." It wasn't a lie. Lucien had no intention of hurting Jeremy himself, but he couldn't speak for anyone else. "Where is he?"

"He's meeting Harmond in Pacifica, team headquarters, in about half an hour."

"Thank you." Lucien motioned to the door. "Now go and don't talk to anyone."

Baker hesitated and looked about to say something but left without a word.

Lucien groaned. "Who do you know who can get to Pacifica and fight off a bunch of Harmond's steroid cases?"

"I would have recommended Sky Warrior, but, you know."

"Yeah."

Alexei frowned. "I have an idea. Have you heard of swatting?"

"Ah, I don't think so."

"It's something people used to do, or maybe still do. It's when a not-so-funny prank is initiated on unsuspecting people. Someone calls the police to say there's a person with a gun threatening people or another scenario they dream up. The police dispatch the SWAT team only to find out there are no armed people."

"That's a horrible thing for people to do, and dangerous. So, you want to get the cops to Pacifica?" Lucien smiled. "It's terrible, but in this case, it's devious and fantastic. We should tell them one of the Neanderthals is a prisoner and is being threatened. That way they'll take Rock with them."

"That's not so far from the truth, my friend. Aside from being shot, I'm enjoying our forays together."

"Yes, the being shot part takes the shine off it. Tell me honestly, do you think Marlowe is okay?"

Alexei nodded. "I do. I think you'd feel it in your bones if she wasn't."

Hopefully, he was right, because losing her at this point would be soul-crushing. Lucien picked up the phone and stared at it for a moment. This would be the only chance to save Rock. He glanced at Alexei and dialed 911.

"Nine-one-one, what's your emergency?"

"Oh, my God! There are men at the Neanderball headquarters in Pacifica with guns! They're going to kill one of the Neanderball players! They're shooting people! They said they'll shoot anyone who gets near them. Hurry!"

"Yes, sir. I'll dispatch the police immediately. Please give me your name."

He hung up and drew in a deep breath. "How did that sound?"

"You made a believer out of me."

"Now we sit back and wait."

Alexei poured a cup of water and took a sip. "We need a police scanner."

"I must have left it in my other jacket pocket." Lucien stood and rolled his neck. "Do you think you can walk?"

"Well, I am pumped full of morphine." He edged to the side of the bed and pushed himself up. "There, you see."

"I can't wait here. You heard the nurse. We should be up and walking. So, let's go for a walk to Pacifica and watch the show." He helped his friend into the wheelchair by the bed, grabbed the cell phone, and opened the door. "I've never been to Pacifica before, but this seems like an appropriate time. We'll have to put our heads together and come up with a plan to get there and get Rock."

"All in half an hour."

"All in half an hour." Lucien smiled and pushed Alexei into the hallway, grabbed two pairs of scrubs from a laundry cart, and hurried to the elevator. While waiting, he checked the phone and saw a new message.

Reinforcements on site. Rescue in progress.

He showed it to Alexei. "Change of plans. We're going to the vineyard. I need to make sure Marlowe is okay."

Chapter 37

Changing out of the flimsy hospital gowns into the scrubs he stole proved more awkward than Lucien had imagined. But he managed, after pressing the elevator emergency stop button for a few minutes to help Alexei. The piercing alarm hurt, but by the time the elevator resumed and made it to the first floor, his ears stopped ringing.

Alexei laughed. "I always wanted to pretend to be a doctor."

"It suits you. Lean on me."

They supported one another, which must have looked strange as they shuffled through the lobby in scrubs and booties. Alexei paused, leaned on a bank of seats crowded with visitors and patients, and continued a moment later.

Outside, Lucien flagged a waiting taxi. "I'm not about to tell them we don't have any money."

With a smirk, Alexei flashed a black leather wallet. "We do. Credit cards, too."

"I never even saw you lift it. Either you're better than you used to be or I'm worse."

"Bit of both I suspect. People are careless and shouldn't leave their jackets on empty chairs when pickpockets are lurking nearby."

"Quite true." Lucien smiled and helped his friend to the taxi.

After giving the driver the vineyard's address, he leaned back. "How are you feeling? I shouldn't have let you leave the hospital."

Alexei clicked his tongue. "You didn't *let* me do anything. I came willingly because I wasn't about to let *you* go alone."

"Fair enough. We're not exactly an intimidating pair, are we? What if they're still fighting when we get there? We have no weapons."

"Things have a way of working out." Alexei rifled through the stolen wallet.

The Bay Area morning traffic was typical, which would make the journey longer than Lucien had hoped, although it gave him time to think about how to help Sky Warrior's team and find Marlowe. And get to Pacifica in half an hour. An idea flashed into his head.

"Driver! Can you make a detour, please?"

The driver glanced in the rearview. "Sure. Where to?"

He gave directions to the weapons warehouse Marlowe had used.

Alexei stared at him, waiting for an explanation. "My friend, where are we going?"

He kept his voice low, "Remember that warehouse Marlowe went to and got the guns, zip ties, and whatever else she had in that duffle bag. I'm hoping I can do the same, without getting shot in the process."

"I remember some serious-looking fellows had it guarded."

"Right. I'm hoping they take a second to listen."

Alexei patted his arm. "Then I'll wait in the taxi."

"Thanks."

"No problem."

He wasn't really upset because Alexei deserved a break from the danger. As the taxi drove through the streets, drifting fog from the bay partially blotted out the sun. Lucien leaned back and imagined happier times when he'd drive to work in the morning fog and the only thing to worry about then was whether he'd produce results to keep the funding coming. Gene therapy had been the ultimate goal, but that had long flown out the window.

"Excuse me, are you sure this is the place?" the driver asked as he parked the taxi on the street in front of the warehouse.

Two men wearing tactical gear and automatic weapons slung over their shoulders paced back and forth in front of the entrance. Probably the same guards who were there last time. They'd let Marlowe through without any trouble.

"Yes, this is right. Please wait." He winked at Alexei, got out, hunched over from the increasing pain now that most of the medication had worn off, and headed directly to the warehouse.

As expected, the men both grabbed their guns and aimed them at him, looking him up and down. He held out his hands and stopped.

"I'm a friend of Marlowe Dunham. She needs help. She's under fire from a squadron of militia not far from here. Please."

The men looked at one another and back at him.

One of them spoke, "You're that Neanderball guy. Marlowe works with you. And now she's in trouble? Because of you?"

"Yes, on all accounts." His throat had dried out, making it impossible to swallow. "Can you please help us? We're headed to *Maison de Vin*. If you know Sky Warrior, he's there helping us and he's been wounded."

The men spun around and went inside, the metal door slamming with a clank behind them. Not more than a minute later, they returned, followed by a group of heavily armed men with frowns set on their stony faces. They climbed into two Jeeps. Lucien nodded and went back to the taxi.

Alexei cocked his head. "I don't know how you did it, but well done."

"For a minute there, I thought they were going to kill me."

"But they didn't."

"No, they didn't. And now we have our own team of fighters." He told the taxi driver to go.

The driver hesitated and turned. "Mister, I don't know what's going on, but I'm not about to break the law. I have to ask you to get out."

"Drive." Lucien slapped the driver's headrest. "Now."

The driver shook his head. "Those men have guns. I'm not going anywhere."

Alexei climbed out of the car and went to the driver's side. He opened the door. "Get out then. We don't have time for your whining. Out."

"No."

A moment later, a Jeep filled with Marlowe's friends pulled up and glared at the taxi driver, who gasped and got out. Alexei climbed in and Lucien got into the passenger seat. Taking the lead, they followed the directions on the taxi's GPS while Lucien kept an eye on the men behind them. When they were within a half-mile of the vineyard, gunshots echoed and smoke hung in the air over one of the buildings; the cellar.

Alexei pulled over and waited until the Jeep came alongside.

The driver of the Jeep hopped out and motioned for Lucien to put the window down. "You're no good to us, so please stay put and we'll handle things from here."

Lucien nodded and held up the phone. "This other woman, Sami, has been texting updates. The last message said reinforcements were onsite."

"Not enough reinforcements apparently. We've been monitoring as well, but I didn't know Sky Warrior or Marlowe were involved."

"Oh. Let me know when you find Marlowe."

"Roger that." The guy strode to the Jeep and got back in. He drove off fast, followed closely by the other Jeep, up the vineyard's driveway, and stopped at the main entrance to the cellar.

The squad of armed men spread out, taking positions in various places until they evidently received orders to enter the building. One man broke the door down with a small battering ram and they all rushed in. Lucien leaned forward as if being closer to the windshield would give him a better view. There were several loud bangs followed by sirens in the distance.

"Oh, shit. The police." He reached over and honked the horn.

"I don't think they can hear that, my friend." Alexei turned and peered down the road. "The police were bound to be called with that racket going on."

"I know, I thought of that, but it slipped my mind until now."

As the sirens grew louder, the gunfire slowed, followed soon by an eerie silence. Two men in military fatigues rushed out only to be shot in the back. They collapsed and Vitaly strolled out, fired one shot into each of the fallen men, and continued toward the taxi. Lucien gasped.

Vitaly nodded to Alexei and got into the back seat. "I heard you were here in the taxi."

"Are you injured?" Alexei turned in his seat.

Vitaly shook his head. "A minor wound to my arm."

"Good, good." Alexei sighed and turned back around.

Lucien found his voice and twisted around to see Vitaly, "What the fuck! You killed two of Harmond's men!"

With a shrug, Vitaly laid his gun on the seat. "They were the ones who shot your woman, Marlowe. I thought you wouldn't object."

"What? Marlowe's been shot? How ... is she ...?" Lucien felt sick, no longer concerned with the bodies outside.

Vitaly continued, "Not dead, Dr. Roux. Wounded though. They cornered her. She held out as long as possible until she ran out of ammunition."

"Where is she? Why did the shooting stop?"

"As you see, I dispatched those two bastards after the men with you stormed in and said you and Alexei were out here. They distracted those snakes long enough for us to get the upper hand. Sky Warrior is alive but in bad shape." Vitaly leaned back and closed his eyes.

Lucien opened the door and got out. "I have to find Marlowe."

"I know you do. Go. I'll try to hold off the police." Alexei flashed a smile. "Be safe, my friend."

"I'll do my best." He jogged on shaky legs, holding onto his side and pushed through the pain. He made it to the building in no time.

Inside, the stench of gunpowder mixed with the unmistakably metallic tang of blood hung heavy in the air. Bodies were strewn in every direction, some wearing fatigues, others in tactical gear. He didn't know where to go, but when he saw movement at the far end of the building, he hurried, hoping it was Marlowe. Instead, he found Sami, clutching a rag to her arm. She saw him.

"Dr. Roux," she approached. "Follow me."

She limped to a stack of pallets and motioned behind them. He held his breath and followed. A body lay face down, a puddle of blood all around. His breath came out in a forced exhale. Sami touched his shoulder and pointed beyond the body.

"Marlowe?" He rushed to her.

She slumped against the pallets, blood on her face and clothes, but she was conscious. "What the hell took you so long?"

"Rush hour traffic." He dropped to his knees and checked her over. "Where were you hit?"

"A bullet caught me in the side, under my vest. Got one in the leg, too." She looked up. "Sami dragged me to safety and killed that fucker before he finished me." She pushed his hand away. "Wait a second, why are you here? You should be in the hospital. And why are you in scrubs?"

"Alexei and I—"

"Alexei. I should have known."

"No, this is my idea. Alexei and I found out that Rock's been taken to Pacifica by Baker's son, Jeremy."

She groaned. "Son-of-a-bitch. That's why Rock wasn't here. And I haven't seen your brother in a while."

"Don't worry about him. But it gets worse. Harmond is going to take Rock to be experimented on so he can still have his super-Neanderthal soldiers." He unstrapped her vest and found the wound. "Can you walk?"

"Of course I can." She took his hand and straightened unsteadily. "So why aren't you at Pacifica?"

"I was on the way but figured I should come here and make sure you were all right. And I thought it would be a good idea to grab whoever's left here that isn't dead or wounded to help. Harmond's men will be at Pacifica, and a SWAT team." He supported her as they made their way out of the building.

"SWAT? What are you talking about?"

"I'll explain later. There's a medic team here somewhere and that's our first concern." He waved to Sami, who rushed over and pointed to a guy with a medical bag.

After tending to Marlowe and calling for an ambulance, the medic hurried away to treat the other wounded. The sirens in the distance weren't getting closer. It had to be Alexei and Vitaly delaying them somehow.

Instead of an ambulance, a helicopter swooped down and settled onto the lawn in front of the cellar. Two men jumped out with a stretcher and Lucien waved to them. They came over and loaded Marlowe on. Several other teams with stretchers began collecting the wounded.

"I have to come with you." Marlowe winced as straps were tightened around her body.

"You're in worse shape than I am. I'll meet you back at the hospital, with Rock. Promise me you'll comply." He waited. "Promise me."

She sighed. "Promise. But listen, Édouard escaped with three muscle-types when I first got here. I want that little shit."

"I told you, it's taken care of. Those were Fenwick's goons." He turned away for a moment. "I'll see you soon." He kissed her forehead and hurried away to find the guy who'd driven the Jeep. "Hey, can you round up as many people as you can? We've got to get to Pacifica and save one of the Neanderball players. That's what Sky Warrior hoped to do." By name-dropping, maybe they'd be more willing to help.

"I know. He filled me in. Lead the way."

"Great. Ah, I don't have a car. My friend, Alexei, took the taxi to head off the cops."

"Ride with us."

"I'm sorry, but I don't even know your name." Lucien extended his hand. "I'm Lucien."

The guy nodded but didn't shake. "Jimbo."

As Lucien got into the passenger seat of the Jeep, he saw Sky Warrior on a stretcher being loaded in the copter with Marlowe and several others. Sami climbed in and sat in one of the seats. It looked like she'd had a chat with Marlowe. Maybe that's what it took for them to mend their differences.

Jimbo put the address of the Neanderball headquarters in the GPS while two guys jumped in the back. Two other Jeeps and one pick-up truck roared to life and drove to the Jimbo. Lucien finally felt confident that he'd wrestle Rock away from Harmond once and for all. The sirens soon stopped and while Lucien was curious about what Alexei had done to keep the cops away, he knew he'd have that discussion another time.

The drive to Pacifica from the vineyard would be well over half an hour on a good day, but with traffic, it would take at least an hour. They'd spent almost forty-five minutes at the rescue, so the plan had rapidly fallen apart. Unless the SWAT team kept Jeremy Baker and Harmond trapped, there was no hope.

"Jimbo, you don't have a police scanner, do you?" Lucien glanced behind at the caravan following them.

"Roger that." He reached down and flipped a switch.

Lucien smiled. No wonder Marlowe stayed in touch with her mercenary friends, they were equipped for anything. Back in the day, they would have been excellent compatriots to take along on capers. Although they were a bit heavy-handed.

The scanner picked up chatter about calling in extra units to the Pacifica headquarters. Good news, because it meant Harmond hadn't gotten away and had to be fighting or causing a stand-off. Either way, Rock wasn't missing in action.

"Can you go faster?" Lucien leaned forward, peering straight ahead at a red traffic light. "Run it."

"Yes, sir." Jimbo floored it and zipped through the intersection without incident.

The other vehicles did the same, dodging a few cars that had started to move on their green light. He watched Jimbo, amazed at how calm he was. Ice water in the veins is what Alexei called it.

"Ten minutes out, Lucien." Jimbo rounded a corner, pushing everyone to the right.

Lucien shut his eyes, grabbed the dashboard, and thought about Rock. Was he sick, scared, or angry? Soon he'd be free, but of course, getting Thomas Baker to relinquish his formal adoption might be tricky. Then again, he did seem apologetic for all he'd done.

Shouts and the sound of engines running made Lucien flinch and open his eyes. No doubt about the location of the headquarters. The street was packed with squad cars, unmarked black sedans, and a huge SWAT van outside a large estate surrounded by black wrought iron fencing. The elaborate gate, emblazoned with gold lettering that spelled out Neanderball, was closed.

Jimbo stopped the Jeep and motioned for the others to pull onto the shoulder. "Lucien, hold tight, I'm going to strategize with the team."

Lucien nodded and undid the seatbelt to relieve the pressure on his wound. While Jimbo talked to his friends, the police continued to mill around the front gate. They had a sniper positioned on top of the SWAT van. Several other cops with long guns flanked the gate, staying out of sight. It felt like watching a movie and for a second, he felt disconnected from reality.

When two men dressed in green fatigues came out of the house and strode toward the gates, their hands exposed to show they had no weapons, the police moved in. One cop with a bullhorn ordered them to stop. They complied, but a voice Lucien recognized bellowed from the grand entryway.

"You have no business here!" Harmond shouted.

The cop responded, "Surrender your weapons and unlock the gate! We know you're holding one of the Neanderball players hostage!"

"I'm General Maxwell Harmond and I order you to vacate the premises. We don't have anyone as a hostage."

Jimbo came back to the Jeep and shook his head. "He thinks he's God."

"Pretty much. He's the one who's trying to take the Neanderball player, Rock." He glared at Harmond, hoping his anger would travel.

Jeremy Baker strolled out behind Harmond and raised a bullhorn to his mouth. "I'm the co-owner of the Neanderball team and nothing is going on here. We have a sick player inside and he needs rest. Leave now or I'll file a complaint with the police chief, the mayor, the governor, and anyone else I can think of."

The cop paused and said something to the officer next to him, then continued, "Come to the gate so we can talk."

Jeremy handed the bullhorn to Harmond and pushed past, swaggering like he owned the world. Lucien had misjudged him like Thomas had. Jeremy had become brazen, and since joining up with Harmond, seemed to have gained a sizable amount of overconfidence.

"Who's that little ass?" Jimbo asked.

"One of the team owners. I didn't think he had it in him to join with Harmond." Lucien sighed.

"You know, I worked under Harmond in Afghanistan. He's a dick." Jimbo paused for a moment and returned to his men.

They huddled and several sprinted to the side of the estate. Lucien watched as they scaled the fence using a brick support column, kept low, and headed for a stand of cypress trees and shrubs. Jimbo came back.

"What are they doing?" Lucien asked.

"Harmond's predictable. He always has the same security detail. I know them. They'll be focused on a frontal assault. We'll breach from the rear." Jimbo reached under the driver's seat and pulled out a pistol. "Hang tight." He hurried away to his men.

"The rear? Wait, how?" Lucien wished Alexei was with him. At least he'd have someone to talk to.

While Jeremy spoke to the cops, a black Mercedes crept down the road. It passed by but slowed and backed up beside the Jeep. Thomas Baker wound the passenger window down and looked at Lucien.

"This your doing, Roux? Are you trying to get my son killed? You swore you wouldn't hurt him."

"Mr. Baker, he's not being hurt. The police are talking to him." He got out of the Jeep and went to the Mercedes. "Why are you here?"

With a heavy sigh, Baker said, "To talk some sense into my boy. Rock doesn't deserve to be treated like a ... a ... commodity. He should be with his brothers to spend whatever time they have left together."

"I agree with you." Lucien pointed at Jeremy. "Go and tell him to bring Rock out. This doesn't have to end badly for anyone."

"Roux, the players in the ICU," he paused and looked away. "They died a few minutes ago. The others don't have long either. I don't even know if Rock is still alive."

"I have to believe he's alive. Do what you can. Please. I've got to see Rock." He went back to the Jeep and paced.

Baker drove close to the patrol cars blocking the road and spoke with the nearest cop but wasn't let through. He got out of the car and yelled to his son.

"Jeremy! It's Dad!"

Jeremy waved his arms. "Dad, tell these morons that this is team headquarters, and nothing is going on!"

Lucien kept his eyes on Jimbo and his team but lost sight of them as they sneaked through the landscaping. He hadn't a clue what they were planning, which frustrated the hell out him. One thing he did know, he had to keep everyone out front occupied. He left the Jeep and stood by Baker.

He raised his hand so Jeremy would see him. "Jeremy! It's Dr. Roux. May I speak to you?"

A cop got in front of Lucien. "Sir, you have to stay back."

Jeremy stared at Lucien for a moment. "Let him through!"

The cop hesitated but ended up standing aside. Lucien went to the gate.

He forced a smile. "What's going on here, Jeremy? Can you bring Rock out so I can make sure he's not sick? You know what's happened to the rest of the team, don't you? Your father informed me."

Baker rushed up beside Lucien. "Son, let me in."

Jeremy dropped his eyes. "Yeah, I heard. I told you, they were my friends. And Dad, Harmond told me not to let anyone in."

"That's bullshit. Open the damn gate." Baker grabbed the gate and shook it.

Lucien stayed calm. "I remember that the players are your friends. But listen, General Harmond wants to do genetic experiments on Rock. Is that what you want your friend to go through? Doesn't he deserve better?"

Jeremy looked up. "Yeah, but he'll die like the others unless Harmond fixes him with some new research he has. Rock can stay alive."

"No, that's not what Harmond wants. He wants to use Rock to create enhanced Neanderthals. He doesn't care if he lives or dies, so long as he gets what he needs. Help me get him away from Harmond." Lucien looked past Jeremy. Where was Jimbo? "Let me examine Rock."

Thomas Baker stared at Lucien. "You want Rock for yourself so you can continue your own experiments."

"Not at all. My experiment failed." Lucien looked back at Jeremy.

For a few seconds, Jeremy shuffled his feet and glanced around. "No, I don't think so, Dr. Roux. We can still recover some of the money we're losing. Harmond said he can do something with the genes to fix Rock and then clone him. We'll have a delay in the games, that's all. You'll see, it'll be even better."

"What will? Enhanced players? Seriously? Think about what you're saying, Jeremy. These aren't playthings, they're people. When the embryos were given too much growth hormone, it accelerated their bodies to the point where their bodies are failing, and it accelerated the cancer. Surely you can see that." He saw a moving light through one of the top windows in the house. He had to keep everyone focused on Jeremy. "I made a mistake. Don't you make one, too."

With a slow shrug, Jeremy motioned to his father. "Dad and I will keep Neanderball going, with better players who won't die from whatever you did to them. You're the problem here, Roux, not us. Harmond has your research. We don't need you."

"I developed the sequencing, Jeremy. It took me months to get it right. Harmond's trying to do the same thing in days. Let me see Rock."

"No. Officers! This man is the one trying to hurt the Neanderball player we have inside! Help!" Jeremy smiled and shrugged again, then turned and ambled back to the house.

Lucien backed away.

The nearest cop glared at him but let him go by. Nobody said a thing and the hush was almost worse than the shouting. He leaned against the Jeep and alternated between watching the house and scanning the fence. After about another ten minutes, the police gathered in a large group. Several got into the squad cars and drove off, while the rest stayed where they were.

He turned at the sound of a car approaching, ready to hide behind the Jeep if necessary. A dark blue Lexus sedan drove up the street toward the house but stopped short of where he stood.

The driver's side door opened and Alexei stepped out, dressed in a light blue suit. "I hoped you were here."

"Alexei. I'm not sure what's going on." He went to his friend and explained the situation.

Together, they walked down the street, out of view, and stayed close to the fence. The cops milled around, but after a short time, the SWAT van drove away.

Alexei tapped his arm. "Look over there." He motioned to the trees. "I see something."

"It better be Jimbo with Rock." Lucien peered at the landscaping but didn't see anything. "Are you sure?"

"Well, perhaps my eyes are playing ... there!"

Sure enough, three men appeared from within the stand of trees, but Rock wasn't with them. Neither was Jimbo. Lucien waved to them. He saw two of the men were injured as they hobbled over, supported by the third man.

They scrambled over the fence and after helping his friends to the Jeep, the uninjured man went to Lucien.

"We're going back in but have to do a little patch-up first."

"What happened in there? Did you see Rock? Where's Jimbo?" He felt Alexei's hand on his shoulder.

The mercenary continued, "Rock's there, with Jimbo. They're in the basement. I've got a schematic of the house and there's an exit from the basement into the backyard. We made it out, but that's when the Harmond's men got us. Something hit us when we tried to get them out. Two of my guys have wounds, burns. Jimbo's still in there. We supplied him with weapons, but he can't hold them off much longer."

"We got shot with that weapon, too. What can I do? There's got to be something ..."

"Dr. Roux, Harmond has at least thirty of his guys patrolling the house and the grounds. We barely made it *inside* without being seen, and you see what happened when we stepped out. They were waiting for us. There had to be a warning system we didn't see."

"My apologies. I know you're doing everything possible. How are your men?" Lucien glanced over at the men as they were wrapping gauze around their legs.

"Each took a graze to the leg, but not a bullet. I don't know what weapon is, but it burned and cauterized the skin."

Lucien turned to Alexei. "Now that they know we've mounted a rescue, they'll be scouring the place inside and out."

"True." Alexei looked around. "Nobody here knows me. Or at the least, won't recognize me as I've only been your accomplice." He smirked. "I convinced the police at the vineyard that we were shooting a movie and the gunfire was only blanks."

"And that worked?"

"You know me, my friend, I have an honest face. Give me a moment." He winked and strolled to the gate.

"Alexei, wait. Alexei!"

Too late, he was out of earshot.

"Dr. Roux, the only chance we have of getting to Jimbo is if the guards move off somewhere else. There are too few of us and too many of them. We'll do what we can, but we need help."

"Alexei is working on something." He wiped his brow. "Do you have an extra gun?"

"Sure." He handed Lucien a pistol. "Don't get yourself killed."

"I'll do my best." He concealed the gun in the waistband of the scrubs and followed Alexei.

He looked back and saw the men scrambling back over the fence again. They were wounded, but still willing to fight, taking up the mantle of Sky Warrior. If anybody survived, it would be a miracle and that's exactly what they needed. Miracles, however, happened to other people.

He half-jogged to his friend, who chatted to several officers.

Thomas got through the gate and walked to the house with his son. Any allegiance he might have had with Thomas slipped away. Greed had won.

"Ah, my friend, we were discussing how Neanderball is better than football. You agree, right?"

"Sure. Sure it is." He pulled Alexei away. "What the hell are you doing?"

"Attempting to bond with the officers. We'll need their firepower."

"They're not going to charge in there." Lucien lifted his shirt an inch. "I have a gun, so maybe I can get inside..."

Alexei smiled. "No need for such heroics, my friend."

A high-pitched whine broke through the quiet.

Lucien cocked his head to locate the sound. "Is that a ...?"

Alexei nodded. "Drone. Vitaly is quite the pilot. He's going to do a little surveillance from above to get the lay of the land."

Lucien raised an eyebrow. "And?"

"And, then he'll know where he can land a helicopter."

Lucien shook his head. "Are you serious? This is madness. Jimbo and Rock are trapped in the basement. They can't get out because they're surrounded by Harmond's men."

"The helicopter will create a distraction. If Jimbo can get Rock to the helicopter, we're home free." Alexei smiled again. "It's a police helicopter. It's unlikely your General Harmond would fire on the police."

Now Lucien smiled. "Not bad."

About a hundred feet up, the drone flew toward the house, but before it got more than halfway, it exploded and fell burning to the ground. One of Harmond's security team crouched near the door of the house with the weapon balanced on his shoulder.

Lucien's smile vanished. "Son of a ..."

Chapter 38

Lucien stared open-mouthed as the remains of the drone smoldered on the front lawn. Alexei pulled him away as the remaining cops swarmed to the gate, weapons drawn. A few seconds later, the whomp-whomp of a helicopter caused everyone to look skyward.

"Vitaly?" Lucien watched the copter approach, low and slow.

"Indeed. Hopefully, he got enough aerial coverage from the drone. We need to get a message to your mercenary friends to mount the rescue now."

"How?"

Harmond strode out and stared up at the helicopter. Even at a distance, Lucien saw Harmond's fists balled and his shoulders stiff. The general called inside and one of the soldiers came out with Rock bound in a straitjacket with what looked like a dog collar and leash around his neck. The soldier handed the leash to Harmond. Rock stood straight, his eyes staring ahead.

"Harmond! You can't do this! Let him go!" Lucien rushed forward.

With a chuckle, Harmond jiggled the leash. "I officially own this creature. He's been signed over to me." He turned to go back inside but stopped and shouted over his shoulder. "Oh, Roux, you should be happy, this one isn't sick. He's a prime specimen."

Lucien grabbed the gate. "What you're doing is immoral, illegal, and a crime against humanity!"

Harmond laughed and disappeared inside with Rock.

"Isn't that the same thing you did, Paleo?"

He spun around. How had Fenwick slithered onto the scene without being noticed?

He caught his breath. "Yes, Beatrix, I committed the same crimes and I've more than paid for my sins, as you know. I'm trying to make amends by setting Rock free."

"Oh, I know. And it's commendable. Stupid, but commendable."

"Why are you here?" He held up a hand so Alexei would know everything was all right. "To gloat at my continued failure?"

She shrugged. "I've already done that. You do seem to fail at everything, don't you? It's sad, really. Consider me a curious observer. I can't wait to see how this turns out. I rarely get the opportunity to see a conclusion." She looked past him to the residence, reached inside her jacket pocket, and took out a small black box. "Here. This disables that nasty laser weapon. It interferes with the charge."

He took the box and immediately pressed a red button on top. "How? And ... why?"

"Told you. I'm an observer, but I also believe in fair play. Guns are one thing, but that weapon isn't supposed to be here. It's a loaner. A test model, not for public viewing."

Lucien understood. "You brokered a deal with Harmond for that weapon?" As loathsome as Fenwick was, she did have a warped sense of right and wrong. He glanced at Alexei and showed him the box. He turned back, but as quickly as she'd appeared, Fenwick vanished.

Alexei hurried over. "What was that all about?"

"She's a bit pissed off that Harmond is using that laser thing. This switched it off, I hope." He handed the box to Alexei.

"That woman does pop up in the strangest places. Where did she go? I glanced away for a second and didn't see her anymore."

Lucien shook his head. "No idea. Maybe she flew off on a broomstick."

Harmond rushed back out, tugging on Rock's leash. Behind him, Jimbo, with his arm in a makeshift sling, pointed a gun at the General's head. The next men out were Jimbo's friends, who stood on either side of Harmond. The helicopter hovered above the roof. Rock lunged forward and knocked Harmond to the ground, then lashed out with his foot, catching Harmond on the jaw.

Jimbo said something to Rock and dashed back inside. The teen Neanderthal stood, glaring down at Harmond. The helicopter banked left and descended toward the front lawn.

Lucien shouted, "Rock! Get to the helicopter and we'll get you out of here!"

The helicopter gracefully touched down on the lawn, the rotor wash blowing leaves every which way. Rock made a move that yanked the leash from Harmond's hand, but in the straitjacket, he couldn't do much else.

Alexei tapped Lucien's shoulder. "Vitaly said all is clear, but they have to get into the copter now before the police realize it's a ruse."

"Okay, okay." He waved his arms. "Rock! Get into the...!"

A single shot rang out and the helicopter lifted off a few feet and slammed back down. Vitaly slumped forward onto the controls, causing the machine to roll to the left as the rotor blades tilted. Everyone ducked or ran for cover, except for Rock. Lucien dove to the ground beside Alexei.

The rotors dug into the lawn with several chunks flying off and embedding themselves into a nearby tree and the side of the house. The engine whirred and eventually stopped. Nobody moved. Rock walked toward the gate as gunfire erupted from inside the house and Jimbo's men ran back inside. He stopped, turned, and charged in behind them.

"No! Rock!" Lucien got up.

The cops were dazed, which helped when he jumped into the nearest squad car and rammed it into the gate, breaking the hinges. He floored it and sped up the driveway, past the helicopter, and stopped only a few feet from the doorway.

With no plan, he climbed out and went inside. The grand foyer had marble floors, an immense crystal chandelier, and a lavish spiral staircase. But the grandness was marred by several dead bodies, blood spatters, and bullet holes that peppered gilt-framed artwork. Jimbo lay face down, his head caved in on one side and his shirt drenched in blood.

"Rock!" Lucien ran through the house, ignoring the stabbing pain in his side, and stopped in a dining room. "Rock!"

"Lucien. Rock in here."

He stepped into the kitchen. Rock had a cast iron frying pan clutched in his hand as he stood over a soldier. Blood dripped down the pan and onto the floor. The straitjacket, on the floor, had been torn to pieces.

"Rock, are you hurt?"

"Rock not hurt. Rock got hands out and ripped up coat."

"Yes, I see that. We have to get you out of here."

Rock dropped the pan onto the soldier's body. "You have blood. You are hurt."

Lucien looked at the scrubs. "No, well ... no. I'm fine." He exhaled. "I can't believe you're here. Finally. Alexei is outside. Come on. We should go out the back, there are cops everywhere and Harmond's men are somewhere."

"I come. We go. Where Marlowe?"

"She's okay. Wounded, but she's in the hospital. We'll go and see her."

"Rock like that. *I* like that." He looked around and grabbed an apple from a basket on the counter. "Apple good. I like apples."

"Oh. Okay." He refused one when Rock offered. "I don't have much of an appetite right now."

With a shrug, Rock took a bite and stomped from the kitchen. Lucien withdrew the gun from his waistband and caught up. They made it to the back door when someone shouted. Lucien spun around and fired a shot, hitting the wall beside one of Harmond's soldiers.

Rock shoved Lucien aside and barreled toward the guy, head down in a full charge. The weight of his body knocked the soldier to the ground, but he still managed to get a shot off. In the span of a single breath, Rock had pummeled the man's face into an unrecognizable mass of bloody tissue and broken bones.

"Rock! That's enough." Lucien opened the back door. "Rock, come on."

Rock stood over the body, his fingers dripping blood.

On shaky legs, Lucien took him by the elbow. "We've got to go, Rock. It's too dangerous to be here. I'll get you somewhere safe and you can live however you want. No more Neanderball."

Rock took a raspy breath and turned. "I no go."

Lucien lost all the breath in his lungs. The soldier's shot hit Rock dead center in the chest. Blood seeped out and spread onto his shirt. Lucien's vision blurred through his tears. Rock wobbled but remained on his feet.

"Rock save Lucien from man with gun."

"Yes, you did." He wiped his eyes and wrapped an arm around Rock's massive body. "We'll get you to the hospital. But we've got to hurry."

Rock shook his head and smiled. "No more raccoon pizza for Rock." He swayed and fell against the wall. "You leave Rock. You go."

"Never."

Sliding down the wall, Rock settled on the floor. He reached out and placed his hand on Lucien's shoulder. "Lucien Rock's friend. Forever friend." He tipped sideways.

Lucien sat and cradled Rock's head on his lap. "Forever friend."

Rock looked into his eyes and with a strained breath, said, "Lucien free Rock's brothers. Promise."

Lucien nodded. "Of course. They'll be free."

Rock closed his eyes and touched his wound. "Rock win final game. Rock play no more." He opened his eyes, focused on Lucien, and smiled. His once-bright eyes dimmed and faded into an empty stare.

"Yes, Rock, you won. You beat them all."

Chapter 39

Lucien shivered in the cold, sterile interview room, Rock's blood caked all over the scrubs. Handcuffs chaffed his wrists, but the physical pain was nothing compared to how his heart throbbed. He sat, empty, devoid of any emotion.

For hours he sat, chained to the metal loop on the table, with a single photograph of Rock's body in front of him. The agony of the photo was exactly what he needed. He welcomed it. It gave him the raw reality to stay grounded in what had happened.

He looked up at the sound of a knock. The door opened and a man sauntered in, someone from his memory, but who was it? A colleague, a friend, an enemy? The latter most likely. It didn't matter.

"Do you remember me, Dr. Roux?"

Lucien stared.

"I'm Simon Basten from the French Consulate."

"Oh." Lucien turned his attention back to the photo.

"Dr. Roux. Dr. Roux."

"What?"

"Please look at me." Basten sat opposite, flipped the photo upside down, and slid an envelope across the table. "Take it."

It took a moment for the haze to wear off. Lucien put his hand over the envelope. "What's going on? I'm done. I have nothing left in me."

"That's what I hear."

Lucien opened the envelope and pulled out his passport. "Thank you, I suppose."

"Listen carefully to me, Dr. Roux. You have a one-way ticket to France waiting for you at the Oakland terminal, under the name on the passport. Tomorrow, Air France, ten in the morning. Use it." Basten stood and walked to the door. "Shame what happened." He knocked on the door and left when a cop came.

Lucien flipped open the passport. It was his photo with the name Jean-Paul Benoit. He sighed and tucked it back into the envelope. What did Fenwick want now? Everything was done now, all of it.

The door opened again and a police sergeant stepped in but held the door. "You're free to go, but you're not to leave the state. I don't know what the hell happened in Pacifica, and I've got to say, your statement hasn't made it any clearer. The detectives on the case said you can go for now, but they'll need to interview you again. Good luck." He waited while another cop came in and took off the handcuffs. "Sign out at the front desk."

Lucien took the envelope and the photo, but the cop with the handcuffs shook his head and snatched the photo out of his hands. He shuffled from the room, found the front desk, and signed a form.

He stepped out into the chill of the night and stared up at the moon. He had a way out of the country, but should he take it? What if Fenwick had a twisted game in mind and planned to have him arrested at the airport trying to flee? Then again, would it be so bad being locked up? It's what he deserved. The ultimate punishment.

A horn tooted.

"My friend! Over here." Alexei waved from the driver's window of a white Lexus. "Hop in."

"I want to walk."

"Plenty of time for a walk later. Marlowe is waiting for you."

He'd been so consumed with Rock's death that he hadn't thought of Marlowe. He got into the Lexus and leaned back. Alexei handed him a wool blanket and a steaming cup of coffee from a local trendy coffee shop and turned the ignition.

He sipped the coffee, snapped on the seatbelt, and closed his eyes. "He died in my arms, Alexei. It feels surreal. How can he be gone?"

"I'm as broken as you, but life goes on."

"Does it? Should it?" He opened his eyes and wound the window down, breathing in the damp air.

"You have a chance now to start your life over. In France, with your family. They know everything and will welcome you with open arms."

With a grunt, Lucien turned and looked at his friend. "I'll be a fugitive. They'll know exactly where to look for me."

"You haven't done anything wrong. The alias is simply to get you home without the paparazzi and the police interfering."

"Wait. How do you know about the passport? Basten works for Fenwick."

"Used to work for Fenwick. He's mine now. Beatrix and I have come to an arrangement."

Lucien slammed his hand on the dash. "What the fuck, Alexei! You're working with that woman?"

"Not working with. She detests me, but she's taken a liking to you for whatever reason. After Rock's death, she reached out to say she considered downsizing her operation and would only hold onto trusted clients. Basten wasn't needed and he became a free agent. I accepted that deal."

"I'm beyond shocked. How can you trust her?"

"There's no trust involved. This is how the business works. Have you forgotten? She'll stay out of our way, and we'll stay out of hers. An unwritten agreement." Alexei accelerated and drove down the street.

Lucien sucked in a lungful of the night air rushing in through the open window. It revived him. "I'm not ungrateful, but I want this whole nightmare over. How's Marlowe?"

"Recovering. Sky Warrior, too."

"Oh, damn, I forgot to ask about Vitaly. Was he ...?"

"Yes. I arranged to have his body flown home for burial. He was a good man."

"We've lost so much. And for what?" He slumped and wound the window up. He sipped the coffee and watched cars go by. "What am I to do with my life now?"

"You'll figure it out." Alexei drove into a hospital parking lot. "I'll be in touch." He motioned to the hospital. "Fourth floor, room 416. She's waiting."

"Thanks."

"Hold on." Alexei reached into the back and handed him a canvas tote bag. "Best that you slip on some clean clothes. I understand they patched up your wound at the police station. I hope they did a decent job."

"They did, well, a nurse did." He stripped off the scrubs and slipped on a clean T-shirt, running shoes, and jeans, a struggle from the front seat. He shoved the soiled clothes into the tote and climbed out of the car. What would he say to Marlowe? Would she want to listen to his explanation? He needed her now more than ever, to hold her and take comfort in her. But everything had changed and none of them would ever be the same.

He got to the fourth floor and found the room, hesitating for a moment before going in. She was propped up with pillows, looking at an iPad. She glanced up, dropped the tablet, and reached out. He hurried to her and melted in her embrace.

"Oh, Lucien, I'm so, so sorry. Are you all right? Did Alexei tell you?"

He pulled away slightly. "I'm as good as I can be. And yes, he told me about Fenwick and France. Enough of that, how are you?"

She shrugged and kissed his cheek. "Not bad. Sky Warrior is worse, but he's recovering. Sami's staying with him." She paused for a moment. "I'm not coming with you."

"Oh." He stepped back, out of her arms. "Is it Sky Warrior? Are you, you know?"

"What? No. My life's here. I don't want to grow grapes in France. I'm American and my job is at Bay-Gen."

No words came. Not a single syllable. He backed away and reached for the door.

"Lucien, wait. Don't leave."

"There's no reason to stay."

"I'm telling you, I'll be here, waiting if you come back. Go home and see your family. Regroup, rest, get your mind right. Take a long break from this insanity. But if you decide that life isn't for you, you know where I'll be."

He turned and opened the door. "And *you* know where I'll be." He glanced back at her.

"Before you go." She held out the iPad.

He was tempted to leave, but he really wanted to stay for a while longer. "I don't want to see anything that'll remind me of what I've lost."

"I think you will." She waved the iPad. "Take the damn thing."

"Fine." He took it and stared at a headline. "What is this?"

"You need to ask that?"

The headline read: U.S. *Military Accused of Illegal Genetic Research on Neanderball Players.*

"Harmond's been exposed." He smiled and skimmed the article. "He's to stand before the Senate. At least I don't see my name in the article."

"Alexei had something to do with that."

How Alexei managed anything remained a mystery. Lucien wandered around the room and stopped at the window. He needed to go home to France, but he'd miss his adopted home and especially Marlowe. But she had it right, they both needed space to sort things out.

He handed her the iPad, gave her a quick kiss on the cheek, and went back to the Lexus. Alexei drove off without a word. Lucien appreciated the quiet. Back at Marlowe's condo, he took a shower, packed up his clothes, and said his goodbyes to Alexei.

Alone, he sat out back on the bench, jasmine perfuming the air. He listened to the wind drifting through the leaves. The idea of running a new vineyard sounded good at first, but something in the back of his mind kept pushing forward.

Rock didn't die like his brothers, which meant he might have had a mutation that suppressed the Stat3-beta2 gene. If the autopsy results showed no cancer, it'd mean the years of research finally paid off. But at what expense? Rock and his brothers were all dead. The ultimate sacrifice.

"There you are, Paleo."

He jumped up. Fenwick leaned out the back door.

"What the hell do you want?" He took one step and stopped, scanned the yard for an escape route, and realized there wasn't one.

"Relax, Paleo. I told you before, you're not on my radar." She walked toward him, no goons in sight. She seemed different, less intimidating, and wearing a looser-fitting pantsuit. "You and me, we're at a stage of our lives where we need to take stock of our actions."

"What, now you've grown a conscience and you're going to live a quiet life with a houseful of puppies?"

She laughed. "I don't care for dogs. Too needy." She walked past him and sat on the bench. "I have a word of advice for you."

He had a clear escape route through the house. "What advice?"

"Start fresh."

That wasn't the advice he expected. "How? My life is a shambles. And it's because of you."

She shrugged. "Sure. I'm a businesswoman and you were my business. What's done is done. But you have an opportunity to step back from all of this and get yourself a new life. Most people never get that chance." She stared into the distance. "The cutie will wait for you to sort things out." She stood. "It's nice out here, quiet."

"Yes, it is." He noticed her hand in her jacket pocket.

When she withdrew her hand, she had a pistol gripped tightly. She aimed it at him. "Start fresh, Paleo, or I'll put a bullet in your head right here."

He backed away and stumbled on a rock. "I'm tired of playing your games, Beatrix. My bags are packed, but I'm not so sure I deserve a fresh start. Look what I've done. All of the death, for nothing."

She cocked the gun. "You know there's no pre-ordained grand plan, no puppet master pulling our strings. We do what we do, bad decisions and all. Learn from your mistakes and get on with your life. Or give up and let my hollow point end it all."

A small part of him wanted her to end it, but his survival instinct won. Fenwick knew it and wanted to force him to make a conscious decision. What a strange world he lived in.

He turned and walked into the house, calling over his shoulder, "I hope I never see you again." He shut the door and locked it, knowing Fenwick would somehow vanish into the darkness.

That night he slept in Marlowe's bed, the scent of her clinging to the sheets. When morning came, he stared in the bathroom mirror. The hair dye had washed out and he looked like his old self, or maybe his new self. His incision had healed more and for a change, he looked forward to wiping the slate clean and, as Fenwick said, starting fresh. He'd never erase what happened, but he'd make sure to keep all of the good memories of Rock alive.

With his passport in his pocket and a fake ID Alexei gave him, he grabbed his bags and sat on the stoop, waiting for the taxi to arrive.

He reached into his leather jacket to make sure he had enough cash, and touched a smooth object, the flash drive with his research. He held it between his fingers in the morning sunlight. Years of work that culminated in tragedy. A yellow taxi honked. He looked up and dropped the drive back into his pocket.

Once in the back seat and buckled up, he gazed out the window at the condo.

"Where to?"

"Oh, the Oakland airport. International terminal."

"Be there in under twenty minutes." The driver pulled away from the curb. "Hey, did you hear about the Neanderball players? All dead. The team owners announced it."

"I heard."

The driver continued, "They're starting up a new ballgame called Neanderball 2.0, this time with regular people and an actual ball instead of a sack of sand. I don't think it'll be near as good, but what the hell, might as well watch, right? So, what do you do?"

Lucien sank into the seat and wrapped his fingers around the flash drive. "I'm a vintner." He wound down the window and tossed the drive out. "Just a vintner."

END

Acknowledgments:

A huge thank you to my editor, Mayo Morley, whose eagle-eye catches things that only an eagle-eyed editor can! I must also acknowledge the person who fed me the inspiration, unwittingly, for this book. Thank you Dr. Matthew Des Lauriers, my graduate archaeology professor and thesis advisor, who mentioned one specific thing during a lecture about Neanderthals that triggered this story idea. A special thanks to the Ojai Writers Group members who critiqued my chapters. And of course, I acknowledge the readers who take the time to sit down with my books.

About the Author

Born in Sydney, Australia, Sofia Diana Gabel is a multi-genre author now living in the Pacific Northwest. Her published works include novels, novellas, and stand-alone short stories as well as inclusions in anthologies. She holds two bachelors degrees and a master's degree in Archaeology, with additional coursework in creative writing. In addition to writing, she loves hiking forest and coastal trails, hanging out with family, and traveling as much as possible. She's a wanderer at heart and finds it hard to settle in one place for long. And why should she? There are so many places to explore!

Don't miss out!

Visit the website below and you can sign up to receive emails whenever Sofia Diana Gabel publishes a new book. There's no charge and no obligation.

https://books2read.com/r/B-A-GPBBB-HWPPC

BOOKS 2 READ

Connecting independent readers to independent writers.

Did you love *Neanderball*? Then you should read *War and Money* by Sofia Diana Gabel!

Fifteen-year-old Dax, low-status and rebellious, never expected to be thrust onto the battlefield to fight aliens for Global Command. But she was hand-picked by Commander Viteri and torn from her family forever. Reluctant to take lives and skeptical of the true motives behind the conflict, Dax embarks on a perilous journey to uncover the secrets hidden within the wars. She bands with her squad of fellow misfit soldiers and an understanding alien to find the reason why Global Command refuses to end the alien wars. As survival becomes her greatest challenge, she is forced to navigate the treacherous path in front of her in search of the truth before it's too late.